MW01147836

OUTSIDE
ACCESS
DO NOT OPEN

BOOK FOUR: CONSUME

The fourth & final installment in the post-apocalyptic saga

As Finnian Bolles lies near death from a tragic accident inside the newly discovered — and long-since evacuated — tenth bunker, his fellow travelers in the post-Flense apocalyptic world must face the possibility that the objects injected inside of them, the very same objects responsible for decimating Humanity four years earlier, might not be enough to repair the damage in time to save his life.

Meanwhile, they must decide whether to carry on searching for the elusive Bunker Twelve, the so-called source of the objects, the Flense, and the cure, or just give it all up and return to the relative safety of Westerton Army Base. But with so many questions being left unanswered, including the fate of the missing Bunker Ten residents, the group cannot agree on a plan. Can a once-hated enemy give them what they need to move on? Or will they finally succumb to ravages of the Flense without ever learning the truth about Bunker Twelve?

Make sure to look for the companion series
THE FLENSE

Hundreds die in a fiery train crash in northern China. A cargo ship smuggling refugees is lost to calm seas off Libya. Entire villages in Ghana are abandoned overnight.

Contracted by a prepper group to investigate a series of seemingly disconnected global tragedies, a young medical reporter, Angelique d'Enfantine, uncovers a disturbing pattern: each event is preceded by the sudden spread of a mysterious ailment and is followed by the appearance of a man dressed in black and silver who witnesses claim is the devil himself.

Each event is more grisly than the last. As the risk to her life grows, Angel begins to doubt that the tragedies are harbingers of an impending biblical catastrophe, but rather practice runs conducted by a fanatical organization bent on global annihilation. Could her sponsors be using her to advance their own paranoid agenda?

The story begins in China . . . .

ALSO BY SAUL TANPEPPER

GAMELAND
Deep Into the Game (Book 1)
Failsafe (Book 2)
Deadman's Switch (Book 3)
Sunder the Hollow Ones (Book 4)
Prometheus Wept (Book 5)
Kingdom of Players (Book 6)
Tag, You're Dead (Book 7)
Jacker's Code (Book 8)

Golgotha (GAMELAND Prequel)
Infected: Hacked Files from the GAMELAND Archives
Velveteen (a GAMELAND novelette)

Signs of Life (Jessie's Game Book One)
A Dark and Sure Descent (GAMELAND prequel)
Dead Reckoning (Jessie's Game Book Two)

Collections
Insomnia: Paranormal Tales, Science Fiction, & Horror
Shorting the Undead: a Menagerie of Macabre Mini-Fiction

Science Fiction
The Green Gyre
Recode: T.G.C.A.
They Dreamed of Poppies
The Last Zookeeper

Scan for more information:

website: http://www.tanpepperwrites.com
email: authorsaultanpepper@gmail.com

CONSUME

BOOK 4 OF THE BUNKER 12 SERIES

SAUL TANPEPPER

BRINESTONE PRESS

PUBLISHER'S NOTE

This book is a work of fiction. Names, characters, places, and incidents either are the product of the author's imagination or are used fictitiously, and any resemblance to actual persons, living or dead, business establishments, events, or locales is entirely coincidental.

Published by Brinestone Press
San Martin, CA 95046
http://www.brinestonepress.com

Copyright © Saul Tanpepper, 2020

LICENSE NOTES

All rights reserved. Without limiting the rights under copyright reserved above, no part of this publication may be reproduced, stored in or introduced into a retrieval system, or transmitted, in any form, or by any means (electronic, mechanical, photocopying, recording, or otherwise), without the prior written permission of both the copyright owner and the above publisher of this book. The scanning, uploading, and distribution of this book via the Internet or via any other means without the permission of the publisher is illegal and punishable by law. For information contact Brinestone Press.

Set in Garamond type
Cover credit and interior design K.J. Howe Copyright © 2020
Images licensed from Depositphotos.com and K.J. Howe

ISBN-13: 979-8-60-578889-8

What if the cure is worse than the disease?

"Heroes always die in the end," Bix grumbled, as he angrily wiped Finn's blood off his hands. "Every single fucking time. That's how the world works now. The only guys who survive it are the bad ones."

CHAPTER

01

THE ASSAULT WAS RELENTLESS, AND FINN WAS TOO—

crushed
skull
crushed skull

—weak to resist, always had been. He saw that now. Too weak and too damaged. Try as he might, he couldn't stop it, couldn't ward off the attack on his senses, the endless intrusion of their garbled, clashing voices—

too much blood loss

—raking at his mind like the filth-ridden claws of the—

fractured spine

—infected, stripping the tender flesh of his soul. Awful, bitter words—

collapsed lung

—spoken in anger and despair. They assumed he was too far gone to understand, too deep in his—

organ failure

—death spiral to appreciate how much it was killing themselves to say these things out loud. But he knew. He didn't want them to fight, not for him. He didn't need their pity.

and almost certain brain damage

STOP IT!! he wanted to shout, but he was powerless, paralyzed.

And so they kept arguing, over who was to blame and how all this might have been prevented. And whether it was better to put him out of his misery or let him suffer.

torture

That was the thing. How would they know the misery he suffered? They hadn't a clue.

listen, everyone, the trauma's too great
too great
trauma's too great

Truth be told, there was no pain anymore. He was actually quite comfortable now. Warm and weightless. No physical sensations to speak of, not since the agony had gone away, suddenly lifting and moving off, like sand lost off a beach after a storm surge, leaving a numbness in him so immense it felt like a gathering of something new, rather than the absence of everything.

They were right, though, about the severity of his injuries. It didn't mean he wanted to hear it, not because he was afraid anymore, but because of the pity, the helplessness. He knew all about that and didn't want them fighting over him now. It wasn't worth it. He didn't want their feeble attempts to save him be the last thing his brain registered before he went. For this to be how they remembered him.

They . . . .

What were their names again?

He thought he'd had them within his grasp just a moment before. Now . . . nothing, a void. Not just set aside, but erased.

Death was the soul consuming itself. Sometimes it took a little while.

Keep it together, Finn. Focus.

At least he remembered his own name. At least he wouldn't die not knowing himself.

nothing we can do for him anymore, bren

Bren. Yeah. That name sounded familiar: Bren.

And . . .

Damn it, what was—

Bix. It was Bix.

He supposed it should bother him, everything coming to this, and yet it didn't. Not really. That's what he told himself.

Bren's face floated up out of the swamp of his thoughts, musty, fading— her smile, her touch, the color of her eyes. He couldn't remember what color they were anymore. Br—

Br . . . ?

Bright.

Losing their sharpness. Losing substance. Fading.

No, wait. Please. Not yet.

Not so soon.

The image disintegrated, as if consumed by hoarfrost on a window made filthy with the dust of decayed memories.

He remembered in some distant way that he loved . . .

someone

who?

Her: br . . .

Something. It was gone, an echo of a memory, meaningless now. Bland and tasteless, this thing called love. He was pretty sure she loved him back— had loved him, anyway, but in the innocent way children love each other without really understanding the full meaning, without knowing love's fullest dimensions. Its boundaries and limitations. Children think love is immeasurable, and it's not. There were places it can't reach. Places it shouldn't. Dark places.

He felt so old now all of a sudden, as if death was not the thief of time, but rather life was, and here was the final accounting of all possibilities that could never be.

They never had a damn clue. That's what life in the bunker had done to them. It kept them alive, but it hadn't allowed them to live.

Maybe she'd have a better chance of figuring it out now for herself, of actually experiencing real love, once he was gone. And she was free of him. She . . . .

Damn it, what was her name again? He really wanted to know.

It didn't matter anymore.

He felt no remorse. She was dead, too, just as dead as he was. She and all the rest who remained in the world. They just didn't know it yet.

Or so he kept telling himself.

Her face drifted away, and after a while was replaced with another, boyish, acne-ridden.

Bix, of course.

His name fetched easier from the trash pit of his brain and stayed longer. But it was also losing resolution, feeling more like notes in a soggy old schoolbook floating in the gutter, the ink bleeding but still legible. That quirky smile and those damn impossibly white teeth with the gap in the front. The constant joking around. The laughter.

Would he miss that, once all was said and done?

Other faces paraded after, sometimes other names, but he was having trouble holding onto them.

Har—

Har—

—der to think.

Harder to focus. And he felt colder all of a sudden. Icy. Suffocating.

Then a roaring sound, and he felt like he was whooshing away now, faster and faster, his soul stretching to infinity.

To infin—

In—

finn?

Finn!

CHAPTER

"**WHAT'S HAPPENING?**" **BREN SHRIEKED. SHE** launched herself out of the chair and toward the bed. "Someone do something! *Please!* Finn! He's turning blue!"

"Get back!" Harrison Blakeley shouted. He kicked the chair out of the way and tried to reach Finn. "Bix, get Bren out of here!"

Bix pulled her into a bear hug and dragged her screaming toward the far wall of the medical bay. "Dad?" he cried. "He's dying! Finn's dying!"

"He's seizing, son. Nothing we can do. Just give us some room so nobody gets hurt."

Bren pulled an arm free and made a move toward the bed again, then reeled back in horror as Finn's upper body lurched upright, his face twisted in agony. Bloody vomit erupted from his mouth and arced across the room. Before the others could react, he collapsed back onto the mattress, still convulsing, hammering the bed frame against the wall.

"Someone grab his arms and legs!" Harrison roared. "Hold him down!"

Eddie leapt onto the bed and took hold of Finn's ankles. Jonah threw himself across Finn's chest, ignoring the muted grinding sounds of the shattered ribs beneath him. Both men barely managed to keep him on the bed as Finn bucked and twisted in his delirium.

"You're crushing him!" Bren shrieked. "He's choking!"

"Turn him on his side!"

"Watch that IV line!"

"Never mind that!" Harper said. "We can put a new one in."

He raced over to the crash cart and started yanking drawers open, strewing supplies everywhere. "We need to get him intubated. He's going hypoxic!"

"No one here knows what the fuck you're talking about!" screamed Bix.

"Oxygen," Harper said, panting. "I need to stick a tube down his throat into his lungs."

"You're not a fucking doctor! You're going to kill him!"

"I learned how to do this in the bunker, basic emergency medical training. Now move! I need to get this in!"

"Since when is sticking a tube down someone's throat basic?"

"He's turning blue, so if you have a better idea—"

"Enough, you two!" Harrison shouted at them. "We're losing Finn, so just do something! Anything!"

"Here, hook up one end of this," Harper said, throwing a package of coiled tubing at Jonah and gesturing toward the gas outlet mounted on the wall. "The green one is oxygen."

"We don't even know if it's still working," Jonah said, but he ripped the package open with his teeth and slipped one end over the chrome nipple beneath the float valve and twisted the knob wide open, eliciting a loud hiss of escaping gas.

Harper situated himself at the head of the bed. "Turn it down a little," he instructed Jonah. He reached forward just as the seizure ended. Finn collapsed back onto the bed and lay still.

"Is he still breathing?"

"Shallowly. But yeah."

They all knew it was a miracle Finn was breathing at all. He'd lost far too much blood in the past hour and his injuries were too great for anyone to survive. It defied all reason. Even the nanites inside his body couldn't possibly stem the bleeding, much less repair the damage in time.

For the briefest of moments, Harper worried he was doing more harm to Finn than helping. Even if he did manage to get the tube down his brother's throat and into the lungs, the best it would do was prolong the torture, delaying what they all knew was inevitable. There was no possible way he'd survive the night.

But he angrily dismissed the thought. He couldn't just give up, not now, not when they'd finally found each other. The last four years had felt like a rollercoaster ride of dread and denial, at times believing he was alone in the world, other times certain his family was still alive and out there waiting to be found. Deep down, he'd always known this was a fantasy, but he'd refused to relinquish hope.

And now the fantasy had come true, and he felt like it was about to be stolen away from him again. He couldn't give up. He wouldn't.

He gripped the shiny metal pharyngeal speculum he'd retrieved from the bottom drawer of the cart and guided it gently into Finn's mouth, sliding it in as far as it would go. When he had last practiced this, he and the others in his bunker — *two years ago now?* — they'd all laughed about it. No one had wanted to be the one with the sensitive gag reflex; no one wanted to be the one to vomit in front of the others.

There'd been that one kid, Mickey Decosta, who'd never taken any of their training sessions seriously. He kept joking about other orifices he'd like to insert the device into, the perv. And where was he now? Dead. Or he might as well be.

They all were.

But this wasn't practice. This was the real thing, and despite all of the attention and genuine desire Harper had paid to get it right during the training, he still felt like he was going to screw it up somehow, hasten his brother's death, increase his suffering.

"Is it in?" someone asked. The question registered at the very fringes of his mind. It was the tall one they called Jonah doing the asking. Jonah reminded him of Mickey in a way, although he couldn't really think why. He just got that feeling about him, that Jonah thought he knew everything he needed to know already and considered everything else a waste of time. In the few hours that had passed since Finn's accident, they hadn't really interacted, there hadn't been time, yet Jonah already felt so damn familiar to him.

"Harper, is it in?"

"Not yet," he muttered. "Give me a moment." He lifted his eyes from the bloody, mangled mess that was his brother's face and stopped when his gaze reached the chest, waiting to see if it would rise again. It did, abruptly lifting, a shallow tenting of shattered bones, more on one side than the other, then collapsing again with a wet, rattling exhale. They waited for another inhale, but it didn't come.

"He's not breathing!" Jonah shouted. "Damn it! What did you do?"

"Nothing!"

"Get away from him!"

"I got this!" Once more, Harper carefully guided the tip of the rigid plastic tube through the groove in the device, unspooled another length from around his fingers, and slowly slid the next few inches through the thick fluid pooling in Finn's throat. There was a twitch, a spasm of the muscles in the neck, and for a fleeting moment Harper feared Finn's teeth would suddenly snap shut on his fingers, severing them.

Too late for a bite guard, dummy.

He focused instead on the tubing, praying it was in the right place, in the trachea and not the esophagus, and that it didn't kink. He was going purely on faith and theory for how this was all supposed to work, but he'd never actually put any of it into practice on a real person. None of them had.

9

The tube refused to go in any farther. He wasn't sure why. He tried to calm himself, tried to remember what he'd been taught: *Lift the chin; insert the speculum with a smooth, downward, rotating motion; slide the tubing in along the shiny metal groove.* But it still caught, bent, reversed itself.

He extracted the speculum fully this time and reinserted it, applying extra pressure against the base of Finn's tongue. There was a soft *pop* and the metal device abruptly dropped to the hilt without resistance. Finn's jaws clamped down reflexively. Air gurgled up from his lungs.

Harper gave it another try, threading the tubing into the hole, forcing himself to go slowly. This time, it slipped in without binding up.

"Is that it?"

"Bag!"

"What?"

He gestured frantically to the crash cart. "Big blue rubber ball, bottom drawer!"

Harrison found it and threw it over. Harper quickly attached it and gave the bag a squeeze. Finn's chest inflated, still lopsided, and just as quickly released, air whistling out through the tubing. "We're in," he declared. He gave the bag several more quick pumps, watching each time for the telltale rise and fall, then paused to see if Finn's brain would take over again, resuming respirations on his own. "Is the oxygen on?"

"Yeah."

He removed the bag, then reached blindly for the other end of the tubing, attaching it to the piece he'd just inserted into Finn. "Crank it up a little. Someone check his pulse."

It took a minute for the dark blue to bleed away from Finn's lips. Then suddenly they flushed bright red. Satisfied, Harper slowly withdrew the metal speculum from Finn's throat, careful not to disturb the tube. He finished by securing it with medical tape against his brother's cheek.

"Pulse is weak, rapid," Eddie confirmed.

"How's the IV?"

"Looks okay," Harrison Blakeley said, letting out a shaky exhale. It had taken them far too long to find a vein in the first place, precious minutes lost while Finn's blood drained from his body. They had nothing to replace it but electrolyte solution, so they pumped him full of that, and dextrose for good measure, not sure if it would help or harm. At least his blood pressure had stabilized.

"Put a fresh bag on."

"Are you sure it'll help?" Jonah asked. "Gotta be almost pure salt water running through his veins by now."

"Just do it!"

"Look at the blood everywhere!" Jonah shouted back.

"I said do it!"

Harrison stepped up beside Harper and gently placed a hand on his elbow. "Calm down, son. We're all doing the best we can. No one wants Finn to die, but . . . ." He didn't finish the thought. He didn't have to.

Harper's eyes skipped from one unfamiliar face to the next, all still strangers to him save for Missus Abramson. He turned to look upon Finn's broken body. It killed him knowing how much pain he must be feeling. The best thing he could do was just let him go, but he couldn't. He wondered if they should give him more morphine. He had no idea how much was enough, and how much was too much. Err in one direction and Finn would suffocate, drowning in his own blood. Err in the other and prolong the torture.

He wiped the sweat from his forehead and nodded. "Okay."

"What now?" Jonah asked.

"What can we do?" Eddie replied. "We wait."

"For what?"

"For the next emergency, and we deal with it the best we can. Then the next. And the next after that."

"Yeah, but for how long?"

"Until something changes."

CHAPTER

JONAH SETTLED ONTO THE FLOOR BESIDE BIX. "WHY do you insist on torturing yourself like this?"

"Take a hike, Resnick."

It was the first chance any of them had to stop and catch their breath since finding the bunker. Hell, the first chance they'd had since leaving the house outside of Salt Lake City early that very morning. So much had happened since then that the house felt like something from the distant past — months, or even years ago already — and not just a handful of hours. So horrific were the events of that afternoon that the imprint left on their minds would not likely fade very soon, if ever. How was it possible that so much had happened in just a single day?

"Sitting here stewing isn't helping anyone."

"And this is?" Bix scowled and started to get up.

"Come on, man. Don't be like that."

"I'm going to check on Bren. She's—"

"Leave her be," Jonah said, and placed a hand on Bix's arm. "She needs space right now. She's in shock. We all are."

"Not you. You seem fine to me. You're already talking about moving on."

Jonah tilted his head back, shut his eyes, and immediately opened them again. He felt like he might be sick. "Someone has to think about what we do now."

Bix rolled his eyes, but he settled back onto the floor anyway, privately grateful for the distraction from the dark thoughts he'd been entertaining, even if it was Jonah doing the distracting.

He stared off into the gloom at the other end of the small room, into the corners where the light coming in from the hallway couldn't reach. He could just make out the bloody pile of rags in the corner, the body underneath, and he felt his rage growing again.

"You think I'm heartless," Jonah said, "but I'm not. Sometimes you just have to put your feelings aside so they don't control you."

"I never said you were heartless. Dickless, on the other hand . . . ."

Jonah gave him a confused look.

"It means you have no dick. It's right there in the name: *dick-less*. Less dick. It couldn't be more clear."

"Look, just because I sided with your father and not you doesn't mean I agree with his decision."

"Yeah, it kinda does."

"Not about this, but—"

"Grow a spine, Resnick. Make a stand."

"It's not just your decision alone. Or his. Or even mine. None of us gets to decide who lives and who dies."

"You're wrong! That's how it does work now, Jonah. That's the world we live in! If I don't like your face, I pull out my gun and put a big hole in it. Plain and simple." He reached behind him, pulled out the pistol tucked into his waistband, and aimed it."

"Bix, don't."

Harrison Blakely stepped into the doorway, blocking the light from the corridor. "Put that away, son. And come on. I need you two."

"I'm not going anywhere with this loser."

"Please, just put aside your differences for now."

"He started it," Bix muttered.

"I don't care, son. It's time to get back to work."

"Stop calling me that! I'm not a child!"

"Just come with me, both of you."

"And just leave him?" Bix demanded, gesturing into the darkness. "Someone's got to keep an eye on that piece of crap."

"Adrian's not going anywhere, not as long as he's tied up."

Bix's scowl deepened. "You don't know him like I do, either of you. You weren't there at his ranch. You didn't see the shit he did to me and Finn. He's pure evil. That's why we have to kill him. Now."

"I'm not having this discussion again," Harrison said, impatiently.

Bix sighed, then pushed himself off the floor using Jonah's shoulder as a brace this time. He was disappointed when it didn't elicit a complaint.

They went to the stairwell, where Harrison paused to catch his breath. The infection that had spread through him over the past couple of days had taken a lot out of him. The antibiotics he'd received that morning had helped a little, but they just weren't as efficient as the nanites the others had in their bodies.

"One thing we can do while we're waiting is find out what prompted these people to leave the bunker. Eddie's already searching level by level, but it's become clear they didn't leave in a hurry— not a lot of dirty dishes and uneaten meals, few abandoned clothes and personal belongings, no blood. Everything points to a planned and orderly exit."

"And yet they left nearly all of the food."

"I think they took only what they could carry. And that's informative, too. The amount they left behind gives us an estimate of when they abandoned this place."

"The door was forced open."

"From the inside, Bix, and the latch was carefully, systematically dismantled. They didn't leave in a panic."

"And walked right into a massacre."

Harrison shook his head. "We don't know if the bones we found out there are theirs. They could belong to the people who worked the mine. They might've been caught out in the open during the Flense. And we can't be sure what took them out, either. It could be wolves."

"That'd have to be one hell of a pack," Bix said.

"How do we figure any of this out?" Jonah asked.

"I want you, Bix, to go through the video recordings in the watch room, assuming they're still there. The room's on the second level, just like it was in Bunker Eight."

"Why do I have to do it?" Bix complained. "What about Jonah? I was guarding Adrian."

"I have another job for Jonah. It's a bit more . . . physically demanding."

"Oh, and I'm too weak? I see how it is."

"That's not what I meant." Harrison's face was haggard. He'd always looked older than he really was, but at the moment it really showed. "It's Seth. Kaleagh asked that we bury him. Properly."

"After what he did to Finn?" Bix growled "He doesn't deserve a proper burial."

"We don't get to decide that, Bix. Bren and Kaleagh do. And, frankly, I think it'll be good for the rest of us, too."

"If he hadn't shoved Finn into the elevator shaft—"

"It's not up for discussion, Bix."

"Why, because father knows best?"

"No, I—"

"Let's just stop pretending it matters anymore, *Dad*. None of this matters anymore!"

They glared at each other for a moment. Then, as calmly as he could, Harrison said, "We don't always get the chance to do the right thing. We do now. So Jonah and I are going outside and burying Seth, and I'm asking you to go check those videos."

For once, Bix had nothing to say back.

CHAPTER

THAT EVENING, **B**REN AND **H**ARPER STAYED IN THE
medical bay to watch over Finn. The rest gathered in the
kitchen, all except Adrian, who remained locked up in an
empty storeroom on a lower level. Despite the horrific
events that had transpired earlier that day, they tried to eat.
Or at least they went through the motions of having a meal.

Finn's condition had stabilized since the seizure, reaching
a sort of indeterminate stasis. He was neither improving, nor
getting worse, which did little to alleviate anyone's anxiety.
His condition could change at any moment, without
warning. In fact, they all expected it. To Bix, it felt like being
perched on the slippery rail of a ship in the middle of a
hurricane. The eye of the storm was over them at the
moment, and it was calm, but the wind was going to pick up
again sooner or later, and he would slip. But in which
direction?

The meal of steamed rice, stewed tomatoes, and canned
beef was the first decent food they'd had in weeks. And
there was plenty of it, too, since the cans were all banquet-
sized, meant for large groups of people, not just the seven of
them— eight, if they wanted to include Adrian, although no
one was inclined to bring the murderer a plate or stay while
he ate. The food cans sat on the counter by the stove, still
three-quarters full. The razor-sharp lids angled upward,
waiting to slice a stray arm.

Jonah had arrived last, his hair still dripping from his shower, his skin red from scrubbing. He had carried Seth's body outside on his shoulder wrapped in bed sheets from one of the dormitory rooms, but some of the blood from the head wound had leaked out and soaked the back of his shirt. The one he wore now, retrieved from what was left behind in one of the dormitory units, was a little too small.

If the question were ever asked, and they were to answer honestly, few of them would claim to be upset that Seth was gone. After all, how many times had the man betrayed them to cater to his own selfish purposes?

"You don't have to eat it," Kaleagh told them, her voice heavier with exhaustion than lack of food or sleep could explain.

"And you didn't have to cook."

"I had to do something while you—" She let out a whimper and left the rest unsaid.

"Well, anyway, thanks," Harrison said. "Better than anything we've had in a very long time." He tried to give her an encouraging smile, but he doubted she even noticed. She just stood there at the end of the table wringing her hands and staring off over their heads at nothing.

"Kaleagh, it's—"

"Finn's going to be okay," she said abruptly. She nodded stubbornly to herself, then turned away.

The others exchanged mute glances, not knowing how to respond. Was she trying to make herself feel better, convincing herself that Finn would pull through, despite all the evidence against it? Or was it for Bren's sake? Either way, it seemed terribly unfair.

"We don't blame you for what happened," Harrison said. "Nobody does."

She fidgeted with the dishcloth for a moment. They could see her wringing it in her hands. Then she slowly turned and slid into the seat at the table next to Eddie.

19

"I could have stopped it," she said. "All of this, from the very beginning. Seth could have. He should have told you about his work, about how he tried every day for years to find a way to eradicate the Flense. Nothing took. Failure after failure. You didn't see, but I did. He blamed himself. By the time that man showed up from Bunker Two, Harper's bunker, he'd already decided there wasn't a cure and never would be. That's why he refused to leave with everyone else. It was safe inside. It was the only safe place left to be away from the Flense."

The confession had been unexpected, and left everyone speechless for a moment. Finally, Eddie asked, "What do you mean he worked for years? Are you talking about *before* the Flense hit? He knew it was going to happen?"

Kaleagh shook her head. "Not the Flense. At least, not that I am aware of. No, I meant that he was doing experiments, in secret, inside the bunker afterward, and—"

"In the bunker?" Bix cried, and pushed himself upright in his chair. "What the hell kind of experiments? On who? Us?"

"Let her finish," Harrison said, and nodded for her to continue.

"He thought the answer was simple, something to do with altering the way the nanites behaved by changing their shape. He had this saying, 'Function follows form.' He knew it always bugged me, because it was the opposite of the old biology axiom."

"How?" Eddie asked, confused. "These experiments— how was he testing his theories?"

"I never knew any of the details. He refused to tell me, saying it was for my own protection. I know he made it sound like I knew more than I did, that day you all left the bunker, but I really didn't."

"Did anyone else know?" Eddie asked. "Who else was he working with?"

"I bet you Jack Resnick knew," Bix said, pointing an accusing finger at Jonah. "Why else would he have killed Doc Cavanaugh? She found out what they were doing, so they had to stop her!"

Eddie placed a hand on Bix's arm and told him to settle down. "Let her finish," he quietly said.

Kaleagh shook her head. "Jack didn't know anything. Nor did Gia Cavanaugh. As far as I knew, it was just Seth. He said the whole thing was too dangerous to share with anyone. That's why he did his experiments in a secret locked room away from everyone in the bunker, in case something ever happened to him."

"What locked room?" Harrison asked. "Where?"

"I don't know."

"What the hell *did* you know?"

"Bix, please."

"That he was terrified. I think it sort of drove him crazy after a while. You never really saw how paranoid he was. It's why he always kept his distance from everyone else. He constantly worried about sabotage."

"He actually believed someone would try to stop him from finding a cure? To the end of the world? That's some paranoid shit."

"Bix!"

"Was there anyone in particular he feared most?" Eddie asked, tiredly.

"Charlie Darby. Seth never trusted him, especially when he was one of the ones who decided to stay behind when you and the others left."

"Chip Darby?" Eddie said, surprised. "Who else?"

"Rory Newsom."

"Both were engineers," Eddie mused. "That's . . . curious."

"But you need to realize, Seth arrived at the bunker paranoid. He trusted no one, not even me. The only person I ever heard him say he could trust explicitly was the old man."

"What old man? Sato Fujimura?"

"No, someone from before. Someone he'd worked with."

"Did he ever keep notes, records, while doing these experiments?" Eddie asked.

"Yes, but I assumed he destroyed them once he stopped trying to find the cure."

"But you don't know for sure if he actually did stop, do you?" Harrison said. "They could still be hidden away inside the bunker."

"So hidden that no one ever accidentally stumbled upon them or his experiments?" Eddie asked, dubiously. "Seems unlikely we would have missed the signs."

"Not if his secret lab was someplace we never thought to look."

"You and I have been all over that bunker, Harrison. We know every nook and cranny there. And we're not the only ones. Abraham Bolles was—"

"But is that true? There were all those empty rooms we never bothered with, the ones for the people that never made it."

"No, it was someplace else," Kaleagh said, "not on the residence level."

Harrison thought about this for a while, then asked, "Had Seth ever been to the bunker before the Flense? Did he pre-arrange a visit there with anyone, have preexisting knowledge about the layout?"

Kaleagh shook her head. "No. I'm certain he didn't even know it existed until the day we arrived."

"How could he not know about it?"

"I don't know. I wasn't privy to the phone calls he was getting. He was out of the country when it all started, dealing with an issue at an off-shore manufacturing plant."

"For the nanites?"

"Maybe. I think so, yes. He couldn't ever talk about it. He just called and said he was coming home earlier than expected. I remember thinking to myself that he sounded upset. And when I asked what was wrong, he let slip that the place might've been intentionally destroyed, and he was worried about the backup plant."

"Backup plant?" Harrison asked. "For making more of the nanites? Where?"

"It was somewhere out west. He'd mentioned it to me once before, said it was out of his jurisdiction. Anyway, he called to let me know he wouldn't be getting his usual layover in Atlanta, and that I shouldn't pick him up at the airport, like I usually did. It was our routine. I'd go get him, we'd get Bren from school, and we'd go out to dinner. He said he didn't know when he'd get home, or how, but I should just wait."

She reached for her glass before remembering it was empty. Eddie got up and filled it for her.

What had first come out of the faucet hours before was black and smelled musty from lack of use. But after flushing the pipes for several minutes, it ran clear again and was drinkable.

Kaleagh's hand shook as she took the glass from him and sipped.

"A few hours later, he told me he was about to land in New York. There was a lot of noise on the call, and I was worried, because the television had been reporting problems there and in other cities. I asked him why New York, and he said he had to go talk to this old man, that it was the only way to stop something bad happening. It was very important. I remember the call distinctly, because he wanted me to get Bren out of school early and take her home and stay there. He also told me to pack a couple duffel bags with enough clothes for the three of us. 'As much as you can fit,' he said. 'And pack the camping equipment in the car, too.' "

"Camping equipment? Why would he need that if you were going to the bunker?"

"That's why I don't think he knew that's where we were going."

"And none of this struck you as strange?" Bix said, incredulously.

"Of course it did. All of it did, particularly after what I saw on the news. And there was something in his voice, something— He was clearly terrified. So I just followed his instructions." She sighed. "I know you never thought very highly of him. You all blamed him for the problems we've had. Maybe he deserves some of it, but not all. Maybe I deserve some, too."

"We're just trying to understand," Harrison assured her. "The more we know what happened, the more we'll be better prepared for what comes next."

"Prepared?" Bix asked. "For what, Dad? What do you think is going to happen next?"

"If we can find Seth's notes—"

"He said there's no cure," Jonah reminded them.

"Well, until I see definitive proof of that myself, I won't believe it. I can't."

"So, we're just going to give up on Bunker Twelve?"

"We've hit a dead end on that, Bix," Eddie said.

Harrison stood up. "And all the more reason to find those notes. If Seth had inside information about the company's operations, manufacturing facilities and such, those notes could contain clues to where they and the twelfth bunker might be hidden. And whether they're one and the same."

CHAPTER
05

HARPER TRIED TO SLIP INTO THE KITCHEN WITHOUT drawing everyone's attention, but all eyes turned to him anyway, although they just as quickly turned away to focus on something else. His likeness was too painful of a reminder of what waited for them downstairs. And what they were very likely to lose.

He took the first seat he came to, a few tables away, and said nothing, feeling like an intruder, an imposter, despite his blood relationship with Finn, and they still hadn't accepted him into their fold. It crushed him to think his only hope of ever being welcomed among them depended on the impossible chance Finn would survive.

They weren't outwardly hostile toward him, but their manner made it clear they weren't comfortable having him around, either. He supposed it was understandable, like being tormented by the spirit of someone who'd recently passed. Or, in this case, someone standing on death's doorstep. He was a reminder of something they weren't yet ready to accept and didn't want. The thing was, he knew exactly how they felt. They were suffering because of what had happened to Finn, but so was he. They were just too wrapped up in their own grief to see how much he was suffering, too. And he had no one to share it with.

He had sensed the strongest resentment coming from the Abramson girl, Bren. She hadn't spoken a single word to him, not since the accident, and not even when they finally had a chance to take a breather. He'd saved Finn's life, yet he felt like she blamed him for taking it. And what hurt him the most was the fact that her father was more to blame than he was.

Of course, her father was the one who'd died, so maybe that had something to do with it. There was definitely some resentment there on her end.

He'd been sitting with Finn when she showed up at the door to the medical bay. He'd assumed she'd joined the others in the kitchen to eat, so her arrival took him by surprise. Nevertheless, he'd made room for her. But it was like she didn't even see him, like he was a ghost. Except, she was the one doing the haunting, drifting in like a lost spirit, her face as drawn and colorless as one, and he realized she was still in shock. But by the way she physically avoided him, it was obvious she knew he was there.

She'd planted herself down in the chair on the other side of the bed, grabbed Finn's hand, and began to speak, telling him he was going to be alright now because she was there for him. This sent a wave of emptiness sweeping through Harper, leaving him as hollow as the promise she'd just made. It didn't make him angry, just sad and confused. So, after a few minutes, he got up and left.

That was the hardest thing he'd ever done. He was suddenly overwhelmed with the certainty that he would never speak to his brother again. A sense of loneliness came over him, more powerful than the loneliness he'd ever felt inside Bunker Two.

He made his way to the stairwell before collapsing, his emotions finally getting the better of him. He wanted to cry, to lash out at the injustice of it all, but he was unable to produce even a single tear. Eventually, the smell of food and voices drew him to the others.

They greeted him with the same indifference, their silence an invisible wall as impenetrable as bulletproof glass.

"Look," Jonah eventually said, apparently resuming whatever subject they had been discussing, "I'm all for finding a cure, I really am. *If* one exists. But we need a plan that makes sense. We need better protection. And we need a clear objective."

"We've always had a clear objective, the cure, and if that means we keep looking for Bunker Twelve, then—"

"No, we haven't always. I mean, no offense to Harper, but the moment we learned about him and it became Finn's mission to lead, we've had one disaster after another. Again, no offense."

Harper shrugged. Although he wanted to defend his brother, he was grateful his presence was at least being acknowledged.

"I'm sure if Finn could speak right now," Jonah continued, "he'd agree that we need to break this run of extremely bad luck we've been having."

"You don't know that!" Bix cried. "You don't get to speak for him! In fact, you're probably glad about what happened. You always resented that people followed him and not you. You're just like your dad."

"You're wrong."

"No, you're wrong, because Finn's going to make it." He angrily stabbed his fork into his food.

Jonah shook his head. "No one will be happier than I, if Finn pulls through."

Harper cleared his throat.

"If?" Bix exclaimed. *"If?"*

"We need to be realistic about his chances. For god's sake, he was bleeding from his ears, Bix. He was vomiting blood. You don't need to be a genius to know what that means."

"Shut up."

"Bix, listen, the swelling in his brain? How many broken bones? His spine, ruptured organs? I mean, he's going to be paralyzed—"

"I said shut up!"

"—crippled. And brain damaged. And—"

Harrison loudly cleared his throat, putting an end to Jonah's gruesome recitation. They didn't need him to tell them what they already knew. "We all know what happened, so obsessing about it isn't helping."

"It's okay," Harper said. "And he's right to be realistic. My brother's in terrible shape. His chances are miniscule. But I just . . . ." He exhaled and shook his head, but couldn't think of what else to say. "I'm not ready to give up hope yet. I can't. I just—" His voice cracked, and he couldn't go on.

"No one is ever ready," Eddie said. "Not for something like this."

"Yeah, well, we've seen some damn crazy shit happen to people," Bix said. "You were burned over ninety percent of your body, Eddie, and we all expected you to die. Nobody thought you'd live, much less come back as strong as you have."

"Don't make this about me," Eddie began, before Jonah interrupted him.

"That's different, Bix, and you know it."

"How's it different? It's not. It all comes down to the nanites. We know what they can do, how good they are at fixing people back up. How many times have we seen them work, and how quickly, too? Look at the Wraiths, what they go through, and yet they still survive. These things inside our bodies — well, *your* bodies — they make you almost superhuman. I mean, that's what they were developed to do in the first place, right? They were made to stop people from getting sick, from dying from injuries. Finn's got them, so maybe—"

"Bix," Harrison interjected.

"We honestly don't know if Finn will live," Eddie said. "I personally think it's about fifty-fifty right now."

"That high?" Kaleagh asked, surprised.

"All I know is that without the nanites, he'd already be dead. So we know they're doing something. I survived an accident that should have killed me within an hour — that *would* have killed any of us before the Flense — so there is good reason to believe Finn has a better chance than we might be willing to accept."

"See that?" Bix exclaimed. "That's all I'm saying!"

"I'm pulling for him," Eddie went on. "We all are, even Jonah. But we have to accept how bad it is. *If* he survives, there will be significant . . . challenges."

"Sure, *if* Finn survives," Jonah said, "and *if* he's not paralyzed. *If* he's not severely brain damaged, it'll be weeks— no, months, before he's able to do anything. My point is, we're not helping ourselves by sitting around and waiting for him to get better. He may never do that. We've got other things to worry about right now."

"Like what?" Bix demanded. "We might as well wait here. It's as good a place as any. And we can't leave anyway, not without transportation."

"If this place is as good as any, then why did the others leave it behind?"

"Because they were stupid."

Jonah shook his head. "What we should be doing is gathering up all the food and supplies and taking them to our people at Westerton." He hooked a thumb in Eddie's direction. "At the very least, it's unfair to keep him and Hannah apart."

"Thanks, but I'm capable of making my own decisions," Eddie said. But he nodded. "I do, however, agree with the plan. They need the food more than we do. There's enough of it here for hundreds of people to survive on for another three, four, maybe five years. That should be our first priority."

"Go ahead, then," Harper offered. "I'll stay here with Finn. He's my brother, my responsibility."

"That's not what I meant," Jonah said. "We're not going to split up. You're with us now."

"Just exactly how are you going to take anything anywhere?" Bix demanded. "Do I need to remind you our truck is sitting dead as a doornail five miles from here? You plan on magically whipping up another bus?"

"In that regard, I may have a solution," Harper offered. "There's a maintenance depot just south of here. It's filled with buses and other vehicles. Some of them may still be functional. Plus, there's Father Adrian's pickup——"

"Don't call him that!" Bix snapped. "That piece of shit human being doesn't deserve the respect of a title, at least not one like that."

Harper nodded warily. "His truck's stuck in the sand on the road by the main gate, about a quarter mile from here. It works and has enough fuel to get us back to that settlement north of Salt Lake City. It just needs to be dug out."

Jonah stood up. "Then it's settled. Eddie and I will get the truck and bring it here."

"Well, the caveat is it might not be there anymore," Harper said. "There was another guy with us. He might have taken off with it."

"Maybe next time lead with the caveat," Bix muttered.

"Adrian has the only key, so the chances of that are slim."

"Ever hear of hotwiring?"

"Let's hope this other guy hasn't," Jonah said, getting to his feet.

"There's one more thing," Harper added. "Well, two."

"There always is," Bix grumbled.

"First, this other guy? He has a gun."

"So do we. And the second thing?"

"Fa— Adrian's sister. We left her strapped inside the truck. Assuming this guy, Charlie, didn't already kill her— and I doubt he would, since he's too scared of Adrian."

"We've dealt with Wraiths before," Eddie said.

Harper nodded. "Yeah, but this one's angry and hungry."

CHAPTER

KALEAGH REMOVED THE CHAIN, BUT DIDN'T immediately open the door. She waited a moment, her ear pressed against the cool surface, her body tensed for an attack. But there was no sound from within, no suggestion of life. She carefully set the chain on the floor beside the door and twisted the knob. The latch clicked, released. She stepped back, gun raised in her hand, and pushed the door wide with her foot.

Adrian was still on the floor, his back against the far wall, and his legs splayed out before him. He raised his hands up, wrists bound, to shield his eyes from the sudden glare of light from the hallway. A miasma of old sweat and dried blood drifted out.

"Get up," she said, snarling down at him.

He lowered his hands and squinted up at her. Everything about him was rumpled and filthy. He looked like a forgotten pile of rags. "How long y'all plan on keepin me in here?" he drawled. There was no trace of anger in his voice, no sense of expectation, just resignation. Kaleagh found it deeply suspect. A normal person would not have given up so easily. And from what she knew of this man, she'd expected him to be a lot more defiant.

"I said, get up."

"Ain't gotta go again already," he said. "Could use somethin to drink, though. Throat's dry."

Kaleagh thrust the gun toward his head. "I'm not going to tell you again."

He still didn't move.

"Do not test me."

"Where's the boy?" he asked, and tilted his head to look past her into the empty doorway. "Thought y'all was supposed to do this in pairs?"

"Harper is . . . busy. It's just me."

Something flickered across his face, a flash of fear, she thought satisfactorily. She wanted to do to the murderous bastard what he had done to her husband. What he had done to countless others. He was the devil and had no right to live, but Harrison had been adamant that they keep him alive, at least for the time being, and Eddie supported him.

"So, this is it, eh?" he asked. "This is how it ends for me?"

"You should be so lucky," she growled. "If it were up to just me, I'd shoot you right here, right now, between the eyes. I could do it, and no one would care. They'd be happy to be rid of you."

"You know I only fired in self-defense."

"Don't you dare!" she spat, and stepped farther into the room. He flinched at the sudden movement, but didn't look away. "You don't get to explain yourself," she hissed. "You came here to kill us all. That was your plan."

"Now, that ain't true, ma'am. I was just lookin fer—"

"Shut up! You shut your damn mouth!"

He frowned but held his tongue.

"Now," she growled, "I said get up."

He still didn't move. "How is he?" he asked instead. "The boy, Finn? He's still alive, ain't he? I couldn't believe he fell. But t'weren't my fault."

Anger swelled inside of Kaleagh. She'd been warned not to get too close to Adrian, not to engage him. To never allow herself to be alone with him. She was in too delicate an emotional state, and he was too sly. That's what Harrison told her, that Adrian had a way with words, an ability to lull others into complacency. But she wasn't delicate or a fool. She was strong, stronger than ever, seeing more clearly now than she ever had before. This evil man should have been the one to die, not her husband. He was the snake, the liar, the con man.

She wished she'd known all this the first time they met, back there in the other bunker, when he'd shown up at their door and tried to sweet talk his way inside. She'd thought they were just desperate men — desperate for food, shelter, medicine — men who wouldn't do harm because harm was what she thought they were running away from, and so she'd pleaded with Seth to let him in. He'd refused.

It didn't take long for the real Adrian to show himself, to resort to force and violence. He had his people take some of the other bunker survivors away and killed. The rest were to be used for leverage, especially Bren. Kaleagh hadn't understood why at first, not until a boy that looked just like Finn appeared, except it wasn't Finn, and she started to get a sense for how it was all connected.

What kind of man does those kinds of things to people because of a boy?

Someone who doesn't deserve to live.

She trembled, standing there in the doorway, all of her strength and fury concentrated on the trigger of her gun, wanting to squeeze, willing herself to wait. In a moment of clarity, she realized that she would do it, that she actually *wanted* to do it.

But the moment passed, and she was unsure again, unsure of why she was even here. What was she doing?

Avenging my husband's murder.

The idea had been there all along, masked by her own shock and uncertainty, thwarted by reason and practicality and the fact that she wasn't a coldblooded killer. All it had taken to break through was a single, random moment of idleness, when her mind, no longer distracted by the mundane tasks of survival, recalled the agonizing details of her husband's death. The tears had come in a rush, and she'd collapsed to the kitchen floor, unopened cans rolling from her hands, and water rushing unheeded into the sink. The gun she'd been given for her own safety, tucked into her waistband, felt hot and heavy against her skin. Before she knew what she was doing, she'd come down here.

Five days had passed since Seth's death. She hadn't wanted to confront the truth, that killing the man who murdered her husband was all she thought about, day and night. The group had discussed it — all but Bren, who she had insisted be left out of it — and only Bix and Jonah wanted to get rid of him, although Jonah agreed with Harrison to wait. Her own thoughts had remained private. But they all knew how she felt.

So the vote stalemated at three to three, and the tiebreaker lay unconscious in a bed, clutching to life.

And now, here I am, taking matters into my own hands, forcing the matter with violence.

She'd always known it would come to this. She raised the gun again, aimed for the wedge of pale skin where two tangled masses of filthy hair parted over his forehead.

You can't.

They knew she was capable of doing it. That's why they wouldn't let her be alone with him, not even for a second, why she was always supposed to be with someone else. Right now, it was supposed to be Harper, but she'd convinced Harper to help Harrison outside.

So here she was. She could shoot him right now. She would. Just stand here and squeeze the trigger and blow the bastard's brains out. A fitting end.

It won't bring Seth back.

No, neither would it bring back any of the others. But it would make her feel better.

No, it won't, Kaleagh. It won't. Don't do it. Don't be like him.

She realized her hand was cramping, the muscles at war with themselves. She took in a deep breath and forced herself to relax. Adrian seemed to sense her hesitation, and the corners of his mouth curled upward just the tiniest bit. She couldn't tell if he was taunting her.

"I ain't got nothin against y'all," he assured her. "Nothin personal, no how. I was tryin to help the boys. Ask. I found them wanderin the wilderness, vulnerable to the ferals. Saved their lives, me and Jenny, my poor sister. We took them in, fed them, gave them a safe place to stay. Y'all looked fer her out there, right, my Jenny? Lookin for my truck? Y'all need a truck to leave, so—"

"I don't want to hear you right now," she whispered. "You make me sick, you and your sick little games."

"Experiments," he corrected. "They was experiments. I was studyin them, the ferals, figurin them out. There's ways to control them."

"I don't believe you. No one does. You're a liar."

"Not no one. The other boy's father believes otherwise. I know things, I just have to wait for the right time to—"

"Shut the hell up."

"Ma'am, we both know the only way this is goin to end is with a cure. Your husband told me hisself, back there at the dam." He paused, as if gauging the turmoil he was stirring up inside her. "We all want the same thing. I wanna know what's causin all this mess. I wanna make it stop, or, if not stop it, then stand up against it. All my experiments was fer that one purpose. That's what I was doing, studyin, seeing what makes them tick. Them and us. But work like that takes resources. How else was I supposed to do it? And all I've learned I am happy to share with y'all. By combinin our knowledge, we can—"

"There's no sharing," she said. "There's no cure, so there's nothing you know that can change my mind."

"Now, y'all don't know that. I know lots of things, like the kinds of machines that make them stop dead in their tracks, and the kinds that make them madder'n hell. I know where there's more of 'em, a truckload down south of here, and—"

She laughed bitterly. "Whatever you think you know, my husband knew it already and more. He knew there wasn't a cure. But even if there was, you killed him. What you were doing, your so-called experiments, were no more sophisticated than what six-year-old boys do to bugs, tormenting ants and leeches with magnifying glasses and table salt."

He shook his head. "It's something 'lectrical in the brain. Your husband, Seth, said—"

"Keep his name out of your mouth!"

His lips stretched, formed a grimace. "Give me a chance. I know I can help y'all find the cure. Or, if not that, then a way to stop 'em."

She shook her head. "Lies. All lies." She stepped back and placed a hand on the knob, both to brace herself, but also because she'd suddenly become aware of how vulnerable she'd allowed herself to be, standing so close to him. The room was small, barely eight feet on edge, and he could have easily thrown himself at her, taken her out at the knees, knocked her down and grabbed the gun.

She raised it again, as if to discourage such thoughts.

"Well," he said, "I still ain't gotta pee. But my throat's real parched."

She stared down at him, blinking away the tears. Why the hell had she come here? Why alone?

To kill him.

She thought she could do it. She wanted to.

But she realized she didn't have it in her.

He got to you.

No, that wasn't it.

It is. He planted doubt about the cure. As long as there's a chance, he knows he's safe.

She yanked the door shut. She could hear him inside, asking for water again. She wrapped the chain around the handle, secured it, and quietly returned to the kitchen to finish making dinner.

CHAPTER

BIX COULD HEAR JONAH STOMPING DOWN THE STAIRS IN his boots. There was a distinctive rhythm to the way he walked. It was subtle, just the slightest of differences between the left and right, a fraction of a second hesitation followed by the merest of scuffs of the other heel, but it was enough to know that it was him.

They hadn't spoken to each other in days, partially because of the argument that first night, but mostly because he resented that Jonah's prediction about Finn was looking to be more accurate than his own. He wasn't getting any better. In fact, his condition only seemed to be worsening— no more seizures like that first day, but they had had to resuscitate him three times now. And the last time it happened, Harrison had actually said out loud what they were all thinking: "I don't think we should try anymore. It's torture."

It took a toll on them all, but it hit Bren especially hard, turning her into an emotional wreck. She couldn't sleep, and she refused to leave Finn's bedside. Harper was having a hard time, too, although he hid it better. For some reason, this seemed to infuriate Bren, who blamed him not just for the accident, but for Finn's failure to recover. Bix couldn't understand it at all. It wasn't Harper's fault. None of this was.

The stairwell door opened and the sound of Jonah's footsteps grew louder. They stopped just outside of the room.

"Got yourself a cozy little set up in here, don't you?"

Bix didn't respond. He was too burnt out from staring at the monitors for hours on end to put up much of a fight. In fact, he wished they could just set their animosities aside, at least for now. It took too much effort to stay angry.

"Wish I could sit on my ass all day."

"Oh, you mean instead of lying on your back like you actually do?" Bix threw back, regrets and best intentions all but forgotten. "Because that sounds *soooo* rough."

"Sure, if you like oil and rust falling into your eyes and mouth all day," Jonah replied. He and Eddie had been working on the buses in the maintenance depot down the road for the past few days, but they hadn't had any success getting anything to run. He shuffled in, pulled the other chair closer and sat down. "Anything?"

Bix shook his head. "Remember that stupid show the Rollins boys used to binge watch over and over all the time, the one everyone else in the bunker couldn't stand?"

"You talking about Jacob and Jareth? What the hell was it? Some stupid reality—"

"Keeping Up With The Cardassians."

"It's pronounced Karda*sh*ian, with an s-h. Cardassians were an alien species on—"

"Like the Kar*dash*ians weren't alien. Anyway, you know what I mean."

"Right. Well, what do you expect from a couple of prepubescent boys?" He chuckled. "Funny how those video disks just up and disappeared from the library one day, never to be seen again."

"I never thought it was possible, but I finally found a show I hate even more. It's called, *Keeping Awake While Nothing Happens.*"

"How much have you watched?"

"I'm a month in, and all I can think is, man, these people must have been batshit crazy to leave a perfectly good bunker and all their food behind to venture out into the Flense."

"Don't be so harsh, Bix. Those people are probably dead now. Or Wraiths themselves."

"So I'm supposed to feel sorry for them?"

Jonah shrugged. "Just saying we shouldn't judge until we know what happened."

Bix glanced over at him, his eyes rolling. Blood splatter stained the front of Jonah's coveralls. "Caught some action today, eh?"

None of them had reported seeing any Wraiths since their arrival, but they couldn't assume there weren't any out there. For example, Charlie, the man Adrian and Harper had come here with, was still unaccounted for, as was Adrian's sister, Jennifer. Neither had been with the pickup truck when Harper and Eddie got to it. All they'd found was a chewed up seatbelt and blood splashed on the outside panel of the door. Either Charlie had shot Jennifer, or she had gotten free and killed him. They could both be dead and dragged off by wolves or Wraiths. Or they were both Wraiths now, doing Wraith things. Waiting to make the rest of them into Wraiths, too.

"No action," Jonah said, glancing down at his shirt. "It's Eddie's. He sliced his hand open trying to remove a heat baffle on the bus we were working on. He didn't even notice until I told him he was dripping on me. Of course, by then, it'd stopped and was already starting to heal."

Bix cringed. "Gross."

"It's a good reminder to keep my mouth shut."

"I've been reminding you to do that for years."

"Why aren't you watching the playback at higher speed?" Jonah asked, switching the subject. "Or is 10x as fast as it goes?"

"I've tried faster, but the system's crap and keeps freezing up, and takes an hour to reboot. Why else would I still be on the first month?"

"Any activity?"

"Saw a mangy looking coyote. Lots of crows. Rats and mice and raccoons. Oh, and oddly enough, a cute little white rabbit, like it was someone's pet."

"I was talking people, bozo."

Bix reset the playback to the beginning. "Close to four hundred went in." He checked his notes. "Three hundred and eighty-eight, to be precise. A bunch were just kids, some even too young to walk, had to be carried in. Maybe a hundred, hundred ten teenagers."

"They all seem pretty cool with what's happening."

"Yeah, no panic," Bix agreed. "Walking in, all in orderly fashion, parents and children holding hands. It's almost like a cult." He pointed to one child. "Dolls in backpacks, pillows. A few old people, too, but not many. It's like they're going in to see a movie, not spend the next five years trapped in a hole in the ground."

One elderly couple had reminded him of the Fujimuras. Sato and Asuka had been well liked in Bunker Eight, fair and honest people, if not also a bit intimidating. They and a few others, like Dominic Green and Chip Darby, had been senselessly gunned down outside their bunker. It infuriated Bix that their murderer was still alive, and that it was within his power to find justice for them. His own damn father had vetoed his wish to punish Adrian, but that wasn't half as bad as Jonah agreeing with the decision. They just couldn't understand how unfair it was to the people he'd slaughtered, people they'd once called friends. The man was a waste of oxygen.

"No Wraiths chasing them in," Jonah observed.

"Not like us on the day we arrived."

"And we still don't know what drove them to leave."

"What if they never did? There's a reason for that barrier at Level Ten. And the broken elevator. What if they're all still down there? What if they're infected and just waiting for us to break through?"

"Down there without food?" Jonah said. "Doubt it. But that's why Eddie's keeping the barricades in place, just in case. Besides, someone had to take those survival kits out of the lockers."

"Maybe it was scavengers."

"Maybe."

"Well, there have been a few Wraiths up top. Not many, but some." He checked his notes. "Seventeen on the cameras so far. Might be sixteen. There was one that was naked, all chewed up. Might've been one I'd already counted earlier that came back. The rest were dressed in work coveralls."

"Miners."

"Yeah, but I haven't seen any since Day 23, so I think they all wandered off to look for food."

"And your dad still doesn't know about those bones out by the fence?"

"He's counted seventy-seven skulls so far. All have been chewed on. But he can't say by what, or whether they're workers or they came from inside the bunker."

Jonah thought about this for a while. "We don't know how many people were here on the worksite before the bunker people came, plus visitors, family."

"Yeah, and the damn cameras are so limited. Whoever put them in must've been high or something, because some of the views don't make sense. Besides the two doors, locker room, and main gate, there's four views of just random crap.

Like this one of the corner of a rooftop. What the hell good is that?"

Jonah shrugged. "Might've been knocked out of alignment by the wind. Is it possible to skip forward? You know, to spot-check later dates."

"Dad wants to know the actual date they left, how many, and how they were acting."

"I know. But you can get there faster without watching every single minute. Jump ahead in the locker room view. Find a point *after* they left, when the lockers are open. Then split the difference. If the lockers are still shut, jump ahead some more. Rinse and repeat. Much faster than taking it day-by-day."

"Damn it," Bix muttered. He should've thought of that, and probably would have if he weren't so worried about Finn. It was worse that Jonah had figured it out for him. He'd never hear the end of it now.

"May I?" Jonah asked, and reached over to bring up the command window. "Okay, based on the amount of food left, we think they left within three or four months of arriving, right? So, jump ahead to four months." He typed in a date and hit return. The screens refreshed, showing the new views, which were the same as the old ones. The quality of light in the images differed, but the scenes remained the same. He pointed to the locker room image. "No change. All the doors are still shut, which means they hadn't left yet."

He changed the date to a full year out, and this time the differences were readily apparent. The locker room appeared just as he and Bix had found it, now more than a week before. "So now we know they left sometime between four and twelve months. Let's split the difference. Check at eight months."

"Still open."

"Six months?"

"Open."

"Five."

"Open," Bix said, growing excited, despite himself. He pushed Jonah aside and entered a new date a week past the four-month mark, then tapped the return key. "Closed."

Jonah stood up and placed a hand on Bix's shoulder. "So, there you go. In a matter of minutes, you've narrowed it down to a roughly three-week window. Try four months and two weeks next. I'm outta here."

"You don't want to stick around and see?"

Jonah chuckled. "I have to get out of these clothes. And I need food."

"Hey."

Jonah turned in the doorway, his eyebrows raised in expectation.

"Thanks."

"You'd have figured it out soon enough." Jonah's eyes twinkled mischievously. "Maybe after another month."

"Bite me, jerkwad."

Bix watched him leave, waiting until his footsteps faded away before turning back to the monitors.

"Maybe he's not so bad after all," he mumbled, then swiveled around to check behind him, suddenly certain that Jonah had sneaked back and heard the admission.

He typed in a date four months and ten days after the bunker residents' entry. The locker room doors were shut. The window was now small enough that he decided to just play the footage back at 10x speed, the fastest the system would allow without freezing up. Shadows flickered and swiveled across the otherwise static views. Night fell and the exposures automatically adjusted, turning from earth tone colors to shades of silver, then finally switching over to the ghostly greens and whites of night vision. He skipped ahead eight hours. Morning arrived. Shadows shrunk. And then, just as he was going to skip ahead again, the front door of the bunker opened and people started streaming out, moving jerkily because of the accelerated rate.

Bix slowed it down and watched as the locker room began to fill. They retrieved their survival kits, no urgency in their movements or on their faces. Some of the adults were even smiling encouragingly at the children. Bix wished there was sound to hear what they'd said. The last people finally exited the bunker, shut the door, and retrieved their own packs.

After that, the locker room emptied out.

"Four months, eleven days," Bix noted. He then replayed the entire exodus, counting the people as they departed the bunker. The number was shy by over a dozen from when they'd entered months before.

"Where the hell are the rest of you?" he wondered aloud. "Did you stay behind? Why? Or did something happen to you? Did you leave already and just not take any kits? Or did you leave later?"

It bugged him that he didn't know, in part because it meant he had to keep watching the recordings, but also because Eddie wouldn't agree to open up the unexplored lower levels as long as there were bunker residents unaccounted for.

"At least most of them left voluntarily," he mused. "Although to where?"

And why.

And what happened to them?

He replayed the day again. This time, he noticed one man in particular, who seemed to be the leader. He wore a much larger backpack, and an object that looked like a fishing pole protruded out through the top of it.

"Not a lot of fishing holes in the area."

He was about to jot this detail down, when he heard a shout from the stairwell. Harper was screaming for everyone to come quickly.

Bix leapt from his seat and raced down the hallway, his heart pounding in his ears. "Is it Finn?" he yelled. "What happened? Is he okay?"

Harper's voice faded as he ran down the stairs toward the medical bay. The hard concrete walls distorted his words beyond recognition, but whatever he was saying, it didn't sound good.

CHAPTER
08

THEY FOUND BREN DRAPED OVER FINN, SOBBING uncontrollably. She had his shoulders in her hands and was trying to sit him up, but she was too weak. Self-neglect over the past week had sapped all of her strength, and the most she could manage to do was jerk his limp body from side to side.

Harrison went to her and tried to lift her away, but she lashed out at him, shrieking at everyone to leave her alone. The sounds of her weeping filled the room, drowning out the beeps and chirps of the medical equipment.

"Bren," Eddie said. He sat down next to her and gently placed his hands on her shoulders. "Bren, stop. You have to let him go."

"No!" she cried. "No! He was just here. He was just here! Finn!"

They all turned to Harper for explanation.

"He woke up," he said, breathlessly. "Bren was talking to him. She said his name and he opened his eyes."

"It was just a reflex," Harrison said. "He's been in a coma for—"

"Bix?"

They all stopped and turned back toward the bed. Bren jerked upright. "Finn?" she whispered.

"Bren?"

His eyes flickered open, tried to focus, then closed again.

Harper stepped quickly over to the monitors and checked the screens. "Heart rate's forty-two," he said. "Pressure's critically low."

"What should we do?" Bren asked.

Harper shook his head. "Adrenaline?"

"I don't think that's a good idea," Harrison said, putting a hand on his shoulder. "Let him rest. There's nothing we can do. If he wakes again—"

"I'm staying," Bren said. "Finn needs me!"

Bix pulled over a second chair. "Me, too."

Harper joined them, effectively blocking access to the adults, as if they feared they might do something harmful. Eddie glanced at Harrison and tilted his head toward the hallway. The two men left. Kaleagh didn't follow.

"What's going on?" Harrison asked Eddie, once they were out of earshot.

"I'm worried."

"About Finn? We all are. Or do you mean the kids?"

"All of them, of course, but—"

"Look, Eddie, I've had my doubts about Finn recovering, but honestly, this feels different. Maybe, just maybe, he's finally out of the woods."

"Oh, he'll survive," Eddie said stiffly. "I have no doubt about that now."

Harrison looked surprised. "Really? Then what's the matter?"

"Back there in Bunker Eight, after I was scalded. You remember that?"

Harrison nodded. "How could I forget? Ninety percent of your skin boiled off. It was literally touch and go for a while."

"That's the point. I should have died, but I didn't. Finn should have died, and now it looks like he'll survive, too."

Harrison's confusion deepened. "We all knew it was possible. We've all seen what those things inside you can do.

But you'll have to excuse me if I'm being a bit thick. Some of us don't have the level of experience you have with them."

Eddie winced, sensitive to Harrison's situation. Neither he nor Bix had received the injections and so were nanite-free. While it meant they were immune to the Flense, they also did not have the benefits the nanites brought. Harrison's recent infection, from a relatively superficial injury, was just one example. In a sense, they had to be a lot more careful than the others not to get hurt.

"I think Finn regaining consciousness, however transiently, is a sign he's past the worst of it," Eddie said. "Every day he lives is another day those things inside him get to repair what's broken."

"So I'm not understanding your concern then," Harrison asked. He glanced past him toward the doorway. "Are you worried about Bren having unrealistic expectations about his recovery? Because I've spoken with Kaleagh about preparing her, making sure she takes better care of herself first, but also—"

"Frankly, I'm worried about all of us, not just Bren. None of us knows how Finn might . . . how he might change, once he's fully recovered. Once he's back among us."

"Physically?"

"And emotionally."

To Harrison, it seemed almost incredible that they were now talking about Finn as if his death was a sure thing, but to actually think of him fully healthy again, brain and spinal cord damage repaired, no longer suffering from multiple bone fractures and internal bleeding. Wasn't it a bit premature to worry about how the trauma might affect his personality?

"I'm listening," he said.

"I never told anyone this, but when I was recovering, and for months afterward, I wasn't in a very good place. I mean, physically, my body was repairing itself just fine. But emotionally, I was a train wreck. I was unsure of myself, angry, half the time uncertain of who I was. Or worse, *what* I was. At times, I was out of control, lashing out when I didn't mean to. I was totally aware of it, yet I couldn't seem to stop myself or rein in my emotions. I felt like an observer, a passenger inside my own body. I didn't know where the recovery would end up taking me."

"Well, first of all, you didn't know about the nanites, so of course it would mess you up wondering how it was all possible. It didn't make sense. But Finn—"

"It continued long *after* we became aware of them. I felt like the only reason I was alive was because of something supernatural and that I didn't really deserve to be here. Even worse, I feared I was losing myself, becoming something that wasn't me. And at the same time, I was terrified that I'd lose it all and go back to being the way I was before, that my physical strength and abilities would all be taken away. I worried about it night and day. It ate me up from the inside."

"You're worried that Finn will go through the same emotional rollercoaster?"

"Maybe not exactly the same, but something like it. It's inevitable."

"He might, or it might be completely different for him. You're two different people, different ages, different life experiences. And the circumstances of your accidents are different. We don't even know what the injuries might have done to his mind, much less be able to predict how his recovery will proceed."

"At this point, I'd be surprised if we see anything less than a full recovery, both physical and neurological. Emotional, however . . . ."

"What are you thinking?"

"It's going to be hard on him. The one thing that helped me keep my shit together was my daughter, Hannah. Having her to look after, to make sure she was safe in this world, kept me focused. If I hadn't had her to keep me grounded, I know I would've gone insane. Finn doesn't have that."

"He's got Bren. And Bix. And now Harper."

"I have no doubt the bonds he shares with them are strong, but it's not the same as having a child of his own to really focus him, make him rise above. A child, especially one as vulnerable as Hannah, puts things on a whole different plane. I mean, you should know what I'm saying, being a parent yourself— not that Bix hasn't proven himself capable of taking care of himself, but—"

"Bix is a lot more self-reliant than you know. He spent most of his childhood fending for himself."

Eddie simply nodded at this, not wanting to pry. Harrison had alluded in the past to both he and Bix's mother not always being there for him. "My point," he said, "is that there are sacrifices you're willing to make when it's your flesh and blood. You put them above everything and everyone else, even yourself. You find yourself taking extraordinary measures."

"Like staying away from Hannah? You're afraid that you'll hurt her because of your strength?"

Eddie hesitated.

"You never could. And neither could Finn. We're all here for him, supporting him. We'll get him through anything he's going to have to deal with."

Eddie nodded reluctantly. "I hope you're right."

"Well, we won't know until we cross that bridge, will we? And there's a heck of a long way to go before we even come to it."

CHAPTER 09

"IT'S AN ANTENNA," HARRISON SAID, STEPPING INTO the watch room the next day.

Bix swiveled around in his chair. He had spent the better part of the morning poring over the video records from after the bunker residents' main exodus, trying to determine if the people still unaccounted for had left. So far, they hadn't, and his eyes felt like they were bleeding. "What's an antenna?"

"The thing sticking out of that man's backpack—antenna, not a fishing pole."

"How do you know?"

Harrison dropped something onto the table. It was long and thin, crusty with sand, and appeared to be broken in half. "They're parts to an antenna," he said, showing Bix how they screwed together to form a single six-foot long rod. "Specifically, it's a homemade antenna for a mobile phone or radio. I found it buried by the fence near the bones."

"This morning? You went out alone?"

"I was careful, Bix."

"You know the rules. No one goes anywhere outside the bunker without a lookout. That was your own rule, remember?"

"And who decided to leave the bus and walk half a day through Wraith-infested territory alone?"

"That was before we knew how bad it was out here. Besides, you could've stopped me that day. Why didn't you?"

"Finn needed you."

"That's it?"

Harrison thought about this for a moment. "I guess it's because I realized I can't always be here for you. The day will come when—"

"Don't talk like that."

"Well, as I said, Finn needed you then, and right now he needs his brother, and I wasn't about to pull Harper away so he could watch me dig around in the sand."

"You could have asked me."

Harrison chuckled, then coughed to clear his throat of phlegm. He still hadn't recovered entirely from the infected bite, which worried Bix. With all the antibiotics he was taking, he should've gotten better by now. "I promise I won't do it again. But after you showed me the recording last night, I remembered seeing something out there. I needed to know."

He shifted a pack off his shoulder and set it onto the table on top of the broken antenna. Whatever was inside rattled heavily, like there were a lot of large metal pieces. The fabric was stiff and almost colorless from exposure to the elements. Otherwise, Bix recognized it as the same bag the man in the recording had been wearing the day they left. The same unique patch of an angry bulldog was stitched onto the front.

"Found this buried close by."

Bix pulled it closer. One of the straps was stained, and he realized it was old blood. He opened it up and found a large boxy object inside. The side panels were vented and several dials and switches were mounted on top. The casing was painted dull green. It had cracked open, and wires and electrical components spilled out.

"Looks like the antenna might've snapped off at the base," Harrison said. "This tells us they were attacked very quickly after they left."

"Wraiths," Bix muttered.

"Or wolves. There's also a large battery pack. No good, obviously. The terminals are corroded and the acid's leaked out. And this." He held up an old-fashioned wired handset.

"What good is a mobile phone?" Bix asked. "Would any of the cell towers still work four months after the end of the world? And who would they call?"

Harrison shrugged. "I agree about the networks being down, but this is actually a radio, meant for short range communication, not a phone. I'm going to ask Eddie to take a look at it, see if he can get it working again. If not, we'll have to wait until we get back to Westerton. Stephen Largent knows more about this sort of stuff than either of us."

"Who would they be talking to?"

"The people they left inside here maybe? I don't know. One thing's almost certain, however. We can now say with confidence whose bones I've been counting. I mean, I was beginning to suspect after I'd recorded the hundredth skull, especially with so many of them being on the smaller size."

"They didn't get very far. Guess that's not surprising, since they were on foot."

"Which reminds me. Have you seen Eddie? Are they back yet?"

"Jonah said they might be late. They're close to getting one of the buses to run. If you ask me, it's about time."

"It took Jonah months to get the bus at Bunker Eight working again. I have faith in him. If anyone can do it, he can."

Bix didn't want his father seeing how the comment irritated him, so he swung the chair back around. In doing so, he accidentally knocked the backpack onto the floor.

"Careful, Bix!" Harrison yelped, and stooped down to gather what had fallen out.

"Have you seen this?" Bix said, snatching a small thin book out of the pile. The paper was yellowed and stiff with age and covered in handwriting. In some places, the ink had bled, but most of the text was still legible. "This looks a lot like the one Finn had. Same size, same type of cover on it."

"Let me see." Harrison carefully pried it open and studied the writing. "Looks like the journal Abraham carried around. If this is the bunker leader's, it might give us some answers."

"Like why they left? Were they running away from something? Or toward?"

"That," Harrison said, slipping the book into his jacket pocket. He swept the remaining items back into the bag. "And why they blocked the lower levels."

CHAPTER
10

THERE WAS GOOD NEWS THAT EVENING, ALTHOUGH IT didn't come as a result of Harrison's dive into the bunker leader's journal. Or from Eddie and Jonah's efforts at the maintenance depot down the road. The announcement came from Bren, who informed them that Finn was awake again and starting to talk. He still hadn't said much, just whispered her name and a few random words. But she considered it a big deal, because he recognized her right away. "I think he's actually happy to see me," she said.

In contrast, Harper's appearance by his bedside had caused Finn to become agitated.

"He might be confused," Harper reasoned. "He could be suffering from amnesia and not remember anything that happened in the moments prior to the accident. He might not realize I'm really here."

"It's pretty common after a traumatic event to lose memory," Eddie acknowledged. "I'd be upset if I woke up and saw what I thought was myself standing beside me."

They wanted to go down to the medical bay and visit Finn, but Harper resisted, asking that they give him a little more time before trying. "He needs his rest."

"He's right," Bren agreed, surprising the others. She still hadn't warmed up to Harper. None of them really had, but Bren's interactions with him had been particularly downright frigid. "Mom's with him now, and that's enough."

She plopped herself down at the table and heaved a deep sigh. The toll of her vigil was written all over her face. She looked more haggard than ever, but when she smiled, it still managed to brighten the room. "And I'm so grateful to Harper," she added, eliciting surprised looks from the others. "He's actually been so helpful. I think Finn's going to be okay."

"I haven't done anything you haven't," he said, modestly.

She shrugged, leaving them all more confused than ever.

Bix prayed she was right. He wanted Finn to be healed sooner rather than later, fully rather than partially. Maybe once he was, then maybe they could all go back to the way things were before. He was getting tired of feeling so lost and alone. And it wouldn't feel so awkward all the time, like it was now with Harper. His trying so hard not to step on anyone's toes was starting to get on their nerves. Finn had never been like that. He didn't try to please everyone all the time.

They lasted only until after dinner before deciding to visit Finn. He opened his eyes the moment they walked in, but it took him awhile to focus, and a long time to recognize each of them in turn. The struggle was apparent on his face, and the truth of his long road ahead became painfully clear. He was able to recall Bix's and Jonah's names without much difficulty, but was unable to come up with Eddie's and Mister Blakeley's.

Harper held back, choosing to remain out of Finn's line of sight. He said he didn't want to upset his brother again.

Finn was weak and almost completely dependent on their help. They quietly cheered when he lifted his arms to grasp their hands. No one missed the fact that there was no movement from the waist down.

"Let him rest," Harrison quietly told them, after barely a quarter of an hour had passed. "At least we know now. We can all breathe easier."

"Easier," Eddie solemnly echoed.

Missus Abramson asked that she be the one to continue watching over him, finally putting her foot down and insisting Bren take care of herself for once. "You're wasting away to nothing, honey. Get a shower and some clean clothes."

"I want to stay, Mom."

"You smell. Bad."

"Mom!"

"There's a pile of leftover clothes in the hallway on Level Three. Take whatever you need. I even found underwear."

"*Mom! Eew!*"

"You've been wearing the same ones for weeks now, and the last time I looked, they had holes."

Bix snorted. Bren covered her face in embarrassment.

"Just throw the old ones away. They're not worth saving."

"Okay! Okay, Mom! I'm going! Just stop talking!"

* * *

They eventually found each other again in the library on the first level, which they had converted into a communal dormitory, filling it with mattresses from the residence level two floors down. Bix kept trying to convince Jonah to join him in a game of cards, but the older boy declined, claiming he was too tired. It was an obvious lie, because instead of settling down to sleep, he and Eddie got into a discussion about their work out at the maintenance depot.

"Everything's in terrible shape," Jonah complained. "Engine parts missing, hoses cracked. No power to run the tools. And even if we do get something to work, where are we going to get any usable fuel?"

"Can't we just make more, like we did before?" Bix asked.

"No more trying to get the diesels to run on crap cooking oil," he said. "We wasted a bunch of time working on two engines before realizing they were air-locked and the injectors shot. I think someone intentionally ran them dry so no one could use them again."

Eddie nodded. "We removed the filters and tried to blow fresh diesel from Adrian's truck through the lines to reprime the engines, but it was no good."

"They can't all be that bad," Bix said.

"Some actually look pretty decent under the hood, but then you've got to deal with gelled up diesel inside the tanks."

"What I can't figure out," Eddie said, "is what happened to the buses that brought the bunker residents here. Close to four hundred people, so there had to be, what, between six and ten buses to carry them all? Where are they now? Where did they go? They wouldn't have just dropped people off and driven away, would they?"

"Another mystery," Harrison mused, distractedly. He was focused on the book he and Bix had found earlier in the day, trying not to tear the delicate pages as he pried them gently apart. It looked like he was in for a long and painfully difficult process.

"Someone could have scavenged them," Bix said.

Eddie shook his head. "If they came here looking, they would have found the bunker, like we did."

"Maybe they used them to bus out the miners. What do you think, Dad?"

Harrison got up. "I'm going to the kitchen. Got an idea how to peel the pages apart without causing more damage."

"You should try steam," Bix called after him.

They watched him go, then resumed their conversation.

"Look," Jonah said, "we've got just about enough fuel in Adrian's truck for one trip back to Haven. I think it might be best to just give up on trying to fix up another vehicle and instead use what we have to get back up there. It's just over two hundred miles, and we should be able to make it in a day, assuming we don't run into trouble in Salt Lake City. We can trade some of our food and supplies for another vehicle, maybe even weapons."

"I don't like that idea," Eddie said, speaking in a way that indicated he'd already been through this before with Jonah. "We don't know those people. How can we trust them? At the very least, they're going to want to know where we got the supplies."

"We trusted them before."

"Don't confuse desperation with willingness. We needed them, used them, and now we're in their debt. Besides, you remember what that guy Shaw said. They won't sell us guns and ammunition."

"They gave us the Hummer with the fifty cal and enough ammo to—"

"Loaned, not gave, in exchange for bringing Adrian back to them."

"So we hand him over."

"That's not happening," Eddie said. "Harrison believes he's useful to us."

"Dad's wrong. The only thing Adrian's useful for is target practice."

Eddie winced. "Maybe so, but I trust your father's judgment. Who I don't trust is the people in Haven, so I'm happy to just stay the hell away from there. For now anyway."

"There's more than enough supplies here to trade."

"There's at least a thousand people living inside Haven. Once they see what we've got, they're going to want it all."

"So we hide it."

"Where, Jonah? How?"

"Okay, then what do we do?"

"We keep working on getting a vehicle to run. If we get desperate, we can try to de-gel some of the diesel. We can use it for the pickup. We make a beeline for Westerton, two or three of us, get their trucks and come back. Three days there tops, two if we drive straight through. Be back in, what, a week at the most? The rest can hunker down here and be with Finn as he heals."

"And what do we do with Adrian in the meantime?" Bix asked. "The longer he's alive, the more dangerous he becomes. You know he's got nothing to do down there but plan his escape. And what he'll do to us if he does. He won't just take off. He'll stick around until he's killed us all."

Eddie muddled over this for a while. "We take him to Westerton. I'm sure we could handle him for the trip. Then we lock him up there until he agrees to help us. If he doesn't . . . ."

"Does that mean killing him?" Harper asked, speaking up for the first time.

Jonah shrugged. "We'll all sleep better knowing he isn't going to slit our throats in the middle of the night."

11

BIX STAGGERED DOWN THE DARKENED HALLWAY
moaning and clutching his stomach in agony.

He hadn't noticed that the automatic lights were on in
the kitchen, just as he didn't see his father's empty bedroll.
In fact, it hadn't been used at all during the night, but he
wouldn't have thought anything of it anyway. Everyone's
schedule was messed up. There were guard shifts to cover
and people randomly getting up to check on one thing or
another, whether it was Finn, or the access doors, or their
prisoner. Plus, there were the usual visits to the bathroom or
the kitchen for a glass of water or canned juice.

He staggered in and collapsed into the first chair at the
table closest to the door.

"Bix?" Harrison said, glancing up in alarm. He was
leaning on one of the tables, writing on a notepad. Loose
sheets of paper were scattered everywhere. "Bix, you okay?"

"My stomach," he whispered. "Starving."

Harrison grinned at the melodramatics. "I'll cook us up
something in a bit."

"How long have you been up?"

"All night. Finally figured out how to separate the pages
without tearing them." He held one up, the page carefully
sliced out of the journal and draped over a baking rack to
dry. "Steam did the trick. And patience. Lots of patience."

"Isn't that what I suggested?"

"Was it?"

"Um, yeah." He waited for his thanks, but realized with irritation that it wasn't going to come. "So, it's readable then?"

"The ink's smeared in places, and I did get some bleed-through. But most of it's legible. Once the pages dry out completely, they might be easier to read."

Bix got up and went over to the industrial-sized refrigerator. "Anything useful so far?"

"Barely started digging into it, but yeah, I think so."

The inside of the fridge still smelled of bleach and mold. They'd discovered it filled with growth the day of their arrival from food left behind. Lack of moisture and oxygen had starved the growth of vitality, turning it into a brittle black powder. Missus Abramson had spent days scraping it out, then scrubbing the walls clean, but the stains and smells stubbornly persisted.

He considered last night's leftovers in the bowl on the middle rack. The only other thing in there was a steel jug the size of a small trash can half-filled with reconstituted milk. He wrestled it out, sniffed the contents, then set it onto the counter.

"If you want to wait, I'll whip us up some scrambled eggs and pancakes," his father said, still absorbed in his work.

"Sounds good." He grabbed the biggest bowl he could find and a spoon from the industrial dishwasher and took them over to the lineup of canisters next to the microwave ovens. Missus Abramson had filled them with different kinds of breakfast cereals from the sealed bags in the larder. He mixed several different kinds together before adding the milk.

"But you're going to eat anyway?"

"I said I'm starving," Bix snapped.

His father straightened up and stretched, cracking the bones in his back. "Everything okay?"

"Why wouldn't it be?"

"You just seem a bit . . . like you didn't sleep well."

Bix took the bowl back to a different table, studiously avoiding eye contact. He was curious about the journal, but acted like he didn't care. Why should he, if no one was going to give him credit for anything? He'd seen the book first. He'd recognized how similar it was to Finn's. He'd suggested using steam to separate the pages. It would be nice to get thanked for something.

Harrison sighed. "Well, it would seem there was more to the bunkers than we realized."

"Like what?"

"We think that—"

"And who's we?"

"Harper," Harrison answered, uneasily. "He helped out a while."

Bix's face pinched. He scanned the kitchen, suddenly certain Finn's twin was going to appear out of one of the corners where he'd been lurking.

"He's not here, Bix. He left for the medical bay an hour— Damn, *two* hours ago," Harrison corrected, checking his watch. "Guess I lost track of time."

"If you wanted help, why didn't you come get me?"

"You were sound asleep. And it's not like I asked for Harper's help, he just showed up on his own, said he couldn't sleep."

Bix muttered something about kissing ass under his breath. His father clearly heard it, because he walked over and placed a hand on Bix's shoulder. "If you're mad about yesterday, I'm—"

"I'm not mad!"

"Is it Finn, then?"

Bix shoved another spoonful of cereal into his mouth and crunched it into mush.

Harrison heaved another sigh and went back to the other table. "So, we have this theory that—"

"Is he your new pet project? Harper? You see him all alone and can't help feeling sorry for him. 'Now there's another pity case that needs my help.' Is that it? Poor lonely Harper. You're just not happy unless you have someone to save."

"You were never a pity case to me, Bix. Someone had to take responsibility for—"

"You didn't."

"Bix, the way things were going with you and your mom, I couldn't just let you flounder."

"You know how much I relish these father-son pep talks, *Dad*."

"Be thankful you have someone to—"

"I'm old enough to take care of myself! I don't need you! I was doing it for years before you came and butted in on me and Mom."

"You blame me for her leaving?"

"We did just fine before you showed up!"

"Really? All those nights of you sitting alone backstage while your mother was touring? You didn't seem fine to me."

"Well, you can be happy now, because she's dead, so there's nothing more to say about it! And anyway I don't care."

Harrison decided not to push it. He didn't know what had brought this up now. Was it Finn's brush with death? Was it his own? He hadn't told anyone how much the recent infection had affected him, but he sensed Bix knew. When it came to old world diseases, he was more vulnerable than most. Living protected inside the bunker had made him forget that.

Luckily, they'd found this place in time. If they hadn't, Harrison knew he would have died, leaving Bix alone. It was something he'd been trying to prepare the boy for since the day they'd escaped the Flense, but he now wondered if he'd been a little too coy about it. The bite, as minor as it had been, was a stark reminder that the both of them — not just him — were just one tiny accident away from catastrophe. Being around people who seemed almost invincible didn't help.

"So, what's this theory about the bunkers?" Bix grumbled.

Harrison studied the boy's face for a moment, noticing for the first time how much it had changed in the past few months. It hardly seemed possible that he was a young man now. "Well, for starters," he said, turning back to the papers, "they might not have all been a bunch of random people just trying to escape the Flense and wait it out. In fact, I think they found out about the nanites very early on. They might even have known about them before arriving."

"How?"

"Harper told me there were people in his bunker working on a cure, just like Seth Abramson was also doing in ours. So why not here, too? It would make sense."

"Missus Abramson said there's no cure," Bix said, hoping to glean his father's thoughts on the matter.

"That's what Seth told her, but what if he was wrong?"

"Jonah doesn't think he was. He says a cure is a pipe dream."

"Jonah's just tired of chasing around for one. We all are. But I won't stop believing we can figure it out."

"He's got Eddie convinced, too."

"Eddie's . . . conflicted."

"They'd both have us head straight back to Westerton today if we had a vehicle ready to go."

"Is that what's bothering you?"

"I couldn't care less what Jonah does. He can do what he wants. If he wants to go back to Westerton, let him. At least he'd be happier there than here."

"Do you honestly believe he'd be happy living out his life behind a fence? What kind of existence is that? Why wouldn't he want there to be a cure?"

"I don't know! Why are you so stubborn there is one?"

"Because I— There *has* to be one. We just have to find it. And if we can't, then . . . well, then we make one."

"And what if it's impossible?"

Harrison shook his head. "I spent a lot of time talking it over with Harper. I know, I know, but we should listen to what he has to say. He actually knows a lot more about this mess than we do."

"So, why hasn't he said so? Why is he keeping secrets?"

"He's not. We just haven't given him much of a chance — or reason — to share."

"That's bull crap. Nobody's told him to keep quiet."

"Nobody's encouraged him to share, either."

"Good thing you were around to do it then," Bix grumbled spitefully, but he knew his father was right.

Harrison stepped back over to the table and picked up the pad of paper onto which he'd been transcribing the legible journal's pages. "I want you to look at something," he said, sifting through the sheets until he found the one he wanted. "See this?"

It appeared to be some kind of list. The item at the top was crossed out. "These are codenames for all of the bunkers. There's ten listed, but Harper says there's actually eleven. Another was added to replace one that was destroyed in a fire. It just wasn't finished before the Flense hit." He pointed to a notation on the last item. "Notice something?"

"Caco-three," Bix said. "That's the code Harper used to send us here. So, he didn't come up with it on his own."

"Exactly. It's the chemical formula for calcium carbonate, aragonite. I asked him how it was possible he knew the code, and he said he'd seen this same exact list in his own bunker leader's journal."

"Harper was a bunker leader?"

"No, but several people in his bunker had access to the journal. The guy who showed up at our front door when all this started was one. That's how he knew about us. Harper assumed that the situation was the same in our bunker and was counting on at least one of us recognizing the code for Bunker Ten, *this* bunker."

"Mister Bolles never mentioned any of this to us."

"I don't think he knew what the notations meant. Remember, he took over when the original bunker leader, David Gronbach, died suddenly. It was just days after we arrived, so maybe he was never properly briefed."

"That explains why we were so unprepared," Bix grumbled. "Everyone in Harper's bunker knew about the other bunkers. They got access to the leader's journal. They had all this medical training that we didn't."

"You can't blame Abraham or Gia for those things. I think they both got thrown into roles they weren't prepared to take on. When I mentioned to Harper that a second bus never arrived, he said the people on it were probably more scientists meant to help Seth work on the cure, like the arrangement in his own bunker. Unfortunately, we'll probably never know the truth."

"We should ask Missus Abramson."

"And I plan to." He shrugged. "In the meantime, I think we can better appreciate how well we managed, given the circumstances. You and I certainly have nothing to complain about, since we weren't even supposed to be there in the first place. We were lucky to be in the right place at the exact right time."

"Why *were* we there?" Bix asked. "Why did you suddenly decide to take us on that road trip? It wasn't even on our way to Seattle to meet Mom."

He hadn't thought about that horrific day in ages, partly because dredging up those terrible memories was too painful. For months afterward, he'd had nightmares. It took a long time to accept that he'd never see his mother again, not in any recognizable state, anyway.

He glanced down at the list through the tears pooling in his eyes. The other bunker codenames meant nothing to him. He supposed they were left intentionally vague, so the average person wouldn't be able to easily decipher them.

"We got lucky Kari figured out that symbol," he said. "If she hadn't, we never would've found this place. And Harper."

Harrison sucked in a shaky breath. "We had no right to figure any of it out, no right at all. It took every single one of us, not just Kari."

He turned and walked over to the sink and leaned on it for a minute. Bix felt suddenly ashamed at the way he'd yelled before. And for mentioning Kari. He hated seeing how much it hurt his father.

"Kari was the one who always pushed us to keep going," Harrison said, his back still turned. His voice was thick with emotion. "But when she died, it shocked me like nothing else ever did. I was done. I told myself no more. And so, that last night in the house, I was ready to tell Eddie it was time to put an end to this crazy undertaking of Finn's. We both had serious doubts about the wisdom of chasing after someone as violent as Adrian, even to save Harper. But then I saw how much you believed in Finn and stood by him, and it reminded me of her determination. I realized I couldn't give up, either."

"You got bit," Bix said, quietly. "You could've died."

"That's a bit of an exaggeration."

"Is it?"

"Well, I'm better now." He turned. "And Finn's recovering, too. We almost lost him, but he's coming back. And now, after finding this journal, I can't explain it, I feel reenergized, more focused and hopeful than we probably deserve to be. I feel like we're supposed to do this." He laughed self-consciously.

"Are you sure someone didn't switch out your antibiotics for something a bit . . . stronger?"

Harrison wiped a tear from his eye and smiled. "You better finish that cereal before it gets soggy. Or soggier, anyway."

"Do you think the bunkers had a way to communicate with each other?"

"Why do you ask?"

"That radio thing you found."

"Oh, I doubt it. I don't think the signal would reach more than a few miles."

"It's just that Finn once told me he'd overheard his father talking to someone inside the watch room, except he was alone. He was telling someone about Eddie's accident right after it happened."

Harrison frowned, puzzled, then snatched the weathered notebook off the table and flipped through it, no longer being careful not to tear the paper. On a flimsy page, still moist from steam, he found what he was searching for. "I didn't know what this was a list of before, but it's so obvious now. Check out the eighth item down."

The journal's previous owner had scratched out a pair of letters and replaced them with a different set.

"DG?" Bix asked. "AB?"

"David Gronbach, our first leader."

"And AB for—!"

"Abraham Bolles. And since Finn's dad didn't take over until a couple weeks *after* we were all sealed up inside, how did the leader of this bunker know? They were talking to each other!"

Bix spun around and headed for the door.

"Where are you going?" Harrison asked.

"The phone in the watch room! That must be it! That's where Finn's dad was—"

"It's gone, Bix, dismantled. I already checked."

"Why?"

"The handset I found out by the fence, I wanted to know where it came from, so I searched until I found it. The phone in that room is the only one that's missing."

CHAPTER

"IT'S A FAIR REQUEST AND DESERVES AN HONEST response," Harper said, replying to Jonah's demand that he tell them everything he knew and leave nothing out, not even the tiniest detail.

"So, you admit you haven't been honest," Bix said.

"No, I wanted to share, but there hasn't exactly been the right time. I mean it's . . . complicated."

"It's not complicated," Bix said, bluntly. "You just tell the truth."

"He will," Harrison assured everyone.

They were all in the kitchen, and, as promised, Mister Blakeley had prepared a breakfast of eggs and pancakes, both reconstituted from shelf-stable powders using reconstituted milk. He served them up with thick fried slices of canned ham. The texture of the meat was off, but it was still a decade shy of its 'Best used by' date.

"Where do I start?" Harper wondered aloud. "Maybe a little background first."

Bix groaned.

"Take all the time you need, Harper," Eddie told him. "We're not going anywhere."

Harper sucked in a deep breath and slowly let it out before answering. The pinched look on his face made clear that the memories he was asked to recall were painful ones. They were for each of them, but these memories seemed particularly difficult for Harper. "I was at my Young Genius internship, at a company called Quantum Telligence, and we were—"

A loud crash from the stove caused everyone to jump. Harrison quickly apologized for the interruption, and retrieved the gallon-sized metal pitcher that had slipped from his grip. The impact caused some of the pancake batter to spout out and splash onto his apron and into his hair. Luckily, he managed to rescue most of it. "Did you say Quantum Telligence?"

"You've heard of it?" Eddie asked.

He hesitated before answering. "If I'm remembering correctly, they were a wireless tech company before the Flense."

"That was actually a small part of their business," Harper said. "They sold a few branded products, very niche, innovative type stuff. But their main focus was information processing, everything from science and technology, to economics, agriculture, social sciences, politics. They hired some of the best minds and developed some of the best artificial intelligence in the world. Their main customers were governments."

"Oh my god," drawled Bix, "this is so fascinating I might pass out from excitement. But what the hell does it have to do with Bunker Two? Or Twelve? And the cure?"

"Give him a chance to tell it his way, Bix," Harrison said, wagging the spatula at him. "As Eddie said, we're in no rush here."

"Well, it was fascinating, at least to me," Harper said, defensively. "A lot of these people were my heroes, so it was really cool to be able to meet them in person, people thinking about global issues, like climate change and pollution, food distribution, poverty."

Bix's face pinched. "You were a freaking freshman in high school. Fourteen-year-olds aren't supposed to be thinking about how to save the world. Not normal ones, anyway. They're supposed to be sitting around playing video games and figuring out how to hack into porn sites on their school computers."

"Eew!" Bren exclaimed, but Jonah burst out laughing.

"Oh, sorry," Bix snapped, "Mister I'm-too-busy-for-fun-because-I-have-to-skip-school-and-help-my-brother-chop-stolen-car-parts. Explains a lot."

"Like what?"

"Like why you're such an ass."

"Bix!" Harrison exclaimed, horrified.

"It's all right, Mister B," Jonah said, and turned back to Bix. "Remind me again how your porn hacking skills have helped us out? At least I was able to get us a vehicle working so we could leave Bunker Eight."

"Oh, right. So why are we stranded now?"

"We're getting off topic," Eddie said. "Harper, go on."

"I wasn't a freshman," Harper said, correcting Bix. "I was a sophomore. And I don't know if you remember, but there were a lot of people my age starting to rise up in anger at do-nothing governments. We were facing *real* existential threats. This company, Quantum Telligence, was right in the thick of it, tracking emerging global risks to human survivability. They were trying to understand how they might spread so we could head them off."

"Yeah, great job," Bix noted, ironically. "Guess the brainiacs at Quantum Leap—"

"Quantum Telligence."

"Whatever. They weren't all that brainy after all, were they, if they never saw this coming."

"Bix," Harrison said tiredly. He was in the process of removing another batch of pancakes from the stovetop. "Would you please—"

"Like some more pancakes? Yes, thanks for asking!" He raised his plate. "Fill her up!"

"I'll take them!" Bren said, jumping in front of him.

"You?"

"They're for Finn," she explained, and grabbed the plate from Harrison's hand.

"Finn?" Bix said, gaping after her as she hurried out.

Everyone knew it was too soon to try Finn on solid food, but no one stopped her. Getting him nourishment had been a growing concern, especially after he pulled out his feeding tube. They doubted he could chew, much less swallow, but if Bren could somehow manage to get him to eat, the better for them all. After making such a miraculous recovery, the last thing anyone wanted to see was Finn wasting away to nothing.

"Still a couple little ones left, Bix," Harrison said, scraping out the last of the batter and dribbling it onto the hot griddle.

"Gimme!" Bix cried. Snatching the spatula off the counter, he flipped the undercooked pancakes over, smashed them down till they sizzled, then transferred them onto his plate before anyone else could claim them. He promptly drowned them in artificial maple syrup.

"It'd be quicker if you just drank the batter straight from the can," Jonah remarked. "Cut out the middleman."

"You're just mad because I got these before you."

"Yeah, I'm jealous of that pouch you're growing there, buddy."

"It's fuel storage. Underneath is a lean, mean fighting machine."

Harper's gaze volleyed between the two, his eyes widening with each exchange.

Bix shoveled the last oversized forkful into his mouth, then washed it down with a full glass of neon orange drink. When he stood up, he looked a little woozy.

"Uh oh," Jonah said, smirking. "Maybe eating them half raw wasn't such a good idea."

Bix's face turned pale. He hiccupped, swallowed, then let out a belch so loud it rang off the stainless steel fixtures.

Jonah waved his hand in front of his nose.

"I'm ready for lunch," Bix said, patting his stomach with satisfaction.

"May I continue?" Harper asked, exasperated.

"By all means," Bix replied, crumbs stuck to his chin. He returned to his seat with the milk jug wedged precariously into the crook of his elbow and another glass of reconstituted orangeade. "Although, fair warning, unless the fascinating part comes soon, I might fall asleep."

"Ignore him," Harrison said. "I don't know what's gotten into him lately."

Bix grabbed his stomach and shook it. "Pancakes. Are there any more?"

"I'm not making another batch."

"*As* I was saying," Harper tried again, but this time it was Missus Abramson who stopped him, worried that Bren would miss what was said. Harper slumped in his chair, defeated.

"We can catch Bren up later," Eddie decided. "Go ahead, Harper. And just talk over the boys. When they're at each other's throats, we know things are normal. It's when they're nice to each other that we need to start worrying."

"We're not at each other's throats," Bix said.

"Yeah, I once tried to wrap my fingers around Bix's neck, but there was too much slack to get a good grip."

"The day you get a grip is the day I start going on a diet."

"Seriously, Harper, just ignore them."

Harper reached unsteadily for his half-empty glass before remembering he wasn't thirsty. Besides, the milk had a weird taste to it. "I thought I won the internship based on the essay I'd submitted, but it turns out my parents probably bribed someone to get it for me."

"Why does that not surprise me?" Jonah said, rolling his eyes. "Rich people always—"

"We weren't rich," Harper countered. "There was a reason for it, and it wasn't for my educational benefit either. I'm sure you've heard about VivVIx." He spelled the name out for them. "They're the people who sold everyone their spots in the bunker."

Eddie leaned forward in his chair, frowning. "They were the agency I used."

Harper nodded. "If you bought a place in one of these bunkers, like my parents did, that's who you went through."

He glanced over at Jonah, eyebrows raised in silent inquiry, but Jonah just shrugged and said he'd never heard the name before. "Sorry. Dad made all the arrangements for our little father-son staycation. I was out of the loop."

"As usual," Bix retorted.

"Well, they had a convincing sales pitch, until my parents found out that the company behind VivVIx was a radical survivalist group known as 6X."

"Yeah, I've heard of them," Jonah said. "They were this doomsday cult, believed humanity was the reason for a new global extinction event."

"The sixth in Earth's geological history," Harper confirmed. "6Xers believed humans were on the endangered list."

"Oh, I get it!" Bix exclaimed. "They're called 6X because of the sixth extinction."

"Yeah, genius," Jonah retorted. "Did you also catch the hidden meaning behind VivVIx?"

"Duh," Bix replied, unconvincingly. "It's so obvious."

"So, 6X terrifies people with threats of extinction," Harrison grunted, "then they make a killing selling spots in survival bunkers. Welcome to the evolutionary pinnacle of the free market: parasitism of the weak and vulnerable. No wonder your parents were skeptical."

"Well, I wouldn't call 6X a radical cult," Eddie said, somewhat defensively. "They didn't stand around on street corners screaming 'The end is near!' and hand out flyers with biblical passages on them. Most 6X followers were successful, well-to-do, well-adjusted folks in the mid and upper tiers of society."

"Methinks he doth protest too much," Bix mumbled, causing Jonah to snort coffee through his nose.

"They didn't sell bunker spaces to naive people in public seminars where you got a free buffet-style lunch just for attending," Eddie persisted, "but on expensive golf courses and in corporate boardrooms. The people who bought them were well-educated, hardworking, sensible folks."

"Maybe you were, but my dad was anything but sensible," Jonah said.

"The point I'm trying to make is, 6X's predictions turned out to be pretty damn accurate."

"But they were just predictions then," Harper said, "based on conjecture and fear and a little science. Before my parents agreed to part with their life's savings for the questionable safety of the bunkers, they wanted to know whether there really was something to the claims. Was it a scam, or was the science solid?"

"So, they arranged to get you access into a doomsday think tank to find out what the experts thought about the threat to humanity?"

Harper nodded. "I didn't realize it at the time, but yes. And it worked. Adults don't censor themselves as carefully when they're around teenagers. They don't think we're paying attention. The secrets they discussed around me would make your toes curl."

"And did you know about the bunkers at the time?"

"Not at first. I wasn't even aware my parents were using me to infiltrate this company. They planted all these questions in my head, which I unwittingly regurgitated to my mentor at Quantum Telligence."

"Well, you obviously gave your parents what they needed to hear, since they went ahead and bought a couple of spots."

"And were trying to buy two more," Harper said, nodding. "For months, my internship was all we talked about at dinner almost every night. I thought my parents were just interested in what I was learning. Turns out they were—"

"Batshit crazy?" Bix offered.

"Don't be so dismissive," Harrison warned. "Your mother and some of her bandmates were survival fanatics, too— off-gridders, paranoid, anti-government."

"And you fit right in with them."

"How so?"

"You lived in a van, never trusted the authorities. You were anti-vax."

"I was never anti-vaccine, Bix. I just didn't trust the government when it came to the new flu shots. I knew they weren't telling the truth about them. Try and convince me my instincts were off."

"I'm glad you brought that up," Harper said. "Turns out the flu scare was actually a carefully crafted 6X PR campaign. It started years earlier, when they began to circulate stories about how bad the flu was and how many people were predicted to die because the traditional vaccine just wasn't cutting it anymore, and how there was a need for something new, something a lot more effective that would protect everybody, before it was too late."

"Fearmongering," Jonah said.

"And laying the groundwork to justify putting the nanites into everyone."

"Whoa, whoa! Wait a minute! Are you saying 6X developed the nanites, too?"

"Not them, no," Harper said.

"Then what the hell do you mean by that?"

"The official line at QT was that the flu scare was nothing but fake news. My mentor even gave me a copy of this white paper they sent to the World Health Organization warning people the numbers didn't justify panic. They didn't name 6X outright, but it was clear that's who they were targeting. Want to guess what effect it had on 6X's credibility?"

"Not good," Jonah offered.

"That's what my parents initially thought, too, which is why they were ready to pull their money out. But the crazy thing is, it had the opposite effect, as if the attention somehow validated the hype. Suddenly, everyone was wondering if there was something to the warnings. More and more people started wondering if maybe they should reserve spots in the bunkers before it was too late. VivVIx's stock price soared. Instead of driving people away, that report and the very public feud that followed raised interest in survival bunker living."

"Even bad publicity can be good sometimes," Eddie noted.

"VivVIx wasn't the only one to benefit. Quantum Telligence's global advisory role also rose."

"Are you saying the two companies conspired with each other to inflate their values?" Harrison asked.

"Yes."

"You have proof, Harper?"

"Not directly, but our bunker leader, Jenkins Rappaport, was some sort of hotshot high up in the Quantum Telligence organization before the Flense. He wasn't the only QT person at Bunker Two, either. There had to be at least thirty experts with us."

"For being so critical of 6X, Quantum Telligence sure had a lot of believers."

"Was Quantum Telligence Seth's employer, too?" Eddie asked Kaleagh.

"Mech inVivo," Harrison replied for her. He looked up when the conversation failed to pick up again right away. "What? Seth told us the day we left Bunker Eight."

"How do you remember a detail like that?"

He shrugged. "Mech inVivo sounds exactly like a company that makes microscopic machines to be put inside our bodies. Just makes sense."

"Seth never mentioned the names of any companies to me before that day," Kaleagh said. "He always refused to say who he worked for, because the company was extremely paranoid about everything— competitors stealing their trade secrets, poaching their employees. He wouldn't even tell me the names of other people he'd met or worked with. He said that everyone had their own little sandbox to play in, and trying to find out what was happening in other people's box was a big no-no."

"Sounds suspiciously to me like the government," Eddie said, and everyone immediately agreed. "Surely, you would have heard about VivVIx, though. They would've sold you your spots in the bunker."

Again, she shook her head. "We didn't buy spots. In fact, I don't think we were even supposed to be in the bunker at all."

"Ha! I knew it!" Bix said, jumping out of his seat. He jabbed an accusing finger at Jonah. "I knew we weren't the only ones who'd stowed away on this little funhouse ride!"

Jonah's father, Jack Resnick, had always begrudged Bix and Harrison for, in his words, "weaseling their way inside the bunker." He made sure to remind people every chance he got that they hadn't paid a dime for the privilege, and he brought it up whenever convenient, like when it came time to assign the nastiest of the chores.

"I meant that it wasn't pre-planned, us having spots," Kaleagh said. "The day it happened, Seth finally got home from his overseas trip. I didn't recognize the car he was driving, although I barely cared about that by then. I was going crazy because of all the news on the TV. Everything was a mess everywhere. Some of the channels weren't even on the air anymore. I tried calling my sister in Reno, but I couldn't get through. At one point, Seth went outside and shut off the gas to the house. He kept saying he wanted to be sure it would still be standing when we got back, and all I kept thinking about was the gas leaks and explosions that had been happening recently. Of course, it was more than that. Schools and businesses were being put on lockdown. The military was activated. Roads were barricaded. Then, out of the blue, he gets a call, and he tells us it's time to leave. I begged for us not to go out there, but he said it was too late and we couldn't stay. We took back roads, guided by the GPS on his phone. I drove while he tried to get updates on his email— until that stopped working. We only knew where to go because he'd been sent an address."

"The evacuation center?"

"Yes. After we arrived, he spoke to some people and we were put on a list. We got on the bus just like everyone else. You know the rest."

"So, let me get this straight," Eddie mused. "Seth worked for a company that was part of a bigger organization developing the nanites, which we now know was responsible for the Flense. Plus, a think tank employs all these experts monitoring global threats. They tell people there's nothing to worry about, but they all end up inside the same bunkers built and sold by a survivalist group that these so-called experts characterized as nut jobs. Is anyone else thinking what I'm thinking?"

"That it's almost lunchtime?" Bix asked. He was in the middle of making another batch of orangeade.

"No, dummy," Jonah said. "That all these different groups were part of a huge conspiracy to con people out of their money. But thank you for playing. We have some lovely parting gifts for you."

"Not just conspiring with each other for profit, Jonah," Harrison said, "but maybe even parts of a single larger organization that made it happen."

Eddie grunted in agreement. "Different arms of the same deadly octopus."

CHAPTER
13

"OCTOPUS?" BREN ASKED, STEPPING INTO THE kitchen.

"The one that started the Flense," Bix explained, unhelpfully.

"The Flense was started by an octopus?"

"Yes, in a garden under the sea."

Bren's look of confusion intensified.

"*People* started it," Harrison clarified. "A company with multiple arms, each one flipping the disaster coin and betting on opposite outcomes simultaneously."

Bren turned to her mother. "Are you talking about Dad? Did he start it?"

"No, honey. Of course not." She went over and tried to take the plate from Bren, not noticing that it was empty.

Bren pulled it away. "I'm not done yet. I just came up to get some more."

"Finn's eating?" Harper asked. "Is he talking?"

Bren shook her head. "Very little. He wants more, though."

"Do you think I might . . . ?" Harper began.

"I think if we all went down to see him, he might perk up a bit."

"Everyone, just stop!" Bix cried. "You guys can't drop a bombshell like this and then act like it's nothing! You *knew* all this?" he accused Harper. "You knew who started the

Flense all along? Does that mean that you — *they* — whoever — know how to stop it?"

"Bix, not now," Jonah said, standing up.

"What do you mean not now? We have to—" He stopped himself and turned to Bren. "Finn's talking?"

"Sort of. He ate everything I took down for him. He asked for more, but I don't know if he means more food or more company. So, I thought we should give him both. He really needs more interaction anyway. So far, it's been just me most of the time, and I don't think it's enough to help him. I don't think *I'm* enough. He needs more stimulation. Maybe it'll help his recovery."

"But you're not sure," Harper said. He looked hurt that she could so glibly discount the time he had also spent with Finn, albeit only while he slept. Harper's presence still tended to upset him.

"You all have been avoiding him. Even you, Harper. You go down there, but you stay out of sight. I don't think it's good for him. He needs to *see* us. He needs to hear us. He needs human contact."

There was a moment of silence as the truth hit home. Each of them had their own reason for avoiding Finn, whether it was guilt, as in Missus Abramson's case, or something else. For Bix, it was his refusal to accept the seriousness of the accident and the possibility that Finn might never get out of bed again, much less remember how close they had once been as friends. For Eddie, it was this crushing sense of foreboding knowing the difficulties that lay ahead for the boy. Jonah had convinced himself that the only way to get over the ache of personal loss was to accept the worst possible outcome, but that ache returned tenfold each time he heard Finn's name.

Ironically, the one person with the most invested in Finn and the most to lose, Bren, had remained unfailingly by his side, even sleeping on a stack of folded blankets on the floor.

It had been she who attended to the most private, most personal of Finn's needs, not as a girlfriend would, but as his nurse. Not even Harper could claim as much.

And then there was Harrison, who worried that Eddie might be right, not so much for Finn's wellbeing, but for Bix's. Bix was emotionally falling apart right before his eyes, and he couldn't do anything to stop it.

He and Eddie exchanged wary glances and nodded, as if simultaneously reaching the same conclusion.

"All right," Eddie said at last. "We'll come down. We can continue this discussion there. It would be better to include Finn anyway."

"We don't even know if he'll be able to understand what we're talking about," Jonah said. "If he's—"

"Do not say it!" Bix warned.

"I'm just saying that he might be—"

"You're the one who's brain damaged!" Bix shouted. He slammed the pitcher of orangeade onto the table and glared at Jonah. "Finn's not brain damaged!"

"That's not what I was going to say," Jonah said. But no one believed him. Caution regarding Finn's recovery had been his constant refrain for the past ten days.

"He's eating, okay?" Bix threw back. "A week ago you thought he was a goner, and today he's eating freaking pancakes and asking for more, for Christ's sake!"

Jonah backed down, shrugging.

"Speaking of which," Harrison said, cutting into the tension with an attempt at levity, "I was saving these for myself, but Finn probably needs them more than me." He reached into the oven and pulled out a plate and swung it out of Bix's reach to give to Bren.

"Let me just wash up real quick and we'll all go down. Eddie's right. We should be having these talks together now, downstairs in the med bay. Finn deserves to be present, whether or not he's in any condition to understand or remember what's being discussed. We're assuming he can't, or doesn't, or won't, but we're wrong to exclude him in any case."

He switched the stove off, then rubbed his hands under the faucet before drying them on a clean corner of the apron, which he dropped onto the table to soak up the orangeade Bix had spilled. Bren asked the others to bring what was left of the drink and some milk, ignoring her mother's assertion that they would upset Finn's stomach.

They found him in the same position they'd last left him the previous evening, sitting up in bed, his face slack and his eyes staring glassily at a spot near the opposite wall. Over the past week and a half, Bren had done a remarkable job keeping him clean, changing his sheets, combing his hair. Even shaving the shadow of growth on his face, which couldn't have been easy, given the wrecked state of his body. His skin had dried and tightened over his cheekbones. Yet flaps of loose skin dangled below the line of his jaw. His eyes had sunken far into their sockets. Tendons stood out on his neck like taut metal cables.

The open sores on his scalp and arms had healed, and even the scabs were already flaking off. The bruises — numbering initially in the dozens before each one ballooned in size and merged into one massive, indistinguishable purple hematoma — had now begun to fade, leaving his skin tinged yellow. His torso, so noticeably twisted from the suspected spinal fracture just days before, had nearly completely realigned. That he was recovering from injuries that would have left him paralyzed, if not dead a dozen times over before the Flense, seemed like a miracle, but the others knew there was nothing miraculous about it. Billions of microscopic machines circulated through his body, busily recycling damaged cells into the makings of new ones at an unnatural pace. It took a massive amount of energy, and all of his molecular reserves had long since been depleted.

Those same nanites saving his life were now consuming healthy tissue to effect their repairs. Each day gone by rendered Finn a little more into a skeleton. He looked like many of the Wraiths they had encountered on the road, and that alone had a marked effect on everyone.

But the ultimate cost, as Eddie silently feared, was yet to be realized.

"Finn?" Bren said in a low, soothing voice. She sat down on the edge of his bed and placed her palm gently against his face and guided it toward her. "Hey, sweetie. I brought you some more breakfast. Do you think you can eat some more?"

He didn't respond. He didn't seem to be aware of her touch or even her presence.

The others watched from where they stood near the doorway, some twenty feet away. They didn't move, didn't make a sound. They simply waited.

"Mom?" Bren said, turning. "Can I have the plate?"

Kaleagh stepped tentatively forward. She extended the dish, leaning away, as if she expected Finn to reach out and grab her. The plate teetered unsteadily in her trembling fingers. "They're kind of dry," she whispered, and looked back at the others for help. "Should we put some syrup on them?"

No one had remembered to bring any.

"Just give them to me like that," Bren said. "He'll be fine." She took the plate and set it on Finn's lap. He didn't react to the pressure. "Finn, sweetie? Are you hungry?" She waved a pancake under his nose, then touched it to his lips.

Nothing happened at first.

"It takes him a moment," Bren said quietly, and tried again. "Sweetie? Come on, you need to eat something. You need your strength."

His lips gave the barest of twitches. Then, eliciting quiet gasps of surprise from the others, his tongue extended from the jagged gash that was his mouth. It touched the fried batter and stopped, seemingly stuck to it. Then he slowly began to lean forward, his head tilting downward and the angle between upper and lower jaws expanding. His mouth engulfed the edge of the pancake, then suddenly snapped shut with a clack. Everyone flinched in surprise, everyone but Bren, who had expected this and remained still. She'd curled her fingers inward to avoid Finn's teeth.

Again, nothing happened immediately. Finn's jaw didn't work the chunk of pancake inside his mouth. Bren lowered her hand with the remaining bit to her lap and waited.

Finn suddenly wrenched his head to one side, then the other. He repeated this once more. Then he leaned back and started chewing.

"Jesus," Jonah whispered, a look of terrified fascination and revulsion on his face.

Bix elbowed him hard in the side and warned him to shut the hell up.

Finn chewed a moment longer, then swallowed. His Adam's apple bobbed several times before a golf ball-sized shape slid down his gullet. He blinked, and his eyes flicked once in Bren's direction, although not fully, before returning to the far wall. He opened his mouth and an eerie sound came out.

"What the hell?" Bix said. "Was that him asking for more?"

Bren turned to them with a smile and nodded triumphantly. "You see? He's still in there. He's hungry. He's getting better."

Bix exchanged glances with Jonah and his father. The looks on their faces said it all. This wasn't normal behavior. In fact, it was terrifying. What the hell was Finn turning into?

"Anyone else want to try?" Bren asked.

"Moooore . . ." Finn moaned. He leaned forward and opened his mouth again. Spittle and pancake crumbs

dribbled from his chapped lower lip and fell to his lap. Bren reached over with a tissue and wiped the string from his chin. She raised the remaining bit of pancake and touched it to his lip. The unnerving sequence repeated itself, this time with shorter pauses between movements. Finn was slowly awakening.

"Go on," Jonah said in a low voice to Bix. "You're his best friend."

"What?" Bix said, jerking away. "No."

"I'll do it," Harper said. He strode halfway into the room, then hesitated, suddenly uncertain, fearful that Bren might tell him no. Feeding Finn was an intimate act; would she grant him even that?

He reached for the plate, and she nodded, stood, and handed him the last little piece of pancake in her hand. "Watch your fingers," she whispered, and stepped aside so he could sit.

"Moooore . . ." groaned Finn, with greater urgency. He leaned forward even farther, his eyes still fixed on the same invisible spot. His jaw clacked shut, then opened again. *"Moooorrrre!"*

Harper sat, gave the others a skeptical glance, then turned to his twin. "Hey there, Finn," he said, his voice shaking. "It's me, Harper, your brother. Remember me?"

"Moorrrrre . . . ."

"Okay, yeah, sure." He carefully positioned his fingers around the edge of the pancake wedge, then lifted it toward Finn's mouth.

This time, there was almost no tentativeness, no tasting. The moment it touched Finn's lips, he lurched forward and closed his mouth over it. Harper flinched, but to his credit he didn't jerk away. Finn gave his head a violent shake and began to chew.

"Finn? Can you hear me? I'm here," Harper said. A tear escaped one eye and rolled down his cheek. "I should have been here more for you, I know, but—"

"*Moorrre . . . .*"

Harper swapped the tiny crescent of uneaten pancake for a whole one. He folded it in half and tucked his fingers once more. Finn gave no indication he'd heard Harper or knew he was there.

"*More . . . .*"

The dried pancake cracked and a piece tumbled into Finn's lap.

"More."

"Okay, just give me sec—"

"More! More!"

Harper lifted another pancake toward Finn's face, but before he could feed it to his brother, Finn's arm shot up and knocked it out of Harper's fingers.

"More!" he bellowed. "More! MORE! *MORE!*"

Harper scrambled to pluck another piece off the plate, and ended up accidentally knocking everything onto the floor. "Here, Finn," he said, picking up one of the pieces. "Here!"

"Careful!" Eddie warned, and rushed forward to help.

"*MORE!!*"

The hand that had knocked Harper's arm before, reached up again. Finn's fingers wrapped themselves around his brother's wrist and squeezed.

"*MORE!!*"

"I'm trying to, Fi— Ow! Stop! You're squeezing too tight!" He tried to jerk his arm away, but Finn's hand was locked in a death grip. The struggle unbalanced Finn and he slumped forward against Harper, his jaw still clacking open and shut. Harper tried to push him away, but he still wouldn't let go.

"Stop! Someone help me!"

Eddie was the first to reach the bedside. He grabbed Finn's arm and started to pry the fingers off.

"MOOOORE!" Finn roared.

"Help us!" Eddie shouted to the others.

There was a muffled crack, and Harper shrieked in pain. He stumbled backward, away from the bed, and fell to the floor. Finn flopped back against his mattress, convulsed once, then sagged into the pillows. The fire that had burned in his eyes a moment before was gone, extinguished in a blink. His face went slack, his eyelids drooped, and he grew still.

Harper slumped to the floor, cradling his broken wrist, and sobbed.

Finn's jaw dropped open, and his tongue emerged, sampling the air, ready for the next mouthful of pancake. *"More,"* he whispered. *"Moooore."*

CHAPTER

THIS TIME, UNLIKE BEFORE, THERE WASN'T ANY MOVE-ment right after the world grew light. The change in routine confused her. But finally, two of the—

men

—food appeared. It was much later than she'd expected, but it confirmed the pattern in her mind, and the confusion passed.

They went inside the hard, burnt-smelling—

truck

—beast. She didn't like the beast. It was loud and it moved very fast, faster than she could run, and whenever she saw it, her vision turned small, like she was deep inside a tunnel, and she curled up into a ball and lost all desire to hunt.

Each time this happened, bubbles of recognition burped to the surface of her mind, where they would burst and release fleeting glimpses of clarity:

food = men
beast = truck

But the swamp of her thoughts would quickly reabsorb these truths, leaving her with no lasting impression of what these things meant, of the distinctions between them. She knew only that the first was somehow associated with the second, and together they made an ache inside of her that grew a little bit each time she saw them.

There was that sound and the smell the—

truck

—beast made, of death and danger, the opposite of life and existence, and so it compelled her to remain hidden. She did remember being inside of the beast's belly herself, before, terrified, unable to escape its jaws. Hungry.

So so hungry.

But she had escaped from the beast, escaped and eaten too, and those memories had given her a sense of power over the

truck

and

men

Then—

memory

—instinct forced her to flee, and time and caution and a full stomach had worn down her resolve, and she grew afraid once more.

She had sated herself already.

She would eat again when the time was right.

When the aching, gnawing emptiness that had so filled her middle returned.

And the cautious fear went away.

There was no need to take risks now. She could wait until the beast was asleep, when the food was vulnerable.

She grew tired after that, no longer compelled to hunt by those urges within her. So she found a place to rest, deep in the large hole, inside the tunnels, one inside of her, the other without. It wasn't the safest of places, but here she could heal, grow strong again. But she found that with growing strength came a return of the gnawing ache and she knew she would have to hunt once more for—

man

—food.

The new food had appeared while she was sleeping, rousing her from her stupor. She'd crawled up and watched them, the ache of hunger still just a memory and the ache of caution still vivid, and she was not driven to flee from herself or her hiding place toward them. The food moved out of sight, but she remembered. It was a pattern. She need only be patient.

She couldn't see them, but she heard them, heard what they were doing. And when they came back, their scent was different, smaller.

Later, after they had gone away, and their smell faded, grew stale, she ventured out for a look. The food had gone into the ground, in a different place than before, and the ache in her belly flared and faded. She would leave it alone for now, let it rest. It wasn't time to feed. Not yet. But soon.

The next time the light returned to the world, the food returned. The pattern reset. They moved quickly, passing her resting place, making tiny shuffling noises and smelling of fresh meat and potential, and she thought again about hunting. But it still wasn't time. Her middle remained engorged from all she had consumed before, many cycles of the—

night

—darkness and—

day

—light before.

After a bit, the beast reappeared, and the food was there, fresh—

men

—food, teasing her with the smell of its flesh, so she started to emerge. But then the food escaped with the beast, dwindled from view. She watched, alarm growing, fear drowning in the ballooning new hunger within her. She still didn't like the—

truck

—beast. It scared her.

So, she slept again, not waking until the light had gone away. Her middle was full enough, and she was warm enough, for now.

And the beast returned, the pattern reaffirmed. It passed her spot, and the food left it and went into their own hiding place. The pattern still held.

So she napped, and more light and dark happened, and she heard the

truck

leave and return. She wasn't so alarmed anymore, because she had learned the habits, her prey, this repeating pattern they always followed. She napped.

She remembered the other food, left behind, how differently it smelled, how it did not have the protection of the beast, as if taunting her. Her mouth was dry, lips chapped, and she could taste its festering flesh on her tongue. But she wasn't hungry enough yet to finish what was left. Still wary, she did not feel compelled to leave her spot right away to consume the

men.

But soon the fullness in her middle became neutral. Darkness and light and food and beast cycled, until one time she woke and the hunger was full within her, a different kind of fullness that was both emptiness and everything, a rage, and the fear had been driven completely away. She felt restless again, ready.

Light grew stronger, building like the hunger within. She watched. And waited for the food and beast to return, for the cycle to repeat.

And just as it had before, it did.

It was time to feed.

No. Please, no.

I can't.

But there was no denying it. She must feed.

She would.

CHAPTER
15

"FINN DIDN'T KNOW WHAT HE WAS DOING," BIX insisted. "You can't blame him for something he wasn't aware of!"

He, his father, and Jonah had moved to one of the storerooms down the hallway so they could speak privately, leaving the others in the med bay. Bren refused to leave Finn's side, determined to feed him until he was either full or fell asleep again. Her mother also stayed behind, ostensibly to tend to Harper's injury, but really to keep an eye on the couple. Eddie lingered as well. He'd given no reason, but it was obvious. He stayed within earshot of Finn's bed.

"That's the problem, Bix," Jonah countered. "He *doesn't* know what he's doing. He's not rational, so we have no way of reasoning with him, no way to know what he'll do next. And he's strong. Like Eddie. Maybe stronger."

Harrison shook his head. "Look, boys, we knew there'd be . . . setbacks with Finn's recovery. Eddie predicted as much days ago."

"Setbacks?" Jonah said. "You call what happened in there a setback? For Christ sake, Mister Blakeley, Finn *snapped* Harper's wrist without even trying, just grabbed it and gave it a flick and it snapped!"

"He didn't mean it," Bix argued. "He didn't know! He'll get better!"

"Yeah, Bix, and that's what scares the crap out of me. He's barely even moving now, and look how dangerous he is! It's going to get worse."

"Don't say that!"

"Did you forget what happened to Eddie in the days after he regained his strength? He wasn't himself, either. He was literally climbing the walls. He escaped his isolation, and we had to put the bunker in lockdown because we thought he'd attack and kill us."

"Except it wasn't him who attacked anyone, was it?" Bix accurately pointed out. "It was your father! Besides, Eddie's perfectly fine now."

"You're both right," Harrison said. "And also wrong. Yes, there were a few days when Eddie wasn't fully in control of himself. He could have been dangerous, but he never hurt anyone. Maybe we were lucky then. Will Finn go through the same process and come out the other end like Eddie? We don't know. One thing I do know is, Finn didn't mean to hurt his brother."

"Thank you," Bix said.

"Which means he's not himself, so we will need to be vigilant until he—"

"Finn can't even get out of bed!" Bix pointed out. " I won't let you tie him up. Or lock him up. And I'm pretty sure Bren won't either."

"We don't know how long this will last. Finn's already much stronger, and he doesn't know what he's doing. He could hurt someone badly without knowing it, without *wanting* to."

"Until he can walk, I don't see the problem."

"The problem," Jonah said, "is what happens if he does recover his legs?"

"*If?* Are you hoping he doesn't?"

"No, jeez, of course not, Bix! I'm asking what happens once he's mobile but still isn't himself? How do we control him then? We really don't know everything these nanites can do to a person, but we sure as hell know enough."

"You want to lock him up?" Bix cried. He grabbed Jonah by the shirt and forced him against the wall. "I told you before. Don't you ever talk about Finn like that! He's not an animal!"

"I didn't—"

"He's not a Wraith, either!" Bix screamed and slammed Jonah back again so hard that his head connected with a loud smack. "That's what you're thinking! Isn't it?"

"Bix, stop!" his father said. "Stop before someone else gets hurt." He tried to get between them.

Jonah pushed Bix off and held him at arm's length until he could clear his head. He could have done worse in retaliation — he had the advantage over Bix, being both taller and stronger — but he didn't. "Look," he said, panting, "I don't like this anymore than you do, but let's be honest here, for our own safety as well as Finn's. We have no idea what's going to happen with him physically. Will his spine ever heal? Maybe. I really hope it does. But what if his brain doesn't?"

"It will."

"If this were a normal recovery, like in the days before the nanites, you know perfectly well he'd never have lived a full day. Even with the best surgeons keeping him alive, he would've been a vege—"

"Don't you dare say it!"

"Boys, listen to me," Harrison said, swatting Bix's hands away from Jonah.

"No, I won't!" Bix howled. He pushed his father, and pointed a finger at Jonah's face. "You said it yourself. This isn't a normal recovery, so stop comparing it to one. We don't know what's going to happen. But I do know this: Finn doesn't have a mean bone in his body."

Jonah stepped to the side, angrily yanking his shirt down and smoothing it out. "You know I'm right, Bix. I can see it in your eyes. You're afraid. You don't expect him to ever be the same, not like he used to be, not even close."

"You're wrong!"

"Boys, calm down!" Harrison ordered, ineffectively. "I'm not going to ask you again."

"I'm his best friend. I know him better than anyone else here."

Jonah locked eyes with Bix. "Then why haven't you spent any time with him? Since he fell, you've come up with every excuse in the book not to—"

"*Liar!*"

"Am I?"

"I've been busy with the video!"

"Busy?" Jonah snorted. "You should've been done with that days ago! You're procrastinating because you know I'm right, coming up with lame excuses that—"

"I'm not procrastinating!"

"No? Then why'd I have to show you an obvious solution to make things go faster?"

"And there it is. I wondered how long it would take for you to make it all about you. You just can't stand it not being about you!"

"I don't give a crap about that!"

"Oh, yeah? What's your excuse then? You're the one who's supposedly in love with him."

Jonah glared at Bix. The skin on his neck flushed bright red.

"You two take a break from each other," Harrison said. "Right now!"

"Yeah, I think that's a great idea," Jonah sniffed, and headed for the door. "How about we make it permanent!"

"Do not leave this bunker alone!" Harrison ordered.

"I'm not wanted here. Nobody wants to listen to what I have to say, so why should I stay?" He dug into his pocket and extracted the truck key, then reached for the doorknob.

"Jonah, do not— Wait a minute!"

"Let him go, Dad," Bix said. "He won't listen to you anyway. He's just like his father."

Jonah whirled around, his face twisted in fury. He raised his finger and opened his mouth, but then thought better of it. He left without saying another word, slamming the door shut behind him.

"What is it with you two?" Harrison asked. He sounded more tired than upset. "You need each other. You get along just fine sometimes. Why can't you boys get along all the time?"

Bix glared at his father. "Maybe if you'd stop calling us boys, that'd be a good start!"

"I didn't mean— Bix, wait!" He watched him take his own leave, resisting the urge to repeat his warning to stay inside the bunker. He had a reasonable expectation Jonah would comply, but not Bix. Telling him one thing when he was like this would only make him do the opposite.

The door swung shut, leaving Harrison alone. The click of the latch was loud in the small space. His eyes swept the room, yet saw very little, too blinded by frustration. He'd tried to be the father Bix had needed growing up, but their relationship had always been tenuous at best, as if they both knew the shaky foundation it was built upon. Much of it had been for show, a way to insulate the kid from those who might judge— Janice's bandmates at first, then the other bunker residents. He knew what it was like to be abandoned, a loner, and he didn't want that for Bix. Over time, the act had become habit, but it was still just an act. Harrison wasn't the father Bix needed, he could never be. And a part of him never actually wanted to.

He waited, sensing that Bix might still be in the hallway, possibly waiting to see if Harrison would come out, ready to concede empty points to the boy just so they could go back to pretending. Bix reminded him of his own father, who had been just as proud and stubborn, except with the added cruelty that the man didn't give a damn if he inflicted pain on others, including his own children. In fact, he'd taken special pleasure in that. And that alone was a big reason why Harrison gave the boy so much latitude; he didn't want to be like his own father.

He reached for the knob but stopped short of grabbing it. He squeezed his fist tight, until he could feel the nails digging into his palms. He wanted to feel something besides powerlessness, but he couldn't deny that's where he was at the moment. He turned instead and grabbed the closest object off the nearest shelf and hurled it at the back wall, not heeding what it was or caring that it might break. It was an uncharacteristic loss of self-control that he immediately regretted. The bottle struck the back shelving unit halfway up, shattering more jars and sending glass shards raining to the floor.

Unsatisfied, he reached for something else. He wanted to smash everything, destroy it all until it was gone, render everything into pieces too small to ever put back together again. But a sound coming from the vent near the ceiling stopped him cold. It came again, little more than a cough, and he froze.

Then the source of the cough spoke, an eerie disembodied voice that sent shivers down his spine:

"Now are y'all ready to talk?"

CHAPTER

JONAH SLAMMED THE DOOR SHUT AND INSERTED THE key into the ignition, but he didn't start the engine right away. He just sat there for the next ten minutes, fuming. How could Bix not see what was so damned obvious? Why did he refuse to face facts? Finn was never going to fully recover. He was never going to be the same again. Why couldn't they all just accept that?

But he also knew that Bix had been right about his own behavior since the accident. He'd used every excuse he could to avoid checking in on Finn; they both had. It was too painful to see him lying there in that bed, unmoving, his face a blank slate, not just inscrutable, but devoid of any coherent thought. Without recognition. Without . . . soul. The terrible injuries he'd sustained were no longer so apparent, but every time Jonah looked at him, he couldn't unsee them— the twisted and broken limbs, the horrific bruises and swelling, the bleeding. He felt the pain as if it were his own. It was all too much for one person to bear. No medicine could restore Finn to the way he was before, no technology, not even the nanites. How could it even be possible?

"Maybe it is," he whispered, arguing with himself. "I don't know."

He raised his hands to his head and cradled it. He wanted to cry, yet refused to submit to the urge. He knew what his father would say at times like this: *Be strong. Don't be a pansy.* He was glad the man was out of his life now, and yet a part of him longed for the strength he'd always demanded from both him and his brother, John. Ironic, wasn't it? Before the Flense, Jonah had wished with all his heart to escape the man and his impossible expectations, his narrow-mindedness, his intolerance to any perceived vulnerability. But then again, he'd gone and stuck them both inside a bunker, showing the world his true character. He was the very thing he despised— weak and afraid.

It was because of his father that Jonah had suppressed the person he truly felt he was. It wasn't until after Jack died, and he was suddenly free of all those unrealistic restrictions, that Jonah realized how much he missed the structure his father had built in their world. He wanted that order back in his life. He wanted to be free of the responsibilities and expectations his independence gave him.

"*Look at you,*" he whispered angrily into his hands. "*Romanticizing the past. Your goddamn father was a tyrant!*"

Maybe that's what this world needed, a tyrant, someone to take charge.

No, stop it. Stop rationalizing.

What was it Seth Abramson had said about the man? *If something didn't fit into Jack Resnick's world view, he rejected it.* It certainly made life easier to navigate when everything adhered exactly to your narrow-minded ideology. It made everything simpler. And made it easier to dismiss everything that didn't fit.

"No!" Jonah shouted, and slammed his fist into the truck's steering column, sending out an anemic bleat from the horn.

Pathetic. Just like you, Jonah. You're weak.

"No," he growled, and stabbed again at the horn. The sound rippled through the compound, across the open ground and into the scar of the mining pit a hundred yards away. It echoed off the walls, sounding more optimistic than the circumstances warranted, a cheerful burp of a sound. It only infuriated Jonah all the more. "No, goddamn it!" he shouted, punctuating each syllable with another punch at the horn. "No!"

A flash of movement in the mirror outside the passenger door caught his eye. He stared at it for a moment, not daring to breathe, then flicked his gaze to the rearview mirror.

Nothing.

He spun around to look out the back. All was still. Nothing suspicious to either side of the truck, as well. He was alone. The compound was abandoned. Nothing could survive out here in such barren conditions for long, and it had been a long, long time since there had been anything here to survive on.

"Seeing things that aren't out there now? You act all big, but you ain't shit. Just a paranoid little shit feeling sorry for yourself."

Now *that* sounded like something his father would've said to him.

"Buck up, you little shit."

He reached over and turned the key. The engine roared to life, rising in pitch and volume as he applied pressure to the gas pedal. It was one of the few pleasures left to him in this world, feeling the torque of a powerful engine revving beneath the hood, drawing the front end down, then the release as he let off on the accelerator again. According to the fuel gauge, he still had slightly more than half a tank, enough to get back to Haven, where he could exchange some food for a fill up. A few more roundtrips to the maintenance depot, maybe a half dozen, were all they could spare. Any more than that, and the Haven option would be off the table.

They still hadn't managed to get another vehicle operational just yet, but he was fairly confident they were close. They'd found an old prison bus with the keys still inside, a work order taped to the door requesting repair of a cracked windshield. He hoped that meant the engine had been in working order when it was left there. Tapping on the fuel tank, he determined it was almost full, but a quick inspection confirmed his fears. The diesel had gelled. The lines and filters were frozen.

It wasn't unexpected. They'd found other vehicles in the same condition. Coming up with fuel wasn't so much an issue, as they'd been able to get away in the past with a less-than-ideal concoction of kerosene and vegetable oil in place of refined diesel. It kept the engine running, although it did a job on the lines, clogging filters and stinking like the worst greasy spoon diner ever. This time, however, the issue was a bit more complicated. They had ample supplies of vegetable oil, but no kerosene. And while de-gelling the diesel was feasible, there were several more steps before the engine might run. But he realized it was the best chance they had.

He hadn't told Eddie of his plan yet, in part because of the considerable risks involved in building a fire around a big tank of highly flammable, potentially explosive gel. Eddie was cautious and would tend to err on the side of safety, and Jonah was too impatient. He'd located just about everything he'd need for the experiment, including a case of anti-gelling agent that would help, although not entirely solve the problem. He'd pull the filters and pumps and use the agent to get them patent again. The tank was the main problem. Heating the fuel while it was still inside was the tricky part. It would require igniting a pan of diesel-soaked sand under-neath, diesel he'd have to remove from the truck he was sitting in now. Precious diesel they wouldn't have to escape this place, should his plan fail.

He was pretty confident he could get it to work. Not absolutely, but close. Maybe ninety percent, close enough that it was worth attempting rather than delaying in favor of a trip to Haven instead. "Grow a spine, take a chance," he muttered to himself. He doubted it would be what his father would advise, but it's what his brother John would say.

He put the truck into gear and steered it toward the road leading in from the gate. He made it as far as the last barrier inside the compound when the engine stalled. Three attempts to restart it failed.

He was at least five hundred yards from the safety of the bunker door, a hundred from the nearest building, a mobile home that might have served as the mine's receiving office, back in a different world. He checked the mirrors once more, then scanned outside each window.

The sun was peaking, not directly overhead, but several degrees to the east and a whole lot more south. The air was still chill from the frigid night; frost still bleached the ground in the shadows that wouldn't see direct sunlight until spring. Nothing moved.

He popped the hood latch and got out, grabbing the toolbox on the seat beside him. At the front of the truck, he took another look around him, then hoisted the hood up and propped it open. The engine ticked as it cooled. He stared at it for several seconds, trying to decide what the problem might be.

He did not see a shadow disengage itself from a building halfway between himself and the bunker. He didn't see or hear the crouched figure make its way toward him.

CHAPTER 17

GIVEN WHAT THEY HAD WITNESSED THAT MORNING, Harrison found it unsettling that Kaleagh would leave her daughter alone with Finn, yet she was gone by the time he returned to the medical bay an hour later. Eddie was still there, however, pretending to work on a piece of medical equipment, but really keeping an eye on the couple. Kaleagh, he informed Harrison, had gone back upstairs to clean up the breakfast dishes and prepare for dinner.

"Seems odd."

"Surprised me, too," Eddie confessed, glancing toward the bed where the two teenagers lay sleeping side by side. "But then again, so did your decision to allow Bix to go off after Finn when we left the bunker."

"Or your decision to leave Hannah?"

"You know those aren't equivalent."

"The truth of the matter is, Eddie, we can't always be there to protect them. The best we can do is prepare them."

"But we should protect them as long as we can."

"And who is protecting Hannah now?"

Eddie's face pinched in frustration. "She's safe where she is. Anyway, trying to justify Kaleagh's decisions now by our own is a fool's errand. She's. . . ." He shrugged.

"Fragile? We all are, Eddie."

"I was going to say lost. Ever since Seth died, she's been in a state of shock. She was always in his shadow, did what he said, never defied him, especially when it came to raising Bren. He's left a vacuum."

Harrison nodded. The couple had always been in lockstep with each other, especially when it came to Bren. They both vocally disapproved of her relationship with Finn, even more so after the physical nature of it became too obvious to ignore. But inside the bunker, their hands were tied. Short of locking Bren up in their quarters twenty-four hours a day, there was little they could actually do to keep the two of them apart.

Now . . . ?

Well, this seemed like her tacit acceptance of the reality Seth had always tried to deny. Or it could be her losing her grip on the truth of their current situation, adrift psychologically, too numb to fully appreciate the physical danger Finn represented.

For the moment, though, there didn't appear to be any imminent threat to Bren, so Harrison told Eddie he'd take a turn watching them if he'd go and check on the boys. "They're having a tough time with everything," he said. "And right now they're both furious with me."

"*Persona non grata*, eh?" Eddie chuckled. "Been there. You worried they might do something rash?"

"I just don't want them leaving the bunker alone, especially Jonah, not in the emotional state they're in."

"The boy does have a touch of his father in him," Eddie commented, but left before Harrison could ask him to clarify which one he'd meant.

He pulled a chair to the side of Harper's bed and sat down. "How are you feeling?"

Harper cocked an eye open. He was still pale, and sweat glistened on his forehead. "Okay," he croaked. "Considering."

"Can I get you anything?"

"Mister Mancuso already got me some pills."

111

"You don't want anything stronger?"

Harper gave his head a slight wag. "No thanks, Mister Blakeley."

"You know you don't have to be so formal with us, right? It's Harrison and Eddie. And Kaleagh."

Harper nodded.

"I need to ask you something. You up for a chat?"

"About?"

"I've still got a lot of questions— what happened at your bunker, what you know and how you learned it, the so-called cure. We never got a chance to finish what we started upstairs."

"What happened to having everyone around together?"

"I don't think that's going to happen anytime soon now."

Harper raised his head up off the pillow. He winced when the movement translated down his shattered arm. He reached over and gently reset it on his lap, panting through the pain. Kaleagh and Eddie had immobilized the wrist with a splinting board and wrapped it in gauze from the cabinet. If their recent experiences were any guide, the arm would be stable in the morning and fully healed in a few days, a week tops. But they all knew, Harper included, that as the nanites inside his body got to work he was likely to suffer a lot worse before the break healed, particularly in the next twenty-four hours, when the damaged ends of the splintered bones broke down and started knitting back together again.

"You think Mister Abramson was right," he said, as the spasms subsided. "You don't believe a cure exists, do you?"

"What I actually believe is irrelevant," Harrison said. "I know what I know, not what I don't, so right now I need you to help me fill in some of the gaps. I want you to tell me everything— why you believe there's a cure, why you believe there's a twelfth bunker, and what you think our chances are of finding them both. Just give me what you've got."

Harper turned his head to glance past Harrison, who followed the gaze to the adjacent bed. Bren and Finn still hadn't moved. Their heads rested on the pillow, their foreheads touching. She had his hands clasped in her own, their fingers entwined.

Harrison got up and drew the privacy curtain between the beds shut.

"Now more than ever," he said, sitting back down, "we need to know how close we are to fixing things."

"Because of what Finn did to my arm?" Harper quietly but pointedly said.

"Not specifically." He sighed. "But yes, that too."

Harper studied Harrison's face for a moment. "Mister Mancuso — I mean Eddie — already warned me about what to expect as Finn gets better, from both a physical standpoint and an emotional one. Are you worried that what happened is a sign of some sort of mental . . . damage?"

"I think it's premature to conclude anything right now," Harrison replied. In truth, the incident that morning did worry him, but what prompted this discussion had more to do with the things Adrian had privately confided in him just a few minutes before. "I'm not sure how much we can extrapolate from Eddie's experience. We don't know if Finn will go through the same."

"Well, I know he didn't mean it," Harper pressed. "He'd never hurt anyone, not intentionally."

"I know that."

Harper continued to scan his face for several seconds. "I'll tell you what I know, but I want your word that you'll let *me* take care of my brother. He's my family, my responsibility, and if he's not capable of making decisions for himself—" He cleared his throat. "I'm the one who gets to decide what to do."

"Fair enough, Harper. I give you my word. Nobody's going to do anything to Finn without your say so. But you also need to understand that what we're talking about is larger than you or him or anyone else in our group. It's bigger than all of us put together. It's about everyone still left alive on this planet, the survivors of the Flense, not just those who are still human, but also the ones the nanites have turned into killers. We need that cure. We have to destroy these things they put inside of everyone. It's our duty to seek it out, wherever it may be, and employ it to the best of our abilities. When the time is right, of course."

"Right now, my brother is my focus."

"And we all want him to recover as much as possible. But we can't afford to let it stop us, either."

"Easy for you to say. It's not your sibling. You can't really understand."

"You might be surprised how well I do."

Harper nodded thoughtfully. "So, you do believe there's a cure."

"Let's just say I have reason to doubt Seth's claim."

"What reason?"

"Call it a feeling."

Relief slowly settled onto Harper's face. "And the others?"

"Jonah and Bix are . . . ." Harrison stopped and shook his head. "Right now, the group is divided on the subject. That's why this is just between us for now. Trying to have that discussion with everyone would be counterproductive."

Harper took his time to consider this, leaving Harrison to fidget impatiently. He pushed himself up higher in the bed so he could sit more comfortably. The effort clearly caused him more pain, but he declined the offer of help. Once he was repositioned against the pillow, he took a sip of water from the cup beside him. His hand shook, and any color that had returned to his face was gone.

"Okay," he finally said, "where do you want me to start?"

CHAPTER

THE SUN HAD LONG SINCE RISEN ABOVE THE OLD tailings of the original pit mine, but while the yellow desert all around thawed, down inside the manmade crater where the air stood still, the shadows remained half frozen. Most of them, anyway.

Under the hood of the truck, Jonah was sweating. Fat droplets dripped off his brow and spattered into the dust below.

He stopped his work long enough to pull off his jacket and toss it into the cab, taking the opportunity to recheck his surroundings. Nothing had moved in the twenty minutes or so he'd been stranded, and he'd grown convinced the movement he'd seen earlier had been nothing more than a trick of the light, or perhaps a stray breeze kicking up a dust devil just long enough to pass across the view in his mirror. Compounded with the low angle of the sun and his height-ened state of anxiety, of course his imagination was going to operate at an elevated level, expecting the worst. It was better to be overprepared for nothing than unprepared for something.

The longer the sun beat down on the hood, the more oppressive the bubble of air trapped beneath it became, unexpectedly humid and laden with the smell of rain, despite the near-cloudless sky. There was not a whisper of sound, nothing but the crunch of his own boots on the gravel and the air passing into and out of his lungs. He knew that things would soon change, as the day progressed. The weather the past few days had been increasingly unsettled in the afternoons, threatening rain and winds. He could sense the storm coming.

Over the next half hour, the sky confirmed his prediction, shifting from stark white to blues to purplish gray. A few thunderheads appeared out of nowhere, and began to climb high into the sky. An occasional low rumble caught his attention, and he'd glance up again. He figured it might be another hour before the storm arrived.

He'd narrowed down the cause of the engine stall to the airflow system. The most obvious problem was the filter, which was badly clogged with dust, caked nearly to the point of being useless, and so he'd spent the better part of the past ten minutes carefully dislodging the crumbly mess and tapping the dust away so it could be reinstalled. In all his efforts to get another vehicle operational, he'd forgotten to maintain the one they already had. Or, rather, it was Adrian's neglect, as the issue had clearly been building for a long time. Still, he should have paid better attention. He should have done a thorough inspection of the truck from the start. If they lost it, they'd be stuck out here. And while they had enough food and water to last them for a very long time, and while the site's remoteness almost guaranteed a greater level of safety and security than they were likely to find elsewhere — from both the infected and uninfected — the place was far too empty and far too creepy for his liking. He couldn't wait to be gone.

He angled the open pliers into the cramped space and positioned them over the ends of the first pinch clamp so he could remove the hose that fed air into the engine. The other end was located in a recess near the back of the compartment and access to it was even more restricted. Someone with thinner limbs, like Bix, would have an easier time of it, but Jonah's forearms were almost too thick. The opening was uncomfortably snug. He reached blindly down into the space and felt around for the ends of the clamp, then squeezed his eyes shut as he carefully positioned the jaws of the pliers over them. He didn't know why shutting his eyes helped visualize what was physically impossible to see, but it did. It gave him a clean canvas on which to picture what he hoped was happening.

He carefully squeezed the handles and felt the tension as the pliers engaged the clip. He could feel the clamp begin to open. All he needed to do was loosen it a little, then wiggle it away from its mount. Then he could remove and inspect the hose and clean out any dust and sand that had managed to get past the clogged filter.

He cracked open one eye, paused to listen, and quickly scanned the area around him as far as he could see. He hadn't heard anything, but the timer inside his head had instinctively gone off, reminding him that it wasn't safe to forget how exposed he was. Sweat dripped from his hairline down his cheek and into the collar of his jersey. He ignored the tickle and waited.

No sounds. No movement.

He redirected his focus on the hose and applied more tension to the pliers. There was a quiet crackle as the stiff wire ring released from the surface of the rubber hose. He gave it a wiggle to test its give, then gently rotated his wrist about a quarter inch. Hard metal edges dug into the back of his hand and into the muscle of his arm, but it was nothing he wasn't used to.

With a snap, the handles suddenly slammed shut. Pain flared at the base of his forefinger and raced up his arm. He let go of the tool and yanked his hand free to inspect the injury. Where the pliers had pinched him, the skin puckered out, angry and purplish white, but there was no blood. He gave it a shake, rubbing the wound with his thumb until the sharp pain turned to a dull throb, then checked to see where the pliers had fallen.

They were deep down inside the engine compartment. He had to lean over even more and stretch as far as he could, yet his fingertips barely managed to brush the end of one of the handles. Grunting and pushing off on his toes, he was still unable to grasp the tool enough to extract it.

"Stupid piece of crap," he whispered, and pulled his arm completely out.

He stood for a moment, panting in frustration, trying to decide what to do. A sprinkle of moisture hit his forearm.

Sweat or rain?

He glanced around and noticed several dark spots in the dust on the surface of the truck and adjusted his calculation for the rains to arrive to less than thirty minutes. The weather was changing faster than he'd expected. He needed to reassess the situation.

One option was to crawl beneath the truck to retrieve the pliers from underneath, but that would require unbolting and removing the skid plates, which would take a good ten minutes. There was enough clearance to fit underneath, so he wouldn't have to deal with jacking the truck up, but lying flat on his back in the dirt out here, ankles exposed and vulnerable, wasn't something he relished.

"One more try," he muttered, and stepped away from the truck for another safety check. His eyes swept past the dried blood on the passenger side door and window frame. *We really should wash that off,* he thought, but then realized a good hard rain would do the job for him anyway. He turned his attention past the back end of the truck and over to the closest buildings. He paused, straining his ears, then began to circle the vehicle, scanning every corner and shadow of the compound within view, taking his time to make sure he was fully alone. No movement. No sound. So why did he feel like he was being watched?

Because you're paranoid.

"All right, buddy, let's do this," he muttered aloud, and hiked his sleeve up above his bicep. His voice sounded deflated beneath the hood, as if the compromised ventilation system had sucked all the air out. He set the toe of one boot against the rim of the tire and reached down into the darkness once more, again closing his eyes to visualize the wayward pliers nestled in the cranny. The back of his arm scraped against the protruding ends of the pinch clamp, but he ignored the discomfort, even though it intensified as he reached even deeper through the opening. "There you are, you son of a bitch. Come on. There it is. Gotcha. Now, and— Damn it!"

He could hear the dreaded clunks as the pliers dropped back down into the space.

"One more time."

They hadn't fallen quite as far this time, and he was able to pinch the tips of two fingers around the serrated jaws and lift. He carefully worked the tool free until the handle was fully in his grasp, then began to retract his arm. The pliers caught, and he nearly lost them again, but managed to manipulate the tool through the narrow space. He was nearly out when his foot slipped and he lost his balance. He tilted forward over the fender, legs flailing. The sudden motion caused the ends of the pinch clamp to rake across the back of his hand like a hot metal poker. His yelp shattered the silence.

The pain was horrendous, but his fright was greater, and he froze, waiting, listening, while his hand burned and throbbed. And then he heard it, the faintest of sounds, still distant: a footfall, the crunch of gravel, followed by another.

And another immediately after, as the slow, careful tread of his stalker turned into the frantic pace of a sprint.

He tried to extract his hand and couldn't. The pliers had fallen again and were wedged tight against his wrist, trapping his arm inside the engine compartment.

CHAPTER

19

"I WANT TO KNOW MORE ABOUT THE CONNECTIONS between the Flense and the company you interned for," Harrison told Harper, "so let's begin with that."

Harper winced reflexively as he shifted positions again, and waited for the flare of pain to subside. "I don't have direct evidence or proof," he said. "I never witnessed anything firsthand. It's just a guess from piecing together what happened."

"Which is?"

"A few days before the breach in Bunker Two, I went down into the deep mine section to look for Mister Rappaport, our leader. He'd go down there on occasion to check in on Mister Hillard."

"Who was?"

"Arik Hillard, the head of the science team searching for a cure. Anyway, I figured that's where Mister Rappaport was."

"Was this Hillard fellow also a Quantum Telligence employee before the Flense?"

"Yes, but like Mister Rappaport, I only met him *after* I'd arrived in the bunker. In fact, everyone on Doctor Hillard's cure team was from another Quantum Telligence site, I think overseas. They seemed familiar with each other, so I suspected they'd all worked together."

"Were there any scientists in the bunker who *weren't* former QuanTel?"

"Several, actually — a few engineers, chemists, a dentist, and even a molecular biologist — but none of them was on the cure team or involved in the bunker research. Not directly, anyway. Hillard would sometimes consult with them on specific things, but always in a very general sort of way, so no one could ever really guess what they were doing. And the deep mine section was off-limits to anyone not on the team. It was all very secretive and mysterious."

Harrison nodded. "And what was this Hillard fellow's role before the Flense?"

"He never said, but there were rumors. One was that he built the Quanum Telligence AI machine from scratch."

"So he was a computer guy?"

"I don't think so. He seemed more comfortable with the biological stuff, but he definitely knew a lot about the system. What seemed more believable to me was the rumor that he had worked in pharmaceutical manufacturing before the Flense. In any case, he led the team, and Mister Rappaport firmly believed Mister Hillard would eventually develop a cure."

"So, did it seem like they already suspected what caused it?"

"They never said so, but yeah. That was my impression."

"What about the rest of the bunker? Did anyone else suspect? Were there rumors?"

Harper shook his head. "Not at first. Just a lot of uninformed speculation."

"So, this company that Eddie believes created the Flense for profit, is now saying they're working on a cure," Harrison mused. "Seems to me that if they created it, they'd make sure to have a contingency already in place. It doesn't make sense."

"You think they were faking making the cure? Why would they pretend?"

"Control of the bunker population," Harrison said. "Hope can be a powerful tool, whether wielded by the masses or used against them. That's why it's so valuable. Your leaders may have thought they could control you better by keeping alive the possibility of a cure. People will behave if they have something to hope for. Without hope, there's no reason to remain civil and submissive."

"Some people did believe they were lying to us about it. There was always a level of distrust."

"Any specific reason why?"

"For starters, they didn't tell us about the nanites right off. We found out about them on our own."

"How?"

"It was about a year after we arrived. One of the teachers cut her hand on a piece of broken glass, not seriously, but enough that she needed to see the doctor. That probably would've been the end of it, but she had this idea to teach us about the composition of blood— you know, looking at the different types of cells under a microscope, learn about our immune system, that sort of thing."

"This was the first chance you'd had to look at your blood? No one had ever cut themselves before inside the bunker?"

"Well, of course they had. There'd been minor injuries, but none that required more than a simple bandage or ice. We never really gave it much thought that we always healed quickly. We accepted at face value that the vitamin shots they gave us on the way to the bunker were responsible for our quick healing."

"That's how it was in Eight," Harrison noted. "There was this constant nagging suspicion that something was off, because everyone was always so damn healthy and healed quickly. But no one ever had much of a reason to check our blood until Eddie's accident, and that was after we'd been locked up for three years."

"Your doctor didn't know about the nanites?"

Harrison shook his head. "But yours did?"

"Apparently so."

"Were they another Quantum Telligence employee?"

"Doctor Praeder? He must've been, although he wasn't on the cure team. To be honest, he wasn't that close with any of them, but when the teacher asked if she could borrow his clinical microscope for the lesson, he refused. He gave her a weak excuse that it was too valuable an instrument to risk getting broken, even though she said he could be the one to do the lesson."

"Then how did you discover the nanites?"

"We made our own microscope. The teacher turned it into an engineering challenge. She asked if we could make something powerful enough to see blood cells using the stuff we already had access to around us inside the bunker. What we ended up with wasn't anything fancy, but it worked. We could visualize the cells at a reasonable magnification. Naturally, we weren't prepared for what else we saw. It was . . . disturbing, to say the least."

"That's an understatement," Harrison muttered.

"Seeing those little black dots everywhere in our teacher's blood, at first we thought she had somehow caught the Flense. She believed it, too, and locked herself up inside her room so she couldn't hurt anyone if she turned. Word quickly got out, and there was a panic. Everyone was running around thinking we'd all be dead soon. Or worse. Finally, Mister Rappaport and Mister Hillard called a meeting. They had to come clean, said that what we'd seen in the blood was actually a new technology, and that they'd been put in us during the government's anti-flu campaign. That was a shock, finding out we'd been duped. We demanded to know what else they'd given us, like on the day we left for the bunker."

"At the evacuation center?"

Harper's face pinched as he thought back. "They gave us the shots on the plane, actually. We'd been told they were vitamins to boost our immunity, but Doctor Praeder admitted that they weren't vitamins, but a technology that was supposed to work hand-in-hand with the *snurbs*. Mister Rappaport confirmed it."

"The what?"

"That's what they called the nanites. The booster was some sort of universal thing that gave them their potency."

"How?"

Harper shrugged. "They never said, just that it worked with the *snurbs* and would give us immunity to every disease known to medicine."

"Except for the Flense."

"They explained that that was because the Flense was previously unknown. It's why they claimed they were the only ones who were qualified to work on the cure, because only they understood how to use the *snurbs* to fight it."

"Did anyone suspect that the nanites — or *snurbs* — were actually responsible for the Flense?"

"Well, yeah. But they insisted they weren't."

"Did you believe them?"

Harper shook his head. "We were all too angry to accept anything they said. They'd put these things into our bodies without our consent. No one ever really trusted them after that. In fact, people started calling for new leadership. They refused of course, saying that they were the only ones who knew how to keep the bunker operating properly, and that our best chance of ever getting out and surviving the Flense would be to just let them do their job. We had no other choice."

Harrison waited patiently while Harper drained his cup of water.

"Things got pretty tense after that, especially after they instituted new security protocols. Then, about a year later, the research team announced that they'd finally made a breakthrough and were confident they had a cure. There was only one problem: They had no way to be sure without testing it on an infected subject."

"A Wraith?"

Harper nodded. "We realized right away they were telling us they planned to open the bunker and send someone out, either to test the cure in the field, or to capture a Wraith and bring it back inside. Either scenario was too terrifying for anyone to contemplate. Just the thought of opening the door was enough for everyone to vote the idea down. No one wanted to risk a breach."

"Even if it meant letting go of the chance to leave the bunker early? You'd already been inside for two years by then and were looking at possibly three more before the food ran out."

Harper nodded. "Yeah, but we'd all witnessed the Flense firsthand. You don't easily forget something like that. We gladly exchanged our freedom for the safety and isolation of the bunker, at least for the time being."

Harrison thought about this for several minutes before asking, "Seth Abramson knew about the nanites in Bunker Eight. People in Two also knew. What do you think the chances are that people in this bunker, Ten, were in on it, too? Think it might be why they left?"

Harper nodded. "I think those chances are high."

"Me, too. That makes it all the more imperative that we find out what they knew and what happened to them. Did your people tell you what was the basis of this supposed cure they had developed?"

"No. They said they couldn't tell us for security reasons, which became another source of suspicion among us. More and more, we started to believe there might be a causal link between the *snurbs* and the Flense."

"And how did the breach occur? Did someone on the cure team try to leave?"

Harper shook his head. "There was no external breach, actually. The research team promised not to unseal the doors. They really had no choice. We outnumbered them thirty to one. It was their way of compromising so we didn't revolt."

"Then how did the Flense get inside?"

"That's the thing, it didn't *get* in. It *originated* from within and got out."

Harrison's jaw dropped.

"That's when I knew," Harper continued. "It's when I realized Quantum Telligence had to be behind the Flense, not just the *snurbs*, whether by accident or on purpose."

"So, did they already have the means to create the Flense and were just saying they needed to get out of the bunker to conceal that fact, or did they recreate the Flense from scratch?"

"I don't know."

"Are you sure it started inside? Maybe someone opened—"

"No, it was them. It was nearly another year later, but you know how it is inside the bunkers. Nothing changes from one day to the next. We were just as distrustful of them as ever and followed their movements carefully."

"You're absolutely certain no one unsealed the bunker?"

Harper nodded. "They intentionally infected one of our own people to test the cure."

Harrison felt the blood drain from his face. *"Christ."*

"This was a couple days before the outbreak, when I went down to the deep mine section to find Mister Rappaport," Harper said. "I needed access to the journal for a door code. There was supposed to be a sentry on duty twenty-four-seven whose job it was to make sure only authorized people had access to the lab. They were armed, and they didn't play games. But on that day, there was no one at the desk. I figured he must've gone to the bathroom or something. Any other time, I would've waited there for him to return. If you were caught breaking the rules, the punishment typically involved some sort of confinement and restricted rations. We had this one guy, Dalton. He was a troublemaker. They'd lock him up for a day or two for doing something, and after he got out he'd behave for a while. But then he'd do something else that would get him locked up again, over and over. He never learned. Or he just didn't care."

Harper gestured for the cup of water on the bedside table, but it was empty, so Harrison had to go refill it from the faucet. He took the opportunity to check on the young couple in the adjacent bed. They were still asleep.

"Anyway," Harper said, resuming after his drink, "I would've just waited there for the guard, but as I said, we were all very suspicious of the cure team. Curious, I snuck in and actually made it pretty far before I started hearing people talking. Someone said Dalton's name and told him not to resist. There was these muffled sounds and a loud crash, like someone was struggling and knocked a bunch of medical instruments onto the floor. Then I heard Mister Rappaport ask if he was ready and Mister Hillard said, 'Bring over the signal generator.' "

"Signal generator?"

"That's what he said. Then, 'Stand back, over there, behind the wall. You don't want to be exposed.' There was a sound, like an electric zap, and everything went quiet. A minute passed, maybe two. I don't know exactly. It seemed like a long time. Then I heard a new noise. I knew right away what it was. You never forget that sound they make when they're agitated. When they're stalking you."

"They?"

"Wraiths."

"And it was this Dalton fellow?"

Harper nodded. "I didn't know what they'd done to him, or how, but it seemed obvious to me what was with them down there now. I couldn't understand it at all, and I was probably in denial, so I turned right around and got the heck out of there. Went straight back to the sentry station. They had an intercom there, which I used to call up to the main bunker. I asked them two questions. First, was Dalton in one of the holding cells. They told me Mister Rappaport had gotten him out that morning. The second question was whether anyone had opened either of the bunker doors, whether to leave or to come back. They laughed at me and said I should know better, since none of the alarms had been tripped, which would happen if any of the door seals had been broken."

"They could have bypassed the alarms somehow."

"They could have, but I knew they hadn't. We'd posted our own people to guard the exit points — people *we* trusted — in case Rappaport or anyone on the research team tried to leave."

"A secret exit then?"

"If there was one, I didn't know about it."

"But you still believe they turned this Dalton guy into a Wraith. Why?"

"I was still on the intercom when the sentry returned from inside the lab. His face was pale, and I noticed the clip on his holster was undone, like he'd recently had the gun out. He saw me using the intercom, and chewed me out, threatened to have me put into detention. He looked more angry than worried, like he wasn't aware there was a Wraith back there."

"Did you mention it?"

"Heck no. I didn't stick around. I went straight back to the main bunker and locked myself in my room. You can imagine what was going through my head. But after a couple days, when nothing happened, I started second guessing myself. First thing I did was check if anyone knew what had happened to Dalton. When no one could say they'd seen him, I snuck back down into the deep mine section. This time, even before I reached the sentry station, I could hear that sound again. Except it was much louder this time, and it sounded like more than one Wraith."

"Just that hissing noise?"

"No. This time they were eating, and it was getting louder. I ran. I meant to go back and warn the others, but suddenly people were screaming. It sounded like they were right behind me, then ahead of me, all around. I didn't know how they could've gotten past me. There were other tunnels, side shafts and such, some blocked, but not all. I knew they'd reached the main bunker by then. There was no way to get to the exits, so I ducked into a room and stayed there for the next few days, listening to them hunting and killing through the door. It just kept going, on and on forever."

"You said there were guns. Did anyone shoot them?"

"Not enough to stop the spread. After a long time, things got quiet. Then, after a full day of silence, I dared to open the door. I was starving, thirsty, half crazy. The bunker was empty. I mean, there were bodies everywhere, most of them pretty chewed up. These were people I knew, had talked with, worked with, played cards with. Shared meals with." He stopped and swallowed several times before finishing. "I found the exit doors flung wide open. The survivors had tried to escape. The infected chased after them."

"And that's when you decided to go looking for your brother?"

"At that point, I didn't even know that any of my family had survived the Flense, much less made it into another bunker. I just assumed they'd all died. Sometimes I imagined that they'd somehow gotten to the family's cabin, although I never dwelled on it. I knew their chances hadn't been very good. It wasn't until I arrived at Bunker Eight that I learned about Finn. I knew about the bunkers from Mister Rappaport's journal, so I went back inside hoping to find it and the phone with the maps in it."

"Phone?" Harrison asked. "The guy from your bunker who showed up at our front door had one on him."

"Micheal Williams. He'd taken it with him. That's how he found you so quickly."

"How did he have it? I thought all cellular devices were banned inside the bunkers. How did he manage to have one?"

"It belonged to my mentor at Quantum Telligence. And it was his place inside the bunker that I took. In the chaos of the evacuation after the Flense hit, he didn't make it."

"And how exactly did his phone come to be in your possession?"

"I know how it looks, me taking his spot and his phone, but it wasn't like that. And I actually didn't know about the phone until after we'd been locked up inside for a week. By then, I was too afraid to hand it over, so I kept it hidden. I took the battery out and stashed it in a secret place in my room. We never turned it on, not until after we started getting suspicious about the cure team."

"We?"

"Micheal and I shared quarters. He was the only person I trusted enough to tell. It took a while for us to hack into, and that's when we found the maps, but we only realized what they were because I had access to the journal."

"If he had the phone, how did you manage to find Bunker Eight on your own?"

"It was the closest bunker, and I'd memorized the location. Same with Ten. I redrew the maps from memory as much as I could into Rappaport's journal and set out to—"

"Finn?"

Harrison raised a finger to his lips, cutting Harper off.

"Finn?" Bren repeated. She sounded disoriented, like she'd just woken up.

"Everything okay over there?" Harrison asked.

"Finn?" Bren said a third time, and there was an unmistakable note of alarm in her voice.

Harper and Harrison exchanged worried glances. Harrison leaned over and pulled the curtain back.

"Finn!" Harper exclaimed. He swung his legs off the bed, ignoring the pain in his arm. *"What the hell happened?"*

CHAPTER
20

HARRISON COULDN'T UNDERSTAND WHAT HE WAS
seeing at first. The privacy curtain, which Harper
inadvertently tore from its hooks when his knees buckled in
shock, drifted around him to the floor unheeded. The scene
on the other side made no sense whatsoever.

Bren backed away from the bed, her eyes wide, fist
shoved against her teeth to keep from crying out.

Both Harper and Harrison started to shout at the same
time, demanding to know what happened. But Bren spun
around and, with a stifled cry, flew from the room.

Harrison stepped over and flung the sheets off the bed.
"Where the hell is he?" He looked over at Harper, who had
made his way back over to his bed, his injured arm cradled
against his side. He looked like he might be sick.

From down the hallway, they heard the doors to the
stairwell slam open. Bren's desperate cries followed, hollow
and haunted. They quickly faded as she mounted the stairs.

"Where is he?" Harper panted. "What happened to
him?"

"I don't know. He couldn't have gotten up and walked
out."

"Adrian?"

Harrison's face tightened into a grim scowl. Had he left
Adrian's door unlocked after their talk? He shook his head.
"He's chained up. He can't have gotten free."

"Unless Missus Abramson—"

"No, I was just with him."

Harper frowned. "I think we should check anyway."

"I'm telling you, it wasn't him. And Kaleagh wouldn't try anything."

Nevertheless, Harrison swept past Harper, hoping the sudden doubt didn't show on his face. There was no way Finn could've slipped past them while they were talking and gone deeper into the medical bay. They would've seen him. But he needed a moment to gather himself.

"Okay, then maybe Mister Mancuso."

Harrison shook his head. "Eddie wouldn't have taken him anywhere."

"Then that leaves only one possibility."

They exchanged troubled glances. It seemed unthinkable that Finn had gotten up on his own and walked out. There'd been no sign his paralysis had reversed.

"Whatever happened, why didn't Bren wake up?" Harper asked.

Harrison had no answer. "Can you walk, help search?"

Harper splinted his arm against his side and tried to stand. He winced, but nodded.

"Then come on. He can't have gone far."

They hurried to the doorway, then stopped and listened. The other rooms on the floor, mostly medical supply closets, were shut tight. Harrison couldn't remember if they'd locked them up after checking them days before. Could Finn have gone inside one?

"Elevator shaft," Harper grunted. "Check the elevator."

A new wave of fear swept through Harrison. Could it have happened again? They'd talked about blocking the open shaft so no one else would get hurt, but Finn's accident had been enough of a lesson for them to avoid getting too close to the open doors. "Check those other rooms," he instructed, then sprinted toward the far end of the hall.

He slowed when he reached the opening, then inched his way forward, dreading what he might see. The lights right below him flickered. There was a darkened section, some ten feet down, where a bulb had shattered during Finn's fall.

But the bottom was illuminated enough for him to see that there was no body. The elevator car was exactly where it had always been. There was a large dent on one side, where Finn had landed. And blood splatter. But it was old and dry.

He joined Harper by the stairwell doors. "Up or down?"

"We should split up."

"I don't think that's wise, Harper."

"He's not dangerous."

Harrison considered arguing, but he could see from the boy's eyes that he already knew it wasn't necessary. "Down," he decided. "And we stick together."

"Why down?" Harper asked, as they pushed into the stairwell.

"Gravity," he said. "Path of least resistance. Given your brother's condition, I think it's more likely."

They hurried down the steps, finding no sign that Finn might've come this way. They paused at the doors on the next level, then decided to continue on, all the way to the barricades if need be. If they didn't find him in the stairwell, they'd search each level, door-by-door, working their way back up.

Level Nine held a number of maintenance rooms, including a secondary pump house and self-cleaning water filtration system. It occupied nearly the same position as the boiler room in Bunker Eight. Harrison hesitated before entering, an uncanny feeling of déjà vu coming over him and a premonition that he was walking straight into a trap, like the one that had nearly killed Eddie, now nearly a year before. But unlike Eddie, he didn't have nanites; he was completely vulnerable. If a pipe were to break, if anything were to happen, he would almost certainly die.

But the facility was empty, as were the remaining rooms on that level.

And the next two floors up.

Just as it had been in Bunker Eight, Level Six was where the bulk food supplies were stored. Although the rooms would normally be locked and accessible only by coded keypad, they had broken into them before finding the journal with its access codes, and the doors no longer latched. With no need for such security measures here, it hadn't been an issue. They didn't have to worry about sabotage or hoarding.

Now Harrison wished they were still locked.

There were five doors on Level Six, and all the rooms behind them were large. All contained shelves from floor to ceiling, behind which anyone might easily find concealment. The two rooms on one side of the hallway held dry stuffs, including consumables such as soap and paper towels, as well as clothing and bedding. The food was divided into three rooms on the other side. One held cans of sauces, condiments, oils, vegetables, meats, soups, and even cases of beverages. The middle room, kept at reduced humidity, temperature, and lighting, held bags of grains and industrial sized boxes of crackers, cereals, pasta, and sealed packages of sugar and flour. The third room was refrigerated.

"Lights are on inside," Harrison whispered to Harper, when they reached the cold storage unit. The door hadn't been shut properly. Through the opening, they could see a tiny sliver of the interior, but far too much remained out of sight. "Ready?"

Harper nodded.

Harrison pressed a palm on the door and slowly pushed it open. Cold air rushed out, carrying with it the aroma of cheese and other long-life foodstuffs.

"Finn?" Harper whispered.

Harrison lifted his hand behind him, palm out, fingers extended, to signal Harper to keep silent, then gestured for him to shut the door all the way. He didn't want anyone sneaking up on them from the hallway.

On the nearest shelf was a heavy duty utility knife for opening packages. He grabbed it, extended the razor blade, and handed it over to Harper.

"What's this for?"

"Just in case."

Harper frowned, but accepted the weapon. He watched as Harrison slid a multi-tool from his belt, then nodded.

The refrigerated room was narrow and long, nearly the same dimensions as a small mobile home, and it was divided into several compartments, each presumably on a different electrical circuit with its own refrigeration system to prevent widespread spoilage in the event one unit failed. The compartments were accessible through a series of doors with magnetic seals.

They made their way past the shelves, approaching each aisle and peering into the next with caution. They found nothing unusual before reaching the next door. Harrison paused to listen, but the noise from the cooling fans overhead prevented him from hearing anything through the insulated wall. He grabbed the handle and, as quietly as possible, pulled it open. It yielded with a crackle and a hiss of escaping air.

"Lights on in here, too. Someone's been here recently."

They stepped inside and made their way toward the last door in similar fashion.

"Look," Harrison said, gesturing at the second row of shelves. Several items had been knocked to the floor. Some of the bottles were broken, their contents leaching through the bottom of the cardboard box they were in. A sweet smell drifted to their noses. "Smells like pickles. Think he got hungry?"

Harper frowned. "Maybe. But how would he know to come straight here? Did he know about this level before he fell?"

"Same exact arrangement as Bunker Eight, and Finn was in charge of food inventory. He might be on some sort of autopilot, going off muscle memory."

Harper shook his head. "I still can't believe he's walking, much less standing up on his own."

"And how's your wrist?"

Harper glanced down at the splint on his arm and attempted to make a fist. He hissed in pain. "Hurts."

"Yeah, but you can flex your fingers without screaming now. Those nanites work fast."

He tipped his head toward the next compartment, and they made their way past the spilled food. Once more, Harrison pulled the door carefully open. The lights flickered on. "He's not here."

"Then where is he? We didn't pass—"

They heard the outer door bang open, then bounce against the wall. There was a scraping sound, a bang, and something brushed against the other side of the door behind them. Harrison pushed past Harper and raised the multi-tool with its short blade before him. It suddenly felt inadequate. He braced himself, then shoved the door open.

There was a blur of movement and a shriek.

"Kaleagh?" Harrison said, pulling back. He tucked the tool quickly into its sheath. "I nearly stabbed you! What are you—"

"I broke some bottles," she said, gasping. She pointed at the mop and bucket she'd rolled in behind her. "I needed to clean it up. Why are you here? What happened?"

"We're looking for Finn."

She gave him a confused look. "I don't understand."

"He's missing."

Her face went pale. "Bren, too?"

"They were asleep. When she woke, Finn was gone. Bren ran upstairs." He made for the outer door, gesturing for them both to follow. "We thought he might be down here."

"I don't— But, wait. How would he be down here?"

"We think he— It's possible he's regained his legs."

"Oh my! Bren might be—!"

Harrison grabbed her arm. "She was okay. She went looking for him. Eddie and the boys are up there, too. They might've found him already."

He was trying to calm her down, but he couldn't hide the concern on his face. Kaleagh raced out of the refrigeration unit and made for the stairs, the others trailing behind. They didn't even reach the door before they could hear Bren yelling from the stairwell, screaming for her mother. Eddie's voice joined in, calling Harrison. The cement walls distorted their voices, but the urgency was unmistakable.

They met on the fourth level landing, all of them panting. Bren ran to her mother and buried her face in her chest, weeping with relief.

"What's the matter, honey?"

"It's awful," she sobbed.

"What happened?" Harrison shouted. "Where is everyone? Where's Bix and Jonah? Eddie, where is Bix?"

There was a dark look in Eddie's eyes, but he wouldn't answer. "You'd better come with me," he said, gesturing. He held an electrical cord wrapped around one hand, the end stripped of the rubber, as if he'd yanked it out of an appliance. There was only one reason he would do something like that, and it was to use it to tie someone up. Or some*thing*.

"Is it Adrian?"

"Just come." He bounded up the stairs to the next landing, then stopped and turned abruptly back toward the women. "Bren, I think it'd be best if you took your mother back down to Five. Get in the medical bay and lock the door. You hear me? Wait there until we get back."

"What is it?" Kaleagh asked. "Bren, what's happened to Finn and the boys? Did he— Honey, what did he do?"

"Just stay there. Do not follow us," Eddie warned them. "You don't want to see this." He gave Bren a stern look, and she nodded reluctantly and took her mother by the hand. It was clear she'd already seen what Eddie intended to show Harper and Harrison.

The three men hurried up the stairs, climbing until they reached Level One, but Eddie didn't stop there. "Where are we going?" Harrison asked. "Damn it, Eddie, answer me! Is it my son?"

"I don't know where they are," Eddie confessed. "I think they might've left the bunker."

"Did Finn go after them? Have you seen Finn?"

"Yes. That's where we're going."

They'd reached the front door of the bunker by then, but before opening it, Eddie paused. He started to say something, then stopped and regarded them for a moment in grim silence. It was all the preparation Harrison and Harper needed. They braced themselves and nodded that they were ready. Eddie pulled out his pistol, put his shoulder against the door, and shoved it open. They piled through, ready to take on whatever met them on the other side.

The first thing they saw was the blood. Then they saw Finn, and he was covered in it. He turned and slowly blinked at them, his face completely devoid of emotion. He was on his knees, kneeling over a body.

"Finn?" Harper gasped.

Finn straightened up slightly and his face twitched in recognition. Harrison reeled back in horror. But he quickly realized Finn wasn't smiling but grimacing.

"More," the boy grunted. "More."

Harper stepped toward him, but Eddie yanked him back. "Stay away!" he hissed. "Don't touch anything!"

"Is that—?" Harrison gasped.

"It is," Eddie said. "It's Adrian's sister."

"She's . . . alive?"

Finn had her by the wrists, his knee planted squarely on her back. She wasn't struggling very much, not at first. At the sound of their voices, however, she'd begun to fight. But Finn was too strong for her.

She turned her face to the men and hissed. Thick black gore dripped from her lips and chin, and her teeth were glistening crimson. She let out a bloodcurdling screech filled with fury and hunger.

Eddie tossed the cord to Finn, who caught it deftly in his free hand, and he began to wind it around the Wraith's wrists.

"Which one did she get?" Harper asked, choking.

Eddie shook his head. "I don't know."

CHAPTER

21

"OH GOD," HARRISON MOANED. HE CLUTCHED HIS head and reeled back in dismay. "Oh god. Bix? Did she get——?"

"We don't know yet," Eddie quietly told him. "I couldn't find either of the boys. I was on my way up here when Finn came out of nowhere and slammed into me just as I was opening the door."

"You didn't hear him?" Harper asked.

"I wasn't expecting it. He was fast, and quiet. Knocked me to the floor. By the time I got back to my feet, he'd already slipped out the door. I went after him, and that's when I saw this. I had no idea she was out here. I think she knew we were inside and was waiting. Finn saved my life."

"Is any of this his blood?"

Eddie sucked in a sharp breath and shook his head. The blood trail led up the passageway to the outside. "Not his. Nor is any of it hers. Neither of them have any visible injuries."

Harrison pushed himself away from the wall. "I need to find Bix, find out if she . . . ." He swallowed, unable to finish.

Eddie nodded. "But not alone. As soon as we've dealt with her, we'll go." He pulled out his gun, ready to kill her.

"No," Harrison said, and put a shaky hand on Eddie's arm. "Not yet."

Eddie stared at him in disbelief. "She's a killer. We can't risk—"

But Harrison was adamant.

"Why?"

"Adrian knows more about the Flense than he's saying. She's leverage. And we'll need her, once we have a cure." He swallowed again, still blinking rapidly like a man in shock.

"We're not keeping her."

"We're wasting time!" Harper hissed, shaking them both. The sudden movement roused Jennifer, and she started to lash out again. Finn's hold on her was too strong, and she quickly gave up and fell silent again.

"Fine," Eddie said. "I'm immune. I'll take care of her. Harper, cover me." He handed his pistol to the boy and stepped over to Finn.

"More?" Finn inquired. He seemed to comprehend what they were talking about. His actions proved he understood the situation and was able to distinguish friend from foe. He also appeared to know that Eddie, like himself, did not need protection from the Wraith's touch. He just couldn't vocalize any of this himself.

"I'm immune, too," Harrison said shakily. He took a tentative step closer.

"That's why I need you to take Finn back inside and get him cleaned up. I think he'll let you, as long as you tell him what you're doing. Take his clothes, seal them in a bag, make sure no one else comes in contact with the blood. That goes double for you, Harper. Do not touch anything. I don't know how contagious this blood is, but we can't take any risks. After you're finished with Finn, Harrison, let Bren and Kaleagh know what's happening. As soon as we've secured the Wraith, Harper and I will search outside for the boys."

He knelt down and placed a knee on Jennifer's back. Finn didn't move right away, but then it seemed to click, and he stood up, turned, and began walking back to the door of the bunker.

"Harper. Cover me in case she gets loose. This blood's still slick. If she bites me, shoot her, not me."

"I'm not sure I—"

"Just keep it away from my head," he said, binding her ankles. "If I'm hit anywhere else, I'll heal."

"Biiiissss...." Finn hissed from the doorway.

Eddie glanced over, then at Harrison. "We'll find him, Finn. And Jonah. I promise. Now go. You did good."

* * *

With Harper holding the pistol, Eddie finished lashing the Wraith to a metal pole inside one of the empty buildings outside the bunker. She was panting heavily, out of breath from struggling, but also from the gag he'd forced into her mouth so she couldn't chew her way through the restraints.

"She can't breathe."

"She'll be fine," Eddie replied grimly. He still couldn't understand Harrison's insistence on keeping her alive. The reasoning he'd given was weak at best. On the other hand, he still trusted the man's judgment. So, even though he suspected that Harrison's capacity to think clearly was compromised, he accepted the decision. Harrison would never do something to put them all at risk, not unless he was sure there was an even bigger reward coming.

He finished checking the knots and nodded to Harper. "Let's go look for the boys."

"You should take this," Harper said, extending the pistol.

"No, you hold onto it." He grabbed a small pickax off a nearby table and dusted it off. It wouldn't provide the same kind of protection as a gun, but it would serve him better at close range than it would Harper. "Ready?"

Thunder rolled ominously overhead.

"I don't know what we'll find," Eddie warned. "If it's them . . . ." He paused and swallowed dryly. "If it's Jonah and he's infected, you cannot hesitate. You *have* to shoot him."

"What?" Harper whispered. "No! I can't kill—"

"In the chest. As many shots as necessary to slow him down. Avoid the head, if possible. The wounds will heal. As long as there's the possibility of a cure, we owe it to him to bring him back."

"And if it's Bix?"

Eddie gave him a grim look. "Bix is immune. If she attacked him— If he's alive, then hopefully it's not too bad. Just don't shoot him, understand?"

"I don't know, Mister Mancuso. I don't know if I can—"

"You can, and you will. And it's Eddie. Never liked the whole *Mister* thing." He meant to give Harper's shoulder a squeeze of encouragement, but stopped himself. His hands were coated with blood. He didn't know which of the boys it belonged to, and whether it contained any infectious nanites, but he couldn't risk infecting Harper. "Stay close."

The wind had picked up, and it made a ghostly sound as it found its way between the abandoned buildings. Eddie kept expecting to hear the loose piece of sheet metal banging away somewhere in the distance, but Harrison must have secured it to prevent it from making any more noise. Something wet struck his forehead and ran into his eye. Rain. He looked up, blinking the water away.

"We'll start over there," he said, gesturing around the back of the compound near the fence line.

They circled the building, moving out of the wind for a moment.

"Truck's gone," Eddie noted.

"Maybe Jonah's at the maintenance garage."

The same thought passed through both of their minds: If Jonah was gone, then the blood had to be Bix's.

They continued onward, reaching the main access road just as the rain came. It started with scattered drops, so that they thought the storm wouldn't be bad. But then the downpour began, lashing them without warning, creating a wall of water so thick they couldn't see more than ten feet in any direction. Eddie was glad to let it wash the gore from his skin, but it limited their visibility far more than he liked, and the noise of the storm rendered his heightened sense of hearing completely useless.

He was angry with himself, and with Harrison, for putting too much trust in the boys. They had all grown complacent, careless, thinking they were truly safe and alone here after only a few days without signs of life other than their own. They'd assumed Adrian's sister had fled into the desert to search for food elsewhere, or maybe been shot and killed, her body dragged off by wolves. But her sudden reappearance proved they could never truly relax, not as long as there was even a single living Wraith walking the planet. Not as long as anyone still had the nanites in their blood. And suddenly he understood Harrison's laser focus on the cure, even if it meant more risk to them in the short term.

"Stay close!" he shouted to Harper over the din of the storm. "And get that gun up! You need to be ready!"

They made their way out toward the main pit area, leaning against the wind, and headed for the gate.

"Which way?" Harper asked, as they took momentary refuge beneath an overhang.

Eddie looked out into the gray. Leftward took them back toward the fence and the steep incline to the desert surface from which they'd arrived nearly two weeks before. To the right, up the rise and past the unseen gate, was the open desert to the south. Straight ahead was the pit, the edge completely lost to view. He stepped out, extending his arms, and rubbed some more of the blood off. The wind whipped over the distant berm, bellowing like a predator announcing a kill, and Eddie was glad for the meager shelter afforded to them down in the bowl. At ground level, the gusts would make it nearly impossible for them to stay on their feet.

"Right!" he bellowed, and gestured. "Towards the road! We'll follow it until we get to the gate, then come back and check the buildings!"

They hurried along, bowing their heads against the buffeting wind and rain, their arms extended to keep the worst of it off their faces. They kept one wary eye on the indistinct shadows of the buildings to their right, the other at the yawning pit.

"The truck!" Eddie shouted, and pointed straight ahead.

"I don't see it!"

Eddie took off running, his feet kicking up mud. He reached the vehicle several seconds before Harper caught up, panting with exertion.

"Are they here?"

Eddie circled the vehicle, wiping the rain off the glass and peering inside. There were traces of blood on the passenger side rocker panel that the rain hadn't finished washing away. But was it new? He shook his head. "Key's in the ignition." He checked the ground, but any signs the boys might have left behind were washed away.

"Why did they stop here?"

"Hood's been popped and dropped," Eddie answered, noting that it hadn't been latched. "Mechanical problem." He glanced around, noting how exposed they were.

He opened the passenger door and stared into the gloom inside. After a moment, he reached in and pulled something off the floor. "Air filter," he said. "Scraped clean." He threw the item back inside the truck, then went around to the front and lifted the hood.

"Is that blood?" Harper asked, leaning closer.

"Don't touch it!"

He pushed Harper away, then gently lowered the hood, letting it drop the last few inches. The rain muffled the sound. He glanced over at the empty buildings with their darkened windows and considered yelling the boys' names, but he had a sinking feeling neither of them was in any condition to respond. Not in the way he hoped.

"What do we do?" Harper asked.

"We stick to the plan," Eddie said. "We check every building between here and the bunker. We keep going until we find them."

CHAPTER

22

"YOU'RE AN IDIOT."

"You're only saying that because it's true."

Bix laughed and tore another strip off his tee shirt and wound it around Jonah's hand to try and soak up the blood. It was a nasty wound, but most of the bleeding had already stopped. A wedge of skin had torn off, starting at the back of his wrist and widening as it drew toward his knuckles. Bix had nearly thrown up when he first saw Jonah's exposed tendons flexing like worms. "Pressure," he said, wadding up another piece of the shirt and holding it against the wound.

"Holy crap!" Jonah wheezed. "Take it easy!"

"Baby. We need to stop the bleeding."

"It's already stopped."

"A thank you would be nice."

"This wouldn't have happened if you hadn't sneaked up on me."

"Well, what the hell were you doing out here all by yourself?"

"What were you?"

"Checking up on you."

"Oh, so you're my mother now?" Jonah said between clenched teeth.

"If I were your mother, I'd have switched you at birth."

Jonah sniffed in pained amusement, then yelped again as Bix wrapped another strip of cloth around his hand. "Jesus already! I said it's good!"

"No thanks to you."

"What the hell's that supposed to mean?"

"If I hadn't come along when I did, you'd still be dangling off the side of the truck, bawling your eyes out."

"I wasn't bawling."

"I saw tears."

"That was sweat."

"I heard crying."

"You heard the wind. Besides, I nearly tore my freaking hand off!"

"And who found the missing piece?"

"Who asked you to? I didn't need it."

Bix thought he might remind him about the risk of infection, but then realized it was a moot point, and for a moment he resented his father for refusing to get him immunized before the Flense. He was better off this way, of course, but there were still drawbacks. "It's going to scar."

"Maybe. Anyway, scars are good conversation starters."

"Sure, next time we hit the club, you can show it off to all the gir— The guys."

"That really bothers you, doesn't it?"

Bix got up and reached for the sweatshirt he'd taken off to get to the tee underneath. It was soaking wet and cold, and he shivered at the thought of putting it back on. But standing there bare-chested beside Jonah, made him self-conscious. He was pale and bony, and the few hairs he'd managed to sprout were pathetic. He was glad Jonah didn't crack any jokes about them.

"Weather's crazy, eh?" Jonah said, pushing himself off the dusty floor of the building they'd taken shelter in. The old trailer appeared to have been an office before the Flense. He went over to the nearest window, now covered in grime, wiped it with his good hand, and squinted out. "It was sunny barely an hour ago, and now look at it. Amazing how quickly things can change."

"Not really in the mood for small talk."

Filing cabinets lined one wall, binders full of paper on top. Framed photographs of people they'd never met, now almost certainly dead, occupied the rest of the surface. Ghosts from a lost time, nothing but the imprint of their existence left behind on paper. There was also a desk with letters and forms in an inbox, the printing on the top sheet faded away to invisibility. On one corner of the desk was a wired telephone — Bix had already confirmed the line was dead — and on the opposite corner was a computer monitor. There was no computer, however, just an old dock for the laptop and an empty space where it would have sat. On a small table was a fax machine, dwarfed by a monster of a copier, the edges darkened by grimy hands, a thick layer of dust on top.

The window overlooked a walkway. On the other side was a pair of natural gas tanks painted light blue. Dirt had stained the tops nearly black, but the rain washed some of it off. Eddie had checked the tanks days before and determined they were empty.

Wind buffeted the trailer, shaking it.

Bix joined him by the window. "This keeps up, we're going to flood," he said. "Got to be a lake by now, down in the pit."

"It's just a desert storm," Jonah answered. "I'm sure it'll pass quickly. I give it another ten minutes, twenty at the most."

"We should head back before then."

"Not before I get the truck put back together again." *And running,* he thought, but didn't say out loud. "I could use a hand, if you're up for it. Still need to make sure there's not a clog in the air line."

"I don't know if that's a good idea."

Jonah raised his injured hand. "Don't make me beg."

"The thought did cross my mind."

"Fine, consider this begging."

Bix scowled. "Pitiful." He turned around and began sifting through the papers on the desk.

"What do you have against me anyway?" Jonah asked. "I feel like we get along fine sometimes, but then it's like something clicks and you remember you can't stand me again."

"You're wrong. I can't stand you *all* the time."

"Why?"

Bix sighed. "For starters, you're arrogant. Stubborn."

"I was expecting criticisms," Jonah joked.

"You think you know better than everyone else."

"That's sort of the definition of arrogant."

"You don't listen to other people."

"Now you're just being repetitive."

"Knock it off!"

"Okay, my turn."

"That wasn't the deal."

"You let Finn walk all over you. You're terrified of the possibility of life without him that you'd rather live in denial than face reality."

"And what reality is that?"

"That Finn's never going to be the same. He can't walk. He can't speak. He barely recognizes us, and he probably doesn't remember much. Do you actually believe he'll just wake up one day, get out of bed, and start joking around with you like old times?"

"There's no such thing as old times," Bix muttered. "Not anymore. There's only now. Anyway, why should I even listen to you? A week ago, you were ready to write him off."

"I wasn't the only one."

"Don't you even try to suggest I was!"

"You had your doubts."

"No, I didn't!" He kicked the chair into the wall. "It should've been you!"

Jonah pulled back, his eyes wide with dismay. "Why the hell did you follow me out here then? If that's how you feel."

Bix glared at him for a moment, then stomped over to the door and reached for the knob.

"Come on, Bix. At least wait till the rain stops."

"They're going to wonder where we are and come looking. We should head back."

"At least wait until— Damn it, shut the door!"

Rain gusted in. The storm was blowing hard, raising a racket. Water rushed off the roof in waves, forming a curtain that curved inward, as if trying to reach them. It instantly soaked the thin carpet and made a squishy sound when Jonah joined Bix beneath the overhang. He expected Bix to turn around and go back inside. Instead, he stepped onto the porch and headed for the steps.

"You coming or not?"

Jonah glanced out to where he knew the truck was, but he couldn't see it. Maybe he was wrong about the rain. It didn't seem to be letting up at all. "Fine. But let's go around the back way. It's out of the direct wind."

They jogged down the walkway and turned right at the corner. The slope from the original mine rose up before them, funneling runoff directly across their path. The water was ankle deep and rising, but at least it wasn't windy. Jonah had been right about that.

"Remind me not to come looking for you next time," Bix shouted as they hurried along.

Jonah wanted to tell him to slow down, as the running made his hand throb. They cut across an open area, making for the building with the entrance for the bunker. The distance between them grew. "And here I thought we were having a moment back there!" he shouted.

"Sorry to disappoint you!"

There was a splash, and Bix disappeared. Jonah skidded to a stop. The ground had turned into a lake, its muddy surface boiling from the deluge. "Bix?" He took a step forward, and a head emerged through the choppy surface. "Bix!" The head slowly rolled to one side. The body appeared next, a few feet away, and rolled in the opposite direction.

"BIX!"

Bix exploded through the surface a moment later, sputtering and shouting for help. He didn't seem to know about the corpse floating behind him.

"Grab my hand!" Jonah yelled. He edged carefully forward, testing the ground with his toes. Beneath the chop, the edge of the grave he and Eddie had dug for Seth Abramson days before was no longer visible.

The rotting body floated nearer and bumped into Bix. With a howl of terror, he pushed it away and scrambled out under his own power. "You son of a bitch!" he screamed at Jonah. "You brought me this way on purpose! That's not funny! You're fucking insane!"

Jonah yanked Bix away from the hole, urging him to be quiet.

"I am not going to shut up! You shut up! You goddamn fucking crazy son—"

"Listen to me, damn it! We're in danger!"

"Goddamn crazy— What?"

Jonah yanked Bix around, then released him. He bent down, pulled Seth closer by one shoulder, and rolled him onto his back. Then he fished for the head. Most of the dead man's face was gone, the flesh torn off. As was half of one arm. The remaining muscle was bleached white.

"This hole was dug up," he said. "Something dug Mister Abramson up and started to eat it, and I don't think it was an animal."

The blood drained from Bix's face. He spun on his heels and took off for the bunker entrance, abandoning Jonah with the corpse.

CHAPTER
23

EDDIE WAS THE LAST TO JOIN THE GROUP IN THE kitchen, appearing freshly showered and shaven with the towel still draped over his shoulders. Kaleagh stood at the stove, studiously avoiding eye contact with anyone. She felt indirectly responsible for what had happened, despite their insistence that she wasn't to blame for any of it. Harrison had told her it was his fault for not making sure Seth's grave was deep enough, but she refused to hear him.

"I hope you're hungry," she said, her voice quiet and hitching from the crying she'd done after hearing the news. She brought the pot over and set it gently down on the table, as if it were made of crystal and would shatter at the slightest bump. She lifted the lid, releasing a cloud of steam infused with the aroma of canned stew.

"Has he remembered anymore of our names?" Eddie asked, referring to Finn. "Said anything else since we got him back inside?"

They looked to Harper, who shook his head. "He fell right to sleep and still hasn't woken up."

"Did he . . . eat anything?" Kaleagh asked.

"Canned peaches. But he didn't speak."

"It'll come," Harrison said, "most likely in fits and starts, like his legs. I think the shower and food helped. So will the rest. At least he's moved on from saying 'more' all the time. And he does seem a lot more aware of what's going on around him than we realized, even if he can't communicate with us just yet."

"Bix?" Kaleagh said, pushing the pot toward him. "Eat. You, too, Jonah."

Bix eyed the floating chunks of potato and meat in the stew, and his stomach did a hot, slow roll. He felt like he could take a thousand showers with scalding hot water and scrub his skin until it bled, but he'd never be able to remove every last trace of dead person clinging to him. He was destined to forever have essence of corpse leak from his pores.

He lurched out of his chair and ran out.

"How's your hand?" Eddie asked. He'd meant the question for Harper before remembering Jonah's injury.

They had happened to come on the scene with Bix and Jonah just as Bix took off. Thinking he was running from an infected Jonah, Eddie shouted out in alarm, prompting Jonah to whirl around. Harper fired the pistol, but the unexpected recoil threw him to the ground, reinjuring his broken wrist. Luckily, the shot had gone wide.

"Um, fine?" Jonah said, eye-checking Harper, who nodded in agreement. He turned back. "Sorry you had to deal with Mister Abramson by yourself, Eddie."

Kaleagh slammed the metal lid for the pot down on the table. "I don't know why we don't just kill her," she snapped. "Why are we keeping her alive? After what she did to— After what she—" Another sob escaped her throat.

No one said anything. There was nothing they could do that would lessen the emotional trauma on them all.

"You need to get rid of her," Kaleagh continued after regaining some control of herself. "And her brother, too. I don't care who does it. I don't care how you do it. If you don't, I will."

"I understand how angry you are," Harrison quietly told her. "But we mustn't act rashly."

"Don't you dare tell me what I should or shouldn't do!" she screamed. "That man murdered my husband! And then his sister—" She covered her mouth with her hand and turned back to the stove.

The next several minutes passed in uncomfortable silence. Finally, Eddie leaned over. "I agree with Kaleagh," he quietly said. "We put ourselves at great risk by keeping her alive. And for what? You still haven't explained how you think she could be useful to us."

"I told you, Adrian is holding out. He knows something."

"He's a liar. He's manipulating you."

"I don't think so."

"If he knew where the twelfth bunker was, he'd have already gone there instead of letting Harper lead him on a wild goose chase."

"He wanted Finn. And now he wants that cure, more than ever now that we've recovered his sister. He'll do what we ask to get it. He needs our help."

"There is no cure," Kaleagh asserted.

"He obviously believes otherwise, and I'm inclined to believe it, too."

"Why?"

Harrison's face pinched. "I just need time. Adrian's hinted at a few things. Now that we have his sister, he'll be more willing to share."

"We don't need him. You want to go looking for Bunker Twelve, fine. We have perfectly good people back at Westerton that will help, people we can trust."

"We thought that the last time, and you know what happened. Nobody is completely trustworthy."

"Really? Does that include you?" Jonah asked.

"Don't talk to my father that way," Bix said, reappearing in the doorway. His forehead was covered in a fine sheen of sweat, and he looked pale.

"Look," Harrison said. He got up and walked around the end of the table to where Kaleagh stood. "Adrian's shackled. He's not going anywhere. He can't hurt us. And his sister's tied up, too. She's not going to get free. All I'm asking is that we don't make any decisions about either of them we can't undo. At the very least, let's sleep on it, gain some distance from what happened this afternoon."

"Well, you know which way I'm voting," Jonah said. "I'm not changing my mind." He stood up and went to the door, but Bix refused to let him exit. "You mind?"

"And where do you think you're going?"

"Rain's stopped. Truck's still broken. The offer still stands, Bix. If you're up for it, I could use your help."

He glanced back into the kitchen, defying the adults to stop him.

"It's already getting late," Harrison advised. "Why don't we just start fresh in the morning?"

"You know something?" Eddie said, standing up. "I've got things to do, too." He slid the towel off his shoulders and shoved it into Harrison's hands.

"Like what?"

"Like packing up supplies."

"Eddie, we shouldn't—"

"I think it'd be best if Jonah and I leave for Westerton in the next few days. We'll send someone back to fetch the rest of you and the supplies, but I think we're done here."

* * *

Harrison sat for a long time after they left, deep in thought. Finally, he turned to Harper. "We know that the Flense depends on the presence of nanites, since Bix and I are both immune."

Harper nodded.

"But so are Eddie and Finn. Their accidents altered their nanites somehow, made them resistant. It's like immunity. So, this infection, this virus, can only infect — what? — nanites that *haven't* been activated in some way?"

Harper reflected on this for a moment. "If that's true, then maybe the cure is to activate *all* of the nanites in our bodies. Is that what we have to do?"

"That's not what I'm suggesting. I mean, who'd want to risk trying to kill himself to test that theory? We also don't know if the effect is permanent. It might not be. Maybe the nanites deactivate after they're finished, although Eddie's still . . . ." He sighed, then shook his head. "No, the only way to be sure is to get rid of them entirely."

"From the body?" Harper asked. "That seems impossible."

"It's only impossible until it isn't." He frowned, thinking hard. "I was just thinking about these devices Adrian had. They produce some kind of radio signal that can stop Wraiths dead in their tracks."

"But they don't discriminate. That signal knocks out anyone with nanites inside their bodies, not just Wraiths."

"That's not entirely true. It does differentiate, since the effect is stronger on Wraiths and on people like Finn and Eddie, whose nanites have been challenged to a higher degree. It barely affects people who haven't suffered a lot of injury or illness. And they don't affect me or Bix at all."

"Well, it's not a cure. The effect goes away as soon as you turn the machine off. A cure has to be permanent."

Harrison nodded. "And the only way to do that is to destroy them. But these separate pieces of information are all part of the larger puzzle. We just can't see the whole picture yet. We need more pieces."

Throughout this exchange, Kaleagh had kept her silence — and her distance — but now she joined them at the table. "If you think it might help," she said, "Seth kept records of everything he did. All his notes, studies, experiments. He was careful in that manner."

"Notes? Why didn't you say something before?" Harrison asked.

She shrugged. "He was so sure there was no cure, and I believed him. But I can't . . . . I want to believe there is one. Especially now."

Harrison saw the flash of alarm on Harper's face. It was obvious she was worried about what the nanites were doing to Finn, what they *could* do in the future. And the effect that his changes were having on Bren. But would curing Finn give them the outcome they all wanted?

"You've seen these notes?" Harrison asked. "You know where they are?"

"Maybe, but it would have only been once. It was the day Abraham became bunker leader. I found Seth down on Level Eight. He had a bunch of loose papers in his arms, and what looked like a laboratory notebook. He also had a folder with David Gronbach's name printed on the front."

"The original leader," Harrison clarified for Harper.

"I thought nothing of it at the time," Kaleagh continued, "since he'd died just the day before, and Seth was helping Abraham with the transition. He was always so organized that way, keeping notes."

"Right," Harrison said, remembering how they'd sent David's body over the railing outside Level Six and into the spillway to the river below as a sort of burial ceremony.

"I could see how upset he was. We all were, of course. But this was a different kind of upset. He was . . . . He seemed angry about David dying, frustrated, which didn't seem to fit with the circumstances. It was like he took it personally. When I asked him what was wrong, he said it was all a lie. Just like that: 'A lie, nothing but false hope.' I thought he meant the bunker, which was supposed to protect us, but he shook the folder with David's name on it in the air and said, 'How are the rest of us ever supposed to get out of here now?' "

The others remained silent, digesting what she'd just told them. Finally, Harper shook his head. "And you think he was talking about the cure?"

Kaleagh hesitated, then nodded. "In hindsight, yes."

"But that was so soon after we arrived. When would he have had time to do any experiments?"

She shrugged.

"Well, in any case, he could have destroyed those notes a long time ago," Harrison said.

"It's been at least two years since he gave up," she acknowledged. "But it wasn't like him to thrown his papers away. I can't be sure, but if he saved them, they'd still be in Bunker Eight."

Harrison stood up. "Then that's where I need to go."

"But Eddie and Jonah are—"

"They can drop me and Bix off. It's on the way." He paused, then added, "You two will be safe here with Finn and Bren until we can come back for you."

"*If* you come back," Kaleagh murmured, as he hurried out of the kitchen to find Eddie. She caught Harper's eyes and saw the same skepticism she was feeling in them, too.

CHAPTER 24

WHEN THEY GATHERED FOR DINNER TWO DAYS LATER,
the mood was considerably lighter than it had been in a long
time. It was the first chance the entire group had to sit
together for a meal since their arrival, and a lot of the tension
from the events of the previous days had diminished.

Finn's vocabulary had expanded considerably, too, and
he now knew them all by name, although he still had no
memory of the day of his accident. The physical healing
proceeded at a phenomenal pace, but there were hiccups and
stalls and setbacks. Sometimes he would suddenly stumble
for no apparent reason, or experience localized temporary
paralysis. He'd stare at the offending body part, not in anger,
but concentration, as if willing it to reboot. Sometimes the
simplest tasks he'd already shown proficiency in confounded
him, or he'd forget what he was doing. Once, they found
him quivering in bed and crying out, as if in agony, but when
they roused him, he woke without pain or memory. The
episodes were always frightening for the others to witness,
but they didn't seem to phase him for more than a few
minutes.

The most troubling aspect of his recovery was his
appetite, which put even Bix's to shame. Nothing, it seemed,
could satisfy his cravings.

They kept hoping to see signs of the old Finn, but he
remained stubbornly absent. On the other hand, there had
been no more manic episodes like the one that resulted in

Harper's broken wrist, which was healing as quickly as they expected, that is to say, a lot faster than normal.

Bix had helped Jonah get the pickup truck back to running, and he reminded Jonah of it every chance he got. With a little guidance, he had singlehandedly — a word he used often and with emphasis whenever the opportunity arose — cleaned out and reassembled the pickup truck's entire air filtration system. The fix had worked, although the engine still coughed and hesitated, as if it wanted to stall. Jonah suspected a faulty control valve sending error messages to the computer.

"That's the problem with these late model cars," he complained. "Give me something from before 1980. No computers, all mechanical, and a lot more reliable."

Eddie had also managed to get the prison bus in the maintenance depot running after Jonah de-gelled the diesel inside the fuel tank and lines. It took a considerable amount of effort and came at great risk, as they'd had to resort to burning whatever they could find to warm the maintenance bay up to the point where the paraffin decrystallized.

And frustrated with so many unanswered questions, Eddie had finally decided on his own to break through the barricade between Levels Nine and Ten to figure out why the previous bunker residents had erected it. The smell of stale air and rot hit him the moment he shoved open the door.

As it turned out, part of the adjacent pit mine had collapsed, probably during an earlier heavy rainstorm. The slumping had taken out parts of the bunker system— luckily without disrupting any essential functions. He didn't find the missing residents, but it seemed likely they had been buried beneath the rubble. Certainly a tragedy, but it was a relief to everyone to know it wasn't anything more sinister.

And then there was Adrian. Just as Harrison had predicted, he agreed to cooperate after finding out they had his sister. He even promised to help with whatever chores they had. "I just want what y'all want," he told Harrison and Eddie. "Y'all have my word, I ain't gonna cause no problems. Now, how about these restraints?"

They left them in place.

That was one thing they could all agree on, leaving him bound and locked inside a room. Surprisingly, he accepted this judgment without argument, conceding that after all the evil things he had done, he wouldn't trust himself either. "But I hope y'all will eventually find it in yer hearts to forgive me one day. After livin in such a harsh, lawless world for so long, fighting fer survival amongst the criminal element, I guess I'd just lost my perspective. I want to thank y'all for helpin me find my way back to the path of righteousness. And fer savin poor Jenny."

"He's not fooling anyone," Jonah said, after Harrison relayed Adrian's overly submissive and self-deprecating performance to the others at dinner the previous evening. "And I still think it's not worth the risk to keep either of them around, much less both."

This time, however, and much to everyone's surprise, Kaleagh sided with Harrison in advocating restraint. She wouldn't say what changed her mind, and insisted she still wanted them both dead, eventually. "But if he ever even thinks about not holding up his end of the bargain," she warned, "I'll kill her myself, and he can watch. He doesn't get a warning."

On this, Harrison agreed.

"So, what's our plan for leaving?" Jonah asked, settling in at his spot at the table.

The group looked to Finn. It was his first attempt at feeding himself, and they were all trying not to make a big deal out of it. He was determined to do it all without any help. He tried to pick up the spoon and promptly dropped it noisily onto his plate, splashing soup. Bren reflexively reached over, but he pushed her hand away. He tried again, then stopped. "Bun . . . ker," he said, struggling to form the words. "Tuh tuh tuh—"

"Twelve?" Jonah asked, impatiently. "Bunker Twelve?"

"Cuh cuh cuh—"

"Cure?"

"Give him a chance to finish," Bren hissed. She turned to Finn. "Are you saying we should keep looking?"

"Yuh yuhsss." He bobbed his head.

"Maybe we should wait until you're fully recovered," Harper said. "Besides, we still have no idea where it could be."

"Muh uh uh muhp."

"Map?"

"There's no map for Twelve."

"Our best chance for either a cure or Twelve may be Seth's notes," Harrison said.

"Bunker Eight?" Bren asked, looking apprehensive. "Do you really have to go back there?"

"We're *all* going, honey," Kaleagh said. "Now that we have two vehicles and Finn is well enough to travel, there's no reason for us to stay here."

"But I don't like that place."

"We'll stay only as long as it takes to find your father's notes."

"Tuh tuh tuwelfff."

"Eight first, Finn," Harrison said. "Then out to Westerton to let them know where this bunker is so they can come and pick up the supplies. Then we resume our search for Bunker Twelve and the cure."

This seemed to satisfy him. He bobbed his head and reached for the spoon again. He didn't seem to notice or care that the others were waiting, silently cheering him on.

For a little while, the only sound was the scrape of metal on plastic.

"I know I keep asking this," Jonah said, first to break the silence once they'd all had their fill. "But what's our timeline for leaving?"

"We'll need to pack enough supplies," Eddie said.

"We have enough food and stuff ready to go to last us a week," Kaleagh said.

"Plus as much as we can carry for Westerton, including medicine."

"We have enough fuel for both vehicles?"

"Both tanks are full, plus as many containers as I could find. There's still about a hundred and fifty gallons left to transfer. I want to take it, too, since if we leave it, it might gel up again."

"That should be enough to top off a couple of the army trucks on base," Eddie noted.

They all turned to Finn. "S-soon," he stuttered. "Toot-too-morrow. Kay?"

They all exchanged glances. It was probably too soon for Finn to travel, but his eagerness was infectious, and they were all anxious to get on the road. Besides, it might actually help him to be moving again.

"Day after," Harrison suggested. "We'll spend tomorrow pulling out the extra supplies and loading them on the bus. Plus, I want full checks on both vehicles. Then, weather permitting, we'll leave first thing the next morning."

"How long will it take to get there?" Bren asked.

"To Bunker Eight? We could push it and arrive by late in the evening, but I think we'd be better off taking our time, playing it safe, taking the long way around and avoiding Salt Lake City altogether. We'll sleep in the bus, since it's got wire on the windows. Barring any mishaps, we should be there by noon at the latest the day after."

Finn jerked his hands up twice before they realized he was trying to clap.

"I'm with Bren," Bix said. "I can't say I'm thrilled about going back there, but I'll be even gladder to leave here. Something about this place gives me the creeps."

"More," Finn said, nodding enthusiastically and sliding his empty bowl toward the pot. "More."

* * *

The sun had been up barely an hour when they closed the outer door on Bunker Ten and shoved a large cabinet in front to conceal the entrance. The place may have remained undiscovered for more than four years, but it didn't guarantee anyone else stumbling upon it and finding the stash of supplies still inside, supplies that were sorely needed by the people they'd left behind at Westerton Army Base, weeks before.

Next-to-last to board the bus was Adrian, his wrists tied behind his back and his ankles linked together by a short pipe through which a chain had been passed. Eddie had welded metal ankle cuffs to each end that couldn't be easily removed. A metal collar was attached around his neck, and another chain linked it to the bindings around his arms.

"What if we're attacked?" Adrian asked Harrison.

"Then I guess you're Wraith food," Jonah shouted from beneath the hood, where he was checking the engine one last time.

"Might I see my sister?"

"Look out the window."

"No, please."

Harrison dragged him off and took him over to the bed of the pickup truck, where Eddie had placed her. Beneath a tarp to protect her from the elements, she was also shackled and wrapped tightly inside several blankets, around which he'd wound enough rope that she'd never be able to escape. She had fought him like a wild animal, but quickly calmed once he laid her in the truck bed. Now, as Harrison pulled back the tarp, she renewed her fight, hissing through the gag Eddie had forced between her teeth, and trying to wriggle her way out of the restraints.

Harrison watched Adrian's face for a reaction. He expected him to get angry and protest the treatment, but he simply nodded and told her that it was all going to be okay. "It'll be better soon, angel," he said. He turned to Harrison and offered a mumbled thanks, then shuffled his way back to the bus. "Y'all done right by her," he said to no one in particular. "Fer that, I am eternally grateful." He collapsed into the front seat without saying another word.

Harrison and Bix got inside the pickup, started it up, and pulled out. Jonah, now in the driver seat, polished the stray dust off his pistol as he waited for everyone to settle in. Then, pointedly making eye contact with their prisoner in the rearview mirror, he stowed the weapon in a makeshift holster within easy reach beside him. They held each other's gaze for several seconds, then Adrian nodded and turned to look out the window.

"Everyone set?" Jonah called.

Eddie was in back checking the straps on the supplies, which now occupied the place where several rows of seats had been removed. Boxes and barrels filled the space from floor to ceiling.

"We're good!" he called, and made his way up the aisle to take his seat behind Adrian. "Let's go home."

CHAPTER
25

THEY HEADED EAST ON THE OLD INTERSTATE 80 AFTER passing the truck they'd abandoned at the exit three weeks before. Bix rolled the window down and sniffed the air, but smelled nothing. The sun and wind had stripped away all traces of fried oil smell, and the desert was leisurely burying the metal carcass. Sand had already drifted halfway up the rims.

There were no visible signs that any other vehicle had passed this way recently, no tire tracks, and no evidence that any part of the deserted truck had been scavenged.

Approaching the city, they took other roads to skirt it to the south to avoid the worst of the traffic left abandoned years before, then rejoined 80 on the other side. There had been some discussion about whether they should return the way they had come, since they already knew that way was clear enough of obstructions for them to pass, but in the end Harrison decided it was safer to avoid going through the city, and south was a more direct route than north anyway. Besides, no one was in any mood to fight off the Wraiths that still dwelled among the ruins within the city.

Left unspoken was the worry they might encounter someone from Haven, to whom they owed a debt, payment for which now sat in the front row of the bus. Harrison wasn't yet ready to tender it.

They encountered surprisingly few obstacles during the first two hours. The roads were passable, although sand had blown onto them in many places, or mud had flowed over them. But since the last rain a few days before, the surface had baked as hard as concrete. As they drove, Bix counted the Wraiths on his side of the road. He was up to fourteen to his father's three, most of them clustered near the junction with Interstate 15, which the map said led to Provo some forty-five miles to the south. When first spotted, the Wraiths tended to be far off, drawn out of their hiding places by the sound of the motors. Most attempted to give chase as soon as they noticed the vehicles, but they were no match for the powerful engines and soon fell behind.

"Bang," Bix said, pointing his finger out the window at his fifteenth and pulling his thumb trigger. "I'm whipping your butt, Dad."

"I have to keep my eyes on the road."

The game served as more than a simple distraction. They knew that when they finally stopped for the night, company would not be far behind. The tenacious creatures did not easily abandon their chase, not unless they fell into complete exhaustion or lost the scent. Once they'd keyed in on their quarry, they stalked it relentlessly, and either infected or killed it without mercy.

The group stopped briefly for lunch and to switch drivers. While they ate, Jonah kept watch for signs of their pursuers from atop the bus. They had reached an area of grassland, now dry and turned to gold. Much of it had been pressed flat against the ground by winds and rain. A few scraggly trees dotted the landscape. *It's a good vantage point*, he thought, as he scanned the horizon. *Nothing's going to sneak up on us here.*

"Look out!" Bix screamed, and grabbed him from behind.

"Goddamn it, Bix!" Jonah cried. It felt like every nerve ending in his body was firing at once, pumping massive amounts of adrenaline into his bloodstream. "What the goddamn hell?"

"Boys," Eddie called from below. "Keep it down."

"Aw, there's nothing for miles around," Bix said. "Last Wraith was a solid forty minutes ago."

"Last one you saw."

"I see everything, Dad."

"Would you just grow up?" Jonah grumbled, and returned to scanning the horizon.

Bix laughed. "You should have seen yourself jump. You might want to check your undies for pee pee."

Jonah shook his head in disgust. But he couldn't help cracking a smile, too. It was good to be back on the road again, and by the way Bix was joking around, he was obviously happy about it, too. He'd had a bad feeling about Bunker Ten since the day they arrived, and not just because of the blocked lower levels. Eddie's discovery of the cave-in had done little to calm his anxieties. Maybe it was the dozen or so bodies they believed were buried beneath the rubble. The bunker had failed to do its one job: protect them.

On the other hand, leaving it had been just as catastrophic for the rest.

"Feels strange, doesn't it?" Bix asked. "I mean, after everything we've been through, even knowing what's out here, I feel . . . . I don't know."

"Liberated?"

"Yeah, liberated."

"Well, don't get used to it. Once we get back to Eight, we'll likely have to fight our way inside."

"You're such a buzzkill."

They watched Harrison escort Adrian out to the nearest bush to relieve himself. They could hear the man whine about performing at the end of a gun barrel. Bix's gaze drifted over to the pickup truck and the figure lying beneath the tarp. During the ride with his dad, there had been moments when he'd forgotten their deadly cargo. But then they'd make an abrupt stop or a sharp turn or hit a pothole, and she'd start thrashing about and hissing, and the back of his neck would tingle, and he'd glance through the glass and see the tarp roiling like the surface of the ocean as she writhed beneath it. He'd imagine that she had somehow managed to get the gag out of her mouth and was working on freeing her hands, and she'd jump out and attack them at any moment. But he'd eventually get distracted, or his father would remind him to keep a lookout in front, and he'd forget about her. They'd stop for a rest break and check, but she'd be as tightly bound as before. Eddie had done a good job of making sure she couldn't escape.

She was fighting at the moment. He could see the tarp flapping beneath her kicks.

Standing in the sunlight atop the bus, the temperature felt like it was in the low-eighties, but it had to be over a hundred underneath the tarp, where the air was still and as dry as dust. He almost felt sorry for her.

His father walked over and untied a corner and folded it away so Adrian could see her. She immediately stilled and turned her head, but not toward either of the men. Instead, her gaze swept higher across the scene, stopping only when it found the two boys on top of the bus. A shiver of revulsion passed through Bix. He wondered, if a cure existed, would it bring Jennifer back the way she had once been? Would she remember any of it, what she had done? He recalled with fondness the home cooked meals she had made for them, before they realized how dangerous the couple were. Would she also recall those few decent moments with the same fondness? Even worse to contemplate, would she remember the things she had done while a Wraith? Would she know she'd dug up a corpse and feasted on the decaying flesh? Or would it all be a blank, empty space?

"She made the best fried chicken," he muttered.

"What's that?" Jonah asked, intruding on his thoughts.

"Nothing."

Jonah gestured back the way they'd come. "We'll need to get moving again soon."

There, on the horizon a few miles away, appeared a handful of moving dots, shimmering through the haze of the desert.

"Damn," Bix whispered. "That was fast."

* * *

The pickup stalled about an hour before they planned to stop for the evening. The sun had slipped much of the way toward the horizon far sooner than they'd hoped, and their shadows stretched far ahead of them, as if straining to arrive at their destination before darkness swept over the land. Being out in the open no longer felt so safe, not with so little daylight remaining.

The sky above them was clear, save for a few long, wispy clouds, but the wind had picked up. It blew cold from the east, carrying their scent back the way they'd come. It was not an ideal scenario, and it made them all the more aware of their vulnerability. Between them were only a half dozen guns, and ammunition was limited. Twilight was just another hour and a half away, and the last Wraiths they'd counted were an equal amount of time beyond that.

Jonah and Eddie worked feverishly on the engine, trying to identify the problem. Facing east, they could not make use of the dying light. The gloom and chill beneath the hood too quickly sapped the heat from the engine, as well as Jonah's patience.

"Why don't we all just get on the bus and find shelter nearby for the night," Harrison suggested. "Leave the truck here till morning. Better safe than sorry."

But Jonah stubbornly refused to give up. He inspected the spark plug wires, then asked Eddie to try again. The engine cranked, caught, then rattled into silence.

"Clogged fuel line?" Harrison asked.

Jonah gave him a dark look that made clear he wasn't helping.

"We filtered the fuel," Eddie quietly explained.

"Can I get a light here?" Jonah asked. "Bix?"

Bix handed over one of the emergency flashlights from one of the spare kits the bunker residents had left behind, and Jonah angled the beam down into the engine compartment. He wiggled a few wires and pinched hoses, all while cursing under his breath. The wound on the back of his hand had scabbed over and the scab had since fallen off, leaving a triangle of mottled pink and white flesh that he no longer bothered to cover. At one point, it rubbed against a hot surface, and he hissed in pain.

"I think I see the problem." He reached around behind him and gestured with his fingers. "Duct tape. Give me a piece about a foot long."

When he was finished, he stood back and wiped the greasy, sooty residue from his palms and nodded to Eddie. "Give it another go."

The engine caught on the third try, sputtered, then began to run more smoothly again.

"Hole in one of the air lines," he simply stated.

"Don't look at me," Bix said. "I didn't do it."

"No one said you did," Jonah replied, and pressed the flashlight flat against Bix's chest. "The hoses are dry and cracking. They'll need replacing soon." He lowered the hood and made sure it latched. "Let's get moving."

CHAPTER

NOWHERE FELT SAFE, SO THEY DECIDED TO KEEP GOING rather than stopping to find a place to sleep, and reached the hydroelectric complex of the old bunker shortly after midnight. Eddie was driving the bus when they arrived, and he opted to back in over the dam to make it easier to pull out when they left. And quicker, should escape be necessary. Harrison parked the truck on top of the dam, but left enough room for the bus to pass.

With the engines silenced, the wind in the trees all around them and the rush of water far below was loud in their ears. A full moon lit up the sky, although it remained low on the horizon, and painted the valley in a silvery glow.

They decided to sleep inside the bus and wait for daybreak to go inside the bunker. Harrison volunteered himself and Bix to take the first watch. They seated themselves on opposite ends of the roof so they could monitor both ends of the dam. Each held a rifle on his lap and tucked a pistol into his waistband for easy access. But after ten minutes exposed to the damp, bone chilling wind that whipped up from the surface of the roiling river below, they tugged their sleeping bags on and zipped them up to their chins, their rifles tucked inside with them.

Sitting was impossible, so they stood and rocked from one foot to the other to keep from falling asleep, and stared out into the darkness, searching for any hint of movement. To Bix, it seemed like the longest two hours of his life, especially when the moon slid to the side and disappeared behind the top of the ridge, and the darkness deepened. All but the luminescent spume of whitewater two hundred feet below and the wispy curls of a few clouds overhead were smothered in the blackest of blacks.

He was dead tired and shivering from the cold when Jonah and Eddie finally climbed up to relieve them. Without even bothering to get out of the bag, Bix descended the ladder, freeing only his hands from the wrists up and immediately regretting it when it let in a rush of frigid air. His feet ached, as did his back, and the cold had worked its way to his bones and bladder. He ignored the need to urinate and instead shuffled straight to the door of the bus, hopped up the steps, then collapsed into the first open space he could find. He was out in an instant.

The next thing he knew, Bren was kneeling over him, shaking his shoulder. Morning light lit up the bus, muted by prisms of winter ice that had grown on the dusty windows. Each exhale was a thin fog, each inhale a fire in his throat.

He'd been dreaming he was at a roadside bar, the dull thump of his mother's bass drum coming through the walls, and he was searching for the bathroom with dread, knowing that it would be a disgusting mess of piss, condoms, cigarette butts, and vomit. Seeing Bren had slammed him back to reality. He lurched upright in alarm, bladder problems temporarily forgotten, and asked what was wrong.

"Everyone's already up," she said. "We're getting ready to go inside the bunker."

Bix glanced down the aisle toward the front of the bus. The adults were discussing what to do with Adrian. "Where's Finn? And Harper?"

"Up top keeping watch."

"Finn's on the roof?" he asked, and tried to pull his arms out from inside the twisted bag.

She nodded. "He made a lot of progress last night. He's talking more, lots more, nearly full sentences now. He's almost all better." She looked like she was about to leave, when she stopped and frowned.

"What's the matter, Bren?"

She took in a deep breath, then gave her head a quick shake. "It's nothing. I'm just being . . . . It's silly."

"You can tell me. Did he hurt you?"

"It's nothing, Bix. We're fine. Better than fine, actually. I just sometimes forget that I have to be patient. He'll come back when he's ready."

She jumped up and hurried away before he could ask her anything else.

He fought with the zipper, but it was jammed, and of course it would have to happen when he really desperately needed to get out of the bag. He managed to get to his feet and tried to shimmy it down off his body, but the opening was too narrow to get past his shoulders. "Jesus," he whimpered, and tugged even harder at the zipper, knowing it was probably permanently snagged.

The group at the front stopped to watch as he penguin-walked down the aisle. Jonah asked if he needed a hand.

"Just get out of my way! I have to—" The bag snagged on something on the floor and he went down.

"Would you just stop for a moment," Jonah said, laughing. He stepped over to help him up. "You're caught."

"No shit!" Bix yelled. "Just get me out of this damn bag!"

"No, I mean the bag's snagged on a loose bolt in the floor."

"I don't need a fricking analysis! Just get this off me!"

"Stop hopping around like that!" Jonah replied. He tried not to smile as he worked the zipper free. As soon as it was down, Bix peeled himself out of the cocoon and shoved Jonah out of the way. Watching him pinball down the aisle with his hands clutching his crotch was too much. Fortunately, Bix couldn't hear him laugh over his own groans of relief.

"So, who needs to check their undies now?" Jonah called out the door.

"It's only funny when I say it."

"It wasn't even funny then."

The rest of the adults exited the bus, Harrison ahead of Adrian, Eddie in the rear. They'd agreed to free Adrian's hands, but he remained hobbled by the steel pipe between his ankles. "At least gimme something to defend myself with," he asked, blinking against the harsh sunlight. Harrison disappeared back inside the bus and emerged a moment later with the windshield scraper and told him it was all he was getting, so he'd better make good use of it.

"If you ask me," Bix grumbled, "I wouldn't even let him have his hands."

Jonah nodded in agreement.

"Finn! Harper!" Harrison called up to the sentries. "Let's go!"

The Bolles brothers glanced down, unintentionally striking the same pose. The resemblance was so uncanny that Bix did a double-take. Day-by-day, their likenesses grew closer. Nearly gone were all outward signs of the accident. But gone too was Finn's characteristic tentative look. And his boyish self-doubt. He now stood tall, although still slightly twisted to one side, his shoulders thrown defiantly back. He stepped toward the side of the bus, then into open space. Eddie gasped and stepped forward, but Finn landed on both feet without a problem and acted as if it was the most natural thing to do.

As he passed Bix, they locked eyes, and Bix thought he'd come over and say something, perhaps even give him a hug. It felt like he'd finally returned from a long journey. *He's back*, Bix thought. *Back and himself again.*

Except the old Finn would never have even dared doing something so reckless as jumping off the top of the bus.

Finn stepped to Bix, then passed him by without acknowledgment, not a hint of emotion or recognition on his face.

And suddenly Bix realized what had so affected Bren moments before. She might not say it, but as much as this Finn looked like the old one, he wasn't. This Finn was an imposter.

"Has anyone scouted the loading ramp yet?" Eddie asked.

"I checked as far as the top of the walkway, but I didn't go down," Jonah replied. "That bus Adrian and his men left behind is still down there. If we're lucky, it's drivable, or at least fixable."

"If we're lucky," Bix added, "the bodies they left behind are gone. Because of wolves, I mean," he quickly added, when the others glared at him. "Not Wraiths!" But the clarification came too late.

Jonah nudged Adrian forward. "We should send him to check."

"It weren't me," he squeaked. "It was Cheever who killed them all."

"Who gave the order?"

"Well, I took care of him afterward."

"Figured you couldn't trust someone who betrayed his own people? Once a traitor, always a traitor, eh?"

Eddie sniffed the air. "It's been weeks, and I detect only traces, so maybe . . . ." He turned to Bren and Kaleagh. "Maybe you two should hang back until we're sure."

Kaleagh shook her head stiffly. "No," she said. Fear had settled onto her face, but it wasn't the only thing there. For the first time, Eddie saw a steely determination in her eyes. He knew it couldn't be easy for her to return to this place. Maybe she needed it for closure.

"Go on," Jonah said, shoving Adrian forward again.

"No, please," he begged. "I know now everythin I did then was stupid. I regret it all."

"Shut up. You're not fooling anyone. You want to repent your sins, here's your chance."

"It was Ramsay and the others, not me!" He took a faltering step toward the loading ramp, then stopped and tried to turn.

"We're not buying it!" Bix said, and wrestled him back around. "You're the one who got off on killing."

"Leave him here," Harrison said. "We don't have time for this."

But apparently the thought of being left alone was enough to get Adrian moving again.

The group followed him cautiously down the ramp, separating into two groups when they reached the abandoned bus and converging again at the other end, the site of the horrific scene of Cheever's massacre.

The bodies were gone. Nothing but the blood stains remained, large black puddles on the ground, spatter on the gray cement walls, streaks and smears where the bodies had been dragged off.

"Scavenged," Eddie said.

"Yeah, but by what?" Jonah asked.

"Wolves don't take motorcycles," Bix said grimly. "Last time we were here, there were a good half dozen of them. None of them worked, but still . . . . Now they're gone."

"If they took the bikes, then they probably got what's left from inside the bunker, too," Harrison said.

"All the more reason to keep our eyes open and listen for any noises, human or otherwise," Eddie instructed. "Assume we're not alone."

They stopped in front of the outer bunker doors, dreading the moment they would set foot inside. They never thought they'd ever see the place again, much less willingly reenter it.

"Ready?" Harrison asked the group, and waited for each of them to confirm with a nod. He nestled his rifle into the crook of his arm, then slowly and carefully nudged the muzzle into the thin gap between doors and pulled one open.

Cold air wafted out.

The stench hit them next.

Then came the Wraiths.

CHAPTER
27

EDDIE WAS THE FIRST TO REACT. HE YANKED HARRISON back and shouted for everyone else to retreat. He tried to push the doors shut, but he was thrown to the side.

"Finn!" Bren screamed.

"Get back!" Harrison yelled, and grabbed Bren's arm to keep her from following Finn into the tunnel, where the sounds of a struggle could already be heard. "Jonah! Bix, protect the women!"

"Let me go!" Bren screamed. "I need to help! He's not strong enough!"

From deep within the tunnel came a series of low growls and hisses. There was a soft thud and the snapping of bones. Finn made no utterance of his own. The fight carried out in eerie quiet until a spine-chilling shriek sounded from the top of the ramp.

Jonah and Eddie wheeled around, bracing for an attack from behind, but the sound of flesh hammering metal told them it was nothing more than Jennifer trying to break free.

Jonah already had Kaleagh's arm in one hand, and he turned to reach for Bren's. The older woman had frozen, but Bren evaded him and tried again to get inside. Bix blocked her way, and Harper grabbed her wrist. "Don't," he warned.

"He's dying in there!"

Bix snatched a handful of shirt from the retreating Adrian and spun him around. "Not you, asshole! You get inside there and fight!"

"No! Please!"

"Do it!"

Adrian collapsed where he stood, whimpering and cowering. Bix tried to lift him to his feet, but he refused to stand.

"Forget him!" Eddie shouted. He nodded at Jonah, who stepped forward, and wrenched the door wide open again. Weak morning light penetrated only a few feet into the tunnel, leaving the depths swimming in inky darkness. Vague shapes flitted about in the gloom, the sounds of skin impacting skin all that emerged. The hissing had stopped. The crunching of bones, too.

"Who's got a light?" Bix whispered, joining Eddie and Jonah. As his eyes adjusted, he could make out more of the scrum. Finn was halfway in, still on his feet and struggling beneath the weight of a pair of Wraiths. More emerged from deeper in the darkness, as if spawned by the bunker itself.

Indecision kept the group from moving. There were too many to take on, and who knew how many more just waiting in the shadows. A third Wraith jumped onto Finn, snapping its jaws, searching for soft flesh.

Harrison halfheartedly lifted his rifle, but he couldn't shoot without jeopardizing Finn. The mass of bodies caromed from one side of the corridor to the other as Finn tried to dislodge them.

There was a loud *SNAP!* and one of the Wraiths fell off. Finn stumbled as another immediately took its place. He dropped to his knees, then reached over his shoulder and grabbed a handful of hair. The biting, scratching creature somersaulted through the air, smashed into the ceiling, then fell limp to the floor. In a flash, Finn was on it, raining punches down on its head. Each blow caused its body to recoil like a rag doll.

"Get out of there, Finn!" Bix screamed, triggering an outburst of cries from the others. Finn ignored them all. The Wraiths pulled him farther into the darkness.

"Take this!" Eddie shouted, shoving his gun into Harper's hands. He turned and faced the unknown, hesitated a moment, then sprinted forward, roaring at the top of his lungs.

Darkness swallowed him, too. Then, suddenly, the sounds of struggle ceased. A low, measured inhale followed, accompanied by a pained grunt. Finn's voice drifted out: "More?"

"*Lights!*" Bix whispered.

"On it!" replied Jonah, and he scrambled over to find the switch.

There was a click, and a single unbroken fixture flickered to life, revealing a scene more horrific than they expected.

"Jesus," Bix gasped. He reeled back, throwing his elbow over his face and retching.

The bodies they'd expected to find outside had been dragged in and stacked up against the inner set of doors. It was mostly bones by now, but the smell of rotting flesh told them that not all had been consumed. The worst, however, was the putrid stink of feces, covering nearly the entire floor of the tunnel. Finn stood in the middle of it all, every inch of him covered in Wraith blood. He dropped the last of them onto the heap. Severed limbs and skulls cascaded down the pile and onto the floor. Eddie stood, crouched not ten feet away, unbloodied, unscathed, and unnecessary.

"Okay," he said, stunned. "It's okay."

Bren broke from Harper and ran, but Eddie caught her before she could reach him. "No! You can't touch him. No one touch anything! It's all contaminated. Get back outside!"

"Finn?" Bren called. "Finn, are you okay?"

Finn slowly turned and stepped toward them. Most of his shirt had been torn from his body, and a new gash exposed his muscles from one shoulder to the middle of his chest. "Dead," he growled, and a smile twitched at the corners of his lips. The whites of his eyes and teeth glowed like shards of ice. Thick, black gore dripped from his hair.

No one spoke for a moment. No one moved, terrified by the look of manic glee in Finn's eyes.

At last, a figure blocked the light from the tunnel entrance, breaking the trance. "Yer boy's a beast," Adrian said.

Jonah turned, his own face twisted in rage. "Go shut your damn sister up," he growled. "Before I put a bullet in her brain. If she brings more of those damn things here, it won't be Finn stopping them, but you."

CHAPTER

28

"YOU CAN'T DO THAT AGAIN," BREN CHIDED, AS SHE dressed Finn's wound. "What were you even thinking running into a nest like that?"

The return to the site, as well as the Wraith encounter, had stirred up powerful emotions for everyone. That is, all except for Finn, whose moment of violent glee had vanished as soon as it had appeared. He was now as impassive as ever, and regarded her stoically while she worked, his eyes tracking her every movement. Water dripped from his hair, still wet from his shower. The towel around his waist was thin and frayed.

She laid a hand on his uninjured shoulder and the muscle underneath rippled with tension. "I mean it, Finn. You could have died."

They were alone. The rest of the crew, Adrian included, were off clearing the rest of the bunker, and Bren had hoped that she might finally break through the wall that remained between the two of them. She wanted to reach him where she knew he still dwelled, but it seemed an impossible task, and she didn't know how to do it.

She dabbed at the water droplets on his neck and arms. The laceration had already stopped bleeding and sealed, forming a tough clot. In a day, the scab would begin to peel away and reveal new, pink tissue underneath. Within a week, only a scar would remain as proof of the injury, and that would disappear in about a month, just as the other injuries he'd sustained in his fall down the elevator shaft were well on their way to vanishing.

It wasn't the physical trauma that concerned her anymore, but the psychological. Finn's mental recovery wasn't keeping pace. If anything, it seemed to have stalled. He was as distant, as unreachable, as when he'd first woken up from his coma. She just couldn't seem to be able to find a way to connect with him anymore. It was like all the doors and windows into his soul had been slammed shut and locked, and she feared they might never open again.

A tear slipped down her cheek. She tried to turn away to hide it, knowing it was visible to him. But another part wanted him to see it, and when he failed to react, she swiped angrily at her face and glared at him. No hint of understanding entered his eyes, no acknowledgment of the pain he caused her. A whimper of despair escaped her throat, and this time she turned fully away, hoping he didn't notice. She felt suddenly embarrassed and vulnerable. He grabbed her hand and yanked her around, forcing her back.

"You're hurting me," she whispered.

He didn't let go.

"Finn, please."

"Brehhhn?"

"What's happening to you?" she whispered.

He didn't answer.

"Are we . . . ? What's happening to us, Finn?"

Still nothing.

"I don't know if I can—"

"What?" he demanded.

"I— I love you, Finn. Don't you love me?"

"You don't know," he said. He raised his other hand and made a fist. His knuckles cracked with the pressure. He remained like that for several seconds, then relaxed again. "You don't know what . . . it's like."

"I'm trying to understand."

"I am trying," he echoed, almost mockingly. "I just . . . I can't."

"Can't what, Finn? Can't feel? Can't remember? Please tell me."

At last he released her, and he seemed to crumble. His shoulders sagged and he lowered his face into his hands. "You don't . . . understand. I feel everything. Pain, healing, anger, hatred, love . . . . Death. It scares the hell out of me."

"Love, Finn?" she said, hopefully. "You feel love?"

He looked up at her, as if startled, and reached out. She shied away, but he was too quick. He grabbed her and pulled her to him, slipping off the examination table and pressing himself against her. The towel about his waist slipped to the floor. He didn't retrieve it. He leaned forward and buried his nose in the hollow of her neck, and breathed deep.

She whimpered as their lips met, gasped at the brutality of his embrace, moaned at the vulnerability of his kiss. She gave herself over to the desire that had been building within her ever since they first left the bunker all those months before. She reveled in the familiarity of his body.

And yet he was a complete stranger to her.

CHAPTER
29

"WHAT IS EVERYONE TALKING ABOUT?" BREN ASKED.

Her arrival with Finn into the kitchen abruptly cut short the discussion the others had been having. There were a few uncomfortable throat clearings, and most of them avoided making eye contact with the couple. Bren turned to her mother and saw that her face was bright red, and so she realized that they all knew what had transpired down in the medical bay. She felt her own cheeks flush with heat.

Finn sat down, apparently oblivious to it all.

"Hungry?" Bix squeaked at them. "We're having soup."

"Starving," Finn grunted.

"It's cream of broccoli."

"Okay."

Bix jumped up and grabbed a couple bowls and took them over to the stove, where Kaleagh stood. Dinner was from a can Bix had rescued from the bunker's plundered stores downstairs, which were now nearly fully depleted.

Months before, when the majority of the bunker survivors left, there had been enough food to last the dozen or so people who chose to stay behind at least another decade. Much of that had been left after Adrian's raid, as food hadn't been his primary objective. The uncertainty of who had since come and taken the items put the group on edge. When had they been here? When would they return?

"So, uh, you guys must be famished then," Bix said.

"Gee, what makes you say that?" muttered Jonah.

Kaleagh set the first bowl of soup before Finn. "Here you go. Careful, it's very hot."

He took it from her, hesitated as if trying to remember something, then slid it over to Bren. He leaned over the second bowl and began to feed himself. His attempts were still stiff, mechanical, but markedly more improved since just the day before. Strength had returned to him early, and in spades. The fine motor skills finally seemed to be catching up.

"So, you're feeling better then, Finn?" Eddie asked tentatively. "More like your old self?"

"You might want to ask Bren how he feels."

"Bix," Harrison warned.

"To be . . . honest," Finn replied, haltingly, "I don't know what that . . . is anymore, my old self." The spoon felt far too small for his hand and was taking too long transferring the food into his mouth. He dropped it and lifted the bowl and slurped the soup instead. He barely flinched when it scalded his lips, and when some of it spilled onto his hands, he didn't even seem to notice. "I feel like my . . . insides are changing by the . . . minute. My brain can't catch up. It's very . . . tuh— tuh—"

"Titillating?" Bix suggested.

Harrison groaned.

"Troubling. I don't . . . . It's . . . disturbing."

"It's not the only thing that's disturbing," Jonah muttered darkly.

"Not you, too, Jonah," Eddie said.

"He always has to make it about himself," Bix piped in. "He hates not being the focus of attention."

"It wasn't about him," Finn said dismissively. He drained the bowl, then gestured for the pot. "Eddie . . . knows."

"Um, what were you guys talking about before we came in?" Bren asked, desperate to change the subject.

"Searching for your father's secret laboratory," Eddie said, his gaze dwelling on Finn's face a moment longer. "We were just saying that—"

"I really think we need to talk about what happened downstairs," Jonah interrupted. "Now that we're all together again."

"I'd rather not," Kaleagh muttered.

"Yeah, they're both consenting adults," Bix said.

Jonah rolled his eyes. "I meant Finn going off half-cocked in the tunnel. Oh for Christ's sake, Bix! Stop with the damn innuendos. Him taking on the Wraiths by himself put us all in danger!"

"Later," Eddie advised.

"No, now," Jonah insisted. "We were attacked. We had guns, but instead of using them, Finn goes in and confronts them alone, not knowing how many there were, to fight them by hand."

"Seven," Finn said. "I knew there were seven. I heard their . . . heartbeats."

This shocked them all into silence.

"And we need to save . . . bullets."

"It was totally irresponsible."

"What matters is that he took care of them," Harrison said.

"He put us all at risk!"

"Never at risk," Finn hissed. He set the bowl down so hard that soup splashed onto the table. His spoon skittered away onto the floor. "I did what I . . . had to. Should be thankful."

"What?" Jonah cried. "You want us to thank you? You think you're a hero? You're a damn liability!"

"Jonah!" Eddie barked.

"How are we supposed to trust him when he acts like that?"

"Like what?" Finn challenged, and started to rise out of his seat. He seemed to change right before their very eyes, growing larger, more . . . present. Something was happening inside of him. They could sense it more than see it. "Better than you, Jonah? Is that what you mean? Stronger? Smarter?"

"Unpredictable. Irrational. Impulsive."

"I said enough, Jonah," Eddie growled, and slapped his palm on the table. He didn't notice how the force of it caused the metal to dent, but the others did. "What Finn did was . . . . It wasn't what I would've done. Or recommended. But we need to cut him some slack. He's still finding his way. What he experienced these past few weeks, none of us can fully understand, not even me. One thing we can be sure of, however, is that it's going to take some time for him to figure out. He will get through it. We need to help him."

"Can't help him if we don't survive," Jonah muttered, crossing his arms.

"Finn needs our support," Eddie reminded them all. "For god's sake, he nearly died back there at Ten. We're fortunate he didn't, so cut him some slack. He deserves a little leeway."

He turned to Finn, whose demeanor had turned impassive again. "That being said, Jonah has a valid point, even if it was poorly made. We *all* need to be smart out there, for everyone's sake, and that means not putting ourselves or our colleagues in positions of greater risk. There are better ways to deal with Wraiths than taking them on hand-to-hand. Can I get your promise to try next time to let us deal with the Wraiths as a team?"

Finn said nothing. He just picked up his bowl and brought it to his lips.

"Y'all ask me," Adrian said, speaking up from a table in the corner, "yer boy dispatched them ferals right quick, and none of y'all got hurt. So, no harm, no foul."

"Shut the hell up," Jonah growled.

"Finn took care of them for us," Bren said. "And like he said, no one got hurt. That's what's important."

"Finn got hurt."

"And he's already healing."

"And what about next time?"

"I can handle it," Finn said.

"Next time might not be just seven Wraiths," Eddie quietly advised. "You're not indestructible, Finn. *I'm* not indestructible. We're stronger working *together*."

"I'm stronger alone."

Eddie pursed his lips. He looked like he wanted to disagree, but he didn't. "It's done. Let's just move on."

Harrison nodded. "I agree. We need to stay focused. The cure is what's important."

"You still believe Mister . . . Ay— abra— able—" Finn clenched his fists, his face twisting in frustration.

"Seth's notes are our best lead at the moment," Harrison said.

"For now," Eddie agreed. "We're here, so we might as well look."

"Maybe," Finn said. "I— I—"

"Christ. Just spit it out already," Jonah grumbled.

Everyone glared at him, but he refused to apologize.

"May . . . be. Maybe— maybe a cure isn't . . . the best thing."

They gawped at him in disbelief.

"I would be dead . . . without nanites, so . . . ."

"Don't go there, Finn," Eddie warned. "That's dangerous thinking."

"You wouldn't be dead, Finn," Jonah asserted. "You'd be home. With your whole family. We all would be. The Flense would never have happened, and your father would be alive, and—"

"Yours, too."

"As I was saying before," Eddie said stiffly, stopping them, "there weren't many rooms left unused inside the bunker or hadn't been accessed by at least one of us present in this room at various times, so that fact alone should help us narrow down where Seth hid his work. There were a couple dozen or so unoccupied units on the residence level that no one ever bothered to open up. He might've used one of those, although I doubt it. He would've had a hard time getting in and out of them without being noticed. On the remaining levels, I can think of maybe a half dozen to a dozen rooms. Getting into some of them might be a challenge without the codes."

"Y'all's assumin the man just left everythin behind," Adrian noted.

"Will someone please shove a butt plug in that asshole?" Bix spat.

"Language, Bix."

"I just know if'n it were me, I'da got rid of the evidence."

"Well, it's not you," Kaleagh said thinly. "You and my husband were nothing alike. He documented everything he did very carefully. He had reasons for every experiment, hypotheses based on solid evidence."

"Real scientists don't create monsters," Bren muttered, drawing a sharp look from her mother. "They don't ruin the world, Mom."

"Your father was trying to save it, honey. He's not responsible for the Flense. I know he made some terrible choices afterward, unforgivable choices, but only because he thought he was protecting us. He just wanted to help everyone."

"Was he helping when he pushed Finn into the elevator shaft?"

Kaleagh slapped her daughter hard across the face. "Don't you ever speak about your father that way again!"

"Yikes," Bix whispered, and threw a worried glance over at Finn, who didn't react at all.

"Can it," Jonah said, elbowing him.

"I'm sorry for what your father did, young lady, but he was a good man put in a terrible situation. What he did, he did out of good intentions."

She waited until Bren nodded.

"I've done a mental accounting," Eddie said, pressing on. "Besides the unused, locked rooms on the residence level, a couple to either side of the watch room, and a few in the dungeon levels, where else could he have worked?"

They shook their heads.

"Okay, then I say we start here on Level One and work our way down, checking every room, forcing open every locked door. We search every square in—"

"Not . . . ness . . . nest." Finn growled, his face twisting in concentration. "Necessary. Adrian has it."

"Has what, Finn?"

"Book. Door c-codes."

Adrian's eyes narrowed. "Y'all talkin about that diary I found the night y'all ran from the ranch? Thought nothin of it at the time."

"Where is it now?" Jonah demanded.

"Well, I figured it might be important to y'all, so I kept it."

"Where is it?" Jonah growled impatiently.

"In the truck. Glove box."

Jonah stood up. "I did see a bunch of papers there, but I thought they were junk."

Bix groaned. "Please tell us you didn't throw them away."

"I put them back. I'll go check right now."

"Go with him, son," Harrison told Bix.

But it was Finn who stood up. "No, I . . . will."

"Stay here, Finn. It's just the top of the loading ramp."

"I'm still coming."

"Please be careful," Bren said. "Both of you."

"I'll watch my own back," Jonah said, his eyes locked on Finn's as he walked stiffly out of the room.

"Is that normal?" Harper asked, after the boys left.

"Not that I've ever seen," Bix answered. "For either of them."

Harper shook his head. "Finn's nothing like I remember before the Flense."

"Yeah, well, it's still a huge improvement from what he was just two weeks ago."

The others nodded, but they didn't look so convinced.

CHAPTER
30

"OKAY, SPILL IT," JONAH CALLED OUT TO FINN, WHO refused to slow down. Finn slammed through the stairwell door and into the hallway on Level Four. He'd nearly reached the last security door before the tunnel leading to the loading ramp when Jonah caught up to him. "Finn!"

The corpses were now gone from the tunnel, and the floor had been sprayed down, but the stench lingered.

Finn unwound the chain wrapped around the handles and stepped through, Jonah still tight against his side. A trace of the message Adrian had painted on the wall in the blood of the people Ramsey had slain was still visible: *Salvation or damnation.* At the moment, it felt particularly relevant to Finn, who was in a state of flux between the two.

"Finn!"

He stopped and turned. "What?"

Jonah shook his head. "Stop playing games, man. You didn't volunteer to come up here just to watch my back — or have me watch yours — so what is it?"

"Fresh air."

"I don't believe you. You obviously have something you want to say, so say it."

Finn hesitated a moment, and Jonah thought he might actually open up. But he gave his head a quick shake and tried to turn.

"What the hell is happening to you, Finn? You've changed."

"Nothing's changed."

"Bullshit. Everything's changed."

"You're still you, and I'm still . . . ."

"What? You can't even say it."

Finn glared at him for a moment. "Like Eddie said. I'm still . . . reek— reek— healing. I can't explain it. Not to you."

"Try. I think that's why you asked to go with me. You know I'll take you seriously."

"I— You have no idea what it's like . . . to die, or nearly die, and then come back and be—" He stopped himself.

"Different?" Jonah asked. He stepped forward tentatively. "Or afraid you'll end up the same?"

"Are *you* afraid?"

"Of what?"

"That I won't be the same. Or that I will."

"Everything changes us, Finn, sometimes a little, sometimes a lot."

"Not me."

Jonah sniffed and stepped past him, shaking his head. "You keep telling yourself that. Whatever gets you through the day."

"Exactly," Finn said, continuing on.

Jonah paused for several seconds, then ran to catch up again. "Let's just get the damn book," he said. "The sooner we find Seth's secret room, the sooner we can get back to Westerton."

"Then what?" Finn asked. "Make a cuh— a cuh— a cure? Will that really make things better?"

"For some of us, yeah."

Finn grabbed Jonah's arm. "How can you be sure?"

Jonah shook him off. "It has to."

He turned toward the door, one hand reaching instinctively for the handle, the other curling around the pistol in his waistband.

"Relax. There's nothing out there," Finn said. "You won't need that."

Jonah stared down at the weapon in his own hand. He glanced up at Finn, finally realizing why he'd come. Then he pushed out into the loading ramp, the pistol raised and ready to shoot.

They had moved the broken vehicle, rolling it out of the way after failing to get it running again. Jonah hadn't been able to figure out what was wrong with it, and Eddie thought it was too much of a hassle to try and hook it up and tow it out. There was enough room to bring the bus in almost three-quarters of the way down the ramp. The pickup sat at the top, off to one side, the tailgate lowered, but the tarp was still in place. Jennifer remained tied up inside the bed.

"Why doesn't she make any noise?" Finn whispered, as they made their way up to it. "Why doesn't she call out for help?"

"Call out? Seriously? It's just eat and kill with them."

"I'm not so sure."

"You saying you know something the rest of us don't?" He stopped and turned to face Finn. "When we were inside, you said you weren't sure a cure is the best thing. Were you talking about her or yourself?"

Finn opened his mouth, then seemed to reconsider his answer. "I almost died. I'm stronger now than I was before, thanks to the nanites. Why would I want to give that all up?"

"Because that's not you. It's changed you."

"If I'd taken steroids to bulk up, I'd still be me, wouldn't I?"

"Not the same."

"I fail to see the difference."

"It's not the same!"

The shout carried up the ramp, and the Wraith began to struggle. The tarp ballooned up as she arched her back, then sagged again when she dropped with a loud thud. She repeated this several times, bouncing the truck on its springs. Jonah noticed how Finn flinched, as if he felt each impact himself. After a while, she stopped. The boys exchanged glances before continuing up the ramp.

"I'll look for the book in front," Jonah said, when they reached the truck. "Why don't you check her bindings, make sure they're not loose or chewed through."

Finn sensed Jonah's eyes on his back as he worked the knot on one corner of the tarp. His fingers felt thick, uncooperative. At last it came loose and he lifted the covering away. The moment daylight hit the Wraith's eyes, she started thrashing again. She abruptly stopped, sniffed the air, then slowly turned her head. They locked eyes.

A familiar sensation permeated Finn, an overpowering urge to touch her, not in any intimate way, but simply to make contact. It was the same sensation that had compelled him to run into the tunnel, although it had dissipated the instant the first Wraith slammed into him and bit his shoulder. His instinct to live kicked in, and he'd killed what a moment before he'd merely wanted to connect to, and it hardly seemed possible he could've viewed them as anything but dangerous. After that, killing them had given him immense pleasure. But the act and the afterglow now sickened him.

At Adrian's request, Eddie had removed the blanket straightjacket and retied her spread eagle. She'd been chewing on the wool. Finn extended a finger toward the exposed skin on the back of her hands, just below the wrists. The skin had chafed so badly from the restraints that it had bled. The injuries had since healed, and a new layer of skin had formed over the sore within hours. The thrashing during the attack in the tunnel had stripped it away again, but while the nascent tissue was shredded and the sore remained open, there was no blood. It barely even wept. Her body had adapted to the recurring injuries and shunted all fluids away to preserve them.

He could almost sense her willing him to touch her, and for a moment it made his stomach roil, not just with revulsion, but with a primitive sort of longing, a need to offer comfort. His eyes flicked back to her face, and the sensations faded away. Hidden behind the filthy tangle of hair and road grime, he recognized the woman who, months before, had shown him genuine kindness, even self-sacrifice. He remembered her sympathetic voice, and he wondered if some part of her might still be there inside her mind, trapped and possibly aware. Or was she completely gone, her mind wiped clean, rendered into something more primeval? Had her nanites rewired her brain so it was no longer anything like the one it used to be?

Had his own been similarly rewired?

"Finn! Hey, what are you doing?"

He jerked away, the spell broken. He looked down and saw that he had a hold of Jennifer's elbow, and he released it and backed off as if it were on fire. That urge to make contact now felt like a trick. He couldn't be sure he hadn't imagined it.

Jennifer turned toward Jonah and screeched. She arched her back, stretching herself as much as the bindings would allow, trying to get to him. She could have easily bitten Finn moments before — he'd certainly been close enough — and yet she hadn't. Even now, she seemed not to care about him at all.

"Just check the damn bindings, Finn," Jonah muttered. "And watch yourself. You may be immune, but as Eddie said, you're not invulnerable. Cover her up and let's get the hell back inside."

"Indestructible."

"What?"

"Eddie said indestructible, not invulnerable."

"Same difference."

The words echoed in Finn's mind. Same? Different? He wasn't so sure about that.

"She's losing weight," he said. "She wasn't this thin before."

"She won't starve."

"I'll feed her. Maybe she won't be so aggressive."

"She's tied up. She's not going to attack anyone."

"It's inhumane."

Jonah sniffed. "The only reason she's here is because of Bix's dad. Let him deal with her. Better yet, let Adrian. But if it were me, I'd put a bullet in her brain right now."

Finn turned his dark gaze toward Jonah. "You would do that? She can't help what she's become."

"Maybe," Jonah said, stepping up to Finn. "But it doesn't change the fact that she's dangerous. And if it ever comes down to her or any of us, I'll do it without hesitation." He paused. "You'll find I don't get stuck on sentimentalities."

Finn tugged the bindings around her ankles, checking for slack and removing the last little bit. He didn't do it out of anger or cruelty, but because he knew she'd injure herself less the more restricted her movements were. "She saved me and Bix," he quietly said. "Back there at the ranch, she let herself get infected so we could get away."

"Yeah, after she lured you two in so Adrian could throw you in his cage with others like how she is now."

"That wasn't her."

"And what about what they did to Danny?"

"That was Adrian, too."

"Yeah, well, excuses. She allowed it to happen."

"Maybe she had no choice."

"Maybe. But it doesn't matter anymore. That person is gone now, Finn. This . . . this thing has only one purpose, and that's to kill you. Kill all of us."

"She still has no choice."

"Whatever. We got what we came for," Jonah said, slapping a pair of books against Finn's chest. "Your dad's journal and I'm assuming Bunker Two's. So, if you're done bonding, let's get back inside and start searching."

"And if we don't find the lab or the notes?"

Jonah shrugged. "Either way, we're going to Westerton.

"You don't sound so eager for a cure, either."

Jonah waited for Finn to retie the tarp. The instant it passed over Jennifer's face, she quieted down again. It was like putting a hood over a falcon's head.

"No, I just don't believe there is one."

CHAPTER

31

"**NOPE,**" **EDDIE ANNOUNCED, EXITING YET ANOTHER** room. He grunted unhappily and shook his head as he watched the door swing shut under its own weight. The latch clicked and the light on the keypad changed from green to red. He turned to the others standing in the hallway. "That's the last one. We've checked everywhere."

"No, that can't be," Kaleagh insisted. "There has to be something we're missing. He had equipment, a microscope at the very least. He had his notebooks."

"Which he could've destroyed."

"No."

"It's possible that whoever came and scavenged the place afterward found and took them," Jonah said.

"Unlikely."

"Well," Eddie said, sighing, "we've opened every single door, checked every room on every level, from One to Nine. Unless there's a secret hidden door in the sump chamber on Ten, we're done."

"The tunnels going out the back way then?" Bix asked. "What about there?"

Eddie shook his head. "Maybe if there hadn't been people living there before I'd say it might be possible. But between Hannah and Jonah going down there over the years, they would have known if someone else like Seth was sneaking into that part of the bunker system, especially to conduct experiments. Those people living in the tunnels would've said something."

"They never mentioned him to me," Jonah affirmed.

"We haven't considered every possibility," Harrison said. "We've ruled out inside the bunker, but what if he did his experiments outside of it? There's the powerplant, for example."

"He'd have triggered an alarm if he tried to use the walkway on Seven."

"But not if he used the catwalk on Six," Harrison noted.

"The one from the Keeper Station to the helipad?"

No one spoke for a moment. Those who had been present when their unexpected visitor arrived from Bunker Two clearly remembered the uproar when he was allowed into the Keeper Station via the catwalk. It was also where they'd sent David Gronbach, their own bunker's original leader, over the side after he died.

"I don't think it's very likely," Jonah concluded. "If he was using that route to access the powerplant, people on watch would've seen him on the monitors."

"Not if he was doing his experiments on his own shift."

"Abandoning his watch?"

"The watch room's on Two, catwalk's on Six. Hard to imagine no one noticing him shirking his duty."

Harrison shrugged. "But still possible."

"I just don't see him using the powerplant," Eddie said. "I've spent a lot of time there over the years checking on the turbines, and it's not really conducive for that kind of work. Plus, I never saw anything that suggested anyone else was doing anything there."

"Maybe one of the outbuildings then?"

"I went through them all when I was scavenging for supplies and parts for the bus," Jonah said. "I never once saw anything like that. And most of those buildings stopped having power soon after the Flense. He would've needed a generator to run any experiments."

"There is one other place we haven't considered," Finn said. "And it wouldn't have been picked up by the cameras."

"Where?"

"The electrical conduit on Eight."

"The one that leads to the powerplant, Finn?" Eddie said. "We've already ruled——"

"I know, and I agree. Dad took me through it once to show me the turbines." He saw Harper's face twitch at the mention of their father. "He thought I should be aware of it."

"Well, I've been through that conduit," Eddie said. "It's hot and cramped, so I doubt Seth would've found it useful. But it *is* invisible to the cameras," he acknowledged.

"I remember it now," Bix said. "Hannah showed it to me once."

"My Hannah?" Eddie asked, his eyes narrowing suspiciously. "Why would she? And how did she know——?"

"I showed her," Bren volunteered.

"Oh, this is getting interesting," Jonah said, raising his eyebrows pointedly in Finn's direction. "And how would Bren know about this secret passageway?"

Bren tried to hide her face, suddenly embarrassed.

"The other end was in the floor of the turbine bay," Finn went on, nonplussed. "It locked from underneath, so you couldn't access the tunnel from the powerplant, just from this side."

"Still no place to conduct experiments," Eddie reminded him.

"There was this space just beneath the hatch. It was small, but I remember a panel with signs plastered all over it warning not to touch it."

Eddie nodded. "High voltage signs. I remember seeing it. Abraham thought it might be for the computer servers controlling the plant, which is why we never touched it. If we messed up the automation, we'd be in big trouble."

"There was a large space behind the panel."

"Yeah, for the servers."

"I don't think so. I never thought so."

"A space? Well, if it's hiding anything, I suppose it's feasible, and Seth could've come and gone through the conduit without anyone seeing him."

He turned to Kaleagh, who could offer nothing but a shrug. "Seth never mentioned where he was doing his experiments, and he never provided any clues. He strongly discouraged me from asking about it or trying to find it because it was dangerous— not just for him, but for anyone else."

"I remember Dad's clothes would sometimes be really dirty after he'd be gone for a while," Bren said.

"There's lots of places inside the bunker that could cause that," Jonah noted, "not just the conduit."

"He'd smell like grease and burning electrical wires."

"That would certainly be consistent with him spending time around the turbines," Harrison said. "Certainly won't hurt to check it out."

They followed Finn to the stairwell, then up one flight to Level Eight, where he stopped before entering the corridor. "I'll crawl through the conduit and open the hatch. It'll be easier for the rest of you if you take the walkway on Seven and meet me there."

"I'll go with you," Jonah offered.

"Or maybe Bren might like to," Bix said, snickering.

"Funny, you guys," Bren said, rolling her eyes.

"We'll need something to break the padlock off the electrical panel."

Eddie raised a finger. "Leave that to me."

* * *

"I want to apologize," Jonah said, as they crawled through the narrow passageway. He shouted it, thinking Finn might not hear him over the rumble of the turbines, when in fact Finn could hear him just fine.

"For what?"

"I don't know. Everything, I guess. For always being an ass."

Finn didn't respond.

"Why are you doing this? I mean, I thought you didn't want the cure."

"Doesn't mean I'm not curious," Finn said. "Besides, having a cure doesn't mean I have to use it."

"I mean, it kind of does. No one's safe as long as someone's got the nanites inside them."

"Whatever."

"You disagree?" Jonah said, swearing when his shoulder touched a hot pipe.

"A cure needs to get rid of the Flense," Finn said. "It shouldn't have to kill the nanites."

They reached the end of the conduit at last, which dumped them out into a space roughly eight feet in diameter. The ceiling cleared Finn's head by a foot, but it was crisscrossed by wires and pipes that forced them to duck.

A metal rung ladder occupied one wall, rising to the hatch that gave access through the floor of the turbine room above. Finn could hear voices, so he knew the others had arrived. On the opposite wall was the panel with a half dozen brightly colored labels covering a third of its surface. It looked like a typical electrical box, the metal painted gray but otherwise unremarkable. It was mounted in a wall about a foot off the ground and extended some five feet up and three feet from side to side. A small padlock prevented access inside it.

Finn stepped onto the ladder. "We're here," he said in a loud voice, and reached up and popped the latch. The grate sprung open a few inches. Someone's fingers curled around the edge and lifted it fully away. A moment later, Eddie's boot appeared, dangling in mid air as he searched for the first rung. He descended a few steps, told the others to stay put. "No sense to coming down if it turns out to be nothing." Then he dropped to the floor beside the boys. He had a heavy plumber's wrench in his hand.

"Cozy, isn't it," Jonah remarked. "Just the kind of place a girl wants to be taken for some alone time."

Both Eddie and Finn disregarded the jibe. The last thing Eddie wanted to think about was teenagers having sex, and the idea of Hannah and Bix sneaking about, doing things they were far too young to be doing, did not sit well with him as a father.

He stepped over to the panel, lifted the wrench, and brought it down with a clang onto the padlock. The metal snapped, and the body of the lock fell to the concrete floor.

"I thought you meant you were going to break it off with your bare hands," Jonah said, feigning disappointment.

"Don't be stupid," Finn muttered.

"I was joking."

Eddie gave the latch a twist, disengaging the panel door. "Cross your fingers, boys," he said, and swung it open.

CHAPTER 32

"WELL?" BIX CALLED DOWN FROM ABOVE.

"Well nothing," Eddie shouted back, disappointedly. "It's just an electrical control panel, not a secret room."

"Seriously? Are you sure?"

"I'm coming down," Harrison announced.

They turned to watch him descend. He stopped on the last rung of the ladder and leaned down to see beneath the pipes and cables lining the ceiling.

"Just a panel," Jonah said.

"Dad?" Bix called down from above. "What is it? Did they find it?"

"It's just a damn electrical panel!" Jonah shouted up. He sounded angry. "Just a bunch of damn circuit breakers. Don't even bother coming down. We're coming up."

"Sorry," Eddie said, squeezing Finn's shoulder. "It was a good thought anyway. Come on. We're done here."

Jonah went first, then Eddie. Finn waited for Eddie's feet to disappear into the opening above before mounting the ladder himself. He glanced back and saw that Harrison hadn't moved since stepping over to the panel to inspect it. He crouched there for a moment, not moving, just staring at it. Then, tentatively, the man stuck out a hand and placed his fingertips on it, as if he thought it was an illusion.

"You okay there, Mister Blakeley?"

Harrison didn't answer, just turned around, a puzzled look on his face. "Would you ask your brother to come down here, Finn? Please."

"Harper?" Finn hesitated, frowning. "Okay."

"What is it?" Harper asked, joining them both by the panel a minute later.

Harrison pointed to a small label affixed to the bottom right corner. The printing was scratched and worn, as if someone had tried to rub it off, but the words were still legible. "That can't be a coincidence."

Harper shrugged. "I don't think it means anything. As I said before, Quantum Telligence sold a number of products. Maybe this was one of them."

"Yes, but in wireless communications," Harrison said. "What does that have to do with server hardware in a dam?"

Again, Harper shrugged. "Maybe part of the system is wireless."

"This is an electrical panel. Those are circuit breaker switches. Unless I'm missing something, this doesn't belong here. It makes no sense." He looked at the boys. "Maybe Eddie should give this another look."

"I don't understand," Finn said, stepping over. "What's the problem?"

"This sticker," Harrison said. "We know this company's linked to the nanites, to the Flense." He turned back to Harper. "I've been all over this bunker, and I've never seen a QuanTel sticker on anything else. Not that I can remember, anyway. So why here? Why *only* here?"

"How do you know this company is linked to the Flense?" Finn asked.

Harrison glanced quickly at Harper, but didn't answer. He leaned down even closer to the label. Cautiously, he pressed his thumb in the center of it and tried to peel a corner away with a fingernail. There was a click, and the entire panel shifted an inch into the wall with a mechanical whir. Harrison scrambled out of the way, but nothing else happened.

"Hidden switch?"

"Eddie?" Finn called up through the hatch. "Hey, you guys, don't leave just yet. I think we've found something."

"It's not doing anything else," Harrison said. He got up and reached out, applying pressure against the recessed panel. It wouldn't budge. He tried to shake it. Nothing. The narrow view the newly formed gap afforded offered no clues. Like the panel itself, the box was made of metal painted gray. He pressed his thumb against the label again, but it triggered no immediate response.

After several more seconds passed, the lights on the panel blinked out on their own. There was a sharp mechanical snap, followed by another whirring sound, and the entire thing slid forward again, returning to its original position. The lights, however, remained dark.

"Did you trip a master breaker or something?"

"We still have power," Finn said, glancing around. "So, no."

"And the turbines are still running," Harper noted.

"Press it again," Finn suggested.

"No, wait," his brother said, alarmed. He grabbed Mister Blakeley's arm to stop him. "It might have a timeout function or a safety lock. If we try too soon or too many times, it might lock us out permanently."

"It's reset," Finn said. "The panel lights are back on." He reached down and pressed his thumb into the center of the label, ignoring his twin's warning. Once more, the panel slid inward. Once more it stopped after moving barely more than an inch.

"Maybe there's a sequence to the breakers switches, a code that needs to be—"

"Move," Finn instructed. "Out of the way."

"Don't do anything, Finn. Just wait."

Finn lifted a foot and kicked hard at the center of the panel. There was a loud bang, and several of the plastic switches shattered. The panel shook, but held. The blinking lights went out.

"Finn, what are you doing? Stop it!"

Finn grabbed a pipe overhead, lifted his feet and slammed them into the panel once again. This time, the panel crimped down the middle. More plastic pieces from the shattered switches rained to the floor. A third kick broke whatever was holding the unit in place. With a screech, it shifted inward. Finn leaned over, put his shoulder against the panel, and pushed. It yielded some more, but still wouldn't give.

"Now you've done it."

"What the hell is going on down there?" Bix yelled through the hatch.

Finn inserted his fingers around one edge of the bent panel and tried to pry it loose. There were several more loud snaps and a thud, followed by the sound of a motor grinding and the smell of burning wires. He stepped back as the panel tilted inward, then dropped suddenly a couple inches. He gave it one more shove, and it listed sideways, released, then chunked heavily to the floor inside, where it landed on its back with a loud crash.

"Tell everyone to come down, Bix," Harrison said, stepping over to the hatch. "I think we've found something. Don't know if it's Seth's lab or—"

"It is," Finn declared. "Has to be."

He stepped through the small opening, waving away the thick curtain of cobwebs. He could see perfectly well, despite the darkness inside, and he knew they'd found it.

"Here," Harrison said, reaching for a yellow electrical cord dangling from the ceiling near the opening. "It's a lineman's work light." He plugged it into an outlet, and a string of fluorescent bulbs flickered on.

They were in a large L-shaped room, cement walled, and sparsely furnished. A row of tables sat against one wall, an array of equipment and papers on top. Everything was covered in a film of yellow dust. Finn stepped over to the closest table, picked something up, and blew. "Looks like a notebook," he said, prying the stiff cover open. "There's writing inside."

He handed it back to Harrison, then plucked a small glass bottle off the table. A thick dark slurry swirled inside.

"What is it?" Jonah asked, stepping up beside him. "Looks like motor oil."

"Looks like ink to me," Bix suggested. He tried to jockey his way through the narrow space to get a better look.

Finn shook his head. He wiped the film of dust away from the label with his thumb and angled the bottle toward the light so they could both see it. "Any of this mean anything to anyone?"

" 'Subject 145,' " Harper read. "Nope. 'QT-192NOVO. UNDIFFERENTIATED.' I have no idea what any of that means."

"QT?" Eddie asked. "Quantum Telligence maybe?"

Finn frowned at the two. It was the second time someone had mentioned that name in the last few minutes. But they didn't notice his puzzlement.

"We should ask Missus Abramson," Harper said. "If this is the lab, she might recognize that bottle."

"Label might be misleading," Finn said, taking the bottle back and studying it directly underneath the light. "The printing's been crossed out and something else was written over it. But the ink's faded. I can't tell what it says." He closed his eyes and gently ran a fingertip over the surface, concentrating for a moment before giving up. He could feel the minute grooves dug into the label by the pen. He could almost discern the letters. But they meant nothing to him.

"What's this?" Bix asked, blowing dust off something in the middle of the bench. "Looks like a microwave oven."

"It is," Eddie said, nodding. "Industrial. Same exact make and model as the ones in the kitchen."

"What would someone need with a microwave down here?"

"It's Seth's," Kaleagh confirmed, stepping forward with the notebook. "I recognize his handwriting. This is his journal, or at least parts of it. There are pages torn out, missing."

"And loose pages on the bench here," Bix said, gathering a few.

"That settles it then," Harrison said. "We've found where he did his experiments."

"Or at least where he heated up his secret stash of cheese burritos."

Eddie shook his head at Bix. "We'll know better once we go through all these papers."

Jonah lifted a plastic cover off another object. "Microscope. Label on it says it belongs in the medical lab. Now we know why Doc Cavanaugh didn't have one."

"I miss her," Bix pined, working his way deeper into the room.

"Don't break anything," Eddie warned.

"Jeez, I won't." He wandered around the corner, out of sight. "Um, guys! Please tell me this is just a huge pile of dirty laundry."

They found him standing by the far back wall, old clothes and bed sheets heaped up in the corner. The shape suggested that something was hidden underneath.

"Don't touch it."

Bix ignored him and dug the toe of his foot into the pile, and it began to collapse. Without warning, he spun around, knocking into Eddie, who fell against the table. Several objects clattered to the floor.

"Nice going, Blackeye!" Jonah cried. "We just got done telling you not to break—"

"We have to get out of here!" Bix squeaked, and tried to get past them.

"Now wait a second! Just hold on," Harrison said, grabbing Bix's arms and blocking his way. "What's wrong?"

Bix's face was as white as a ghost's, and his eyes were as wide as dinner plates. "Get out! Everyone, get out!"

"Bix, what did you find?"

Eddie reached over and pulled the blanket off the top of the pile. Then he stepped quickly away.

"What is it?" Harper asked.

"A body."

CHAPTER

33

HARPER WAS THE FIRST TO UNDERSTAND THE TRUE danger the dead man posed to the group. He told everyone to stay away from the body and not touch it, not that anyone was in any hurry to do so, but he was the first to point out, correctly, that there might be a deadly pathogen inside of him.

They scrambled out of the hidden lab and crowded into the tiny space outside of the panel door. Bix was halfway up the ladder before Jonah told everyone to stop.

"Okay, first of all," he said, turning to face Harper, "I want to know what makes you so sure it's a man."

"What?"

"You said *he* might be infectious. And second, we're the ones with the nanites, remember? We're immune to pathogens!"

"Um, excuse me!" Bix said. "Not all of us are."

"First, it was dressed in men's clothes," Harper explained. "And I saw a man's wedding ring on his hand. As for the rest, we can't assume we're immune to everything."

"We don't know what killed him," Eddie said. "But whatever the circumstances, we have to assume it is infectious, as Harper said. It might also be the Flense, which is why those of us with nanites especially should stay away. If it's biological, Bix and Harrison are, at minimum, vulnerable."

"And what about you, Eddie? You're immune to both."

"We don't know that."

"Who do you think it is?" Bren asked, her voice trembling. "One of ours? Or one of Adrian's men?"

"It's much older than that," Eddie said. "It looked like it's been sitting there for years."

Bren's eyes widened. She cupped her hands over her mouth and gasped. "It's been here the whole time? We lived here for years with a dead person?" She looked like she might be sick.

"Christ!" Bix gulped. Some of the color had returned to his face, but it suddenly flushed red with anger. He wheeled around to Kaleagh. "What the fuck was your husband doing in there?"

"Bix, language!"

"Screw that! That's a freaking mummy sitting in there! I touched it with my boot! If it's been there that long, then obviously Mister Abramson didn't care about working near a dead person. What the hell kind of sick mother—"

"Bix, that's enough," Eddie said. "Just everyone calm down. Let's get back in there and gather up all the records we can find— papers, journals, anything that'll tell us what Seth was up to, and who that person might be."

"I'm not going back in there!"

"Just stay away from the body."

"How do we know everything else is safe to touch? Maybe it's all contaminated, even the dust." Bren gasped again and stared at her hands. "Oh my god! Maybe we're all infected!"

"You're not infected. Just cover your mouths and noses. Try not to stir up the dust and breathe it in. Collect the notes quickly and carefully, then head back upstairs."

No one argued. They all wanted to get as far away from that grinning, eyeless skull as soon as possible.

They reassembled in the kitchen, where Eddie and Harrison divvied up the notes between themselves. No one else wanted to touch them, certainly not after they'd scrubbed their hands with scalding water and dish soap. They sat at a different table and waited to see if the men might find something.

Bix was too antsy to sit still and kept pacing. At one point, his stomach growled so loudly that everyone looked over at him. He shrugged, then glanced over at the cans of food stacked on the counter and made a face. After the fourth or fifth such time, he reminded them they hadn't eaten anything since the soup at breakfast. "Isn't anyone else hungry? Anyone? Mind if I open—"

"Sit down, Bix," his father snapped.

Finally, Eddie tapped a page and said he'd found it. He looked up, and his face was drawn and pale. He exhaled shakily and said, "It's David. The body's David Gronbach."

"The first bunker leader?" Jonah asked.

Everyone started speaking at once, but Jonah's voice boomed over the rest, saying what they were all thinking, that it was impossible.

"Well, according to these notes, it's him."

"But we sent Mister Gronbach into the river," Jonah insisted. "We were all there and witnessed it. Well, everyone except for Harper and him," he said, pointing at Adrian, who sat alone at a nearby table, his ankles chained to one of the metal braces so he couldn't go anywhere. "We watched him go over the railing and into the river below."

He searched each face for an explanation, stopping when he reached the Bolles twins, his gaze flicking between them, as if he wasn't sure which was which. "It was your father's decision, Finn. Remember?"

"Of course I remember," Finn replied sharply. "Everyone remembers. There was a huge fight over whether we should open the bunker or not."

"Yeah, because everyone was afraid we'd catch the Flense if we did," Bix muttered. He'd already moved on from the shock of finding the body to the more pressing concern of his empty stomach. He juggled a pair of cans in his hands, and seemed to be weighing which of them to open.

"As I recall, your father overruled us all," Jonah said.

"What are you saying?" Finn demanded. "Are you suggesting my father had anything to do with this?"

"I'm saying that he was the one who sent David Gronbach over the side, and now we have Mister Abramson's journal saying otherwise. So, which is it?"

"How the hell should I know?"

"Or maybe it's a lie. Were they working together? Did your father know about the nanites?"

"No!"

"Right. First Harper, and now your dad."

"He wouldn't lie about something like that," Finn growled. He started to rise out of his chair. "Not to me. Not to anyone!"

"Uh huh. Just like his whole taking over as bunker leader wasn't a complete sham. I mean, admit it. He was completely unqualified for the job."

"You think he *wanted* to do it? He didn't want the responsibility, but he didn't have a choice!"

"We could've had a vote."

"Mister Gronbach specifically asked my father to take over!"

"So we've been told."

"Knock it off, Jonah," Eddie warned.

"Yeah!" Bix said, stepping to Finn's defense. "It always pissed you off that Mister Bolles was the bunker leader instead of your father, so now you're trying—"

"I don't give a crap about that!"

"Well, you certainly did then. And you seemed pretty damn happy when your dad finally managed to steal the position away!"

"I was . . . ," Jonah began to reply, but gave up, knowing it was true.

"Regardless, Jonah's point stands," Eddie said. "As usual, he's just having trouble expressing himself diplomatically."

"And what point is that?"

"The conflicting stories regarding David Gronbach's body. We need to explain that."

"Maybe the notes are wrong. It wouldn't be the first time Mister Abramson lied," Finn said. He didn't notice how red Bren's face became. "But don't ever accuse my father of anything like that unless you have proof!"

"You mean like you just accused Bren's?" Jonah countered.

"*My* father never killed anyone. *My* father didn't lie."

This shut Jonah up again. His own face reddened, and he clenched his fists.

"Okay, Finn, you're right," Eddie said. "But it *was* your father who took charge of disposing David's body. I think it's fair to ask you to think back on that time. Do you remember talking to him about the circumstances surrounding his death and burial? Even how he took over for David? Anything that might give us a clue as to what really happened."

Finn heaved an impatient sigh. "The night Dad told me he was taking over as leader, I remember we were in our quarters. I begged him not to do it, because I was afraid everyone would blame him if things went wrong, as they always did."

"You mean like how Mister Resnick basically blamed him every single day afterward?" Bix said, glaring at Jonah.

"Give it a rest," Harrison warned.

"I told him it was too much responsibility," Finn continued, "especially for someone who knew absolutely nothing about how to run a survival bunker."

"Or a hydroelectric powerplant," Jonah pushed.

"I mean, he couldn't even take care of his own family," Finn said, ignoring the criticism. But he had to stop himself from letting his anger at his father for abandoning the rest of the family get to him. "So how was he going to take care of thirty-odd people? He told me he had no choice. He had to do it. Someone had to step up, take responsibility. 'I didn't ask for the position,' he said. 'Mister Gronbach entrusted it to me.' Those were his exact words."

"And the body? Your father campaigned to get rid of it. He was adamant, despite the near unanimous vote against it."

"I begged him half the night not to unseal the bunker," Finn said. "I told him nobody else wanted him to do it. But he said it was a done deal. Mister Abramson was already prepping the body. 'There's not going to be any further discussion about it,' he said. 'I'll say a few words to the group in the morning, then we'll send the poor guy off. It's the closest we have to a burial ritual, and as much dignity as we can muster under the circumstances.' He said it would be best for morale to do it properly. I asked why we couldn't just lock him in a room somewhere or put him in cold storage. He admitted that if it were only himself here to worry about, he might've done just that. But there was too much risk to everyone else. He didn't want someone stumbling on the body by accident and getting sick."

"Boy, can I relate," Bix said.

"The stumbling part?" Jonah snorted. "You should be used to that by now."

"Says the guy who tore half his hand off."

"That was an accident."

"Yeah, because you were being stupid."

Finn pressed on. "He said we couldn't risk any disease spreading to the rest of us. Remember, he didn't know about the nanites back then. All we knew was that a deadly disease

222

was raging outside the bunker and now one of our own had suddenly gotten sick and died. He didn't want it to spread to the rest of us."

"Still doesn't explain the discrepancy between what we saw and what Seth wrote," Eddie said. "There weren't two Davids, so how could he be in two places at once?"

Kaleagh cleared her throat. "I think maybe I should explain what really happened back then."

CHAPTER

"IT WAS ACTUALLY ALL SETH'S IDEA, NOT ABRAHAM'S.
He was the one who convinced Abe we needed to wrap the
body and dispose of it over the spillway." She took a deep
breath. "He was also the one who said David had
recommended Abraham take over his leadership position,
even though it wasn't true. Seth was supposed to take over."

"What?" Jonah said, surprised. "Why him? And why
would he lie and say it was Mister Bolles?"

Kaleagh stood up and went over to the sink, where she
poured herself a glass of water. Her hands shook as she
brought it to her mouth, and a little spilled out and dribbled
down her chin. She drained the glass in several quick gulps
and went to refill it. But then she reconsidered and brought
it back to her seat empty.

"Kaleagh?" Harrison prodded.

"I don't know Seth's reasons for a lot of the things he
did, why he lied about certain things, but I always believed
he was trying to help us all in his own way, to protect us. I
believe he pushed for Abe to take over instead of him in part
because he didn't want the extra scrutiny he'd receive. Or the
extra demands on his time. Also," she added, glancing
nervously over at Jonah, "he knew that if it were left open to
a vote, Jack would campaign for the position, and he didn't
want to see him win. Even back then, he knew Jack was a
bully. Sorry, Jonah, but it's true."

Jonah scowled, but he gave his head a slight nod. "He was a bully."

"Seth also believed that, out of all the people in the bunker, Abe might be the easiest to . . . ." She winced and shifted in her seat. "Well, he'd be the easiest to manipulate."

Finn's face immediately reddened and the veins stood out on his temples. He looked like he wanted to punch something.

"So, Abraham was just an unwitting accomplice," Eddie quickly summarized. "Are you sure about that?"

"The night Mister Gronbach passed," Kaleagh said, drawing another rattling breath, "Abraham came to me asking for my help. He said he'd accepted the position as the new bunker leader at Mister Gronbach's request. I only found out the truth from Seth later. Abraham said that, as bunker leader, it was his duty to deal with Mister Gronbach's body and asked if I knew where there might be a big enough cloth to make into a shroud. I mentioned I'd ask Seth, and that's when Abraham confessed it was Seth who had come up with the idea of sending David over the side of the dam and into the river."

"So, it all traces back to Mister Abramson," Jonah said. "Are we sure the body downstairs *isn't* someone else's? Maybe one of the people from the tunnels?"

"It's him."

"Maybe Mister Abramson fished the body out of the river afterward and brought it back," Bix suggested. "And speaking of fish, I happened to find a can of tuna, in case anyone is interested in—"

"Sit down, Bix," Harrison said. "We'll eat later."

"Nobody fished anybody out of the river," Eddie said. "I'm betting that never was David wrapped up in that shroud. The whole burial service was a sham, done so everyone would believe we'd gotten rid of the body."

"Why?"

He shrugged. "So no one would wonder what happened to it."

"Then who did we send over the side?" Bren asked.

"Not who, but what," Harrison replied. "Seth said he was going to prep the body. He could have easily substituted other stuff to make it look like one. Not hard to fake something like that, and no one would have been the wiser, including Abraham."

"Are you calling my father stupid?"

"No one's saying that, Finn."

"Why the hell would Mister Abramson want to keep a dead body?" Bix demanded.

"For his experiments, dummy," Jonah said. "Stop fondling those cans and get with the program."

"At least I like fondling cans," Bix said. "What? *He* said it, not me!"

No one spoke for a moment, and not out of shock over Bix's crudeness. They were used to it by now. But because of the implications from these new revelations, which were even more stunning than finding out a dead body had been hidden among them the whole time they'd lived there. Seth's years of deception were a gross betrayal of the trust they'd placed in each other, but they'd all come to terms with it. This, however, was so much worse. It forced them to imagine what sort of sick experiments he might have performed on the corpse.

"Maybe one of his experiments killed Mister Gronbach," Jonah whispered.

"And y'all call my work depraved," Adrian grunted. He cocked an eyebrow at Kaleagh. "I guess y'all didn't really know the man as well as—"

"And *y'all* need to shut the hell up!" Bix yelled. "And apologize to Missus Abramson right now!"

But Kaleagh just shook her head and shrank farther down in her seat, ashamed for her husband.

"Before we judge the man, you should know that Mister Gronbach wasn't just some victim in all this," Eddie said, still studying the journal pages. "According to these entries, he knew what they'd put inside our bodies. In fact, he and Seth started collaborating on a cure before they even arrived here. David told him at the evacuation center they were supposed to meet up with the other members of the cure team, scientists from—" He frowned. "He just writes 'the company.' Kaleagh, who did Seth say he worked for again?"

"Mech inVivo. But in fact he was just a subcontractor."

"You ever heard of this other company, Harper? Mech inVivo?"

"No, just Quantum Telligence."

"You keep bringing up that name," Finn said. He still hadn't been told of its connection to the nanites or the Flense, nor did he know about his brother's association with it. "The one on the sticker downstairs."

Harrison nodded. "Seems all these different companies were tangled up in this together— QT, VivVIx, 6X. And Mech inVivo."

"The octopus," Jonah said, and all but Finn nodded.

"These people clearly went out of their way to conceal exactly what they were doing with these nanites, even from others within their own organization."

"Seth always did say everything was heavily compartmentalized," Kaleagh said. "Each function was kept separate. The left hand never knew what the right hand was doing."

"Sandboxes," Harrison affirmed, to which Kaleagh nodded.

"Sounds a lot like QT," Harper admitted.

"Someone want to explain to me what the hell you're all talking about?" Finn demanded, finally losing patience. "What's Quantum Telligence? And how are you such an expert on it?" he directed at Harper.

"Quantum Telligence was the company I was interning for before the Flense. It was—"

"Hold on! The company on that sticker on the electrical panel downstairs? That's who your Genius Internship was with? And they were involved in the Flense? Why the hell am I just hearing about this now?"

"You were in a coma," Jonah said.

"I wasn't when we were downstairs standing in front of that panel! It would've been nice to know then before I kicked it down!"

"But you did know before," Harper said.

"When? The last time I saw you was before the Flense! You never told me then, either!"

"I'm sure we mentioned the name, Finn. We talked about it at dinner nearly every night. You just don't remember."

"I remember everyone rubbing my nose in the whole damn thing! You made me feel like—"

"You know that's not true. I never bragged about it."

"You didn't have to. You were always so smug. And you made sure everyone else knew about it, so there'd be no confusion who was the brilliant twin and who was the dim bulb."

"Finn, come on. That's not fair."

"It's water under the bridge, boys," Harrison said. "Just let it go. For now anyway. We need to figure this out."

"I am not just going to let it go!" Finn said, kicking his chair out of the way. He seemed to grow in size right before their very eyes, and the look on his face as he stepped toward Harper was nothing if not terrifying.

"Uh oh," Bix mumbled. "I knew this was going to happen if we didn't eat soon. People start getting hangry and—"

"Shut the goddamn hell up about food for once in your life, Bix!" Finn roared. He turned back to Harper. "All these

228

coincidences? You happening to intern at a company involved in the Flense, Dad getting tangled up in the middle of it in here. Mister Abramson. And you!" he said, thrusting a finger at Adrian. "What the hell is your part in all this?"

"Me?" Adrian squeaked. "I ain't no one." His eyes flicked at the others before stopping at Harrison. "I'm just a minor character in this drama. Always was."

"Why do I doubt that?" Jonah growled.

"Yeah, we're not buying it," Bix agreed.

Harrison cleared his throat, silencing them.

"Look, Finn," Harper tried to say, "we don't know for sure that Quantum Telligence was—"

"Was Mom working on it, too? Was Leah? Maybe our little sister was the mastermind of the Flense!"

"Don't be silly."

"So it's silly that I'm just trying to understand what the hell is going on? Because it seems like I'm the only one who doesn't know anything about anything anymore! I'm always the last to know!"

"Welcome to my world," Bix grumbled.

"Finn, there's nothing to know," Harper said.

"Except that you somehow ended up in another bunker when Dad insisted you couldn't possibly have. Dad somehow ended up as the leader of *this* bunker, only we now find out he was supposedly being used. Or was I the one being used? How did all this happen? How did you—"

"Just coincidences, Finn," Harper insisted.

"Am I going to find out that Mom and Leah are safe in another bunker? Maybe Mom was the leader of the last one we found! Are they dead? Are they alive?"

"No! I mean, I don't know."

"Actually," Harrison said, "the initials for Bunker Ten's leader were—"

"I looked up to you, Harper! I trusted you growing up! I revered you. But I don't even know who you are. I don't know *what* you are, and I guess I never did!"

"I told you I had nothing to do with any of this, Finn. You have to believe me. I just happened to be in the right place when the Flense struck. Just like you."

"Oh no, I wasn't in the right place. I was never lucky enough to be. You see, I was *always* supposed to be in the bunker, because Dad and Mom never—"

"Stop!" Eddie cried out, when Finn took a threatening step toward Harper. "I think we all need to take a deep breath and—"

But Finn was beyond reason and too quick for Eddie. He flew across the room and grabbed his brother by the shoulders and lifted him into the air like he weighed nothing. Harper instinctively cradled his injured wrist against his stomach.

"How did you end up inside that bunker?" Finn screamed. "Tell me!"

"I got lucky!"

Eddie and Jonah got to the boys a moment later. They tried to pull Finn off, but he was too strong. He levered an elbow back, catching Jonah on the shoulder, who flipped backwards over a chair. He landed awkwardly on one foot and yelped in pain, then managed to sit up. He cradled his ankle, his face twisted in pain.

The second blow caught Eddie to the face. It would've knocked any other person out cold, but Eddie somehow managed to keep his feet beneath him and his hands on Finn.

"Lucky?" Finn screamed. "That's right. You were always the lucky one. Lucky Harper, leaving me nothing but bad luck and crumbs!"

"That's not my fault!"

"You sucked all the good out of the room just by being there! Until the day I needed you, and you were nowhere to be found! You know where I was when the Flense hit? Home, all alone, covered in my own blood, and wishing I was dead! Dad had to come pick me up from the nurse's office at school because you weren't there for me! You were off traipsing around with the people who put us here in the first place!"

"I've never lied to you, Finn," Harper said, choking. "You know that. You know I never would."

"None of this is Harper's fault," Eddie told Finn, still tugging on his arm.

"You weren't there!"

"He told us, okay?" Eddie pushed. "You missed a lot while you were recovering. Please, let's just stop, sit down, take a break. We'll catch you up on Quantum Telligence and all the rest. Okay?"

Finn glowered at his brother, the tension building in his face and threatening to explode. At last he released him. But he refused to sit back down. Instead, he scowled at everyone and stomped out of the room. No one stopped him. No one followed or even tried. Jonah just sat and rubbed his ankle and glowered at the floor. Bren looked simply mortified. She shrank in her chair, her eyes wide and full of tears, like she was finally now beginning to understand how terrifying Finn had become.

"Um, can I just say something?" Bix said, raising his hand.

"No!" the others chorused.

"Oh, fer cryin out loud!" Adrian exclaimed. "Just let the poor boy eat already. Put us all outta his damn misery."

"Or maybe," Jonah yelled, swinging around in his chair. He reached behind him for the pistol in his waistband. "Maybe we just put you out of ours!"

CHAPTER

35

"OKAY," EDDIE SAID A LITTLE SHAKILY. "LET'S ALL JUST take a deep breath and calm down."

He settled back into his seat and resumed scanning the journal pages, trying to act as if nothing out of the ordinary had just happened, although the proof of it was imprinted on his face in the form of a nasty bruise. Finn's behavior, as alarming as it was uncharacteristic, had cast a much darker pall over their discovery of Seth's notes than the body of their former leader.

Bix handed Jonah's pistol back to him from where he'd retrieved it off the floor. Luckily for Adrian, it had slipped out when he fell, otherwise the man would almost certainly be dead now. Then he returned to his place by the counter, all while resentfully muttering that what he'd wanted to say had nothing to do with food, but never mind about it anyway. No one took the bait, so he eventually gave up trying to convince them.

"Do we have a roster of the other scientists that were supposed to be working on the cure with Seth?" Harrison asked.

"None that I can find," Eddie said, fanning through the journal pages. "Just a mention that they never arrived, leaving it up to him and David to pursue a cure alone."

"The second bus," Jonah said. "They must've been on the other bus."

"Did they know each other before meeting at the evacuation center?"

"No, looks like David introduced himself to Seth there."

"So, it sounds like it was supposed to be the same sort of arrangement that Quantum Telligence had in Bunker Two, with a select team developing a cure while the rest of the folks were just random innocent people. Bunker Ten probably had their own as well. Unfortunately, none of the three journals provides any names. Everything's just initials or codes."

"Too paranoid about anyone else finding out."

"But why put everyone in different bunkers?" Bren asked. "They were all looking for a cure to the same thing, so why not bring them all to one place to work on it together?"

"Good question," Eddie said. "It sounds like they came from different places to begin with, different companies, and they each probably had unique sets of expertise. Different ways of thinking means different approaches to tackling the problem."

"But you'd think it would be better to work together."

"Sandboxes," Kaleagh said.

"It might've been so they couldn't sabotage each other," Harrison added.

"You really think they would do that?" Harper asked, incredulously.

"Why not?" Finn demanded from the doorway. "It wouldn't be the first time someone you trusted betrayed you."

He stepped into the room and took his seat again, ignoring the wary glances from the others. Veins still throbbed on his temples, but he appeared more in control than he had just moments before. He offered no excuses or apologies for his behavior, and no promises about it not happening again, leaving them all to wonder if this would be the new norm, him flipping between reason and violence at the slightest provocation.

"Sabotage aside," Eddie said, "it makes no sense to put all your eggs in one basket. We already know that four of the original ten bunkers collapsed prematurely for various reasons— Two, Seven, Eight, and Ten. And Bunker One was already out of commission before the Flense. That's half."

"And Seth did say he thought the production facility he was inspecting was intentionally set on fire," Kaleagh added.

"Ultimately, separating the groups would've increased the chances that at least one of them survived long enough to find a cure."

"How would we know if one of the remaining bunkers did?" Jonah asked.

"We don't. We don't even know which ones are still intact right now. All we can do is assume we're on our own and figure things out without their help."

He turned back to the papers. "It seems that Gronbach had this theory that the way to end the disaster was to purify the body."

"Of nanites?"

"He calls them something else, but I think so, yes. He outlined how to do it, but Seth strongly disagreed with his method, said it was too dangerous." He leaned back, frowning.

"What are you thinking?" Kaleagh asked.

"Maybe that's what killed him. Maybe they ended up trying David's method and he died from it."

"What exactly did this method entail?" Harrison asked.

"Give me a sec," Eddie said, sitting forward again. "There's a lot of technical jargon to wade through. And I still haven't located some of the pages. Also, these notes aren't always in order." He fanned through the loose sheets on the table before him, then returned to the notebook. "There's a passage here, talks about a process called *chemically-mediated catalyzed disruption.*" He read quietly to himself for several seconds, then shook his head. "I don't really understand it."

"Just read it out loud," Kaleagh said. "Maybe between the eight of us, we'll be able to work it out."

"*Nine* of us," Adrian quipped. "Y'all forget I got experience in this arena."

"The only arena you have experience with is cage fights with Wraiths, you murdering psychopath," Bix retorted.

Harrison frowned at him, but Jonah agreed, demanding to know why Adrian was even allowed to listen in. "I seem to remember a room down in the dungeon that would be perfect for him."

"Look, I don't like him being here anymore than you do, but we can't ignore the fact that he has done work on this, of a sort. He might have some useful insight to offer."

"He's a sadist."

"No one's forgetting the deplorable things he's done—"

"Like killing good people," Bren reminded them.

"And torture," Bix added.

Harrison nodded. "He'll be held to account for his actions. For now, as long as he's of use to us, he stays."

"And when he's not?"

"We get rid of him."

"I call dibs," Bix said.

Adrian gulped, and his face paled.

"Eddie, if you would," Harrison said, frowning at his son.

" '*In evolutionary biology,*' " Eddie read, loudly enough to discourage any further protest, " '*form often follows function. With the S.N.R.B.s—*' "

"*Snurbs,*" Harper said. "That's what they called the nanites in my bunker after we found out about them."

Eddie nodded. " '*With the snurbs, the relationship between form and function is tightly linked. For example, we know that the various snurb functional classes are specifically associated with different morphologies. But there is one form that has the unique property of catalyzing the destruction of all functional snurb superstructures via a process called chemically-mediated catalyzed disruption. Based on Doctor Gronbach's description of this phenomenon, I believe it is similar to wave-pattern molecular dispersion, as the theory is strikingly similar to one I discussed with the Old Man and even witnessed myself in practice once. But David's approach—'"*

"Old man?" Harrison said, turning first to Kaleagh, then Eddie. "Could this be the old man we talked about before?"

She shrugged.

"He said he witnessed it himself," Harper interjected. "Does it say where? When?"

Again, Eddie shook his head. "If he wrote about it, it's not on any of the pages I've seen yet."

He returned to the notebook and continued reading:
" *'David's approach requires highly potent chemical surfactants known as chaotropes, substances that are capable of disrupting the unusually strong atomic forces holding the functional snurb superstructure together, thus reducing it back into its basic components. In this highly disrupted state, the snurbs not only fail to reassociate into functioning bodies, but when subsequently mixed with intact snurbs in the absence of chaotropes, such as those extracted from human hosts, catalyze the further disruption in an unstoppable chain reaction. He says that the mechanism is analogous to the prion-mediated destruction of native, correctly-folded protein isoforms, such as in Mad Cow Disease. He theorizes that these monomers are small enough to be cleared through the body's usual excretory pathways.'"*

"What does that mean?" Bix asked. "Is he saying you poop them out?"

"I think it means through the kidneys," Harrison offered.

"Is that even possible?"

"Seth said he'd observed something like this once before."

"He also said there's no cure."

" *'Doctor Gronbach assures me,'* " Eddie went on reading, " *'that the Groom Lake team proved the first and second parts of this process many years ago, and his own team established its effect in serum extracted from active production sources.'* "

"Groom Lake?" Harper asked. "Yet another arm of the octopus?"

"Or possibly the other production site Seth was talking about," Eddie surmised. He turned back to the notes.

" *'I have previously observed that physiological clearance of monomers is in fact possible. But while we have suitable chaotropic chemicals on hand, we lack the proper equipment to remove them after treating the snurbs so that they can be safely administered into the body. David is determined to try anyway, arguing that the chemicals will be instantly diluted after injection into the circulatory system. Furthermore, any damage these chemicals might cause will be rapidly repaired before the snurbs are completely disabled and removed. He insists we can immediately begin testing using the sample I retrieved in New York.'* "

Finn reached into his pocket and extracted the bottle from the lab. In the chaos following the discovery of the body, he'd slipped it in there and forgotten about it. "I think he might mean this."

Everyone stared at it as he set it onto the table, as if they expected it to do something, like turn a different color. Or start leaking out.

Harrison gingerly picked it up and held it to the light. "I want that microscope," he said. "In fact, I want everything Seth had down there brought up here."

"But what about the body?" Bix asked. "It could be dangerous. You said so yourself."

"I'm starting to think not. But stay away from it anyway. Bring everything else."

Bix shook his head. "No way. No freaking way I'm going back down there again!"

Adrian raised his hand. "Then might I offer my assistance?"

"No. Anyone else?"

"Ugh, not me," Bren said. "I'll do anything but that, as long as I don't ever have to see that horrible thing again."

Bix turned to her, grinning and patting his stomach. "Anything, you say?"

She snatched the can of tuna fish from the counter and pushed it into his hands. "I'll make your stupid macaroni and cheese, but I'm not adding tuna fish to it. That's just disgusting."

CHAPTER
36

"**FINN, WE NEED TO TALK ABOUT THIS,**" HARPER pleaded.

"Why, so you can lie to me some more, like you did about your internship?"

"I didn't lie about that."

"You sure as hell didn't speak up when Eddie pointed out what was on the label of that bottle of nanites. Or on that panel."

Harper's face reddened. "What was I supposed to say? Besides, I didn't know what those letters meant. Q and T could've meant anything."

"Q and T on a bottle of nanites, which the company you interned with was deeply involved in somehow. The company you refer to as QT. You see why I'm skeptical?" He started shoving Harper toward the door of the library. "No thanks. We're done talking."

"I'm not leaving, Finn."

"Then go help Eddie and Mister Blakeley in the kitchen."

The others' interest in Seth Abramson's experiment had dwindled when new insights failed to materialize hours after the rest of the notes and equipment were retrieved from the secret lab. By midnight, they were all begging off.

They'd gone to the library hoping to find diversion, while the men continued their work. But after a few halfhearted attempts at cards, Bren and her mother went off to their old quarters. They had a lot to discuss, given all they'd recently learned about Seth. He wasn't the man they'd known before the Flense, nor the man they thought they'd come to understand afterward.

Jonah had fallen into one of his sullen moods and slipped away when no one was paying attention. Where he went was anyone's guess, and no one bothered to go looking for him. If he was foolish enough to leave the bunker alone again, especially at night, then he deserved whatever fate befell him.

And Bix was asleep on the couch by the stack of board games.

"Then why don't you go find Jonah?" Finn said. "You're part of his gang, aren't you?"

"There's no gang," Harper replied. "And if there's any division between us now, it's because you keep pushing us all away. I mean, it's one thing to treat *me* this way. I'm your brother, and I'll always be your brother, no matter what. But you're alienating your best friend. And your girlfriend is terrified of—"

Finn grabbed Harper's shirt and shook him. "You don't get to come in here and say those things about my friends— *my* friends! Do you hear me? You don't know them. You weren't here for the past four years! You don't know what we've been through. And most of all, you don't know me and what *I* have been through." He let go of the shirt and shoved Harper toward the doorway again. "And don't you ever even *suggest* something like that again. Bren loves me."

"But do you love her? Are you even capable of it? Because you sure don't act like it, Finn."

Finn glared at him. He could have smashed his fist in Harper's face, and while he certainly wanted to, a part of him found the idea so deeply repugnant that it sickened him. It was like a spiteful, dark side of him he'd never known existed had wrested control of his life away from the part of him that had guided his first eighteen years. He tried to make it stop, make it go away, but he couldn't figure out how. The worst part about it, the part that scared the holy hell out of Finn, was that he wasn't sure he really wanted it to end.

"I haven't lied to you, Finn," Harper calmly said. "Not once. I wish you would believe me."

Finn stepped back. He was dimly aware of pain in his palms, caused by his own unclipped fingernails digging into the flesh. His arms felt suddenly heavy, but also powerful, like sledge hammers, and he forced his hands into his armpits to stop them from seeking something to pound into a pulp.

"Please, Finn."

And then, suddenly, the sense of rage and betrayal that had so filled him a moment before, was gone. He didn't know how or why, just as he never knew what triggered the rage in the first place. All he knew now was a sense of helplessness and shame.

"Lies of omission," he said halfheartedly. "You kept things from me." He realized something else then, and a flash of anger returned. "Did *you* know before the Flense that Mom and Dad purchased spots here?"

"Finn . . . ." He sighed, shrugging. "Yeah, I knew, but only days before the end. So what?"

"One was for me, the other was supposed to be for—"

"Leah. Yes, Finn, I was aware of that."

"You know why? It was because they thought we were the two weakest members of the family. They thought you three would have the greatest chance of surviving outside if anything ever happened. You and Mom and Dad were supposed to go hide out in your cabin in the woods. 'Let's just get rid of Finn and Leah. They're the weak links. They'll drag us down.' "

"No, Leah was vulnerable, yes, but they knew you would take care of her. You would do anything to make sure she survived."

"Liar."

"It's the truth. They were trying to buy more spots for us all," Harper said, raising his hands in a vain attempt to diffuse Finn's anger. But he wouldn't let him.

"I don't care anymore. You know why? Because now I'm the strong one."

"You were always strong, Finn. I always believed that. I still do."

"Well, you were wrong then. But I am stronger now, even more than you. I'm stronger than anyone here, even Eddie."

"You have to believe me, Finn. Mom and Dad wanted us all to be together, but by the time they had the money to pay for more spots in here, there were none left. Then, maybe a week before it all started, they were able to secure spots in a new bunker in Canada. They were going to transfer everything to there so we could be together as a family."

"Canada? Is that how you ended up there?"

"No. I ended up in Bunker Two. The new one, Eleven, was supposed to be much further north, somewhere in the eastern part of the country. Mom said it was on a remote lake, deep in some forest. But it wasn't finished before the Flense hit."

"Then how did you end up in a bunker anyway?" Finn demanded.

Harper collapsed into one of the overstuffed armchairs. "I almost didn't. I was at Quantum Telligence's corporate headquarters the day it happened. It was actually my first time visiting there. Usually I'd shadow at one of their satellite sites, but the company had called a meeting of senior managers, including my mentor, to announce reaching an important milestone. We arrived early, so he took me to lunch at one of their on-site restaurants. That's when he received an alert on his phone. He told me that the company's AI had detected a pattern of incidents popping up in social media and telecommunications transmissions. 'Nothing serious, though,' he told me. 'Just proof of our algorithms hard at work, separating the wheat from the chaff.' "

"But they were the first signs of the Flense?" Finn asked.

Harper nodded. "In hindsight, yes. Unfortunately, the data QT was receiving in real time was muddled by a bad batch of hallucinogenic drugs that hit the markets in several cities across the globe simultaneously, causing the AI algorithms to become confused. A report was sent out recommending no intervention was necessary beyond local law enforcement."

"Who was the report sent to?" Finn asked.

"State and federal agencies in the US, the heads of national security all across the world. By the time all this background noise was eliminated, it was too late. The system was unable to respond because of its reliance on mass media networks, and they were the first to go out once the Flense hit. This meant that the program's threat-level assessment algorithm never had a chance to reach its highest category, and it was impossible to stop."

"How did you get out?"

"How did you and Dad?"

Finn's eyes darkened from the recollection: the beat-down by the older classmates that triggered their father coming and picking him up at the nurse's office; the disappointed look on the man's face upon realizing his son had had his ass whipped again; the disgust upon seeing the wad of tissues jammed into Finn's nostrils and another shirt ruined with blood stains; the oppressive air inside the car on the ride home. Then, the crushing emptiness inside the house, after his father left to return to work.

Finn was far more accustomed to loneliness than any teenager should be, but it was so much worse that day. He remembered the way his father had come back, racing up the driveway, brakes squealing, exploding out of the car, screaming Finn's name.

Finn cleared his throat. "We tried to get a hold of you and the others."

Harper nodded. "Yeah, I tried calling, too, but the cell towers were overwhelmed by then. I was stuck at Quantum Telligence during the lockdown. Eventually, they ordered us to evacuate. 'Contingency Omega,' they called it, whatever that was. Alarms were blaring, people were shouting and running everywhere. But it wasn't chaos. They'd been trained for this. But I hadn't, so I just did what I was told, which was to stick close to my mentor. We joined up with a group of senior staff members, who headed for this one exit. It led to the executive parking garage. It was dark by then, but we could see them beneath the lamps coming over the walls, heading toward us. I remember looking over the side and seeing hundreds of them below, coming through the fields, weaving through cars, climbing over them, attacking people."

"The Wraiths?"

"And soldiers." He shivered. "The blood and screams were . . . . Car alarms going off everywhere. We ran to the other side of the garage and were almost to the bus when my mentor was grabbed from behind and taken down. He was right there next to me. I tried to pull him onto the bus with me, but all I got was the emergency backpack he'd grabbed. They all had them, except me. The next thing I knew, I was being yanked inside and the doors were closing and we were driving away."

Harper stopped to catch his breath. He glanced over at Bix, who hadn't moved a muscle since falling asleep. He couldn't tell if he was faking it or not.

"They took us straight to the airport, ignoring red lights and stop signs, sometimes going in the wrong direction. It was insanity. The driver ran over anyone who got in his way. Once we got there, we all just followed directions and got on a waiting airplane. We were in shock."

"Nobody questioned you or asked for proof you were supposed to be there?"

"No, although I did get a few double takes because of my age. I quickly realized what was keeping me from being tossed out was the backpack. That was my ticket. I didn't know where we were going; all I knew was that it was away from that hell, and I didn't care."

He stopped, his eyes flicking from side to side, as if the scene he was reliving in his head was being played out on a screen before him.

"As soon as we were in our seats, they told us to get out the instructions. They were printed on these laminated sheets in different colors. I could see that they were survival techniques and phone numbers to call. Useless by then. There were also bottles of water, some plastic squares — I think they were security keys of some sort — and some packaged protein bars, things like that. Also credit cards and money. The instructions said we had to remove all the batteries from any electronic devices we had with us — cell phones, laptops, tablets, smart watches — and surrender them. Everything. Even wireless earbuds. Someone came around and collected it all in a duffel bag. I didn't want to give up my phone, but they threw this one person off the plane for refusing, so I didn't argue. We were told to find this little plastic box inside our kit. It held a preloaded syringe, and we were supposed to inject the entire contents into our thighs."

"Did you?"

"I had no choice."

"What did they tell you it was?"

"They said it was a booster, to protect us, but that didn't seem to satisfy anyone. Some people thought it might be anti-radiation medicine. Others figured it was antibiotics."

"They told us at the evacuation center that it was vitamins. Was it black, like the nanites we found?"

Harper shook his head. "Clear. They came down the aisles and checked that we'd emptied the syringes, then the lights dimmed in the cabin and we started to taxi."

He pushed himself out of the chair and began to pace, visibly upset.

"Where'd they take you?" Finn asked, refusing to let Harper's anguish erode his anger, despite knowing exactly how his brother felt. It was the same anguish he'd held inside himself for years.

"We landed about three hours later at a remote airstrip and got directly onto another bus. It was pitch black and bitter cold. No light pollution at all, no smell of civilization, and all you could hear was the sound of the wind blowing. They drove us directly from the airport to the bunker."

"No evacuation center?"

"No, straight to the mine. Several other buses had already arrived by the time we got there, and several more came after. They waited until midnight, then locked and sealed the doors tight. That was the last time I breathed unfiltered air until I escaped three years later."

"Nobody ever questioned you the whole time? Nobody ever asked why you were there, alone, why you had a Quantum Telligence backpack when you were clearly just a teenager?"

"There were over four hundred people inside the bunker by then. Only a couple dozen were QT employees, and in the weeks that followed that group kept mostly to themselves. The rest of the people were like us, just normal folks who had bought and paid for spots inside. It was easy for me to just disappear into that segment of the population, and I did, because I was just as terrified as they were. I stayed in my quarters, and didn't even come out for meals. I was depressed. I was sure you and everyone else I knew had died. Terribly. My roommate brought me food."

Harper suddenly stopped pacing in front of Finn. "You don't know how glad I was to learn you were alive. You don't know how hard it's been for me being all alone." He wrapped his arms around his brother, weeping openly now, no longer able to hold back the emotions flooding out of him.

Finn stood there for a moment, torn between turning away in disgust and returning the hug. He brought one hand up. His fingertips pressed against the tender flesh on the back of Harper's neck, quivering from his brother's sobs, and he realized how vulnerable the spine was underneath. He lifted his other arm and enveloped Harper in a weak embrace.

Then, slowly, began to squeeze tighter.

CHAPTER
37

SOMEONE WAS WALKING QUIETLY DOWN THE HALL. THE
soft, shoeless tread would have been inaudible to most
human ears, but it yanked Finn out of a sound sleep. He
listened as they approached, waiting to see if they would
stop.

A half second later, the first tentative knock rattled his
door. He didn't answer right away. He lay there without
moving, just staring straight up, his eyes not focused on
anything in particular. He was trying to remember the way
the tiny room had looked months before, back when his
father was still alive and still the bunker leader and not some
pawn in a massive conspiracy. He wished he could just go
back.

But the past was unreachable.

What's the saying? he thought. *You can never step into the same
river twice.*

Which made the bunker's location all the more ironic.
They'd essentially spent three years frozen in space and time
in the middle of a river, while it rushed obliviously past
them. The world had changed, but they hadn't, not until that
fateful day when they decided to leave the bunker behind.

Finn could still picture the dreary gray walls and ceiling
as they had been the day they arrived, nearly four years ago
now. And then, later, with the surfaces all covered up with
colorful pages torn out of already-outdated magazines,
drawings by the bunker's younger residents, and amusing

bits of product packaging from the shelf-stable foods in storage, their expiration dates set so far into the future that the residents' children and grandchildren could theoretically safely eat it. If anyone happened to still be alive.

Bix had added his own unique contributions to the walls, of course. He had a flair for the perverse, odd photographs and mash-ups that sometimes made people uncomfortable, even Finn. But it was his more profane attempts that could rankle Finn's father, although not enough for him to ask they be taken down. Everyone knew it was a necessary pressure outlet. For most of the residents, papering over every square inch of the stark walls inside their rooms was as much a release as it was an act of protest or denial, as if covering the stark, gray walls could drive back the cold, hard truth of their circumstances and the things hunting them outside.

Many of the decorations still hung where they'd been taped. There was a conspicuously blank space directly above Finn's old mattress. He knew that something important had once occupied it, but for the life of him he couldn't remember what, and this bugged him. The accident had taken chunks of his mind. That they might never be recovered alarmed him, although in a vague, distant way.

The knock came again, and this time Bix called through the door. "Finn? Dad and Eddie want everyone to meet in the kitchen." The handle jiggled, but Finn had locked the door for privacy after leaving Harper the previous evening. He'd needed to get away, to be alone after their talk. Away from Harper's unabashed display of vulnerability. He'd needed to get away from them all, in fact, but the one person he most needed escape from was himself. "Finn, you awake in there?"

"Yeah, Bix," he croaked. "Okay. Be there in a sec."

"You need any help?"

"No."

"I mean, these sleeping bags can be tricky to open and—"

"I said I'm fine, damn it!"

He could still hear Bix standing there, indecisive. Finn didn't understand why it infuriated him so. It never used to.

Bix coughed and shuffled his feet. "Is Harper in there with you?"

An icy sensation flushed through him. "No."

"Well, it's just that no one's seen him and—"

"He's not here."

"Oh. Okay."

Finn waited a few minutes after he left, then sat up and pulled on his boots. He had thought that spending the night in his old quarters might help him recover some of his old self again. But morning found him feeling nothing but anxious and resentful. He didn't know why, except that nothing was the way it should be. He felt like he'd woken up from a terrible dream, only to find that the one he was in was even worse.

He grabbed his jacket and put it on. But before exiting, he took one last look around, stepped over to the far wall and carefully peeled off one of the sheets of paper. The drawing meant nothing special to him, just a crayon sketch that Sammy Largent had done a long time back, when he was just six and everyone's memories of blue skies and clouds were still vivid. The boy had made dozens of such drawings for the bunker residents over the years. This one was captioned MY FAMLY FUHLYNG ONA DRAGIN. The dragon was blowing fire out of its nose at people on the ground. It wasn't hard to understand the context, even if the artwork was crude and the spelling bad. Both had improved considerably over time, thanks to the efforts of his teacher, Missus Abramson. The paper was now stiff and yellow, spotted with coffee that had splashed from a cup Finn's father once dropped. It had soaked into their sleeping pads, and the smell lingered for weeks before eventually fading.

He sniffed the paper — it smelled only of dust — then folded and slipped it into his back pocket as he made his way to the elevator.

Everyone save Eddie was already in the kitchen when he arrived. Finn had run into him in the hallway outside the elevator doors, where Eddie had quickly informed him he was off to fetch something. "Tell the others to start without me," he'd said, and was gone before Finn could ask what it was that needed fetching, what else needed starting, or whether Eddie needed any help.

Adrian stood at the stove, an apron tied around his waist. It was a jarring sight, given that the man had gunned down the husband of the woman standing beside him just a few weeks before, something Finn still couldn't remember but had been told happened. Chains still bound his ankles and rattled whenever he moved his feet, but the metal bar was gone, and his hands were free. He'd been put to work opening cans.

Finn went over to Mister Blakeley, who was leaning over the table with the papers. More pieces of equipment and other objects had appeared since the previous evening, and the collection now occupied nearly half the eating space. "What's going on?" he asked.

"Hey, Finn," Harrison said. He placed his hands on his lower back and arched into a stretch. "How are you feeling? Sleep okay?"

"Yeah. You been up all night?"

He shook his head. "Eddie managed a few hours. I . . . ." He gestured at the retrieved items. "There's so much to go through, and the notes are a mess, not in any order."

Finn felt someone at his elbow and he turned to see Missus Abramson. She pressed a bowl into his hands, and told him to eat. "It's oatmeal. There's syrup and honey over there with the others."

He glanced over. He remembered that he preferred his oatmeal sweetened, but this time he decided he could go without. The flavorings were with the foursome of his peers, who were currently huddled in conversation. He knew that they had seen him come in and sensed that they were purposefully avoiding making eye contact.

"Go ahead, dear," Missus Abramson urged, and gently pushed him in their direction.

He took the empty seat next to Bren, muttering "Hey."

"Hey to you, too," Bren returned, after a slight hesitation. She gave him a tentative smile, then reached over and squeezed his hand, all the while studying his face. The boys just nodded their heads without saying anything.

He caught Harper's eye and asked how he was feeling.

"Okay. You?"

"Yeah. What's up?"

"They have an announcement."

"About the cure?"

Bren took in a deep breath and gave his hand another squeeze. "We're not sure. It's just—"

"We think we might be leaving soon," Bix whispered.

Finn nodded. He could tell from their faces that they were just guessing, and that there was some disagreement among them. "Westerton or Bunker Twelve?" he asked.

More shrugs.

Bix slid over the gallon-sized can of fake maple syrup. It was what Finn had always put on his oatmeal before, but this time he decided to try the honey. "You sure?" Bix asked, puzzled. "I thought you didn't like honey."

"I never said that."

"Okay. But you never ate it before."

"Because of his asthma," Harper offered.

"Just give me the damn honey," Finn grumbled, before adding, *"Please."*

"Well, since you asked so nicely and all," Jonah said, passing it over.

"Now that we're all here," Harrison announced, "I think we can get started. I was hoping Eddie'd be back sooner, but that's okay. He knows what I've got to say."

He was clearly eager to tell them what they'd figured out overnight, but he still took his time refilling his coffee cup from the carafe by the stove and stirring in milk and sugar.

"So, as you know, Eddie and I spent the night going over everything we collected from the lab. Most of the notes made no sense to us. But it was something Adrian noticed that told us what we should be looking for."

"Adrian?" Bix asked. "You're seriously giving him credit?"

"Where it's due, yes. Without his insight, we might have missed or misinterpreted important information. Thanks to him, we now know for certain that a cure was successfully developed and tested."

"They tested a cure?" Harper said. "On who?"

"David Gronbach, our original bunker leader. Just as we'd suspected."

"How can you say it was successful if he's dead?" Bix challenged.

"Because he didn't die from the experiment," Adrian blurted out. "He died from the cure."

"Does he really need to be here?" Bix complained. "He's not making any sense."

"What he means, Bix, is that unrelated consequences of the cure killed David, but not until after he became nanite-free."

"How?"

"Seth describes it here. He believed David's body had grown dependent on the nanites, and removing them left him immunocompromised— vulnerable to opportunistic infections."

"Is that a guess?"

"It's Seth's, based on his observations following the treatment. Eddie and I happen to concur."

"But he wasn't a doctor, and neither are you."

Harrison shook his head. "The symptoms appear to bear it out."

"So, if it worked," Jonah said, "why would he lie and say it didn't? Seems sketchy to me, like we're missing something."

"Seth makes very clear that the treatment did exactly what they expected it to do: broke up the nanites. They even verified it by checking his blood over the next several days. By the end, there were no detectable nanites left."

"And once again, by the end, he was dead," Bix reminded them.

"How did he decide it was an infection and not the toxic chemicals?" Harper asked.

"Because they didn't use any chemicals. They used an alternate method that Seth devised using some of the equipment from here."

Four of the five sitting at the table exchanged confused glances; Finn was the exception. He'd watched the discussion with interest, noting Adrian's reactions in particular. He thought he knew the answer, but he chose to remain silent and see.

Harrison glanced toward the door, exasperation growing on his face, plus a little worry.

"He's coming," Finn said. "I hear him coming up the stairs now."

Sure enough, Eddie rushed in a few seconds later, apologizing for the delay. "Got it," he said, and handed the backpack from Bunker Two over to Harrison. "It was hidden, just as you thought. Also had to redo the bindings on the Wrai— Sorry. On Jennifer."

Adrian spun around at the mention of his sister.

"They were loose?" Jonah asked, giving Finn a suspicious look.

"No. But she's lost so much weight that she managed to get one arm free and was trying to chew through the other."

"Those bindings are made of Kevlar."

"Not the binding, her other arm. She's fine," he quickly added, clearing his throat. "The wound will heal. But the hungrier she gets, the more desperate and unpredictable she becomes. She'll need to eat soon."

"I'll do it," Adrian said. "I'll feed her."

"Planning on offering yourself as the main course?" Bix suggested.

Harrison frowned at him, but said nothing.

"She gets too riled up when you get close to her, Adrian," Eddie said. "I'll deal with her after breakfast."

Adrian hesitated, then nodded and turned back around. The look on his face was inscrutable, but for some reason it raised the hair on the back of Eddie's neck. He didn't like not knowing what the madman was thinking.

"So, are you going to tell us what's in the bag?" Finn asked.

Harrison nodded, but Bren interrupted him. "You still haven't explained why Dad would keep Mister Gronbach's body. Why would he pretend to get rid of it?" She turned to her mother for explanation, but Kaleagh had nothing to offer.

"It was because he needed time to figure out exactly how David died," Eddie explained. "He suspected infection, but until he could verify it, he didn't want to put the rest of the bunker at risk by sharing his findings. He didn't want us demanding the cure for ourselves only to have us all come down with the same infection afterward."

"What kind of infection?"

Eddie quickly scanned the piles of papers and found the sheet he was looking for. "We're still looking for some missing pages, but a few days after giving him the treated nanites, a skin rash appeared on David's lower back. It was accompanied by severe itching all over his body."

"That sounds more like an allergic reaction than infection," Kaleagh noted.

"Not if it's viral. But you're right: Seth initially concluded it was allergies, so he administered steroids. But they only made the symptoms worse. The urge to scratch got so bad that he had to wrap David's hands to prevent him from scratching himself bloody. Four days later, he found David semi-lucid in his quarters. He'd chewed through the fabric to get to his hands. He'd also chewed the tips of several fingers." Eddie gulped uncomfortably before adding, "Down to the bone."

Bren gasped and buried her face in Finn's arm.

"Instead of healing, as they should if his nanites were intact, the symptoms quickly got much worse. He grew feverish, and his urine turned dark, likely from severe dehydration. Within twenty-fours hours, David was completely delirious and started ramming his head into the floor. Seth managed to get him sedated, but his internal body temperature suddenly rose to a hundred and seven. That's when Seth concluded David had come down with a severe infection in his blood. Unfortunately, David's heart failed soon after, and he couldn't be revived."

"And you still believe the cure worked?" Bix remarked.

"Why didn't he try antibiotics?" Jonah asked.

"He did, but he had no way of knowing if they were the right ones."

"Why didn't he ask Doc Cavanaugh?"

"You know why he couldn't, Jonah," Harrison said.

"Seth feared that whatever pathogen killed David might be in the drinking water or in the air filtration system," Eddie continued. "But until he could pinpoint the source, the cure was useless to us. He couldn't run the risk of destroying the nanites we needed to defend against it."

"Dad and I never got sick," Bix pointed out. "We ate and drank all the same stuff you guys did, breathed the same air, and we don't have nanites."

"First, in thinking about Seth's decisions, you have to remember what he knew at the time, or thought he knew," Eddie explained. "He would've assumed you'd been injected like everyone else. Second, David's infection wasn't because he didn't have nanites. It was because his immune system had grown reliant on them, and after he lost them it couldn't recover quickly enough to fight off even the simplest infection. That wasn't something you and your father had to deal with. Your immune systems were already intact."

"That's one possibility," Harrison said. "Another is that David might have had a preexisting condition he didn't know about, some sort of immunodeficiency that was exposed after his nanites were removed."

"That's an important point to keep in mind going forward," Eddie said. "These nanites may mask vulnerabilities in certain people, like diabetes or anemia, and getting rid of them might actually do more harm than good."

Finn nodded.

"So, it turns out Kaleagh was right. Even though Seth knew he had a way to get rid of the nanites, he had no choice but to deny its existence to protect us. Until he figured out how not to make us sick with the cure, he had to deny its existence. His subsequent experiments were focused on finding the source of David's infection."

"So we're supposed to just forgive all the crap he did to us?" Bix snapped. "The people he killed to protect his secret?"

"No," Bren replied defensively. "But maybe stop being so judgmental all the time. My father wasn't as evil as everyone wants to think he was."

Kaleagh placed a hand on her daughter's shoulder, quieting her, then turned to Harrison. "You said they didn't use chemicals. So how did they do it? What method did Seth use?"

"You want to explain, Adrian?"

"The microwave oven," Finn said, speaking up for the first time. "That's what this is all about, isn't it? He used it to somehow change the structure of the nanites. But you don't know how, which is why you want us to go to Westerton, to see if someone there can help you figure it out."

Adrian looked like he wanted to choke Finn for stealing his thunder. "Very good," he said, slowly clapping. "I told y'all I had some practical experience in this regard, and y'all didn't believe me. All them experiments I was doin at my ranch was—"

"Stop calling them that!" Bix yelled. "They were nothing but sick, sadistic games to you."

"Without me, y'all wouldn't have known what to look fer!"

"It's true, Bix," Eddie said. "We now know Seth had the oven modified." He carefully lifted the stainless steel casing off the microwave. "I suspect he might've had help from Danny Delacroix, since he was an electrical engineer and wouldn't have known how to rewire this. Maybe even Chip Darby helped."

"Too bad neither of them is still alive, or we could know for sure," Bix said, glaring at Adrian. "But thanks to him, we can't ask them!"

"Stephen Largent's our next best go-to. He knows a bit about microwaves and all. I'm just a mechanical engineer, so the best I can do is hazard a guess until we get to Westerton."

Ever so gingerly, he began to tweeze apart the exposed wires inside, then he gently pulled a small, nondescript black object forward for them to see. "When Harrison and I were checking this last night, Adrian noticed this. He says it looks a lot like components he found inside those knockout devices he had at his ranch. You have to look closely, but it bears an imprint of the Quantum Telligence logo."

"There's that damn company again," Jonah said, frowning sideways at Harper. "Always at the center of every-thing."

Harper's eyes flicked to Finn, but his brother seemed not to have noticed Jonah's complaint.

"Microwave-generating devices use something called magnetrons," Eddie explained. "Adrian has this theory this little device is the key to making them work in conjunction with the nanites."

"Magna-*whats*?"

"Magnetrons. Eddie's familiar with them, just not how they produce microwaves."

"The magnetron in an oven is designed to operate in a very narrow electromagnetic band, one tuned specifically to excite water molecules. That's how it heats up your food. Nanites, however, are completely impervious to them at that frequency. And yes, we've already checked," he said, gesturing toward the unmodified microwave by the refrigerator. "Twenty minutes on high in one of those had absolutely no effect on a sample of them."

"So, that little black box changes how the Decepticon thing works so it breaks down nanites?" Bix asked.

"Magnetron. And yes. Once we realized that, suddenly all those pages of calculations and scribbled nonsense started to make sense. Seth used the modified oven to treat a sample of nanites, breaking them down in the same way certain chemicals can. And when he injected those into David, they triggered a cascade pathway that led to the destruction of the nanites in his body."

"Are they safe?" Bren asked. "The microwaves, I mean. They're not dangerous like the chemicals?"

"The risk vanishes the moment the magnetron is turned off; they don't carry over in the treated sample. But I doubt they'd do our bodies any harm anyway, not at the levels Seth was using. They're like the signals cell phone towers used to generate."

"Then why didn't they just expose Mister Gronbach to them, rather than a sample first? Or would that not work?"

"That's a great question, Bren. It's probably feasible to do it that way, but it's better to use the microwave oven to pulse a sample first, at least while they're experimenting. Remember, they'd need proof the pulse had the desired effect and not cause some other problem. The oven would contain the signal and prevent incidental exposure, since it's a readymade Faraday cage."

"A faraway what?"

"A device that blocks electromagnetic signals from escaping, Bix. I'm sure if they could build a large enough Faraday cage to fit David inside, they would have done that, eventually, but that requires a much larger magnetron, too, which they didn't have."

"Which brings us to this," Harrison said. He dug around inside the old backpack Eddie had retrieved and pulled out another of the black objects. "This was part of the phone I dug up outside Bunker Ten. Didn't know what it was then, but we now think they used the phone to generate an EM signal, possibly one similar to the knockout boxes."

"But it failed," Jonah said.

Harrison nodded. "So it would seem. It's another question for Stephen. If he can figure out how this was modified, what its purpose was meant to be, then I think we'll finally understand what happened to them."

"But not why."

Harrison shook his head.

"You said those black boxes are similar to each other," Finn said. "How are they different?"

"We think the devices inside the knockout boxes and the one we found attached to the mobile handset at Bunker Ten are pre-programmed to deliver a very specific signal. The one inside the microwave may be more flexible, as it appears it might be controlled by an external source."

"Such as?"

Eddie quirked a smile and dug inside the Bunker Ten backpack one last time. "This."

"A laptop computer?"

"Seth had stashed it away inside the lab — in a cubby behind David's body, if I'm being honest — which is why we didn't find it earlier. I started to boot it up downstairs, but the battery was too drained and it shut down almost immediately." He set it on the countertop beside the other items, and from one side of the Quantum Telligence module inside the microwave, unwound a cable with a loose end, which fit perfectly into a serial port on the computer.

"I'm praying the program that controls this component is on this drive."

"And if we're lucky," Harrison added, "it won't just be the cure, but answers to *all* our questions."

CHAPTER

BIX YANKED HIS PANT ZIPPER UP AND TUCKED HIS SHIRT down inside to keep out the chill, then he turned back toward the vehicles. He peeled away the bandana he'd wrapped around his face to protect against the wind and sleet, then took a large swig of water from his bottle, swallowed half, swished the rest to warm it up, and spit it onto his frozen hands to get the caked mud off.

"Feel better?" Jonah teased.

"I would if I had some decent gloves."

"You look like a raccoon," Finn told him, as he walked past.

"Ha ha."

Finn turned and stared at his friend without responding, and Bix got the distinct feeling from the dead look in his eyes that he hadn't meant it as a joke, but as an observation and nothing more.

"Give it time," Jonah remarked soberly, and patted Bix's shoulder. "Apparently the funny bone takes longer to heal."

"Ha!" Bix barked.

"No, seriously," Jonah said, deadpan, "it's a proven fact." He cracked up at the uncertain look on Bix's face.

"Hey, boys, make it quick!" Eddie called over to them, as he stepped out of the bus. Harper followed him out, but went straight to the back to climb up onto the roof to assume the lookout position. "Check your tires and coolant levels. How're we doing on fuel?"

"We're good," Jonah replied. "We'll make it to Westerton no problem, just as long as Bix doesn't drive us into anymore hailstorms."

"Like I can control the weather," Bix grumbled.

"I told you those clouds looked bad and to stop beneath that underpass."

"Excuse me for wanting to get there ASAP."

"We're all in a hurry to get there, Bix, just in one piece, unlike the truck's windshield." He went over to assess the damage.

"I see your lips moving, Jonah, but all I hear is *'wah wah wawa waa waaah,'*" Bix shouted back.

Half the windshield was missing, shattered by an especially large hailstone that punched clean through the glass and missed hitting Jonah's knee by an inch. They'd had to kick out the spiderwebbed glass so they could see. Although Bix would never admit to it, not in front of Jonah, it was a miracle they hadn't crashed. Instead, he'd claimed it was his insane driving skills that kept them on the road, especially when the storm hit and their visibility dropped to zero in seconds.

The barrage ended as quickly as it started, but the hazards left in the storm's wake surpassed those they'd encountered up to that point. Newly downed tree limbs, uprooted brush blown onto the road, washouts, and mud. Lots of mud, and much of it quickly freezing over. Making sure they stayed on the road meant driving slower than they liked, but if there was a silver lining to the inclement weather, it was that it seemed to have forced the Wraiths into cover. They'd spotted far fewer than expected.

"How's my sister?" Adrian asked, joining them on the ground. He gestured at the tarp covering her, but kept his distance, as he'd been warned. Despite their best efforts to secure it, the tarp had torn and blown loose, and the flapping noise had driven Bix nuts, but he refused to fix it, since it also irritated Jonah. But a downed road sign blocking their way had finally forced them to stop.

"She's fine," Bix insisted, despite not having checked on her. He shadowed Adrian as the prisoner edged his way closer.

As if sensing their proximity, Jennifer started to thrash about, snapping her head back and forth, so that it smashed against the truck bed. Her skin had turned an even deeper shade of gray from the cold, as blood retreated deeper into her body. Her hair, thick with filth and rain, had matted over her face, blocking her vision. She stopped suddenly and sniffed the air, and quieted.

"She smells me," Finn said, startling Bix when he appeared right behind him.

"Y'all have a calmin effect on her," Adrian murmured, still thirty feet away. "Eddie, as well."

But the sound of her brother's voice broke her trance and she resumed her struggles, hissing and tugging against her bindings.

"And you have the opposite effect," Bix said back.

"It's primal," Finn said. "I think she somehow understands she can't infect me." He stepped over to her and extended his hand until it was just a few inches above the woman's face. She spun her head, sniffed, and lay still. "Okay, now you, Adrian."

"Thanks, but no. I'll stay—"

Bix shoved him in the back, prodding him again each time he stopped. Tentatively, Adrian lifted his arm over the bed of the truck, careful not to get too close. "Okay, m'dear," he said in a low, soothing voice. "I promise it'll soon get better fer us all."

Without warning, she lunged upward, arching her back and straining her neck. Her mouth opened so wide it seemed her jaw would dislocate. Adrian recoiled and fell into the mud. The bindings caught and Jennifer slammed back down onto the truck bed. She let out an unholy shriek, drowning out Bix's laughter.

"Hey!" Eddie shouted at them from the fallen road sign. "Stay away from her!"

"I blame myself," Adrian said, and retreated back to the bus, chains dragging in the mud. He looked like the broken, changed man he insisted he'd become.

"Don't believe it for a second," Jonah muttered. "First chance that man gets, he'll put a dagger between our shoulder blades. We should dump them both here and be done with them. I don't care how helpful he's been."

Finn angled his head and frowned at the older boy. "That's his sister. She didn't ask for this."

"From what I understand, she kinda did."

"At least show some humanity."

"That's ironic coming from you."

Finn blinked stoically at the boy, then turned and joined Eddie and Harrison by the fallen signpost.

"Humanity," Jonah spat. "What does he know of humanity anymore?"

Bix didn't say anything.

Jonah sighed and shook his head. "Come on, let's give them a hand. Can't get to Westerton soon enough."

The metal signpost had bent at its base near the ground on the other side of the road and fallen until it blocked all four lanes. The crimp was heavy with rust, so it had happened long before they arrived. Weeds grew from the dirt and trash blown against the sign. Harrison was clearing away what he could, while Eddie tried to lift the crossbar. But it was too heavy, even for him, and a corner of it was embedded within the roadway. It wouldn't budge.

"Hey look, if we go south, we'll hit Roswell," Bix said, circling around to the back side and reading the sign.

"So?"

"Roswell, New Mexico. You know, aliens? We just passed the turnoff." He pointed. "That-a-way."

"We're not going sightseeing."

"Ah, Roswell." Harrison said, chuckling. "The ultimate expression of America's secret obsession with self-annihilation."

The boys exchanged puzzled frowns.

"I remember visiting there once. There was this little roadside joint just outside the town," he reminisced. "Best burger I ever ate. Their signature dish was the Flying Saucer, a half pound patty of ground beef on a thick bun and topped with UFOs."

"UFOs?"

"Unidentified fried objects," he said. The corners of his eyes crinkled at the memory. "They were onions and mush-rooms."

"I don't remember that," Bix complained.

"This was years ago, back when I was a teenager. My first trip to the States."

"The States?"

"Western states, I mean. Came out to visit my sister at university."

"Man, what I wouldn't do for a big, fat, juicy burg—"

"How about we cut the chitchat," Finn said. "Let's get this thing out of the road and be on our way."

"What the hell crawled up his ass?" Bix mumbled.

"Aliens," Jonah answered. "They're searching for their probe."

A screeching sound, far louder than the one Jennifer had produced a few minutes before, came from the direction of the road sign. They saw it lift a foot, then it began to tip over toward them.

"Jesus, Finn!" Bix yelled, scampering away. "What the hell are—"

"Finn, stop! You're going to hurt yourself!" Eddie shouted. He hurried over, grabbed the crossbar next to Finn, and leaned his own shoulder into it.

"I got this!"

"It's too heavy! Put it down!"

Finn strained again, grunting from the weight.

"Holy crap," Jonah said, watching the two in awe. "That thing's got to weigh at least six hundred pounds. Maybe a thousand."

"Guys!" Harper called from the roof of the bus. "You better move it, because we got company!"

"Where?" Harrison called. "How many?"

Harper lifted his rifle and pointed it toward the exit ramp they'd passed a quarter mile back. "I see two!"

Harrison, Bix, and Jonah joined Finn and Eddie at the sign, but Finn waved them off. "Eddie and I got this!"

"But—"

"Go!" Eddie grunted. "Set up a perimeter! Now, Finn, it's almost free!"

Jonah was already running back toward the vehicles, his pistol in his hand. He leapt onto the hood of the pickup, then to the roof over the cab and peered out over the road behind them.

"Come on, son," Harrison said, and grabbed Bix by the arm. "We can buy them some time."

"There's three now!" Harper called.

"I don't see them," Jonah said.

"They ducked down off the road and into the ditch there." His arm tracked a ripple passing through the grass.

"There's nothing to shoot at!"

"Stay here," Harrison instructed Bix. "Make sure they don't get past us. Watch Finn's and Eddie's backs!"

"Where are you going?"

"Up with Harper to get a better vantage point."

"Dad, be careful! It's icy on top of the bus!"

"Eyes on the ditch, Bix! They're moving closer. And get your gun out, for Christ's sake!"

Bix reached blindly behind him, but his fingers were still stiff from the cold. Strangely, he felt little urgency. It was weird to be in this situation again, almost as if he'd forgotten what it was like to go face-to-face with the Wraiths. Not even the incident at the bunker a few mornings ago, or the ever-present risk posed by Adrian's sister, now seemed all that bad. After all, Finn had dealt with the Wraiths singlehandedly, and Eddie had managed to completely neutralize Jennifer. And what was his own contribution? Very little. He felt like supporting cast. Even Adrian had apparently done more to get them back on track.

He glanced over at the bus. *Speaking of the asshole, why the hell isn't he out here helping defend us? The damn coward's hiding—*

"Bix! Look out!"

The shout jolted him like a bolt of electricity, restarting a heart and brain that had gone sluggish. His skin burned like it was on fire. A gunshot followed Jonah's warning, but by the time Bix reacted, the reverberations were already rolling away over the flatlands. He spun around, barely aware of the screech of metal off to his right, his focus drawn to the hissing sounds made by the Wraiths. The long grass growing in the ditches along the side of the road shifted, and a face briefly appeared, then vanished as another shot rang out.

"Shoot it, Bix!" Harper screamed.

"Watch out for the others," Jonah said.

A third shot rang out, this time from the direction his father had taken. Bix heard a startled shout, then the sound of a body slamming onto the top of the bus, and when he looked over, his father was gone. Bix fumbled for the gun in his waistband, but it caught in the hem of his jacket.

Harper fired twice more, Jonah once. The grasses parted again, thirty feet closer than before, and a Wraith burst out from concealment and headed straight for Bix. He yanked desperately at his jacket, cursing his numb fingertips, found the grip of the gun, and pulled.

Another gunshot, and a small spray of mud behind the charging Wraith appeared, doing no harm.

Now it was less than sixty feet away.

Now fifty.

Forty, and it slipped, scrambling over the slick surface.

Another sharp report, and crimson spurted from the Wraith's hip. It stumbled and fell, regained its footing and, almost as quickly, its momentum.

At last the gun came free. Bix swung it around, but it slipped from his grip and skittered over the roadway directly into the Wraith's path.

Thirty feet now and slowing as the damage took its toll on the charging Wraith. It was still terrifyingly fast and laser focused on him, but the limp was noticeably stronger. It stopped and bared its teeth at him. The blood spray from the hole in its side abruptly turned to a trickle. The Wraith charged again, the limp nearly gone.

Twenty feet.

The signpost collapsed with a loud crash to the ground behind Bix, producing a cold, wet puff of air that ruffled his hair.

Fifteen.

Ten.

Bix's last thought, just as the killer leapt, was that it was going to hurt. A lot.

He raised his arm, stumbled backward, and fell, landing hard enough that his teeth clacked, and the wind exploded out of him. His vision turned white.

But the Wraith never hit him. There was a flash of movement, the sound of flesh on the pavement, mud splashing. Grunting. The sound of bones being broken.

He thought he heard another gunshot, distant now. Shouts. The scene remained overexposed to his stunned senses, foggy. He tried to breathe. Straight above him, a bird flew in a lazy circle, a tiny comma slowly gyrating on a blank, gray page.

He couldn't move, but things moved around him. Out of sight. At last, the iron band sprung free from around his chest and air whistled out of him through clenched teeth, followed by a hot breath on his neck that wasn't his own.

"Get up, Bix," Finn hissed. He shoved Bix's pistol into his numb hands and jerked him back to his feet. "Come on."

Another horrific screech hit his ears. He turned, still dazed, and saw Eddie dragging the freed road sign off the road.

Another gunshot from the other side. The rustle of grass growing faint.

Then silence.

"I think I got it," Jonah announced. "I'm coming down to check. Cover me!"

"Dad," Bix gasped. "He fell."

Finn's face slipped into view, a blank canvas, no urgency or concern. "He slipped. Gunshot knocked him off the roof. He's okay."

Bix collapsed to his knees and puked.

"Get a grip," Finn said dully. "It's still your turn to drive."

CHAPTER

THEY ARRIVED AT THE ARMY BASE JUST AS THE LAST rays of light spiked out of the horizon behind them and pierced through the distant thunderheads. Due to the debris on the road, it had been a long, slow, and exhausting drive. The brief encounter with the Wraiths, now viewed through the prism of endless miles of dreary wasteland and boredom and countless stops for obstacles, seemed almost a welcome distraction. Each break had necessitated setting up a perimeter watch while the pickup scouted ahead, and ended up forcing them to backtrack multiple times. When they finally reached the gate and were met by a familiar face, they all broke down into tears of relief, even Jonah. Only Finn stood by, watching dry-eyed, a look of mild impatience on his face.

"You were gone so long, we were sure we'd lost you," Susan Miller said, hugging each of them in turn. When she reached the end of the line, she glanced expectantly at the bus door. Her face tightened as she did the math, calculating their losses.

"Kari's gone," Eddie quietly confirmed. "It's hit Harrison especially hard."

Susan's eyes narrowed when Adrian appeared on the bus steps, her face tightening into a mask of rage. "What the hell is he doing here?" she growled, angrily watching him step down.

"Captured," Eddie told her. "Don't worry. It's under control." She reached for the gun on her hip, and he stopped her. "He will pay for his crimes."

"Damn right he will. Right here, right now."

"He's been useful to us."

"After what he did to our people? To Bix and Finn? How useful could he be?" She turned again, scanning the faces. "I don't see Seth."

Eddie sucked in a deep breath, shook his head.

It was all the answer she needed. "Talk to me," she said.

"There may be a cure. We just need to run some more tests and get some input. And yes, Adrian helped."

She blinked in disbelief. "A cure? But Jesus Christ, Eddie, you know you can't trust him! That lying, murdering son-of-a—"

"I know, but it's Harrison's call, and I trust him."

He gestured at Finn and Jonah to pull the vehicles inside and to shut the gate against the encroaching darkness. "It's been a long day, and we're tired and half frozen. I'll give you a quick briefing, but we could use a hot meal and some rest. Who's in charge?"

"Harry."

"Good. Stephen and the family?"

She nodded. "They're fine. Vincent, too. His leg's fully healed. He and Maria are good."

Eddie turned, searching the crowd that had formed. "Hannah?"

Another nod. "She's well, Eddie. She's . . . she's a strong girl, resilient." She laid a hand on his arm. "But you should know, not everyone is doing so well, particularly those who don't have nanites. They're getting sick."

He frowned. "Why?"

"We're low on medicine. And we've had to put everyone on half-rations. All our stores are low, including fuel, and we just don't have the people to take care of things here, much less go out on supply runs. We're starting to get desperate. But the longer we wait, the weaker we get."

"How many people do we have in total?"

"Close to ninety, maybe a dozen without nanites. There's our twelve, plus you guys and Jasmina and her baby. Nineteen from Bunker Seven. Thirty-three from the base. And stragglers. We're lucky we haven't had any deaths yet, but they'll be coming unless we get help soon."

He nodded. "I see. How about doctors?"

"Two, Jadhari and a new guy, Sagan."

"Good. I'll need to speak with them." He gestured at the bus. "We have food, blankets, clothes, and medical supplies to stave off the worst for now, and there's more where it came from, lots more. Let's gather up whoever's available to help unload."

"How much food?"

He quickly ran the numbers in his head. "For now, enough to last a couple weeks, maybe a month, if we stretch it out. We'll make another run to the bunker for the rest."

"There's nothing there, not enough to justify another run anyway."

"Different bunker, a few days drive southwest of here. The road's rough, and some of it's through infested territory. But it's not that bad. We managed without too much trouble. In fact, the worst of it is the condition of the roads. They're pretty torn up. But the army trucks will—"

"We'll need fuel."

He nodded grimly. It was the one thing they didn't have much of. "How many vehicles do we have in total, not counting ours?"

"Three large cargo trucks, a half dozen smaller vehicles and cars. A few motorcycles, including the ones we collected from the bunker about a month ago."

"That was you?"

"Yeah. It was touch-and-go there for a while. We were attacked, managed to corral a bunch of Wraiths inside the maintenance tunnel."

Eddie pursed his lips. "We took them out."

"We would have, but after the armory went up in flames, we just don't have the firepower. For fuel, there's enough to fill up the big trucks, and a couple of the pickups, but every gallon they use is a gallon less for the generators, and we need the lights and the fence for security."

He nodded. "Can't do much about the ammunition situation, but after we've rested and fed everyone, once we all get our strength back, we'd better organize the scavenging party."

He stepped aside for the bus to pass. The pickup truck followed, the tarpaulin in back glistening with frost beneath the glare of the security lamps. Eddie asked Susan to wait, and he ran over to stop Jonah, who was driving. "Take her over to the maintenance hangar."

"Her?" Susan asked, when Eddie rejoined her.

"I'll explain later. For now, can you find Vincent for me? Ask him to meet me at the maintenance hangar."

"Why? What's going on?"

He leaned over. "I need people I can trust, who won't freak out." He glanced at the retreating pickup truck, then turned back to her. "I told you we need to test the cure before we can treat anyone."

She frowned. "Test it how?"

"Not now."

"Eddie?"

"I don't need people panicking, Sue."

She turned and watched the truck disappear behind the administration building. "What did you bring in here with us, Eddie?" She grabbed his arm and wouldn't let go until he answered. "What's in that truck?"

"There are still questions about the cure. We can't be sure—"

"You brought a Wraith in here?" she hissed. *"Are you crazy? You're putting us all at risk!"*

"She won't escape. I guarantee it."

Susan's eyes narrowed, then she shot a glance over at Adrian. "Who is it, Eddie?"

"His sister. Look, I'm sorry to dump this on you, but we need her."

Susan's lips thinned to an angry white line. "I hope to hell you know what you're doing."

"So do I," Eddie replied, without a hint of irony. "So do I."

CHAPTER

HE CALLED OUT TO HARRISON, WHO WAS ON HIS WAY TO the locked maintenance hangar. The morning sun was at their backs, so when Harrison turned, he had to raise his hand to shield his eyes. "Eddie?"

"That was quite the impassioned speech you made back there," Eddie said, jogging over. "I'm not so sure they would have been so receptive had we not had the Bunker Ten supplies."

"You think I'm bribing them?"

"No, I'm just saying—"

"We have a chance to get rid of the Flense, not just the nanites but the reason for where we are now," Harrison said. He turned and resumed walking. "They know that. They know a cure is the only way we survive. Food has nothing to do with it."

"They're starving. Food is *all* they're thinking about right now. Harry told me they've been subsisting on one meal per person a day for the past two weeks." He shook his head. "I should've been here for Hannah instead of running around. I shouldn't have left her."

"We needed you, Eddie. And Fran tells me she's fine. She's been helping out with the boys. And the Largents' kids, too. Julia's especially grateful to Hannah for keeping them busy."

"You're deflecting, Harrison. Are we absolutely certain this is the right thing to do? We don't want to get their hopes up, only to see them dashed if this doesn't work."

"It'll work." He stopped and turned, frowning. "What makes you think it won't?"

"I don't, but we're making a lot of guesses based on incomplete knowledge."

"I think it's a lot more complete than you realize. Or are willing to admit."

"What do you mean?"

Harrison took a deep breath. "I mean you might have a personal reason to push back."

"Push back? What are you implying?"

"Nothing. Forget I said that."

"When the time comes, I'll be at the front of the line."

Harrison nodded. "Okay. Good."

"All I'm saying, Harrison, is that Seth knew more about the cure than we ever will. But he had serious doubts, and yet you still want to move forward despite this? We're not even sure which of the programs on his laptop is the right one. There are thousands."

"Seth's mistake was keeping his work secret, Eddie, not consulting Gia and the rest of us. David didn't have to die. But we know it worked and we have a plan to address the aftereffects of destroying the nanites. We have access to medical supplies, antibiotics, and doctors." He patted Eddie on the arm. "Have faith."

"You never struck me as the kind who would rely on faith."

Harrison chuckled. "Me? Never. But let's just say that recent events have changed my outlook significantly."

"You talking about Kari's death?"

Harrison shrugged. "I can't deny it affected me deeply. But they all do, don't they? Or they should."

Eddie glanced back toward the mess hall, to the sound of a door closing. "Looks like they're finished eating. You may have some lookie-loos hoping to get a glimpse inside. How long do you think you'll be able to keep her a secret?"

"Long enough. Are the doctors coming?"

"After breakfast, yeah."

They resumed walking, both lost in their thoughts. They passed the burnt shell of the building that had once been the armory. All of the framing save a few boards had collapsed and remained untouched. It was one of three structures that had been torched by Cheever's men, traitors to Colonel Wainwright, who'd died during the mutiny. Luckily, the small medical facility in the center of the compound had been spared. The equipment inside was critical to their monitoring the progress of the treatment Harrison, with guidance from the doctors, would be testing out on Jennifer. But that would not happen until she'd recovered much of her body weight and they'd pre-medicated her with antibiotics. After treatment, the physicians would need to monitor her twenty-four hours a day, including running lab tests on her blood. All told, it might be weeks before they could know for sure. Or it might take months. It was this level of stringency that convinced Eddie that Harrison wasn't just rushing headlong into a cure. Nevertheless, the man's obsession with it puzzled him. He didn't have nanites, so he wasn't vulnerable to the Flense like the rest of them. So why should he even care?

Given that reasoning, why should I? Eddie thought. His answer came to him almost immediately: He cared because of what it could mean for the people he loved. But the answer did little to explain Harrison's own motivation. Kari was gone, and Bix was also immune.

So what was it?

* * *

278

The maintenance bay had been converted into a makeshift hospital, and around-the-clock sentries were posted outside both entrances. Inside, the Wraith had been strapped to a metal workbench, only a thin foam pad from the camp's former weight room to cushion her. Sturdy tie-down straps had been wound several times around her wrists and secured far enough away from her mouth that she couldn't possibly chew through them. Her ankles were also immobilized, and a pair of thick straps wrapped over her knees and abdomen to prevent her from struggling. Most of her clothing, already in tatters, had been cut away and discarded. A tan army issue woolen blanket had been laid over the top of her, not for warmth or modesty, but as a physical barrier against accidental contact. Underneath, her skin had taken on the appearance of a roadmap, her blackened blood vessels pulsing like parasitic worms, rippling across the ridges and valleys of her ropy sinews.

With instruction from the doctors, Eddie had succeeded in inserting intravenous catheters into both her arms and feet. He thought she'd fight, but despite having to stab her multiple times, she didn't even flinch. A half dozen bottles now hung above her, each delivering a different cocktail of antibiotics, antivirals, vitamins, steroids, powerful sedatives, and, at Doctor Jadhari's recommendation, interferon, all from the supplies they'd brought from Bunker Ten. To feed her, a rubber hose was slid down her throat and into her stomach, and through it flowed a thick brown sludge Harrison prepared in the kitchen's blender. She had managed to chew through the tubing twice before they wised up and used a length of PVC pipe to stop her. The bite block was wired into place.

A quartet of medical instruments played an endless dissonant symphony for those in attendance, her vital signs reduced to asynchronous chirps and beeps, numbers, and flashing lights.

Her nanites were apparently very efficient at converting everything they administered into energy and body mass. In just a few days, her weight increased from sixty-seven pounds to ninety-eight. Her color improved, as did the tone and opacity of her skin. Her hair, which had been blotchy from parasites and filth, was shaved off close to the scalp. As it regrew, the bare patches filled back in. She looked almost human again, laying placidly in her sedated state. Yet her mind refused to relinquish consciousness entirely, for whenever someone happened to get too close, she would utter a hiss in their general direction and try to gnash her teeth.

Harrison had taken to watching over her, sharing the duty with Eddie and a few others they felt they could trust. Adrian also never left the building. He slept on a mattress thrown into a corner, out of sight of anyone he might upset. He remained shackled at the ankles to hinder escape, but he insisted he had no interest in doing so at all.

His own transformation appeared to be nearly as extreme as hers. He repeatedly expressed sorrow for the horrific acts he'd committed, insisting the scourge that had ravaged humanity had also, temporarily, stripped him of his. The man he truly was, the man he was trying to be once again, was not the man they had come to know. He'd been possessed with the devil, and only by assisting their efforts would he purge the evil. Now that he was back among civil folk, the true nature of his character was once more allowed to manifest.

That's what he said, but Eddie didn't buy his mewling confessions or promises for a second. He'd never met anyone before who acted with such a strong sense of self-preservation as Adrian. He'd say anything if he thought it would help him survive another day.

As Jennifer regained her strength, so too did the people of Westerton. Jonah organized several local scavenging runs. Each one was meant to last no more than two days, sometimes three, depending on their luck. It had become necessary to extend the search radius from past attempts, as anything closer had been thoroughly plundered. In this way, the camp managed to restock the pantry enough to give them another couple weeks of buffer. One team returned with two large whitetail bucks, their sides fattened by an abundance of foliage from an unusually wet fall. They were promptly butchered by one of the men from Bunker Seven, and the meat divided up for salting, drying, and cold storage. Nothing went to waste.

Usable engine fuel was getting harder to find, but with Susan's expertise in petroleum sciences, they developed a safe method to redistill what they could find to remove any water contamination. "Used to be I'd catch flack for my work," she remarked to the group one evening at dinner. "People would blame me for killing the world by propping up the fossil fuel industry. I actually agreed with them, which is why I'd devoted my life to making the process of fuel production cleaner and more efficient. After the Flense, I never would have predicted my expertise would be called upon again."

After a week, Jennifer's condition had reached a new stasis. Once more, it was up to Harrison and Eddie to announce their plan to the rest of the camp members. They gathered in the mess hall expecting excited anticipation; instead, they were met by an angry mob.

"Tell us what you're doing inside the maintenance hangar!" one man demanded.

"We're preparing to—" Harrison attempted to explain.

"Is it a Wraith?"

He and Eddie exchanged frowns. Had someone been talking to them, spilling details they'd all agreed to keep quiet? Or was it just a lucky guess?

"What are you planning to do?" they shouted. "We demand to know what you're doing!"

Eddie stepped forward, raising his arms. "Yes, we've got a Wraith—"

The crowd erupted, screaming and shouting so no one could be heard. Eddie had to keep waving his arms until they calmed down.

"Are you making the cure from its blood?" one woman screamed.

"No. We only need her for confirmation."

"Her?"

"Yes, it's a female. The only way to know if the cure works and is safe for us will be to test it on her first."

"You don't even know if it works?"

"We're pretty sure, but even with a half dozen of our best educated people poring over Seth's notes and reviewing our plan, we'll only be certain when we run an actual test."

"Seth Abramson was a damn traitor!" Vincent Caprio yelled. How can you trust anything he wrote? He's the reason this happened in the first place!"

Harrison whistled loudly to quell the ruckus. "Seth's not responsible for the Flense."

"Is it true the last person he tried this on died?"

"Please calm down! Yes, the previous . . . subject died, but again, it's not relevant."

"How can it not be relevant?"

"The patient died from an unrelated cause, a health issue that became apparent *after* the nanites were destroyed. We've taken precautions this time to make sure it doesn't happen again."

"It's unethical," someone in the back said. "You can't just experiment on people."

"It's a Wraith," someone else countered.

"They're people, too. It's even worse because you don't have a clue what you're doing. You're just guessing."

A few throats cleared, and the crowd shifted uncomfortably. This certainly wasn't the direction the men had expected the discussion to take.

Harrison tried again. "The ethical issues may have been valid pre-Flense, but the world has changed since then. All the rules have been rewritten. Our species faced a crisis four years ago, and that crisis has only grown worse with each passing day. The survival of our species absolutely depends on finding a cure for the Flense, and then using it to reverse the damage it has done. We are approaching this in the most humane manner—"

"You want humane? Just shoot the bastards," someone yelled. "Pick up a damn gun and put a bullet in its head! That'll cure it."

The crowd erupted in agreement.

"And what do we do when we run out of bullets?" Harrison shouted over them. "That day will come a lot sooner than we realize. What then?"

"Then we outwait them," someone else suggested. "They're not immortal. They can die. We just have to outlive the ones we don't kill."

Most people cheered, but some shook their heads. They either knew how unrealistic it was, or they agreed with the woman who didn't want them to experiment at all: The Wraiths were human, a fact few of them were willing to openly admit.

"*If* we outlive them," Eddie corrected. "They are a lot hardier than we are. They can survive under the harshest of conditions, and we don't even know how long—"

"And we're hardier because of our nanites! Yet you want to get rid of them?"

"Yeah!" someone agreed. "No way I'm getting rid of mine! I don't care if they make me susceptible!"

"Look at you, Eddie!" the first man said. "You're a beast! What'll happen when you get rid of your nanites? You'll become just like the rest of us, weak and vulnerable!"

"He's not weak!" Jonah shouted. "He never was! And neither are we, nanites or no nanites!"

Eddie held up a hand to quiet them. "Hear me out, please. If we do nothing, they will either outlive those of us lucky enough not to become one of them, or they will kill us. We can't live out the rest of our days in fear, behind fences, terrified of something as basic and human as physical contact with each other. And when we're all dead and all that's left are Wraiths, what happens when *they* finally die out? That'll be the end of humanity. They don't procreate. That's not what they do. All they do is spread the Flense to those they can and kill those they can't. Well, the Flense can't spread if *no one* is susceptible, can it?"

"Not if we become resistant to it like you and the boy!"

"And Finn and I nearly paid with our lives for it. Let me tell you, I would never wish that on anyone. It's not worth it. If Finn were here and not out on a supply run, he'd tell you the same thing."

"You're wrong about that!"

Eddie frowned. Had Finn been the one spreading secrets? He'd left the previous morning, and it hardly seemed possible the crowd could keep these concerns to themselves for twenty-four hours. But if not Finn, who?

"I'll admit," Eddie said, searching for and finding his daughter's face in the crowd, "I'm terrified by the idea of losing my . . . my abilities, or whatever you want to call them. I live in constant fear of waking up and finding that all of my strength has vanished. It's a horrible thing to have hanging over you all the time. No one could possibly understand that, not unless you've been in my shoes, seen the things I've seen, and done what I've done. But if this works, if we're able to do this successfully, I promise you, I'll be right there with you getting the cure."

"Well, I won't!"

Jonah stood up. "It's your choice. Eddie doesn't speak for any of us. He only speaks for himself."

"What are you doing?" Harrison hissed.

Jonah ignored him. "This is just a test, right? No one's going to force anyone to do anything they don't want. We've had enough of our freedoms taken away. That's how we got here in the first place. We're not going down that road again."

The men hesitated. This wasn't the outcome they'd hoped for, but they understood what Jonah was doing. These people were terrified of change, even if that change meant an end to the hell they'd been living for the past four years. But after the treatment proved effective, maybe the others would be more receptive.

Maybe.

Reluctantly, the crowd gave its assent, but only after warning the men they would be standing outside with guns, just in case something went wrong. And if it did, they were prepared to shoot anything that came out of the hangar.

Including them.

CHAPTER

41

THERE WAS ONLY ENOUGH ROOM INSIDE THE MAIN-tenance hangar to safely hold a handful of witnesses, although that turned out not to be a problem. Very few of the camp residents were eager for a ringside seat. Eddie assigned rifles to three people and spaced them strategically around the bed so they wouldn't shoot each other. "Use them only if she breaks free of her restraints," he warned. "And try not to hit anyone else."

Under the guidance of the physicians, who stood far enough back to avoid an inadvertent touch or splash of contaminated blood, the two men set up the experiment. The witnesses took their places against the walls. Eddie positioned Adrian in a chair a few feet from the head of the makeshift bed and ordered him to remain silent.

"So, the treatment we'll be attempting helps the body get rid of its nanites," Harrison explained. "The first step is to pre-treat a small sample of nanites under conditions that cause them to physically break down into their individual pieces." He lifted the small glass vial with its precious fluid inside. "The method requires exposing the sample with a very specific kind of electromagnetic radiation."

"Exposing them how?" asked one of the observers.

"With this," Harrison said, tapping the microwave oven.

"You're going to nuke it?"

"The oven's been modified so that it can emit variable frequency EM, which is dictated by a program on Seth

Abramson's laptop. For the record, we're using the program called MDR-14, which appears to have been the one he used on David Gronbach in Bunker Eight."

"You can destroy nanites using microwaves?"

"Not just any microwave, but a very specific pattern and frequency of microwave pulses. Different pulses can have different effects."

"Including causing the Flense?"

"Presumably. But that's obviously not all."

He pointed to a small plastic box on a nearby table. It was scuffed and dirty, and one corner of the casing had been smashed in.

"For example, this device we retrieved from Adrian's compound up north is a simple EM generator. When it's on, it emits a specific signal that acts only on the nanites in the brain, disabling them."

"But that effect is only temporary. It lasts only as long as the device is powered on."

Eddie returned to the microwave oven. "MDR-14 produces a different signal, one that our preliminary tests suggest has an irreversible, cataclysmic effect on nanites."

"Suggests is a far cry from certainty."

Harrison nodded. "Which is why the ultimate proof of their destruction is to then put them inside a Wraith."

* * *

Harper sat in front of the laptop, ready to execute the command-line program MDR-14, which would instruct the magnetron to pulse the nanite sample at a specific frequency for a preset duration of time.

Harrison had prepared the solution, carefully extracting five milliliters of the precious black slurry from the vial and adding it to an equal volume of saline, just as Seth Abramson had outlined in his notes. If it occurred to any of the observers, none of them pointed out the glaring problem they faced should the test succeed, that there was no way they'd be able to treat the entire camp with what was left of the nanite sample inside the bottle.

It was something the men in the room had already discussed privately. As Harrison explained to Eddie, it was why he believed it was critical they find Bunker Twelve. From what he had gleaned reading Seth's notes, and from Kaleagh's recollections, he was convinced the bunker was in fact the backup production site Seth had previously mentioned, not just a safe haven for people. If he was correct, then there should be enough raw material there in storage to treat thousands more, perhaps even millions.

"First, the control sample," he said. "Untreated nanites." He dipped a syringe into the vial, stirred, then pulled the plunger back to withdraw a tiny amount, which he deposited onto the surface of a glass slide.

Leaning over, he squinted through the eyepieces of the microscope and adjusted the focus until the tiny objects came into view. At the lowest magnification, the solution wasn't opaque like the liquid in the vial, but clear, and the nanites were just small, discrete dark specs in a field of blinding white light. He rotated the objective carousel to the highest magnification and adjusted the intensity of the light.

"The untreated nanites, which Seth called undif-ferentiated, have a smooth, almost disk-like appearance," he reported. "For comparison, activated nanites, like those in Eddie, are typically smooth and spherical, but much larger, roughly three times the size of the control sample. We sometimes see variations on their surface."

They made a final check, making sure everything was plugged in and connected, that every piece of equipment was primed and ready to go. Then, when they could delay no longer, Harrison transferred the full five milliliters of solution into a test tube and placed it into the microwave oven. Then he gave the signal to execute the program.

Harper reached over and tapped the ENTER key. Everyone held their breath as several thousand lines of white text began to scroll by on the small black screen.

On the adjacent table, connected to the laptop by a narrow cable, the microwave gave a chirp and turned on. It ran for precisely eleven seconds, then fell silent.

"That's it?" Jonah asked.

"That's it."

Harrison, his hands gloved, opened the door and reached inside. He carefully flicked the dark solution to mix, removed a tiny amount and applied it to the slide, then handed the rest to Eddie to hold onto.

"Now let's see what the treated sample looks like." He positioned the newly deposited droplet within the circle of light. "So far, everything matches with what Seth described. Still small, but definitely expanding in size."

Eddie checked his watch. "Sixty seconds."

Harrison nodded and returned to the slide. "Still growing larger."

"Ninety seconds."

"Looks like they're starting to come apart, right on schedule."

"Minute forty-five."

"And . . . they're gone. Just like that, complete disintegration!" He slid the glass slide once more to the untreated sample. "Control nanites remain unchanged."

"The treated solution has also gone clear," Eddie said, holding the test tube up to the light.

"So far, so good." Harrison backed away from the microscope and removed the slide and set it aside. From one of a pair of labeled test tubes, he extracted a small amount of thick red liquid and touched it to the surface of a fresh glass slide. "I'll be testing what happens when we mix it with

Jennifer's blood first," he explained. "This will be the first time for this test."

Her nanites were considerably more dilute than the bottled sample, but they were much larger and appeared less rigid, almost gel-like as they slowly diffused about within the droplet. The first time Harrison had seen them, he'd nearly choked with revulsion, but after that initial reaction, he found the dark spheres mesmerizing in their own right. They would spontaneously flatten or elongate, as if they had a life of their own. They also had a tendency to clump together temporarily, sometimes forming massive superstructures that were almost visible to the naked eye. In contrast, the nanites from Eddie's blood didn't act that way.

Eddie extracted the contents of the test tube into a syringe, then stepped over and carefully applied a single drop onto the sample of Jennifer's blood on the slide. Everyone waited as Harrison mixed them, then placed it onto the stage and adjusted the focus.

"I just saw one disappear!" he exclaimed almost immediately. "And there's another! They're breaking apart! It's working! It's going faster! Holy cow! It's spreading throughout the sample like—" He moved the glass slide around, searching the entire field.

After a few seconds, he looked up, a look of complete surprise on his face. "I can't find any nanites anywhere! I didn't even have to mix them. It was nearly instantaneous. Definitely not what we expected, but absolutely the outcome we were hoping for."

There was a rumble of relief and excitement. Someone opened the door and relayed the news to the people outside.

"We should test the other blood before we proceed," Doctor Sagan quietly advised.

"Right," Harrison said, as Adrian impatiently demanded to know what other blood. He quickly prepared a new slide with fresh blood extracted from Doctor Jadhari's arm, while

Doctor Sagan explained that it was necessary to test a range of nanites. Ahmad Jadhari, he said, was one of the original Bunker Seven survivors, and his nanites were likely entirely inert, as he was healthy and hadn't suffered any significant injuries that would cause them to activate. If the treated nanites were able to destroy Jadhari's, then it was proof the process wasn't restricted to Wraiths and people like Eddie, but to everyone.

The seconds ticked by with excruciating slowness as Harrison watched the samples merge and then mix under the microscope.

"What do you see? Are the nanites breaking down?"

"Nothing yet," Harrison replied. "They're small and hard to see to begin with."

Ten seconds turned to twenty, twenty to forty. Then a minute had gone by.

"How long before we're sure?" Eddie asked. He was still clutching the syringe with the treated sample.

"Let's give it another couple of minutes, just to be sure."

Harrison repositioned himself over the eyepieces. He barely breathed as he continued to monitor for proof the nanites were breaking apart. And not seeing it.

"That's three minutes now," Harper announced.

". . . and now five."

They waited, and still nothing happened. The doctor's nanites remained unchanged.

"Ten minutes," Harper said. "Maybe it doesn't work on—"

"Wait." Harrison held up a hand. "Wait. They're . . . . They're doing something now . . . expanding, changing shape. I think they're starting to clump."

"Are they turning into Wraith nanites?" Harper asked.

Harrison shook his head. Jadhari's nanites didn't behave anything like Jennifer's. If anything, they resembled Eddie's, growing larger but maintaining their rigidity. The process was painstakingly slow to initiate, although it appeared to be accelerating.

But they still weren't breaking down.

"Fifteen minutes."

"Bigger still, but intact."

"Look, Harrison," Eddie said. "We know it destroys Wraith nanites. Outside the body, anyway. That's something. It's one step closer to a cure. We might not be able to treat ourselves, but we can move forward with testing her."

"I suppose," Harrison admitted, disappointedly. He glanced over at Adrian, who offered no comment.

"We'll figure the rest of it out."

"Okay. Do it."

Eddie swiftly inserted the needle into one of Jennifer's IV lines. His hands shook slightly, but he was careful not to push the syringe's plunger too hard. After the entire contents had been administered, he flushed the line with sterile saline solution.

No one knew what to expect, but they hoped it would be obvious. But nothing about the Wraith changed, not the way she breathed, not her heart rate. She just lay there without moving, the machines continuing their discordant refrain.

A minute passed. Then two.

At five minutes, Eddie extracted a new sample of blood from the line in Jennifer's foot and handed it over to Harrison to examine.

"No change," he reported. "Nanites appear fully intact."

Another sample was removed thirty minutes later. It appeared to contain slightly fewer nanites, but Susan noted it wasn't enough of a statistical change to mean anything.

An hour after the injection, the nanite count was unmistakably less. And a fifth sample an hour after that yielded fully half the original count.

Tempering his excitement, Eddie announced the results to the handful of people still waiting outside the maintenance hangar. "We don't yet know if it's a cure for everyone," he told them, "but it's a start. We'll know better when she—"

The door flew open behind him, and Harrison stumbled out, his eyes bloodshot from staring into the microscope, but they were wide, and his face was flushed. Several people raised their guns, but he quickly told them to hold their fire. "I just rechecked Jadhari's sample," he said. "I was going to discard it, but decided to take one final look."

"What is it, Harrison?"

"They're gone. All of the nanites! It took a little longer, but I searched the entire sample and couldn't find any."

Eddie stood for a moment, puzzled.

"It means the treatment will work for everyone!"

CHAPTER

42

THEY WERE IN THE COMMANDER'S OFFICE DRINKING coffee and poring over the maps, hoping to find clues to where the elusive twelfth bunker might be, when there came a knock at the door. Harry Rollins stuck his head inside.

"You said you wanted to know when she was awake."

"Already?" Eddie asked, surprised. He dropped his feet from the desktop and checked his watch. "It's not even been three hours. We told Doctor Jadhari to wean her off the sedative slowly."

The doctor appeared behind Harry and stepped inside. "I did. But we calculated her renal clearance rates based on normal kidney function. We didn't take into account for nanites accelerating metabolism of the sedative."

"You said she was clear of nanites," Harrison said.

"In the blood, yes, but we cannot know about any nanites embedded within the hard tissues— the liver and other such organs. They would be less accessible than those freely circulating and thus slower to disintegrate. We should have predicted this."

Harrison sighed. "We couldn't have known. Is there a way to check the other tissues?"

"Not without biopsying. Do you want me to resedate her?"

Harrison looked to Eddie for help.

"Has she shown any aggression?" he asked.

The doctor shook his head. "She is awake. Her eyes are open and reactive to light, but that is all the response we have so far. We do not know what to expect. Can we say for sure the treated nanites are capable of crossing the blood-brain barrier? They are much smaller, and so we think they will, but we will never know for certain without taking a tissue sample."

"Of her brain? No," Harrison said. "We just have to wait and see."

"Watch for any signs of hostility," Eddie advised.

"There is something else," Harry Rollins said.

"Yes?"

"People have gathered outside the maintenance hangar again. Some of them are raising questions, doubts."

"Any trouble?"

"It hasn't gotten violent, if that's what you mean, but it feels like it might be headed there. You should also know, Finn's right in there with them, riling people up."

Eddie got up, shaking his head. "I didn't think the scavenging team would be back so soon. Let's see what's up."

The crowd was larger than they expected. Nearly everyone in the camp was there, including a number of people who had voiced opposition to the experiment from the start. Harrison located Bix on the fringe, still dressed in the clothes he'd had on when he and the others left to scavenge. Finn stood up near the front, not saying anything, but appearing to pay close attention to what was. Someone had climbed onto the hood of a truck and was shouting that a cure wouldn't do any of them any good.

"Bix?" Harrison said, stepping up beside his son. "You're back."

"Hey. Yeah, we found a stash of supplies and decided to come back for more people and another truck before it got dark. They're saying you did the experiment and it worked?"

"We're not absolutely sure yet," Eddie said, just as a roar erupted from the crowd. Several people raised their arms and pumped their fists in agreement with whatever had been said. "Stay here. I'm going to talk to Finn."

"When will we know?" Bix shouted over the din.

"Not sure."

"We may never know if she's completely clear," Doctor Jadhari quietly advised Harrison. "Not without brain pathology."

"You mean an autopsy?" asked Eddie.

"It won't come to that," Harrison firmly replied.

"If she doesn't want to kill anyone—"

"Then that's a good sign, of course," Jadhari said. "However, even if she no longer exhibits symptoms, she might still carry the Flense. We must first wait to see if she survives the treatment. There is always a chance she could end up dying like the other."

There was a loud rattling noise, and the crowd quieted. Doctor Sagan stood in the doorway banging his hand against the aluminum siding. He shouted for everyone's attention.

"What did he say?" Bix yelled. "I didn't hear what he said."

Sagan caught sight of Jadhari and gestured frantically for him to approach.

"Quiet!" someone yelled. "Everyone, quiet!"

The crowd parted, allowing the two doctors to confer. Harrison and Eddie joined them at the front.

"What is it?"

"It's the patient," Doctor Sagan said. He extended an arm to block anyone from going inside. "There's been a development, a change in her condition."

The crowd noise diminished further as they waited expectantly.

"Well?"

"She's awake."

"Yes, we know that already! We—"

"No, she's conscious and responsive. And she spoke."

"Coherently?"

"What did she say?" someone shouted.

"I'm sorry."

"What the hell did she say?"

"No, that's it," Doctor Sagan replied. "She said she was . . . sorry. She apologized."

* * *

If Jennifer had said anything else, the effect on the crowd almost certainly would have been hostile. She might have asked for food and received less pity than disgust. She could have spoken her brother's name and found more outrage than compassion. Or tried to excuse what she'd done as a Wraith and been condemned. Any of these things might have won over a few sympathizers, but not many. Instead, the two words she'd uttered rendered them all speechless and put into perspective the stark truth about the Flense that the majority of them had been trying hard to deny, that they weren't the disease's real victims, the Wraiths were.

As Doctor Jadhari would later observe, "There is power in a simple apology to smash down the highest wall."

The woman who had committed horrific acts while under the influence of the Flense, proved two things at once in speaking these words. First, she established that she had been an unwilling witness to the crimes her corrupted nanites had compelled her to commit. It shifted the burden of guilt from her and laid it squarely on the shoulders of the people who had created the disaster in the first place, which most of them had forgotten was where it truly belonged.

More importantly, her apology reminded everyone of something many of them forgot: Wraiths, despite their atrocious acts on humanity, were still inherently human.

She slept most of that first night after waking and nearly the entire day after, and only spoke once more to ask for water. In the days that followed, the waking periods grew longer and more frequent. The doctors removed her feeding tube and all but a single IV line. At first, she ate almost nothing, and asked only to drink. Her thirst seemed unquenchable, and Doctor Jadhari surmised that it was a likely side-effect from the destruction of the nanites. Water was both catalyst and solvent in many biomolecular reactions, jobs her cells now had to perform unassisted.

Adrian remained by her side nearly the whole time, although still not touching her, per Eddie's insistence. He instructed the guards to shoot them both if either of them disobeyed. They couldn't take any chances, since they didn't know if Jennifer might still carry the tainted nanites in her skin and thus be infectious to others. Only he and Harrison were allowed to make any sort of direct physical contact with her. It would remain this way until they could figure out how to safely determine she wasn't contagious.

"As much as I hate to say this, we have to repeat the experiment," Susan remarked one day at lunch.

"Why?" Bix asked.

"Rigor."

"Isn't that what happens to dead bodies?"

"That's *rigor mortis*, Blackeye," Jonah retorted. "But thanks for playing *Are You Smarter Than A Foot Fungus*. Here's your consolation prize," he said, flinging a dish towel in his direction.

"And here's yours," Bix replied, giving him the finger.

"Scientific rigor," Susan said, and turned to Harrison. "Let's review what we learned from the experiment."

"For starters," he replied, "the microwave pulse had a direct effect on the physical makeup of the nanites, and that, in turn, activated some sort of innate self-destruct mode. When we put these pulsed nanites into Adrian's sister, they sought out and destroyed the rest of the nanites. With them gone, the Flense, or at least the symptoms, disappeared."

"Sounds like a cure to me," Bix said.

Susan stood up and began to pace around the table. "But is it? When I was in grad school, way back in the Dark Ages — not a word out of you about it, Bix — my geology advisor frequently reminded us not to assume we knew more than what we could directly observe. If you modify an existing fracking technique and happen to draw more oil from a pocket of shale the first time you try it, that doesn't mean anything until you can consistently and predictably get the same result. There's causation: Does A cause B? There's correlation: Does A accompany but not cause B? And then there's consistency: Does B always happen when you do A? To test that, we need scientific rigor, and that requires an absolute minimum sample size of three. So the test needs to be done at least twice more."

"Why three?" Bix asked.

"A single result might trick you into thinking the outcome you got is meaningful, and that you will always get that same outcome in the future. What happens if you repeat the experiment and get a different result the second time? Now you're forced to choose which of those results is the valid one. Maybe neither of them is. A third trial might give you a result similar to one of the first two, and so your confidence in that particular result goes up. A fourth, fifth, tenth, hundredth trial yielding similar results to each other gives you statistical confidence in your conclusions, but three is the absolute minimum. Put another way, let's say I flip a coin once and it lands on its edge. Without further trials, I might argue the same thing will happen every time afterward, and that the coin will never land on one side or the other."

"But it won't," Bix argued.

"Our experience informs us it won't, because we've all flipped hundreds of coins in our lifetimes. But we have no prior experience with curing the Flense. We can't say with any certainty that what we observed this one time is meaningful. Was Jennifer's recovery the one-in-a-million time the coin lands on its edge? If we repeat the toss, will we get a different outcome?"

"How do you suggest we repeat it?" Jonah asked. "As long as there's any doubt, who's going to volunteer?"

"Who said anything about volunteers?"

"Another Wraith? I'll be the first to admit that we took a huge risk bringing one on base," Eddie said. "It was against my better judgment. You even pushed back against it, Susan. Thankfully, it worked out for the best, but I'm not going to do it again. It's just too dangerous for everyone here."

"Well, you asked for my input," Susan said, "so I'm giving it. I'm not comfortable with making a conclusion based on a single trial run."

"But it's not a single trial run," Harrison argued. "Jennifer wasn't the first. In fact, she validates Seth's prior result with David."

"And David died."

"Because of an unrelated infection. We've addressed that, and overcome it."

"Maybe not," Doctor Jadhari said, stepping over to their table.

"What do you mean?" Eddie asked.

"I am beginning to doubt it was an infection that took out the other patient."

"What?" Harrison asked, startled. "Why?"

"Because our patient is beginning to show the same symptoms, and this despite the antibiotics we have been giving her. I checked, and I am unable to identify a possible pathogen."

"Could it be viral?"

"Blood tests suggest otherwise. However, I have my suspicions what might be the issue."

They followed him out of the mess hall and across the compound, stopping only for one of the perimeter guards to report an increase in Wraith sightings from view of the fence. He was instructed to monitor them but not waste any bullets trying to shoot them, not unless they posed a direct threat. The electrified fence would incapacitate any that tried to get inside.

They reached the maintenance hangar and went in, where they found one of the armed guards pointing his gun and threatening to shoot Adrian if he didn't get away from the bed. Eddie rushed over and threw him back before he could touch his sister. Jennifer's face was frozen in a death mask of agony, her body contorted. Just that morning, she'd appeared almost normal, but her skin was now pale and waxy, and deep, dark circles had formed beneath her eyes. Doctor Sagan said he'd had to sedate her to keep her from scratching her skin off.

Eddie threw Harrison an alarmed glance. "Sound familiar?"

"She is unconscious and now only mildly responsive to pain stimuli," Jadhari added, demonstrating by dragging a blunt screwdriver across the bottom of her foot. The toes curled subtly, but there was otherwise no reaction.

"We've also stopped giving her fluids," Sagan said.

"Why?"

"Urinary output is not keeping up with intake, and her latest urinalysis showed significant metabolic abnormalities, including occult protein. Blood glucose levels are normal, so it's not diabetes. She's showing signs of severe renal stress— kidney failure."

"Is she running a fever?"

"No. In fact, her temperature's low. How sure are we that the other patient died of infection?"

"It's what Seth concluded in his journal."

"But he wasn't a doctor, was he? He had no medical training, no instrumentation, no way of running laboratory tests?"

"No."

"To the untrained eye, a systemic infection seems a logical explanation," Sagan explained. "But this symptomology suggests acute blood toxicity. I think we're looking at either renal or hepatic disease. Her skin doesn't appear jaundiced, so my money favors the kidneys."

"What could be causing it?"

"The nanites."

"They're back?"

"No. I think the kidneys can't handle the fragments. Imagine if someone injected billions of plastic microbeads into your bloodstream. What does your body want to do with them?"

"Flush them out."

"Exactly. And how do you think it does that?"

"Kidneys."

Sagan nodded. "The kidneys, liver, and skin are the key organs for waste removal. Now imagine that those plastic beads all slam into the renal corpuscle — the part of the nephron where large particles are filtered out — and clog it up. Kidneys start to fail. Nothing gets through, including toxins. The body reacts just as we're seeing here."

"Is it treatable?"

"How long did the first patient last?"

"About a week."

"As of now, her condition isn't critical. I can give her some ACE inhibitors to help protect the kidneys, but other than that, all we can do is just wait and see."

"And if she doesn't get better?"

"Assuming the diagnosis is correct, without dialysis or kidney transplant, she'll most likely die."

"No!" Adrian shouted. He burst free from the people holding him back and ran toward his sister.

"Wait!" Eddie yelled, stepping over to block his way. But Adrian was faster. He had his arms around Jennifer's neck before anyone could stop him.

The guard raised his rifle and took aim, but Eddie pushed the barrel away.

No one moved.

"Just wait," Eddie whispered, and began to count off the seconds in groups of ten. "Adrian?" he asked, after a full two minutes had elapsed. "How do you feel?"

Adrian continued sobbing, but he lifted up and turned. "How the hell do you think I feel?" he screamed. "I'm angry! I won't let her die!"

"Well," Jonah said, holstering his own pistol. "I guess we know she's no longer contagious."

"That's not all we know," Bix said.

"What do you mean?"

He went over and grabbed the man's collar and spun him away from his sister. "You goddamn liar. You've been faking your accent this whole time. Who the hell are you really? And what else are you lying about?"

CHAPTER

IT DIDN'T TAKE LONG FOR NEWS OF THE SETBACK TO spread through the camp, but most people didn't seem to know what to think about it. The cure appeared to be a success, since it destroyed the nanites, but what good was it if the patient died afterward?

Another week passed, and Jennifer's condition remained perilous. Her lapses from consciousness grew more frequent and lasted longer. When awake, she would often shriek out in pain, and death seemed imminent. The doctors were forced to keep her sedated.

But while the uncertainty with her was alarming enough, the situation outside the camp was growing even more so. Wraith activity was on a steep rise. Few of the long term residents of the base could remember a time when so many were visible outside the wire. Some people reasoned that it was just a larger swing in the usual seasonal variation caused by a spate of warm days following an unusually cold spell. Others suggested that it was due to the increased vehicular activity from the supply runs Jonah was spearheading. And Susan's petroleum work required that the backup diesel generators run for longer hours. The sound, particularly at night, seemed to carry for miles.

But some people believed that they were drawn to the camp by Jennifer's screams, like a siren calling them to save her.

Whatever the reason, at least the creatures seemed reluctant to approach the wire. Those that did rarely tried again, as it typically required only a single encounter with the electrified outer fence to discourage a Wraith for good. Occasionally, however, one would persist, despite the damage the electric shocks did to its body. Those that didn't recover quickly were easily put down as they lay stunned on the ground. That is, assuming a shooter got to them in time.

A few of the Wraiths seemed to have learned not to touch the wire and instead tried to jump over. But the ten-foot barrier proved too tall for even the strongest of them. They'd hit the fence high up, and the shock would hurtle them back as if they'd been hit by a wrecking ball, sparks flying, leaving a ghost-like imprint of smoke hovering at the point of contact.

The dead were left where they lay until late at night, when someone immune would go out, during the coldest hour, and collect and burn them, which meant it was usually Eddie, Harrison, or Finn. Bix flatly refused and was rewarded with extra sentry shifts.

"It's getting old quick," he complained to Jonah one morning on patrol. "This view. Two damn weeks and I'm going crazy already. I can't imagine doing this for the rest of my life. Sure makes me not want to grow old here."

"You know what's getting old?"

Bix rolled his eyes. "Let me guess: my whining."

"Well, yeah, but not what I was thinking." He pointed toward the lone figure making the same walk a couple hundred yards ahead of them. "The way he's treating everyone, like he's the only one whose opinion matters. The way he treats Bren, have you seen her lately?"

Bix hesitated before nodding. "She's a mess."

"He treats her like shit. And Harper's just enabling him. 'Gotta give Finn time and space to work things out.' He's useless. I mean, what's up with that? You don't see your brother in three years, you think the guy would want to spend time with him, but he acts like he's to blame for Finn's condition."

"He's getting better."

"Finn's too far gone. He's not the same anymore. And he doesn't deserve any of us, not the way he treats us."

"Give the guy a break. He'll come around. Eventually."

"You sound just like Harper. I don't understand why you, of all people, are cutting him so much slack. He treats you like crap, too."

"Because this isn't him! The Finn I know cares about people. He cares about Bren and me and Harper. He even cares about you, although I really don't understand why, considering how much of a prick you've been to him all these years. And when *that* Finn comes back, he's going to—"

"*That* Finn died back there in Bunker Ten. He's never coming back."

"Don't say that!" Bix screamed. He shoved Jonah in the chest hard enough that his feet tangled and he fell. The motion caused his rifle to swing up and around, and the stock hit the ground hard.

"Jesus, Bix, what the hell is wrong with you? I could've shot you!"

"Finn's not dead," Bix growled. "This?" he said, gesturing at the receding figure of his best friend in the distance. "This is just him trying to deal with the fact that he survived. So cut him some damn slack, Jonah. Just give him some goddamn time to come around."

* * *

Finn could hear every word they said, even the ones they whispered. He heard the intensity of emotion in their voices, the depth of their frustration and despair. He felt on some level that their anger was justified. But he didn't feel responsible or compelled to change anything. What was happening had been done *to* him as much as the Flense had been done to the infected, not by his own choices. He wanted to make sense of it all, but in the end couldn't, so he just gave up.

That part of me died back there at the bottom of the elevator shaft, he thought, unconsciously agreeing with Jonah. *There are things the nanites can't repair.*

The pair of sentries walking ahead of him were talking about the cure, speculating whether it was worth the risk to take it if Jennifer survived and made a full recovery, or even a partial one. A part of Finn was glad the woman had escaped the grip of the Flense, not because she'd sacrificed herself for him and Bix. He honestly couldn't seem to bring himself to care about that at the moment. Nor did he have any strong feelings about her condoning Adrian's demented experiments and torture in the past. He just knew that it must be a terrible thing to be trapped inside a body, aware of all the repugnant things it was doing, yet helpless to do anything about it.

He reached the corner and made the turn. Somewhere on the other side of the compound, he heard the sound of a gunshot and the soft thud of a body falling, and he knew there'd be another corpse to take care of later that night. But even as the reverberations faded away, his attention was drawn elsewhere, to the argument taking place inside the maintenance hangar.

He turned again and stepped away from the fence. There wasn't another Wraith for miles around on this side of the base anyway. He knew this for a fact, so he wasn't worried about leaving a gap in the patrol. As he approached the hangar, the crunch of the gravel beneath his boots was ten thousand times louder than the voices leaking through the walls, yet he was easily able to isolate the latter from the rest and focus on it. He marveled at this ability, which, like his other senses, had grown sharply acute since his accident. He could spot a scorpion crawling on the ground two hundred feet away, hear a rabbit sniff from half a mile. He could smell the onions stored inside the camp pantry and the rotten meat stink of a dead Wraith's last exhale as it hit the ground. Even the blood that spilled from the wound and leeched into the sand left a pungent aftertaste in the back of his throat, leaving him to wonder yet again if nanites had their own smell.

He opened the door. It was dark inside the hangar. All of the lights inside were off, save the single small lamp at the desk, where the doctors kept their notes. It took only a fraction of a second for his eyes to adjust from the bright sunlight outside, but in the space of that moment, he had determined exactly who was present and where they were located. He nodded to Hannah sitting quietly in the shadows to one side.

The discussion had stopped the moment he opened the door. Now Eddie spoke, asking if they could help him with something.

"Just checking. How is she doing?"

Eddie didn't even bat an eyelid. He had to know Finn could hear them perfectly well from outside and might even have known he was coming. "The doctor says she's improving," he said, casually. "Kidney functions appear to be returning to normal."

"Has she eaten anything?"

"A few crackers," Adrian muttered, raising his head from his manacled hands.

After being called out by Bix for the fake accent, Adrian's entire deception had crumbled. He confessed to making it all up years before, after their escape from the Salt Lake City Walmart — the accent, his title, everything, all to help him and Jennifer fit in with the band of highwaymen, killers, and thieves, they'd joined up with. The group was returning to their stronghold in the north after a plundering campaign near the Mexican border. Adrian would eventually wrest that stronghold from them and imprison the former owners, then subject them to his experiments. Even after they were all dead, and there was no need to continue with the pretense, he'd maintained it. Why change what worked?

He'd confessed all of this voluntarily, parts of which Jennifer corroborated, but even though he seemed genuinely contrite about the deception, it reminded Eddie and Harrison that they'd extended to him far too much of their trust. He didn't argue when they put the shackles back on his wrists.

"Crackers? I guess that's something," Finn said.

"It's definitely an improvement," Harrison replied, giving Finn the opening he sought. "Things are starting to look up."

"So, you'll be moving ahead with the injections on the others?"

"That's a bit premature," Eddie stiffly answered. "Plus, there's still a number of details to work out. It's not going to happen anytime soon."

"What details?"

"Dosage, for example," Harrison said. "Doctor Sagan is sure we can halve it, maybe even quarter it. The overall process of nanite destruction in the body will take longer, but that's the point. It'll put less strain on the kidneys, spread out the clearance over more time."

"How sure is he?"

"How sure can anyone be without proof?" Eddie asked.

"That's why we need to do another experiment," Harrison remarked. "Like Susan said. It gives us another data point."

Finn turned to Eddie. "Do you think it'll work at such low dosage?"

"My opinion doesn't matter, I guess," he grumbled. It was honest enough to be true, but deftly avoided answering the question, while simultaneously communicating his disapproval to Harrison.

"It's not like we have a choice anyway," Harrison said. "Assuming everyone wants the cure, we'd have to go down to half a mil per person. Seth used nearly half the bottle on his experiments, nearly twenty mils on David. In hindsight, it's almost certainly what killed him so quickly. The five mils we used on Jennifer nearly pushed her over the edge, too. A half mil will be enough to treat everyone in camp."

"Or it could end up having no effect, leaving us all back at square one."

"You're making my case, Eddie. That's why we need to do another test."

"We're not bringing another Wraith here." He rolled up his sleeve. "Inject me instead."

Hannah leaped out of her chair, shouting for her father not to do it. The cry made everyone jump, even Finn. Jennifer grunted in her sleep and turned onto her side.

"Hannah, it's the only safe way to do it."

"No, Dad, let Finn instead. Please, not you! He—"

Finn shook his head defiantly. "Not me. No way."

"Why not, Finn?" Hannah demanded. "Why should it be my father and not you? You need it more than he does! At least he's not mean!"

"Hush, young lady."

"No, Dad, I won't!"

"Why not me?" Finn asked. He turned to Eddie. "Because I don't want it. And, honestly, I'm surprised you would."

"It's not a matter of wanting it, Finn. It's a matter of needing it. I see the harm the nanites are doing to you."

"What harm?"

"You're struggling with demons, Finn, just as I did. I still fight them every day. It's a constant battle, overcoming this dread that the nanites will one day stop working, the doubt that you're better only because of them. Better than you ever were on your own. Well, I'm not better. I'm just . . . different. You may not have begun to consciously have those same doubts, but you will."

"No doubts," Finn asserted. "I'm certain about this, including the fact that I am better than I was before."

"Well, you're wrong."

Finn stared at him for a moment. Then he spun on his heels and walked out. After a few minutes, the men resumed arguing. This time, however, Finn blocked them out. Eddie didn't have a damn clue what he was talking about. He didn't know what Finn was going through.

No one did.

CHAPTER

44

THE FOLLOWING AFTERNOON, JENNIFER MANAGED TO get up out of bed, although she was terribly weak and easily fatigued. Once more, word of her condition spread quickly; it was all anyone could talk about. And a nice distraction from the state of affairs beyond the fence line.

Finn volunteered to relieve the guard watching over her that night, compelled by some undefined urge to speak with her. But she rebuffed his attempts, even refusing to make eye contact with him. She was overwhelmed with shame for what she had done while under the influence of the Flense. He didn't realize that she partially blamed him for the sins she'd committed, not until Adrian spelled it out.

"What you did for me and Bix, the sacrifice, was . . . ," Finn told her. The words felt awkward coming out of his mouth. They seemed reasonable, yet felt flat. His brain told him that expressing his appreciation for her selfless act was appropriate. And yet, at the same time, he wanted to tell her the decision had been entirely hers and so he owed her nothing. "I can't imagine what you must've—"

"Please," she whispered, her voice gravelly from lack of use. "I don't want to talk."

A tear slipped from her eye and streamed down her cheek. He could smell it, the saltiness nearly smothered by the heavy stench of antibiotics and steroids coursing through her veins. He could smell her sweat and the oils on her skin. And ever so often, a faint infusion of something metallic.

He'd detected the same smell in the air when the dead Wraiths were burned.

"Leave her alone, Finn," Adrian requested, but there was no strength in his plea, only resignation. "She's innocent. If it weren't for her, you'd be——"

"No, Adrian," she interrupted. "He's right. I did those things. I'm guilty of everything I did."

"I forced you into this life, sweetie. Those were my decisions, my moral lapses. I own them."

She took in a deep breath and slowly let it out again. "I killed people. I . . . I *ate* them. I don't deserve to live."

She slipped off the bed and collapsed over the trashcan, retching. When she was finished, she brushed her teeth. She'd already gone through a whole tube of toothpaste and a bottle of mouthwash since waking.

"No one's going to punish you for that," Finn told her.

"They should."

"You didn't know what you were doing."

"But I did."

"You weren't in control."

Adrian shuffled over to her and grabbed her shoulders as best as he could. "Look at me," he told her, and waited until she did. "You weren't in control."

"But I——"

The door flew open, and Harry Rollins rushed in, leaving the rest of her thought unspoken. "Finn? Is it just you here? Where is everyone else? We need help by the south gate now! That means you, too!" he shouted, pointing at Adrian. "Anyone who can fight! They're coming!"

"I can't leave my sister. She's in a bad place right now!" Adrian shouted after him, but he was already gone, back out into the darkness. "Finn, please, someone needs to stay with her."

"Shut up." He grabbed the man by the arm and half-carried, half-dragged him along. Adrian didn't put up much of a fight, but he did curse something terrible.

The south gate was at the opposite corner of the compound, out of sight and, for most people, out of earshot, but even Adrian could tell as soon as they exited the hangar that the situation was bad. All of the spotlights were on, throwing parts of the base into blinding pools of light, while the rest remained in the darkest of shadows. Gunshots started to ring out, echoing off the buildings, and rolled across the desert. People shouted. A body slammed to the ground.

"Wraith attack," he grunted.

"What am I going to do?" Adrian asked, pleading for Finn to release him. "Spit on them? Poke them with a stick? Look at my hands, my feet! I can't even run!"

"I'm not undoing your bindings," Finn said and tightened his grip on the man's arm until he yelped in pain.

"I can't leave my sister."

"She'll be fine."

"No, you don't understand. She's emotionally un—"

"We're not running a daycare. She'll get through this, if she wants to live."

"That's what I'm saying, but you're not listening! She's—"

"*Stop!*"

He yanked Adrian back just as a vehicle roared past them, kicking up a cloud of dust. Stephen Largent was at the wheel, one of the men from Bunker Seven beside him in the cab. Four more people were in the bed, each holding a rifle aimed at the sky. Bix was among them, busily loading a magazine with rounds from the box bouncing around his feet.

"Hurry up!" Finn hissed, and yanked Adrian nearly out of his chains.

He sensed the man go for the pistol in his waistband, and he could have stopped him, but he didn't. He was curious. It actually thrilled him to know the man might try and shoot him. It was the first bubble of excitement he'd felt in a long time.

Adrian jammed the weapon against Finn's side and screamed to be let go. Finn turned and gave him a hard stare, but he didn't stop pulling or even slow down.

"I said, let me go!"

"Or you're going to shoot me?"

"One bullet to the head," he said, aiming the gun higher, "and you'll—"

"Kill me, or at least try. And they'll kill you. What do you think will happen to your sister after that?"

Adrian stared at him for a moment, then dropped the pistol to his side. He gaped at Finn in dismay. Finn yanked him again, and he stumbled and nearly lost his balance. The only thing keeping him from falling was the iron grip on his arm.

"You're not even human anymore," Adrian said. "Whatever humanity you once had, it's gone now. Nothing my sister did was ever as bad as what you're doing."

"And why is that?"

"Because these people rely on you, trust you. They expect you to make the right choices. My Jenny couldn't control what she did. But you can."

"You're one to speak. You could control what you did, too, yet you chose to—"

"Nothing I ever did was as cruel as what you're doing now."

Finn didn't answer. He just kept marching. It was nonsense anyway, and a waste of his breath to try and argue.

Roughly half of the adults on the base were already at the gate and spread out along the fence. Everything was brightly lit by the flood lamps, and more people were arriving on foot and by vehicle. The hisses and growls of the Wraiths could be heard between the smattering of gunfire and shouts. "Save your ammo!" Eddie bellowed from somewhere among the crowd. "Make every shot count! Don't shoot blindly into the darkness!"

Finn frowned. He didn't hear the familiar *SNAP* and *CRACKLE* of bodies hitting the electrified fence, although he could hear the chain link rattling. He realized the lights on the outer fence were dark. *"Damn it,"* he hissed. *"The line's been cut."*

He saw through a gap in the crowd the shapes of the Wraiths emerging from the inky blackness of the desert. They moved with incredible speed, materializing like ghosts and racing across the open ground on all fours. They barely slowed when they neared the fence, then leapt, slamming violently into the wire. They didn't try scrambling straight for the top, but instead zigzagged their way up, so it was difficult to shoot them down. Despite Eddie's warning, people kept shooting. And most of the bullets missed.

"Jesus," Adrian said. "Why are there so many? Where did they all come from?"

Finn reached into his back pocket and pulled out the spare magazine and shoved it into Adrian's free hand. "You've got thirty shots total. Make them count." He gave the man a hard shove in the middle of his back, forcing him toward a gap between people at the fence line. He didn't wait around to see if Adrian went.

The Wraith attack appeared to be concentrated about fifty yards to the left of the gate. They were a gray blur, leaping, scrambling, bouncing off, disappearing and reappearing some distance away, confusing the people inside. The chain link shook with each individual attack, jostling the wire and threatening to pull it off the posts. He saw where the power supply had been torn free by their assault.

Another wave of defenders arrived to join the fight, and the air began to crackle even more with gunfire.

Prior to Cheever's mutiny months before, dogs had been set loose in the run between fences. But they'd all been killed or escaped in the chaos. Harry Rollins had increased the number of around-the-clock armed patrols from four to eight when the Wraiths first started appearing two weeks before. He'd argued for raising it again to fourteen just that afternoon, but others said it was too many and they wouldn't get anything else done.

It was now clear that fourteen wouldn't have been sufficient to keep everyone safe. Not even forty would do it.

"There's too many of them!" someone screamed. "We can't shoot them all!"

"Just shoot where it's thickest! Get the rest when they hit the run!"

But Finn knew that wasn't going to work, either. The run between fences was eight feet wide, short enough that they could leap entirely across it. They'd be inside the compound in a flash. They had to be stopped before they came over the top of the outer fence.

He sprinted for the gate, which was no longer the focus of the assault. He felt strong now, light on his feet, fast. He felt invincible. But he was unarmed. All he had to defend himself, all he had to kill their attackers, were his bare hands.

"Open up!" he bellowed at the guard. "Let me through!" As he ran, he swept up a twelve-foot steel fence post from a stack of spares and flung it end over end into the air. It landed on the gravel inside the run with a loud clang, momentarily causing people nearby to stop and look over. "Open it up!" he bellowed.

"Are you crazy?" Stephen Largent yelled back. "You're not going out there!" He turned around again and resumed firing at the horde.

Finn ignored him and charged. Where the gate and main fence met, there was a gap in the concertina wire spooled across the top. He aimed for it and jumped midstride. The inner fence was eight feet high, and he would have cleared it if a bullet didn't hit his plant leg. Pain ripped through him as he leaped, sapping him of strength. The toe of his boot caught the top of the post and flipped him over like a marionette whose strings had been snipped all at once. He crashed into the outer fence halfway down, bounced and slammed into the ground, another flare of pain coming from the shoulder he'd landed on.

He sat up and tried to shake off the dizziness of the impact. Several feet away, a familiar face gaped at him through the fence, the smoking handgun dangling limply at his side. The shooter turned and disappeared into the darkness.

Blood poured down Finn's arm. His pant leg was soaked through, but he could already feel the wound beginning to close off. He pushed himself to his feet, stumbled when his leg refused to hold his weight, and tried again. Filthy, long, bloody fingernails raked his face and neck. He pushed himself off the wire, willing his leg to hold. Somewhere, seemingly far away, he heard people shouting for him to get out of the run. He heard Bix yelling he was out of ammunition. And Bren's anguished cries for him not to be a hero.

The Wraiths had found a new weak point in the outer fence and were focusing their attack there. The wire was beginning to pull away from the posts beneath their weight. Finn limped toward it, dragging his bad leg. He plucked the fence pole off the ground as he went. Eddie ordered him to stop, and when he didn't, the man turned and screamed at those shooting at the Wraiths not to hit him.

Eddie ran to the fence, stopping just feet away. "Finn! What the hell are you doing?"

"Tell everyone to move away. I don't want to be shot again."

He lurched forward, gripping the pipe behind him, then swung it as hard as he could against the outer fence, knocking several Wraiths off. They hit the ground twenty

318

feet out, but almost immediately scrambled upright again and renewed their charges toward the fence. Finn swung again as another body launched over the top. He slammed the pole into its midsection and the violence sent the creature crashing so hard to the ground it's neck immediately snapped.

He was like a madman, taking out the Wraiths that made it over, attacking them without mercy. He didn't feel rushed, and yet he was a blur to those watching. With the main thrust of the assault broken, the rest of the Wraiths scrambled, making them easy to target.

Bodies began to pile up both inside the run and out, and Finn stumbled over them more than once. Then, without warning, the attack ended. The Wraiths gave up and disappeared en masse into the night. Within seconds, they were gone.

A few more gunshots rang out, defenders dispatching the slow and crippled.

Finn dropped the bloodied pipe, his muscles singing from the effort, and collapsed into the dust.

CHAPTER
45

EDDIE PACED THE FLOOR LIKE A CAGED LION, SWEEPING past Harrison with a troubled glance, then spinning around to cast an even more worried look at the body laid out on the table.

"I can't believe you want to do this now, *this second*, after the losses we suffered at the south gate. People need a chance to catch their breath, to recover and regain their balance. This is just going to rip the wound open again."

"If not now, then when?" Harrison asked, rolling the tray with the medical instruments toward the table.

"We've got far graver concerns to deal with right now. We're dangerously low on ammunition. We should be making more supply runs instead of wasting time on this."

Harrison swirled the bottle of nanites. "You think I don't know that? Let me remind you that I'm not the one who needs this cure."

"Don't act like you're doing this out of altruism." He put his hand on the tray, preventing Harrison from moving it. "Ever since Kari died, you've been obsessed. Finding a cure isn't going to bring her back."

"This isn't about Kari, it's about our responsibility to our species. That's why we need to inject him. Now. Besides, I would've thought you'd be happy. Now you won't have to be the guinea pig. Hannah will be glad about that."

"That's unfair."

"We've got an opportunity here, Eddie, a chance to prove again the cure works. And you want to just let it slip by?"

Harrison withdrew a quarter mil of the liquid, half of the amount Doctor Sagan had advised. If it worked, they'd have enough for everyone on base. The liquid was clear because he'd pulsed the entire bottle already, theorizing the monomerized nanites would remain stably in that form. It was something they could easily check using the microscope, and if he was wrong, they could just re-pulse. He wanted to be ready to deliver the cure to everyone else at the base whenever they decided to take it.

He turned, the syringe in hand, and faced Eddie. "You're scared, I know. So am I. But we can't afford to panic because of what happened."

"When the Wraiths start coordinating their attacks, then it's time to panic."

"That wasn't coordinated."

Eddie slammed his palm against the wall in disbelief. "You want to lie about what happened so people can sleep at night?"

"No, I'm—"

"Those things out there, those killers that everyone thought were mindless drones, somehow hit us where we're most vulnerable, dismantling our security system. They went straight for the power supply to the flood lamps and the fence. They attacked us the day before Harry was going to increase the number of guards."

"Coincidences."

"Is it coincidence that they hit our weakest point? This was strategic, Harrison. They pulled back once they saw they couldn't succeed. *After* assessing our defenses. That was clearly a win for them, and we need to be prepared for the next attempt, because it's going to happen again! And next time, we won't have Finn to defend us."

321

"Testing us? You're giving them way more credit than they deserve. What happened was an anomaly, a rare . . . swarm. Someone told me the other day that they think it might be a migratory thing. They could be following the weather. Or the sun. Or the stars. Who knows? But I have *never* seen them act in any way that could be described as coordinated."

"You've seen — what? — a dozen large scale attacks since leaving the bunker? And now you're an expert?"

"Look, Eddie, animals migrate. Droughts, seasons, food. Maybe they're just following another food source."

"Yeah, us."

"We just happened to be in their path. You heard Jonah and Harry report this morning that they couldn't find any sign of them out there. They've moved on, like locusts."

He turned back to the table, picked up the syringe, and stepped toward the Wraith they'd captured the night of the attack. It had been shot three times, once in the neck and twice in the torso. One of the bullets had severed its spine between the shoulder blades, paralyzing it from the waist down and preventing it from escaping on foot. The spinal cord had healed enough since then that the creature was starting to be able to move its toes again. It was currently too disabled to escape, but it wouldn't remain that way for long.

"No prophylactic antibiotics this time," Harrison said. "No sedatives. No nothing." He plunged the needle into the Wraith's neck and injected the pulsed nanites directly into the muscle. The Wraith hissed and tried to snap at Harrison. "Now we wait."

"He's your responsibility," Eddie warned. "Just remember what happened to Jennifer afterward, the psychological toll her recovery took on her. This one's certain to suffer far worse."

Harrison didn't answer. He'd already rationalized what Jennifer had done to herself the night of the attack. They couldn't have known she wanted to kill herself.

"I wash my hands of this," Eddie said. "I've got too many other things to worry about. And once the fence is repaired, I'm restarting the scavenging rotation. Get ready to go with them, because experiment or no, you're at the top of the list."

He left Harrison without another word and made straight for the fence-repair detail, where he found Jonah. "Have you seen Bix?"

Jonah nodded. "He was here, but left when the new shift arrived." He tipped his head to where Finn was digging new postholes to brace the existing fencing. "I was just about to knock off, too."

Eddie sighed. "Those two still not talking to each other?"

"If someone accused me of shooting them and said I couldn't be trusted to carry a gun, I'd probably be angry, too."

"Finn was delirious when he said that stuff. He was fighting us. Doctor Jadhari had to hit him with a massive dose of sedative just to remove the bullet. He didn't mean what he said."

"Doesn't matter. Bix believes it." He glanced over to where Finn was working. "Every day I wake up thinking he can't possibly become even more intolerable, and every day I go to sleep with new proof of how wrong I was."

He turned back to Eddie. "Bix can't see it, but I can. I've had it with Finn. I'm done. And I'm not the only one. Bren refuses to even come out of her room now."

"We need to be patient with him."

"He can kiss my ass, for all I care."

"You know he can hear us."

"I'm counting on it," Jonah retorted.

Eddie was silent for a moment. "You know, speaking of changes in behavior, have you noticed anything odd about Harrison lately?"

Jonah stabbed at the hard dirt with his shovel, wincing from the soreness of digging in it all day. "What do you mean?"

"He just injected the Wraith we picked up the other night. Without a doctor present. And no other preparation."

Jonah didn't react. "So?"

"It's sloppy. He's not even following protocol anymore. He won't listen to reason. He's got blinders on."

"He wants everyone to have the cure, especially after Mister Wilcox got infected."

"Jordan's death isn't Harrison's fault. And it's certainly not justification for proceeding as recklessly as he is."

Jonah sighed. "And if he's right?"

There was a loud clang, followed by the rumble of heavy objects crashing to the ground and cries of alarm. They looked over just in time to see Finn sprinting toward the source of the shouts, no indication he'd been recently shot. Several large rolls of fencing wire, each weighing hundreds of pounds, had broken free of the forklift and fallen onto someone, trapping him underneath. Before Eddie and Harper could take more than two steps to assist, Finn had already lifted the rolls away and extracted the man.

Jonah shook his head, more in derision than appreciation. "Not surprised."

"Be grateful he was here to help when it happened, just like the other night."

"He should've been watching Jennifer."

"What she did isn't his fault, Jonah. Anyway, Sagan says she'll live. She's lucky, healing quickly, not as quickly as before, but quick enough. He thinks there's probably residual nanite activity in her liver that helped counter the drugs she took. He's counseling her now."

"Good to know." Jonah lifted the shovel over his shoulder.

"Before you go, I wanted to ask if you'd put together a team for another scavenging run. Say, four people."

"Bunker Ten?"

"That's still too far away right now. Besides, we need to prepare for another Wraith attack."

"So, ammo then. I can go tomorrow. Sure beats doing this grunt work."

"Good. Make sure to include Harrison."

CHAPTER

THEY WOKE THE NEXT DAY TO A FRIGID RAIN DRIVEN nearly horizontal by a brutal wind. It swept in sheets across the valley in varying hues of gray and limited the scavenging team's visibility to a dozen or so yards. After venturing out less than a quarter mile, they turned back, worried about losing their bearings, although that concern was secondary to the possibility of an attack. While less likely under such harsh conditions, an encounter with a large group of Wraiths would be catastrophic, and Eddie wasn't willing to take the risk.

At noon, when the rain still showed no end in sight, they decided to postpone the trip. The next day dawned dark and ominous. The wind still blew with fierce determination, but there was no rain. Yet once again they were forced to delay. With the temperature hovering barely above freezing and the ground saturated, partially frozen mud became their enemy. It was another two days before they could try again.

Since the attack nearly a week before, no more Wraiths had been spotted outside the fence, and the one inside had lapsed into a coma hours after Harrison's injection.

"Nanite count last night was down roughly thirteen percent from its initial level," Doctor Jadhari reported at breakfast. "It is now down another five percent."

"How solid are those numbers?" Susan asked.

"It is statistically significant," the doctor confirmed. "We're using a counting slide and averaging over multiple blood draws. We are confident of one thing: the nanite numbers are down, at least those within the blood. Where they are going, however, we cannot say. Maybe they are being destroyed, but it is also possible they are relocating into other tissues." He shrugged. "We may have to accept we might never be sure."

"Maybe reasonably sure is the best we can do."

"Assuming the nanites continue to break down at the current rate, I would expect the blood to be completely free of them within two weeks. As for behavioral signals, we have none as long as the patient remains comatose. The real question, however, is transmissibility of the Flense. That is going to be tricky to address. There is just no way we can know without actual skin-to-skin contact."

"And who's going to volunteer for that?" Bix asked.

The doctor nodded. "We can search in the blood all we want and confirm they are gone from that milieu, but it is the nanites distributed at the surface of the body that are likely responsible for transmitting the disease. That would require a biopsy with cytological examination, a microtome for sectioning, and a far more powerful microscope than we have here."

"What about Jennifer? How is she doing?"

"By all measures, she is completely free of nanites and clear of the Flense. Nothing in her blood. No transmissibility, as we already know. Kidneys are recovering. If I were an oncologist, I would declare her cancer-free and the treatment a complete success. But I doubt I will ever be able to say it with regard to the Flense. Besides, we all know her biggest challenge now is psychological. It will likely be far worse with the second patient, assuming treatment succeeds."

Harrison closed the journal where he'd been keeping notes. "And the second patient's kidneys?" he asked, ignoring Jadhari's cautionary words. "Any signs of stress?"

"Nothing to worry about yet. Urine output is normal. Good color. No infections, protein, or other abnormalities so far."

"So, the reduced dosage worked."

"The blood tests do show some aberrant chemistry, but we do not have a meaningful baseline for them anyway. We have no idea what metabolic *normal* is in these creatures."

"People," Harrison corrected. "They're people, not creatures, or monsters, or whatever else we're tempted to call them. They're people. They have a disease. They're sick, and it's not their fault."

No one spoke for a moment, then the doctor nodded. "Yes, of course. I meant no disrespect. This . . . person exhibited out-of-range values for several standard kidney markers before, but they appear to be returning to normal ranges since the injection— normal for us, that is. By every measure, it— *he* appears to be getting better. Best of all, he is not showing any signs of organ distress."

Harrison thanked him, then turned to Eddie, who was deep in thought. "I'd say we have our proof that cutting down the dose works and avoids other problems. It just works slower."

Eddie raised his eyes and nodded solemnly, although his face remained pinched with doubt.

Harrison turned back to Doctor Jadhari. "What's the latest census?"

"As of this morning, all but seventeen people now say they want the cure. Assuming our patient fully recovers at the dosage given, we will have enough to cover everyone, plus have a couple dozen doses to spare."

"And those holdouts, what are their reasons?"

"Six are pre-Flense diabetics. They are unwilling to return to insulin-dependence. One suffered from a neuromuscular condition, and one had heart disease. Understandably, they feel they are better off now than before and do not wish to see past issues return."

"We don't even know that will happen," Harrison said.

"I cannot imagine a way it does not," the doctor replied. "The nanites do not fix genetic defects, only mask them. In any case, it is a terrible decision for them to make for themselves. We cannot force anyone to do something they don't want."

"Yeah, sort of makes me understand where Finn's coming from," Bix said.

"Does that number include Finn?"

Jadhari nodded.

"And you, Eddie?"

Eddie stood up before he could answer and gestured to Jonah and Bix. "I think the ground's dry enough now. Time you boys set out."

"You're not coming this time?"

"Hannah asked me to stay." He turned to Jonah. "Take Finn in my place."

Bix and Jonah exchanged puzzled glances, but to their credit, neither said what they were thinking.

* * *

At Jonah's recommendation, they headed due north. The drive took them over the taller and more forbidding of the parallel ridges bordering the base. Westerton's old-timers could not say whether the roads in that direction were even passable, since previous search parties had opted for the wider, more reliable roads servicing communities to the east and west. But Jonah reasoned that this worked in their favor, increasing their odds of finding places that hadn't already been scavenged over the course of the past four years.

Their route followed a zigzagged path through in-creasingly rugged landscape, barren scrubland, and former reservations. Several times, they encountered an obstacle that needed to be carefully navigated or cleared, a rockslide or a fallen tree. With the oversized tires and high clearance of the army cargo truck, they could get past most of these with little trouble. Other times, the road was completely blocked, washed out, or torn up. One bridge had collapsed, and they had to backtrack and find a way around. Detours cost them at least three extra hours, and the best they'd managed to find was a rusty shotgun without shells in a lonely windswept ranch that had been taken over by a family of badgers. After eight painstaking hours, they had gone barely two hundred miles, and it was time to find a place to spend the night. They had passed into thick coniferous forest by then, and daylight was quickly failing.

They took refuge in a wooden fire watchtower that had somehow escaped an inferno that charred the forest around it some time before. The view from the elevated platform revealed nothing but a rolling gray sea of ashfall for miles around and gloomy white above. As the sun set and darkness swept across the land, they searched for the telltale signs of civilization — campfires, lanterns, even headlights — but the scorched and sooty canvas of the ground below soon melted into the charcoal of night, turning all into a vast black sea. Only when the clouds began to break apart a few hours later, and a few dozen stars of the Milky Way sprayed their dappled light across it in patches, did they fully understand the immensity of their solitude.

The temperature dropped quickly and significantly after that, forcing them to retreat into their sleeping bags. But the night was the coldest they'd experienced in four years, and they found the bags and their clothes woefully inadequate. Few of them managed to get much sleep. And when morning came, they weren't surprised to find that the world had turned white from a heavy predawn snowfall. The sun was an amorphous blob of white caught within the scraggly knuckles of the burned trees, and a few tardy snowflakes made their lazy way to the ground.

Harrison was already dressed when Bix opened his eyes. Harper was up and lacing his boots, shivering from the cold. Only Finn remained sound asleep, apparently unaffected by the cold.

"Do I smell coffee?" Bix called from deep inside his sleeping bag.

"Coffee and oatmeal," Harrison confirmed. He adjusted the heat on the two-burner camp stove they'd brought with them. "Better get it while it's hot."

"Why's it so damned cold?"

"It's called winter," Jonah said. His voice was muffled, but the sarcasm was unmistakable.

"No shit, Sherlock. But *this* cold?"

"The seasonal phenomenon is caused when the inclination of the planet reduces exposure to the sun," Harper offered.

"Also, it snowed last night," Jonah said, without a trace of irony.

"I hate snow," Bix said.

"Oh, that's funny," Jonah retorted. "I can distinctly remember you saying how much you missed the snow and wished you could go skiing again."

"Yeah, when we were stuck inside the bunker. Not now."

"You don't ski," Harrison said over his shoulder.

"Mom took me one winter when I was little, before you showed up."

Harper gave Jonah a puzzled look. "Bix lived mostly with his mom growing up," Jonah whispered. "She was in a band, traveled a lot. Dad showed up when he was twelve or so."

"The first time he showed up was when I was five, actually," Bix said. "Then it was off and on till I was twelve."

"My family skied when I was young," Harrison said, clearly uncomfortable with the discussion. He pulled the pot of oatmeal off the stove, gave it one last stir, and scooped some out into a bowl. "Probably why I could never stand the idea of it."

"He and his dad didn't get along," Bix quietly said, leaning over Harper's other side. "But if we ever fix the Flense, maybe we can learn how to snowboard."

"Sure," Harrison replied. He went over to Finn and shook him awake. "Breakfast and coffee are ready. Get it while it's hot. The sooner we get back on the road, the sooner we can get back home."

"Easy for you to say," Bix grumbled. "It's your turn to drive this morning. You'll have the heater up front."

"Oh, poor baby has to sit in back this time," Jonah said, chuckling. He stepped out of his sleeping bag, stomping his feet and rubbing his bare arms. "Where are my— Oh, what the hell? Very funny, Blackeye!"

"Didn't I tell you last night it was dangerous to sleep in only your tightie whities?" Bix said. "We could be attacked in the middle of the night." He laughed and pointed at Jonah's bare legs as the older boy made his way to the broken window where Bix had hung his clothes to block out the wind. They were stiff with hoar frost.

Jonah shook his head as he retrieved the items, but he didn't say anything. He wouldn't let Bix have the pleasure of knowing he'd gotten the better of him. Thankfully, the clothes weren't very wet. Once they thawed, they'd do just fine. Until then, however, it was going to be damn cold.

He tucked his sweatshirt under his arm and reached for his pants, and that's when he saw the thin ribbon of smoke rising from a spot along the snaking curve of the road they'd arrived on, about a mile away. The road's path was nearly impossible to see beneath the new snow, just a narrow ribbon meandering through the dead growth. "Guys?" he said, gesturing. "We got company."

"Wraiths?"

"People."

Incredibly, Finn was the first to reach him, even though a moment before he'd been snoring deep inside his sleeping bag. "Four vehicles," he said, standing there with as little clothing on as Jonah, yet completely unfazed by the cold. "They look in pretty good shape. Half dozen people, maybe more."

"You can see all that?"

"Tracks through the snow in both directions on the road indicates it's two different parties. One of the vehicles appears broken down. Hood's up."

Harrison joined them. He squinted toward the distant thread of smoke, but couldn't make out its source. "Who's got the binoculars?"

"I do," Harper said. He was fully dressed by now and bundled inside his jacket and knit cap. He went over to the broken window and peered out through the glasses. "I count four vehicles, too, one with the hood up, as Finn said. What should we do?"

He turned to where Jonah had been a moment before, but the other boy had already taken his frozen clothes over to the stove, where he was running the bottom of the hot pot of oatmeal over them.

Finn stared out over the scorched and frozen wasteland a few seconds more, then said, "Looks like a family: one man, a woman, and one child, about eight or nine years old. I think they're in trouble."

"What do you mean?"

"I can't tell exactly. It's too far away, but I'm definitely getting a hostile vibe from the four— no, five other men. One's holding a shotgun and pacing around like he's nervous."

He spun around and stepped swiftly over to his clothes and began to pull them on.

"Whoa, hey there, Finn!" Bix exclaimed. "It's not the time for heroics. You said it yourself, they don't look friendly!"

Before Finn could answer, the sound of a single gunshot rippled across the valley, eventually fading away until they couldn't be sure it was the echo or wind passing over the hills.

Everyone but Finn froze. Then Harper grabbed Bix's arm. "Someone needs our help. And you're saying we should just leave?"

"Yes," Finn said from the other side of the room. He reached for his shirt, not bothering to button his trousers.

"Yes?"

"They have guns. It's too dangerous. We mind our own business."

"But the woman. The kid."

"Strangers. We have to protect ourselves."

Harper turned to the others. "Everyone else think this way?"

They all exchanged uneasy glances. Only Jonah joined Harper in wanting to help. "We have an obligation."

"Sorry, three to two," Finn said. "We're leaving. Now. Before they come here and find our truck."

They gathered up the rest of their belongings and a few of the other items they'd scavenged, then scrambled down the stairs. The wind hit them the moment they emerged through the floor onto the caged stairwell and threatened to freeze them before they reached the ground. There, they dumped what they had into the back of the truck.

Harrison, Harper, and Jonah went to climb into the front, but Finn pulled Jonah to help defend them in back, just in case they were followed. "We're lucky the snow held off until after dark," he said. "Otherwise, they'd have seen our tracks. We have a good chance of getting away without being noticed."

"Or we could have just stayed put," Bix countered.

"The tower's the only structure for miles around," Finn said. "Chances are they'll decide to check it out, maybe even bring their prisoners here."

"Why?" asked Harper.

"Do you really need it spelled out?" Jonah muttered, and gave Finn a disgusted look for even bringing up the possibility.

"They could be friendly."

"Then they don't need our help," said Finn.

"But what if they do, the woman and kid?"

"They're on their own."

"You should try not being so damn heartless," Jonah growled.

"It's not heartless, it's realistic. Now get in. We don't know if they noticed Jonah's clothes hanging in the window."

"They'll hear the truck."

"Can't be helped. And if they follow, we'll shoot."

The engine started up, a loud roar that seemed to expand in the still air until it filled the valley below. They began their descent down the fire trail to the main road, moving as swiftly as possible. The fresh snow gave them no problems. They were easily able to traverse the few fallen trunks and washouts, following the ruts their own tires had made in the mud the day before. There was nothing they could do about the noise.

As they approached the road, Finn jumped out and ran ahead to scout for cars, then waved them forward. "We're clear," he said, and climbed into the back. "Bix, where's your gun?"

"Inside the bag with me. Don't worry, it's loaded."

"I don't think that's a good place for it."

"Yeah, well, and I don't think my fingers are a good place for frostbite, either."

"As long as he doesn't have to pee, he'll be fine," Jonah said.

They turned left onto the main road and away from the source of the smoke. From his place against the right rear tailgate, Finn could see through a narrow opening between the side and back canvas flaps. The strangers' vehicles had left tracks in the snow when they passed this way earlier that morning. The treads were narrower than their own, and in a few places they had slid on the ice, observations that told him a little bit more about the people they were hoping to avoid. He glanced over at Jonah, seated on the other side of the tailgate, his rifle in one hand, which was wrapped inside a spare sock. The other hand held the canvas flap aside so he could also keep watch. Bix was huddled on the bench beside him, his chin buried deep inside the sleeping bag, his eyes squeezed shut.

Finn turned back to the narrow opening. The breeze snatched the fog of his breath and whisked it away behind them. He stared at the tracks. There was something about them, about the way they snaked over the road, like individual strands of twine tangling and coming undone. And then it hit him.

He jumped up, his heart racing. "We need to stop!" he shouted. He turned toward the cab, throwing an arm out for balance as the truck skewed over the icy surface.

"What's the matter?" Jonah said.

"I was wrong! There are two sets of tracks on the road, not one, and not three!"

"What?" Bix asked, alarmed.

"Two sets, Bix! Two!"

"I don't understand what that means!"

"Oh, shit!" Jonah said. He yanked the sock-mittens off his hands and fumbled to ready his rifle.

"Somebody tell me what's going on!"

Finn had nearly reached the front, ready to warn Mister Blakely and Harper that they might be heading straight into trouble, when the truck skidded to a stop and threw him into the hard shell of the cab. His chin slammed against a metal bar, and he stumbled backward.

Even before the tires stopped skidding, he knew they were surrounded. And he could tell from the smell of gun oil that the people blocking their way were heavily armed.

CHAPTER

"THROW ALL YOUR WEAPONS OUT! SHOW YOUR HANDS! NOW!"

Jonah complied immediately, tossing his rifle out, then raising his arms through the opening in the flap. Someone climbed up the tailgate and pulled the canvas cover aside and aimed his pistol into the gloom. Another man appeared farther back, a serious-looking semi-automatic weapon resting casually over one forearm. He shouted, "Everyone out! No stupid shit. We don't want to hurt anyone!"

"Yeah, right," Bix muttered.

Harrison and Harper appeared on the road behind the truck, their fingers laced over their heads. The motor shut off, now in the control of a stranger, and the truck shook itself into silence.

Finn slowly got to his feet. He made eye contact as Jonah climbed out of the truck. Jonah gave his head a slight shake, warning him not to try anything.

"Gun!" the man on the tailgate snapped, and gestured at the rifle on the floor beside Finn's feet. "Pick it up by the barrel and hand it out. Don't try anything, and no one gets hurt."

They huddled the Westerton group on the road and frisked them for more weapons. Four men held rifles on them, while four more searched the cab and the boxes in back. All had small personal radios, which occasionally crackled. A door slammed from somewhere ahead of the truck, and a ninth man appeared. He was dressed in a long, heavily stained trench coat and leather boots. A pistol was strapped to his thigh, and another was within easy reach in a shoulder holster. He carried a sawed-off shotgun in one hand, and idly flipped a butterfly knife in the other. Both hands were clad in fingerless gloves, and the beds of his nails were black with filth.

"Only thing missing is an eye patch," Bix muttered.

The man chuckled and tapped his own cheekbone with the tip of his knife, but it was impossible to tell if he was amused or not.

"How y'all doing today?" Bix asked, assuming Adrian's fake Southern drawl.

"Shut it," Jonah hissed.

"I'm just trying to—"

The man stopped pacing and turned. "Just fine, thanks," he said in reply, his voice loud, yet disarmingly calm. "And how're you folks doing? Same, I hope?"

"We've been better," Jonah said.

The man nodded thoughtfully. "I do apologize for the dramatics. You just cannot tell these days who you might run into out here. Shady characters. Characters from the wrong side of the line, perhaps. Ain't that right, Ghost?"

One of the armed men nodded. The stony mask of his face did not crack, and he didn't lower his rifle. "That's right, boss."

"The wrong side of what line?" Bix demanded.

He received no reply.

The man circled the group, nodding and inspecting them from every angle. He wore a tattered green bandana around his neck, but his head was uncovered, exposed to the bitter cold. His hair was short, except on top, which was spiked and bleached. The roots, however, were coal black, unlike his three-day-old beard, which was naturally white.

He crossed behind Bix and stopped. Then the bitter cold of his knife slithered between Bix's neck and the collar of his shirt.

"Hey!" Bix shouted, jerking away.

"You want to tell me what you're doing in these parts?"

"How about *you* tell us."

"Bix," his father warned. He turned to the man and said, "We're scavenging, just like you."

"Now, that's a lie."

"It's not a lie!" Bix yelled.

The man gave the knife a few playful flips, then closed and slipped it into a pocket in his overcoat. "You may be scavenging, but we ain't. So, yes, it is."

"My mistake then. I assumed—"

"You know what they say about assuming things."

"Got half that right," Bix muttered.

The man grinned and wagged his finger toward Bix. "You folks must be desperate. Pickings are slim-to-none for miles around. Fact, I'd say nonexistent. But I can't blame you for thinking you might get lucky, choosing forest over the cities. Too many ferals there. Lots of cover here. Avoiding the main roads, what with all the patrols. That is why you're not using the main roads, ain't it?"

No one spoke.

Another nod. "Yeah. Okay, look, I know it's hard for strangers to break the ice, particularly under such . . . frigid conditions."

"We don't have anything."

The man spun around, boots crunching on the snow, and stepped over to Bix. "Ah, you think that we are of the . . . criminal ilk."

"Are you?"

"Ain't highwaymen. Ain't murderers, thieves, or rapists, either."

Thankfully, Bix kept his mouth shut this time.

The man shrugged. "But you see, our dilemma is this: We know who we are, but how do we know *you* ain't any of those things?"

"Because we said so."

"And we should just take your word for it?"

"And we should take yours?"

"Got to extend trust to get trust."

"You're the ones pointing the guns."

The man ignored Bix. "You're all a lot younger than the usual folks we find out here. Except you, of course. I'm guessing you're, what? Early forties? No, not quite that old. You the leader?"

Harrison didn't respond.

"At least tell me where you're all coming from. Perhaps we can help you get back."

"A few hours south of here," Harper offered, but volunteered no further detail.

"Now see? That there is a damn fine start. But, you know, I know this part of the world like I know my own face, and if that's the truth, then you boys have been living a lot harder than your appearances suggest. Or maybe you're from even farther south than a few hours, 'cause there sure ain't nothing much for at least a long, hard day's drive. Mostly just a bunch of what used to be federal lands, all of it unsuitable for habitation."

He circled them again, studying their faces, then smiled. "Ah, yes, I see. You are."

"We are what?" Harrison asked.

"A long, *long* way from home." He pulled his shotgun up and leaned it against his shoulder and waited.

The men searching the truck returned and reported that they'd found no more weapons and little else of any value. "Just enough canned food and bottled water to last them about a week max, but no contraband. And no affiliation insignias."

Their leader nodded. He raised a foot and placed it on the bumper of the truck. "Army issue," he said, tapping the end of the shotgun on the black letters stenciled beside his heel. "And how might you have acquired this?"

"Found it at an old equipment depot," Harrison said. "It's where we've been holed up since the Flense."

"Since the what?"

"The Fle— The feral."

The man tilted his head and cocked his eyebrows. "I know some folks who call it that, Flense. Spent time riding out the disaster in some underground shelter." He snorted. "You wouldn't happen to know about that, would you?"

"No," Jonah said. "But we took in a few people a while back, said they were from one of those places."

"I see." The man dropped his boot to the road, then wiped the back of his free hand across his upper lip and spit. "I see," he said again, nodding to himself.

The sound of vehicles came through the trees, and soon they could be seen making their way up the road from the direction of the watchtower. Finn immediately recognized them as the same four he'd spotted earlier, and they pulled up in a line and stopped about thirty feet back from the men on the road. A freshly shot deer was strapped to the hood of one, blood still draining from a hole in its neck, although pink ice crystals were beginning to crust the edges of the wound.

The driver's door of the lead vehicle, a luxury SUV that had seen better days and taken a few bullets by the looks of it, opened and a man stepped out. "That them from the tower, Garth?" he shouted.

The man in the trench coat — Garth — slipped his shotgun into a sling and walked over. "What have you got?" he asked, gesturing to the vehicle in the middle, an older model sedan whose front bumper was held in place with rope. It was the car that had appeared to be broken.

342

"Cracked water line. Probably froze from the cold. We wrapped it pretty good. It'll hold for now."

"And the family?"

"Coming with us."

Garth nodded and craned his neck to see inside the car. "Can he fight?"

"They're both healthy and strong, definitely willing to work in exchange for our services."

"And bleed?"

"Like I said, willing."

"Living on the run will do that to you. You sure the repair job will hold till we get back?"

"Pretty sure, but those tires are nearly as bald as you, boss." He snickered. "There's other mechanical problems, too."

"We'll use it for parts. Write everything down, make sure they get full market value on the trade. Minus debts, of course."

The man thrust a thumb toward the scavenging party. "And them?"

"Armed. Definitely lethal. Definitely *not* starving. And so far not willing to cooperate."

"Affiliated?"

"It would seem not," Garth replied. "But . . . ."

"Yeah. Well, I wouldn't put it past Six to start subcontracting. Or using unmarked scouts, despite the agreement."

"That's my thought. They say they're from way down south. I have my own suspicions."

"We taking them back?"

"It's for the best. Let Cas deal with them. He's got a way with people, getting them to talk."

The other man chuckled. "That he does."

Garth spun around and twirled his finger in the air. "Load them up! We're pulling out. You," he added, crooking his finger at Bix. "You can ride with me."

"But—"

"Relax," he told Harrison. "Can the boy drive?"

"Yeah."

"Good. Plessy, you too." He pointed to the others. "Divide them up, one per vehicle."

"No! You can't separate us!" Jonah said. Ghost blocked his way, but Garth raised a hand to stop him.

"Safer that way, my friend. Safer for all of us. Besides, I ain't blind. Or inhumane. The back of your truck is an icebox, and it would be a shame to lose any of you to the cold. We won't charge nothing for sharing our heat."

"This is a mistake," Finn growled.

Garth turned to him. "Think about it from where I'm standing. It'd be an even bigger mistake letting you go."

"We have people depending on us."

"And so do we."

"Not as many."

"Oh, I highly doubt that."

"At least tell us where we're going?" Harper asked.

Garth leaned back, and gazed at Harper through hooded eyelids. "Someplace a lot safer than here, so close to the line. That is, assuming you ain't affiliated. Still not convince you ain't."

"Now who's assuming?" Bix grumbled.

Garth shrugged, then turned and marched away.

CHAPTER

THEY DROVE DUE WEST THAT ENTIRE FIRST DAY, stopping to fuel up their tanks in places Finn and his group would never have guessed existed. The men holding them captive clearly knew their way around the old highway system, taking routes that were clear of obstructions, avoiding urban areas, and stopping just long enough to switch drivers. The men remained in contact with each other by radio, often communicating statuses in terse staccato bursts that offered aggravatingly few answers to the Westerton group's questions. They were kept separated to prevent them from comparing notes.

Harper had the most success breaking through his guards' tough veneer. After a few hours, they seemed to relax and ignored him. Listening to their banter, he was struck by how civil they were with each other, despite their hardened appearances and gruff manners. They lived in a lawless world filled with constant threats, so perhaps the only thing keeping them civilized was the fact that they had to rely on each other to survive.

An older man, who went by the name Curly, was more talkative than the rest. He drove first, and the conversation centered mainly on Curly's eclectic tastes in music and the arcane collection he kept in the glove compartment, as well as the even more esoteric assortment of trivia about them, which he was more than happy to impart onto his reluctant audience.

At one point, the man sitting beside Harper in the back seat lost patience with the endless litany of useless facts, blurting out, "Who the hell cares where the drummer went to high school, man, or who their sixth wife happened to be? They're all dead now, every single damn one of them, and the world ain't never gonna get no more new tunes."

After their break, Curly moved into the back, and someone else got to choose the music. He was friendly enough to Harper, and confided that he had been a warehouse supervisor in Reno before everything went to hell. "Thank god I never got married and had children. Who wants that responsibility in this world?"

He assured Harper they wouldn't be hurt, and that they'd get their truck and weapons back eventually. "Assuming you are who you say you are."

"Why would we lie?"

"After everything that's happened to the world, why would anyone tell the truth to a stranger?"

Harper took little solace in the man's words after that. But at least Curly was right about one thing: They treated him fairly, if not warmly. They didn't harm him physically or force him into shackles.

As for the others in the other cars, he had no way of knowing if they were being treated with the same regard, although nothing he could see on their faces during their roadside breaks suggested they weren't.

This, however, was its own cause for alarm. What if they were like lambs being led unwittingly to the slaughter, lured into submission so they wouldn't fight when the butcher came to slit their throats? It was a dark thought, the darkest he'd ever had about another person, and he willed himself to forget it. Except he couldn't.

They spent the night in an abandoned used car dealership on the outskirts of Colby, Kansas. The showroom was empty, and the vehicles in the lot had been torched long ago. Curly told Harper that in the weeks after the world blew up, chaos and destruction reigned. Survival was the world's new economy, and violence was its currency. Some of the nihilistic things people had done seemed to make sense — setting fire to anything and anyplace that the ferals might use to hide in — but not all. There was a lot of wanton destruction and senseless killing, people shooting first without considering whether their victim was infected or not. "It wasn't like that where you were?" he asked, seeing the horrified look on Harper's face.

"I saw some of that on the first day, yes. But not afterward. I guess I was lucky and got to a safe place. We just stayed put after that and remained isolated."

"Lucky then, you and your brother there, watching each other's back. Family's important."

"I thought you were glad you didn't have family."

"Never said I was glad, just relieved. Besides, you can't trust anyone like you can your family."

"What about Garth and the others?"

"Oh, I trust them," he said, but there was a dark look in his eyes. He'd begun to rub the crook of his arm unconsciously, as if working the stiffness out of an old injury. "To a degree."

"Did they hurt you?"

The question seemed to startle Curly. "Hurt? Why would you say that?"

He gestured to Curly's arm.

"Everyone pays, one way or another."

"How?"

The man stood up stiffly and flexed the fingers on his hand. "You'll find out soon enough."

* * *

Curly spoke very little the next day. Once again, he started off driving, but this time he didn't even bother choosing the music. He seemed uninterested in conversation, too. But Harper couldn't tell what had changed his mood, whether he was simply distracted or tired, or if he regretted what he'd said the night before. The other men didn't seem to notice the change. They were happy that they could listen to whatever they wanted.

They continued west, chasing their shadows all morning and for a while afterward. It wasn't until they started heading north again, just before entering Idaho, that Harper realized where they were going.

"It's Haven," he said. "That's where you're taking us."

Curly, now in the passenger seat up front, looked back over his shoulder. "What do you know about Haven?"

Another man hissed a warning, but Curly dismissed him. "He was going to guess anyway. Ain't nothing much else between here and the mountains."

"He could be Six."

"It's just—"

"Look," another man told Harper, "if you know about Haven, then you know the drill."

"I actually haven't been there before, just passed by it once."

"Passed by without stopping in? Why wouldn't you?"

They rode on, leaving the snow behind for clear roads and skies, although the temperature remained below forty. Soon, the white-tipped peaks of the Teton Mountains rose into view, fifty miles further on.

They arrived at the outskirts of Pocatello by mid afternoon and began to thread their way through the intricate maze of outer neighborhoods. Barriers erected years before channeled them toward the heart of the city. It seemed insane to Harper that people would opt to live in the very middle of an urban wasteland populated with things that wanted to kill or infect them.

He watched, fascinated by the level of coordination exhibited between the drivers as they sped at breakneck speed through the gauntlet. The caravan contracted, each vehicle separated from the next by mere feet and racing even faster toward the fortress. A wall rose up ahead, yet they continued toward it without slowing. He was told to relax and be quiet.

Curly pointed to the green light mounted near the top of the wall, still a mile away. "Keep your eye on that." Chatter on the radios reached a fever pitch as the other drivers planned their entry strategy. And their escape contingency, should the light happen to turn red.

Shift right. Shift left. Maintain course and speed. Hold. Hold.

Harper struggled to keep from yelling out that they were going to crash, but the placid looks on the others' faces assured him they had done this many times before, and he'd spent enough time with them to know they weren't suicidal.

His was the last vehicle. He had mere moments, a heartbeat, to watch before the wall opened up and the cars ahead of him entered without smashing into it. He swiveled around in his seat as they passed through, and strained his head upward just in time to see the giant panel swing down again. But then he was thrown violently to his right when the car spun suddenly in the opposite direction.

They screeched to a stop less than fifteen feet from another wall, the car rocking on mushy springs, and the engine, already off, ticking as it cooled. The doors popped open and the passengers piled out. He saw Garth stride across the compound toward the massive inner wall, shouting someone's name. The door there opened just as he reached for the knob and someone emerged, a younger man with bright unruly hair and eyeglasses wrapped at the bridge with tape.

"Caspar!" Garth shouted again and extended his arms. "Garth!"

They wrapped each other up in their arms, then locked lips in a lover's embrace.

"Did not expect that," Bix muttered.

"Don't stare," Jonah said, stepping to Harper's side, although he was just as surprised as Harper looked.

None of their captors seem the least bit fazed by the unexpected display of affection by their tough-guy leader. They simply went about their business, removing bags and equipment from the trunks of their cars, signing forms. The Westerton crew and the three family members with the repaired car were told to line up for inspections.

"So, what have we got here?" boomed a new voice, and another man walked out, short and chubby, like an Asian cherub, except there was nothing angelic about his appearance. He wore scuffed cowboy boots, tight jeans, and sported a large silver handgun on his hip. He scanned the lineup, then froze the moment his eyes lit upon Harrison.

Harper glanced subtly left toward his brother, but Finn's face revealed no clues. To Harper's right, he heard Bix whisper, *"Shaw."* It was loud enough to catch the man's attention. He nodded and walked over.

"So, the prodigal posse has returned from the dead at last," Shaw Chao said, a hint of dismissiveness in his Texas drawl. He made a performance of glancing around at each of them and checking inside the empty vehicles. He did a double take when he came to Harper and Finn, his gaze flicking between them a couple times, as if he wasn't sure he was seeing correctly. He made no comment about their resemblance. Finally, he returned to Harrison. "Stop teasing. Let me have him. I mean, I assume that's why you're back, right? You did promise to bring me something back in exchange for the loaner."

"You know these people, Shaw?" Garth asked.

"This is the group we lent the Hummer and roof-mounted 240 a couple months back. Well, some of the group. This one's new," Shaw added, pointing to Harper. "Or is it the other one? Can't tell them apart. But there were others with them." He turned to Harrison. "And where might they be?"

"We lost them," Harrison croaked, adding that they'd died, in case it wasn't clear.

Shaw shook his head. "I'm sorry to hear that, but we did warn you of the dangers."

"About that favor," Harrison tried to explain. "We can't—"

Shaw cut him off with a wave of the hand. "I guess *favor* isn't the most accurate way to describe our mutually agreed upon arrangement, is it? I believe the legal phrase is *contract*, and a contract is binding, is it not?"

"Okay, but—"

"You agreed to the terms."

"What terms?" Harper asked.

Shaw turned to him. "So, you must be the one they went into the city to rescue. Yes, okay, I see it now. Once we've tallied the accounts, you'll be free to go. The rest, I'm afraid, have some business to conduct with us."

"Go where?"

"That's up to you. Haven's arrangement is with the others." He turned back to Harrison, raising his palms questioningly. "I don't see my loaner, the Hummer. Where might it be?" He snapped his fingers, and feigned thinking hard. "That's right, we found it totaled, all four tires flat, axle busted, north of Salt Lake City. What we did not find was any survivors. Might've written you off as dead, vulture food, except the 240 was gone. Of course, someone might've come along and taken it afterward, but the uncertainty was enough to keep the account open." He shook his head, clicking his tongue.

"You asked us to return Adrian to you, if we were able to capture him alive," Harrison said.

Harper's reaction didn't go unnoticed. Shaw swiveled around and wagged a finger at him. "So, you'll confirm he's dead? Is that true?"

"We were attacked by Wra— ferals," Harrison offered. "We lost several of our people, too."

"That is terribly unfortunate." Shaw sighed and shook his head. "Terribly. Now how on earth are we going to square up?" He spun around to face Garth. "Do they have anything to trade?"

"Just the truck."

"Wait!" Jonah shouted. "You can't—!"

Shaw silenced the protest with a loud clap. "That's all?" he asked.

"Yes."

"Hmm, gas guzzler like that won't quite make up for the Hummer." He turned back to the group. "And that 240 was worth a fair mint. I'll need to run the numbers." He gestured to Caspar and the other men. "Take them until I can consult with the accountants."

"We can still trade!" Harrison shouted, as his arms were grabbed and pulled behind his back.

"Of course you can, and you will. We're all about trading!"

"No, you don't understand. We have foo—"

"Adrian's alive," Bix yelped.

"Bix, no!"

"We have him. We'll give him to you, but you have to let us go."

Shaw nodded solemnly. "Alive, eh? Is he— No, that doesn't matter right now, although it does make the calculation a bit easier. Caspar, if you don't mind, take them to the Deseret. Make sure they get dinner, of course. They're our guests."

"Are we allowed to leave?"

"Not just yet."

"Then we're not guests, are we? We're prisoners."

"The debt must be repaid," Shaw replied.

He turned toward the young couple and their child, who'd remained silent throughout the entire exchange. They now looked terrified. Shaw smiled and extended his hands. "My sincerest apologies. You know my name by now, and I'll be honored to know yours. I'm in charge here. Well, this small part of it; Haven's a lot bigger than it appears from between the walls. Allow me to be the first to welcome you to our community."

The man nodded tentatively.

"I understand my people here helped repair your vehicle."

"Y-yes, sir. He said there would be ways to pay you back. And that you'd be fair. We don't have much."

"I don't think you realize how much of value you really own," Shaw said, casting a sly glance at the woman and their child. "But come. First we'll get you settled and some food in your stomachs. Then, when we're ready, we can review the accounts."

CHAPTER

THEY WERE TAKEN THE NEXT MORNING TO A LARGE
meeting room deep in the middle of the walled settlement
and told to sit quietly and wait for Shaw. The moment he
entered, all five of the Westerton group stood up. Harrison
tried to intercept him before he got too far, but the man
swept right past him, ignoring all of their questions. One of
the security detail ordered everyone to sit back down.

Shaw went to the front of the room, sifted through some
papers on the table, then turned and asked if they'd all slept
well.

"Yes, but—"

"Good. Lots to cover, little time." He gestured to one of
the men seated behind him. "Rooms? Meals?" he asked.

"Already on the ledger, sir."

"Excellent." He turned back to them with a thin smile.
"Where would the world be without accountants, eh? Hell
may be overfilled with them, but here on Earth, they keep us
all honest."

"You're making us pay for holding us against our will?"
Finn demanded. "You can't just keep us prisoner!"

"You're not prisoners, you're collateral being held
against a debt. There's a difference. We had an agreement.
You accepted our help, now we have a right to collect. I
thought this was clear to you. What you don't pay, or can't
pay, we will extract in kind sooner or later. It's a fair system,
much better than what we had before, what with paper

money becoming useless and the false faith and trust of a government that didn't even last a full day after the banks collapsed."

"You railroaded us."

"And you still think this is a conversation." He and rubbed his hands together as he paced, warming them. His cheeks had a ruddy glow, as if he'd been outdoors for a while. "What I need to happen is for you to bring me my man, plus a mutually-agreed upon sum as payment for the lost equipment. Do that and we zero out your initial debt, just as we agreed. Do it within, say, the next four days, and I'll even recommend we forgive last night's accommodations."

"Sounds fair to me," Bix said, getting up to leave.

"Whoa, whoa! Hold on there, son. There's still the matter of accrued interest. I can't emphasize how quickly it adds up, and since it's been months—"

"Our agreement was to hand Adrian over to you," Finn said, "that's all. There was never any timeframe discussed."

Shaw laughed. "Don't be ridiculous. Open-ended contracts are a fool's pact."

"We'll bring you the man, that's it. After that, we're done. We don't owe—"

"You're really not in a position to change the terms."

"You might be surprised how wrong you are," Finn growled.

"Don't," Harrison quietly warned. He turned to Shaw. "Would you at least consider telling us why you even care about Adrian? Is this really worth what he did in Missoula?"

"The damage he inflicted on us has had long-lasting and catastrophic effects on our community and elsewhere."

"Elsewhere?"

Shaw sat down on the edge of the table. "He destroyed a critical fueling depot, so the effects have been felt all over the region, from the Rockies to the Mississippi, Mexico to Canada. It's not just Haven suffering as a result."

"So, now you want your pound of flesh. Is that it?" Finn demanded. "Set him up as an example?"

"It isn't about revenge. It's about accounting, about zeroing out the balance sheet. Haven't you figured that out by now? It's always, *always* about accounting."

"Makes sense to me," Bix said, standing up again.

"Sit down!" Finn snapped. He turned back to Shaw. "You still haven't answered why it's so important that we hand Adrian over. How is that going to fix a couple blown fuel tanks that aren't even yours?"

"I know you think of Missoula and Haven as just some isolated outposts in a world that's more dead than alive, but you're wrong. Our communities and a dozen others like it are vibrant, vital links in a complex network of interconnected settlements all over the western part of North America. We depend on each other for trade and protection. Each one of us is like a specialized and essential organ. Take one out and you throw off the body's homeostasis, and that leaves it vulnerable to opportunistic diseases. When Missoula fell, the body was weakened and has since come under attack. If we don't protect ourselves, the parasites will eventually overcome us."

"What parasites?" spat Jonah. "What diseases?"

"The agents of chaos— murder, mayhem, kidnapping, theft. They've always been among us, working to destroy us, destroy our way of living. For the past few years, though, we've managed to hold them back so that they're little more than mere annoyances. The body was healthy and could repel them. But the body has been compromised, and when people lose confidence in the body, it withers. We must reassure the people that it will not fail."

"And Adrian is a parasite?" Harrison asked.

"He is a vector. Our biggest threat is another trade network established on the east side of the Mississippi. They call themselves Brigade Six and, yes, they are just as militant as their name sounds. Fortunately, their members have been typically easy to identify, wearing recognizable insignia on their clothing and brands on the skin of their neck. We've had a longstanding agreement with them, each of us staying on our own side of the river, but the moment word of Missoula's destruction got out, they began sending in their scouts to test our defenses. The men who found you and brought you here were dispatched to monitor their activities."

"We're not with this Brigade Six."

"Clearly. Otherwise, you would already be dead and your bodies sent back to them gift wrapped. Well, the parts of your bodies we can't use. We have expenses, just like anyone else."

"So, are you convinced now?" Bix asked the others, before anyone could ask Shaw to clarify what he meant. "Can we just give them Adrian and be on our way? We don't need him anymore anyway. Hell, we'll even throw in his sister as a bonus. Win-win! Let's go."

Both Finn and Harrison immediately raised a protest. Harper looked like he wanted to say something, but decided to let the others fight it out themselves. Jonah simply crossed his arms and kept silent.

Shaw eyed Bix intensely. "Are you referring to the feral woman he had with him when he passed through here?"

"She's not—"

"Worth the trouble," Harrison said, jumping in before Bix could finish. He didn't know how Shaw would react if he found out they were in possession of a way to get rid of the nanites, but he didn't think it would play to their advantage to share that information just yet. In fact, it might give Shaw yet another excuse to hold them longer, perhaps even demand they hand the cure over in lieu of payment, and they didn't have enough of the treated nanites to help but a few dozen of the thousands of Haven's residents. The man already had all the leverage in this negotiation, despite what Finn thought about his own abilities to get them out of this.

Shaw took his time answering Harrison. His eyes remained locked on Bix for several seconds, waiting to see if the boy would spill anything more. But when it became clear Bix had gotten the message and wasn't going to offer up anything else, he turned to address Harrison. "You still have this feral as well? Why keep it alive?"

"To study. The more we know about them, the better we'll be able to defend against them, predict their behavior."

Shaw seemed satisfied with this. "They are an equally distressing issue for us," he admitted. "After Missoula went up in flames, our patrols encountered more than the usual numbers of the infected. At first, we thought they had just been displaced, but their current behavior makes little sense to us. Perhaps we could barter for some of that information you have gleaned."

Harrison leaned forward, his eyes narrowing. "Behavior?"

"Something else has woken them up, altered their movements in unexpected ways."

"They're migrating," Harrison suggested.

"This isn't the typical spring and fall movement. Usually by this time of year, everything's quieted down. Not this year. This year they appear to be traveling farther, and they seem to be converging somewhere in the south, a few hundred miles from here. Fortunately, it's happening in the middle of our lightest travel season, but we've still had to dispatch riders with travel advisories."

"Salt Lake City?"

"Farther east."

The boys exchanged glances, but Harrison didn't even flinch. "This isn't the first time it's happened, is it?" he asked. "This off-cycle migration?"

"The last time was maybe eight months after the world fell into the toilet. They came from a thousand miles around and took out nearly everyone in its path. That's why you find some cities completely empty. Most of the ferals you see now, for example the ones surrounding Haven, resulted from secondary outbreaks in other safe communities after this mass migration."

"Where were they headed that time?"

"Las Vegas, we think."

"But Salt Lake City is filled with them. Wouldn't they have gone, too?"

"The city was clear for several weeks. You could walk unmolested down State Street from Temple Square to the aquarium. But the survivors there grew careless and there was another outbreak months later. If you think the city is bad, Vegas is far times worse."

"Anyone know what triggered that particular event?"

Shaw's eyes narrowed suspiciously. His answer gave nothing away. "Your guess is as good as mine."

"Then what makes you think this event has anything to do with what Adrian did in Missoula?"

"This is what happens when you disrupt the balance. When you force people to travel along different routes, go into places they shouldn't, clear roads meant not to be used, they will inevitably stir up the ferals."

He stood up, all business again. "Four days," he said. "You will bring this Adrian to me by then."

"Finally!" Bix said, standing up yet again.

But Shaw held up a hand, and the guards moved to block the meeting room's exit. "The last time I foolishly agreed to a deal without upfront payment or collateral, you tried to stiff me. I may enjoy a significant amount of latitude here in

Haven, due to my rank and seniority, but no one is above paying their dues, not even I."

"We didn't stiff you."

"Perhaps. But fool me once, shame on you. I am going to need collateral this time."

"All we have is the truck."

"Which you will need to get back."

"What else is there?"

"Yourselves. Two of you will return to fetch the offender, plus enough to cover the additional expenses. A pair of my men will accompany you. They are authorized to decide what is fair compensation."

"Harper and I will stay," Finn offered.

"Ah, once again, you seem to think this is a negotiation, son. It's not." He pointed to Mister Blakeley and Harper. "You two will go. The rest will remain my paying guests."

"Why them?" Bix asked.

"Because I know they will keep their word and return, one for his son, the other for his brother."

CHAPTER
50

EDDIE PACED THE LENGTH OF THE HALLWAY OUTSIDE his room for the hundredth time, glancing over at the door whenever he heard a noise that suggested Hannah had gotten up and was moving about. Sleep had eluded him all night, his thoughts plagued by worries. And there was certainly enough to worry about. Enough that he was thinking it was time to start panicking.

He had asked Harrison to lead the scavenging team for multiple reasons, first and foremost, because the man tended toward caution, especially when it came to his son. If the crew encountered any unusual challenges, Harrison's natural instinct would be to expect the worst and plan accordingly. He would scrub the four-day mission at the first sign of trouble and return, empty-handed if necessary, before putting the boys into danger they couldn't handle. He had the kind of temperament the boys needed — levelheaded and reasonable, yet firm — which helped to offset their own youthful tendencies toward willfulness, recklessness, and petty distraction. Whatever Harrison decided, he would make sure they listened and abided. They might not like it. They might argue or even get angry. But they would eventually acquiesce. He would do everything he could to get them all back safely.

The other reason was to get him away from here, which would hopefully break him out of this rut he'd fallen into and his growing obsession with the cure.

But now they were long overdue, and Eddie couldn't help but assume the worst.

The storm had hit Westerton on the third day of their absence, just one day before they were due back. It swept in from the north, pounding the army base with gale-force winds that drove the snow down from the highlands and across the desert before piling up it into dunes five feet high in some places, while leaving other areas scrubbed bare. Eddie had worried a bit during the storm, but he had faith in the team. They would hunker down and wait.

The storm passed, yet the weather remained unsettled, the sky pressing forbiddingly low. Another inch of snow fell the next day, the day they were supposed to return, flakes the size of walnuts drifting silently down. Daytime temperatures remained below freezing. The day after was slightly better, mostly cloudy but without wind or precipitation, and the day after that was clear. The nights remained bitterly cold, however, and daylight brought little relief.

The group had taken five days' worth of supplies, which they could stretch out an extra four— assuming, of course, that they had been rationing from the start, which didn't seem very likely. At best guess, they might have six, maybe seven, day's worth of food and water. After that, nothing.

The seventh day dawned bright and unexpectedly warm. By midmorning, most of the snow had turned to slush. Eddie prayed it wouldn't freeze overnight.

He hoped the scavenging team hadn't needed to use their fuel to keep warm.

He hoped they hadn't slid off the road somewhere.

Or broken an axle.

And he hoped they were still unharmed.

He'd risen the eighth morning at dawn and went out to check with the guards if they'd returned over night. They hadn't, but of course he already knew that. He'd left explicit instructions to be notified the moment they showed up at the gate.

An hour after sunup, the roads were nearly dry, so he'd assembled another team to search for them. "Three hours out, three hours back," he instructed Harry Rollins and the mixed crew of former Westerton soldiers and Bunker Seven men. They were to go out in two vehicles, just in case one broke down. "That way you'll still be able to get back here before nightfall if you have any problems."

Twenty-four hours later, the search team still hadn't returned.

He now had to accept that it was a mistake to let the team go north, rather than sticking to one of the more well-traveled roads to the west or east. The reasoning had been sound at the time, but also driven by their need for weapons and ammunition. Sprawling ranches meant guns— for self-protection, hunting, and recreation. Of course the roads would be trickier to navigate, and they'd have to go slow, but that was sort of the point, to scavenge in the places past teams hadn't bothered with.

Nine days had now passed, and it was clear that both teams had perished, and now he was faced with having to tell the community at breakfast what most of them already knew to be true. Hearing it out loud, though, would dash any traces of hope.

Understandably, Hannah had worried about Bix the whole time. Eddie had managed to convince her they were fine, even as late as the sixth day. But after the seventh, then the eighth, and after the second team also failed to return, she'd fallen into despair and stopped eating. Yesterday, she'd slept through every meal, jolting upright each time Eddie entered the room and at random moments in between. She'd ask, always hopeful, if they'd returned. He wouldn't even have to say anything before the light in her eyes would dim, because she could already see the truth in his own, despite his best attempts to hide it. He tried to comfort her during the night. She fell asleep every time sobbing.

It had long surprised him, the staying power of this adolescent infatuation she held for Bix, although he reasoned it probably shouldn't. There had been so few choices for the youngsters coming of age in the bunker, and not many more here at Westerton. The boy next closest in age to her was Jareth Rollins, and he was fully two years younger than she and still showed no interest in any of the girls. Also, she hadn't made an effort to befriend any of the new boys she'd met since arriving here.

Bren remained just as devoted to Finn as Hannah was to Bix. Another surprise, given how callously the boy had treated her affections. Bren dealt with her worry differently than Hannah, though, immersing herself in work, running errands for the base, stocking supplies, washing laundry, cooking. She had always been quiet in the bunker, quiet afterwards, too. But after Finn's near fatal accident in Bunker Ten, she'd asserted herself more and more. Eddie appreciated how much of a fighter she had become, but he worried what she would do when she, too, finally accepted that Finn wasn't going to come back this time.

The door at the far end of the hallway opened, and he spun around to see who it was.

"Ah, Eddie, I see you are up already. I came to deliver to you the update." The man was silhouetted in the morning sunlight, his face hidden in shadow, but both his accent and his scent gave him away.

"Yes, Doctor Jadhari?"

"There is no problem after two days. Everyone is still happily alive and not attacking each other." The man laughed stiffly, before covering it with a thin cough. "I am sorry. I just thought you should know." He turned to go.

"No, wait." He jogged over to where the man stood. "How many so far?"

"Sixty-two. All of them are very healthy, no problems at all. Just like our new Mister Jonathan Doe."

The number surprised Eddie. He hadn't expected it to reach so high so quickly. "John Doe," he mumbled, "not Jonathan."

"Right. Well, he is still not talking, but I think he will be soon, just like our first miracle cure. By the way, she is also recovering well from her . . . incident."

Eddie hadn't wanted to move forward with the injections, especially with Harrison gone, but after the second Wraith woke, their paralyzed John Doe, it seemed like no one wanted to wait. The man's recovery had gone far more smoothly than Jennifer's, likely due to the lower dose of treated nanites, although he had yet to speak a single word. This did not seem to be by choice, as he communicated using hand gestures, but rather by defect, perhaps as a result of having not spoken for a very long time. Most importantly, he wasn't contagious, which, as in Jennifer's case, had been discovered by accident. He showed no signs of infection, whether Flense or otherwise, and had not received any medicine to aid in his recovery.

After the team failed to return on time, demand for the treatment exploded. Eddie worried the camp residents would try to take it by force, so he acceded to their demands, and the two doctors set about administering the injections.

Doctor Jadhari reached into the deep pocket of his white lab coat and pulled out a pair of syringes. "These are for you and your daughter. Inject directly into the muscle of the arm or thigh. It does not seem to matter which."

"You should hold onto them," Eddie said.

"No. There is enough for everyone in the camp right now, but that could soon change, should new people arrive. If they know about the cure, they will want it, too, so you should take yours now before there is no more left. Please, put it someplace safe, if you do not care to use it right away."

"Is it stable?"

The doctor shrugged. "So far, yes. We can always give it another pulse later if you wish to be sure." He turned and tried to leave again.

"What about the others?" Eddie asked. "The ones who don't want it? How many are there?"

"Total untreated as of this moment is seventeen. That includes you two and both of the Abramson ladies."

"Bren wanted to wait for Finn."

Doctor Jadhari nodded. "I have set aside their doses, as well, for them to administer to themselves, when the young men return." He studied Eddie's face for a moment before attempting once more to leave. Again, Eddie stopped him.

"And no negative side effects yet?"

Jadhari frowned. "Are you now having second thoughts?"

Eddie looked down at the syringes in his hand. He couldn't explain his hesitation. If anything, he now had more reason to take the treatment than he had just a week and a half ago, when he'd volunteered out of frustration to be Harrison's guinea pig. It was now clear the treatment worked, and all signs pointed to there being no adverse side effects at this new low dose. But even if there were, it seemed everyone was convinced they could never be as bad as the risk of being turned into a Wraith.

"I understand your hesitation," Doctor Jadhari said, wagging his head. "You are unwilling to give up the abilities they have granted you."

"That's not it," Eddie replied, although he didn't fully believe it.

"It is my opinion that it is foolish to torment yourself over it," Doctor Jadhari said. "Do not wait, especially now, after recent events." He gestured toward the door, bowing his head this time, as if asking permission to leave.

Eddie nodded.

Everything had been quiet in the immediate aftermath of the attack at the south gate, not a single Wraith sighting. But the day after Harrison and his team left, they'd begun to show up again. And since the day of the snowstorm, the number of sightings and shootings along the fence had ticked steadily upward. He didn't know if the weather had stirred the creatures up again. More troubling was the thought they might be planning another attack. It appeared to be the same pattern as in the lead-up to the previous incident.

He knew the assault on the back gate was at least partially to blame for the sudden demand for the treatment, particularly after Jordan Wilcox's infection and his unavoidable slaying. His wife, Sarah, was left without a husband, their children fatherless, and it terrified everyone to think it could happen to any of them should there be another breach. They would rather be torn apart and eaten than to be the ones perpetrating those horrible acts, perhaps on their own family members.

"Keep those syringes in a safe place, Eddie," the doctor repeated from the doorway. "And do not wait too long to use them."

CHAPTER

"WHERE THE HELL ARE THEY?"

"For the last time, Bix, sit down," Jonah grumbled. "You're making me nervous."

Bix ignored him and walked over to the window and looked out onto the motel parking lot. "It's been almost a week. What the hell are they doing? They should be back by now."

"Finn?" Jonah said. "Tell him."

Finn didn't say anything. He hadn't spoken more than a few dozen words to anyone since his brother and Bix's father left to fetch Adrian from Westerton. He'd been too focused on how they might escape from here, should it come to that. In fact, he didn't think Bix and Jonah were taking their predicament seriously enough. They were utterly convinced their people would come through for them, but Finn wasn't so inclined to leave his fate in their hands. It didn't matter to him that he would have in the past. Times had changed, and so had he. They might have left their blood relatives behind, but when it came to making choices about one's survival, people always chose what was best for themselves.

"One day's drive there," Bix continued muttering, as he paced the room. He went over to the door and reached for the knob, but he didn't grab hold of it. "A long day, sure, but still. Plus, one day to drive back, and maybe a day to negotiate and load up supplies. It's been twice that now." He spun around. "Do you think Eddie refused to hand Adrian over?"

"Eddie wouldn't, especially if it meant getting us free," Jonah said. "It was your father's call to keep Adrian alive from the beginning."

"And a damn good thing, too, it turns out."

"I'm just saying, maybe he's the one refusing to let Adrian go."

"Don't put this on him! He'd never put Adrian over me."

"Sure, but the way he's been acting—"

"No, it had to be someone else."

"Who else is going to refuse to trade him? We've all wanted him gone."

"Jennifer wouldn't."

"She has no vote," Finn said. "Besides, if she wants to stay with Adrian, let her come, too."

Bix gaped at him in shock. "She didn't blow up the fuel tanks." But then his eyes widened with a new realization. "Do you think they took off, Adrian and Jennifer? Maybe that's what happened, they escaped, and now they can't find him. Oh, shit. We are so screwed if they got away."

"Bix!" Jonah snapped. "I won't say it again. Sit down and shut up."

"We should have been planning how to get out of here. I knew from the gecko we were in trouble."

"No one could've— Did you just say gecko?"

"What?"

"You said you knew from the gecko. It's *get go*, not gecko."

"No it's not. It's gecko. He sits on your shoulder and whispers in your ear. That's how you know things, from the gecko."

"What? Are you talking about your conscience? Your conscience isn't a gecko. Well, maybe yours is, but—"

"I know that! I'm not stupid. Your conscience is a cricket. The gecko is more like a . . . a guardian angel."

Jonah gave Finn a helpless look.

"Actually, Bix is right," Finn said.

"Ha! Told you!"

"Not about the lizard," Finn said. "You're right that we should've been figuring out how to escape, because something has definitely gone wrong with the exchange. It should've happened by now. Thankfully, not all of us have been just sitting around waiting."

"You have a plan?" Bix asked.

"We can't escape from here," Jonah hissed. "This place is a fortress. To escape, we'd have to get out of our rooms, out of the building, past guards, who knows how far on foot to the walls, then over or through both of them. And that's the easy part. Then the real fun begins. It's impossible."

"It's not impossible."

"Fine. Improbable then," Jonah said. "Let's say we manage to get past the walls. We still have a two-mile hike through Wraithopolis. Remember Salt Lake City? Now picture that, except ten times worse. We lost Kari there, remember? Maybe you two are okay with getting torn to shreds, but there's no way I'm taking that risk."

"They won't eat you," Bix said. "They'll just turn you into one of them."

"Because that's so much better."

"All we need to do is get a car," Finn calmly explained. "We threaten to ram the—"

"Absolutely not, Finn!" Jonah exclaimed. "That's a death sentence for everyone inside the walls. Or worse."

"We're not responsible for these people."

Jonah stared at him, appalled at the suggestion. "You're insane. Both of you."

"We can do it, Jonah," Bix whispered. "We have Finn."

"No," Jonah said, gravely shaking his head. "No, he's not Finn. The old Finn? He couldn't even conceive of something so despicable."

"Shut up," Bix growled.

Jonah grabbed him by the arms. "You know it's true, Bix. Your friend is gone. And what's left, it's . . . ." He sighed, shaking his head. "It's whatever was left when he died. He's not human anymore. He's a freaking machine. He's what the creators of the nanites were probably secretly aiming for when they put them inside us: supersoldiers."

Finn rose slowly to his feet. There was a terrible look in his eyes, so dark and stormy that Jonah realized immediately he'd pushed too far, and for the first time he could ever remember, he was terrified at what Finn might do to him. All he had to do was reach out and grab him by the neck and give his hand a little twitch, and Jonah's spine would snap as easily as Harper's wrist. He could do it, and if he did, there'd be no recovering. Some of the things Finn had done since crawling out of bed back there in Bunker Ten shouldn't be possible, like lifting that street sign. And yet they'd happened.

Finn took a step toward Jonah, but the door behind him opened, and like a switch, the iciness in his eyes vanished. He turned and gazed indifferently at the newcomer.

"Come with us," the guard said.

Another armed man entered the room and quickly circled around the trio. He jerked his rifle toward the door. Finn knew there would be at least one more guard standing outside on the walkway, maybe two. That was the routine on the few occasions the boys had been allowed out of their "guest accommodations." It might look like a standard room in a cheap motel, but it was a cell. There were even metal bars on the windows.

"Where are you taking us?" Bix demanded. "Is my father back?"

The man didn't answer.

They were led down the rusty metal and cement staircase to the ground, then across the parking lot to a waiting van. The drive was short — everywhere inside the wall was only a few minutes from every other place — and when they stopped, the door slid open and they were told to get out.

Shaw stood on the bottom step of a stark red building, his already diminutive stature further diminished by four massive columns of yellow stone. He had his back turned to them and didn't bother to face them when they were brought over. He simply started walking up the steps, expecting them to follow. Not a word was spoken. The boys had no choice but to see what awaited them inside.

"This is bad," Bix whispered, nodding his head toward the inscription above the entrance. It may have been years since the government fell, but the word COURTHOUSE still managed to evoke trepidation.

"Quiet!" a guard snapped.

Two men stood beside the doors. They reached over and opened them so the procession could enter. Shaw marched into the darkened empty lobby without pause, then passed through the inert metal detector. His footsteps echoed against the bare stone walls, further deepening the sense of dread that settled over them.

Another man approached. "Courtroom Four today," he said.

"Four?"

"Large crowd. They're expecting you."

Shaw nodded, then made for the stairs. The guards pushed the boys in the back to hurry them along.

Up one flight, down a hall, through another set of double doors.

The chamber was packed with people. Shaw gestured for the boys to line up against the back wall. He held a finger to his lips, then backed himself up and stood beside Finn.

"All rise!" a voice boomed a minute later, and everyone seated obeyed as a woman entered from a hidden door behind the bench.

"Be seated!"

The woman took her place in the judge's chair. She didn't wait for the din to stop. "Welcome back," she said in a tiny, squeaky voice. "We're here for final judgment in the case of Julia Dehoyen, who was found guilty this morning of breach of contract. Has an equitable assessment been reached?"

A man rose from one of the lawyer's tables. "It has, Madam Chief Controller."

"And what say you?"

"In the matter of Julia Dehoyen versus the Distinguished Community of Haven, on the first count for the crime of breach of contract, the accountants require fair recompense of two pints."

"Pints?" Bix whispered. *"Of what, beer? Milk?"*

Jonah elbowed him into silence.

"And on the second count?"

"In the matter of Julia Dehoyen versus the Distinguished Community of Haven, on the count for the crime of breach of contract, the accountants require fair recompense of one kidney."

A sob rose from the vicinity of the other lawyer's table. Bix craned his neck to see who it was, but the only view he could get was of the back of a woman's head.

"Very well. Sentence in the first part to be carried out immediately. Sentence in the second part shall be two weeks from today."

Bix looked over at Shaw and mouthed, *"What the hell? Kidney?"*

Shaw didn't answer.

The door through which they had entered the courtroom opened again, and a man appeared, pushing some kind of machine covered in dials and lights, and from which a multitude of tubes and wires sprouted. He passed the gallery and through the bar, coming to a stop in front of the woman who had just been sentenced. She didn't resist when he gestured for her arm.

"What are they doing?" Bix quietly asked.

A woman sitting in the chair right in front of him turned and scowled with irritation.

They watched as the man inserted a needle into the woman's arm, then turned on the machine, drawing her blood through the clear plastic tubing. It made a low hum and clicked loudly at regular intervals. This appeared to signal to the witnesses that it was okay to converse quietly.

"They're taking her blood?"

Shaw stepped away from the wall and over to face the trio of boys. "Two pints, to be precise," he said, as if it weren't already obvious. "That's what the accountants calculated would cover her debt."

"What are they going to do with it?" Finn asked. He seemed more curious than disturbed.

"That's a plasmapheresis machine. It's spinning out her blood, separating out its components. Don't worry, the process is harmless. Missus Dehoyen will suffer no ill effects. In fact, the bulk of her blood will be returned to her. The rest belongs to Haven."

"What do you do with it?"

"We have over four thousand residents inside the walls right now, another thousand at various of our outposts . At any given time, a fair portion of us require medical care. Resources are limited, especially medicines, so we've learned to make do with the blood of donors for its curative properties."

"Well, duh," Bix said. "That's because of the—"

"Immunity," Jonah said. The look on his face warned Bix not to say anything more.

Shaw waited a moment, then continued. "This is how Haven citizens repay their debts to each other. We extract what we need from those who fail to meet their contractual obligations."

The boys exchanged troubled glances. It did not appear as if these people fully understood, or were even aware of, what was in their blood, and why some people, but not all, never got sick.

"And the kidney?" Jonah asked. "How does taking that from her help?"

Shaw smiled. "Same thing. Kidneys, pieces of liver, a lung. Our doctors will transplant them into patients who need them."

"You're insane," Bix hissed. "How could you people be so— so *barbaric*?"

Shaw shook his head. "It's neither insane, nor barbaric, my boy. In fact, it's the most civilized thing we can do for our people."

Someone stepped over and handed Shaw a piece of paper. He studied it for a moment, nodded and whispered something into the messenger's ear, then handed the sheet back.

"What was that?" Finn asked, even though he already had a good idea. He'd heard what Shaw had whispered.

"This week's court docket. Given that your debt has not been paid in a timely manner, your case has been scheduled for adjudication. Your hearing and sentencing are set for the day after tomorrow."

CHAPTER
52

THEY FOUND EDDIE IN THE SHOWER, HIS BLOOD-
soaked clothes sitting in a heap on the floor, and the steam
so thick not even he could see through it. He only knew they
were coming by the soft scuff of their approaching feet on
the wet tile.

The swirling clouds of mist and distorted voices
resurrected a distant memory, and for a moment he was back
in the boiler room of the bunker, the damaged pipe spewing
scalding water vapor that enveloped his entire body. He
remembered the excruciating pain, followed by the slow,
agonizing descent toward death. Then the bewildering return
to health.

"Mister Mancuso, is that you in there?"

"Don't touch the clothes! They're contaminated," he
shouted, before remembering that most of the people in
camp were now immune from the Flense.

The new attack had started shortly after one o'clock,
when all but a few were at lunch. A pair of perimeter guards
reported seeing the first vanguard of Wraiths sweep over a
rocky abutment about a quarter mile away. There were less
than a dozen, roughly the same number as had been lurking
about in the frozen arroyos crisscrossing the desert closer to
the fence line. The men had taken to sighting the creatures
through their gun scopes and betting each other how few
bullets they'd need to take them out should they decide to
get any closer, when the entire lot of them suddenly

vanished. This prompted one of the guards to lower his rifle from his shoulder and stare out over the desert, his vision no longer restricted by the scope's narrow aperture, but also unassisted. He squinted in concentration, until his partner asked him what he was doing. "Something's spooked them."

"Or the damn things are messing with us." He, too, lowered his weapon away from his face.

The two returned to their patrol, scanning the barren landscape with more trepidation than before.

Movement caught the first guard's eye, far from where they'd seen the original group. "Hey," he said, and pointed.

It had the hallmarks of a coordinated assault, although it was neither large nor sustained. The Wraiths made a beeline for the fence, right toward the spot of the previous attack. The alarm was immediately raised, and even though the Wraiths were fast, they still didn't reach the barrier before three more guards had joined the first two. The killers came as silent as smoke, racing over the rough terrain. The only sounds were the soft pads of their hands and feet and the crackle of ice breaking on frozen puddles. When the first gunshot rang out, they broke ranks, scattering with growls and hisses. But they kept coming, and were soon leaping for the only part of the fence that still remained electrified.

Nevertheless, they were easily eliminated.

The second vanguard came on the opposite side of camp, attacking the front gate. The response there was slower, and it took the shooters longer to push them back.

It was the first gunshot that drew Eddie out of his nap, and he initially didn't realize what was happening. He'd been sound asleep, the treadmill of worry and guilt that had kept him going for the past several days finally shutting down. His first thought upon waking was that he was napping in his house in Chicago, the sun shining through the window. He could actually smell the fresh cut grass and hear the game on the television, and he reflexively reached to the side to retrieve the beer can he'd set on the coffee table. The crackle of gunfire sounded like the neighborhood kids setting off fireworks in the street. Was it Independence Day? But his arm wouldn't move. It was trapped underneath Hannah's head, and he realized he wasn't in Chicago, and the smell wasn't fresh grass but mud and gunpowder.

He gently extracted his arm, telling her to stay put, when she began to stir. His shirt was still damp from her tears, so they couldn't have been asleep for very long. "Don't go anywhere."

"What?"

"Gunshots at the gate. I'm just going to check."

He stepped out as the first shots from the front gate sounded, and he spun, undecided for a moment, then headed toward the unprotected run along the southern line, where he sensed another group of Wraiths was about to attack.

It took him almost three hours to remove all the bodies afterward and burn them. In the meantime, several of the guards had formed a posse to search outside the wire for any live ones. They went to the dry creek bed and as far as the ridge where the Wraiths had first been spotted, but found nothing but a few scraps of torn clothing, a badly deteriorated shoe, and several piles of hard, black excrement.

After that, no one could argue the attacks were random or chaotic.

"What is it?" Eddie shouted, peering out through the swirling fog of his shower. Another attack, and so soon after the last one? Could it have been a prelude to a larger, more sustained siege? The quality of light coming in through the frosted skylight overhead told him the sun was low on the horizon. It was going to be a long night for everyone, but particularly for the guards. "Hello?"

"They're back."

He sighed. There was urgency in the young man's voice, but, strangely enough, no alarm. "Where is it this time? Which gate?"

"Not the Wraiths, Mister Mancuso. It's Mister Blakeley. He's back. They've returned."

Eddie froze a moment, shocked by the news, then spun the shower tap closed. "All of them?"

"Just him and the Bolles boy, sir. And two other men, strangers."

"Finn or Harper?"

"The normal one, sir."

Eddie's heart sank. *No Finn and no Bix. No Jonah, either.*

"They're at the main gate."

"Well, let them in, for god's sake!"

"We tried. There's a situation. You had better come out."

He stood there for another second, water dripping off his body and draining away. The contaminated blood was long gone, washed into the drain, but the smell of smoke and charred flesh still filled his nose. It was in his skin, even though he'd scrubbed. He reached for his towel. "Okay, give me a couple minutes."

"Yes, sir. I'll let them know you're on your way."

* * *

He was able to convince the Haven men accompanying Harrison and Harper to come inside the base, although he suspected it was his decision to let them keep their weapons more than the promise of a warm meal that decided it for them.

"I'm sure you can understand why we're not happy about this," Stephen Largent told them. They'd gone to the commander's office to discuss the terms, and he stood with his arms crossed over his chest and leaned against the filing cabinet by the door, as if to prevent them from leaving until they came to a mutually agreeable understanding. "You're holding our people hostage over payment for—"

"They're not hostages," the shorter of the two men replied. His name was Curly, and Harper had already advised Eddie that they could take him at his word. He wasn't so sure about the other guy. "They're being held as collateral," Curly explained, "as valuable to Haven as they are to you. Shaw has no interest in harming them as long as you agree to the original terms and hand over the fellow who blew up the fuel tanks in Missoula."

"And if we don't?" Eddie asked. "Hypothetically speaking."

Stephen stepped forward, frowning. "Whoa, hold on, Eddie. Why wouldn't we agree? After what that man did to us at the bunker, what he did to you and the others? To Finn and Bix?" He shook his head in disbelief. "Why would we even consider not doing it? He's a waste of space and supplies. Hell, it's a wonder why no one's taken the initiative and shot him already."

"We don't barter with human lives. There has to be another way."

"Hypothetically," the second man said, rising from his seat and frowning with such intensity that Stephen immediately backed away. The man's name was Bear, and unlike Curly, the reason for his moniker was patently obvious. He was unusually large and hairy. Carpets of black fur protruded from the bottoms of his sleeves, and another thick tuft of hair peeked out from the V in his shirt. "That would be a breach of contract," he growled. "It won't be good for your boys. Hypothetically."

"The deal's already been struck," Curly said, trying vainly to pull his colleague back. "The terms are clear. Let's not muddy the waters here, Bear. We just want what's due us.

Once payment's been made, we'll send all your folks back. Unharmed."

"Payment is due immediately," Bear persisted. "We've already wasted too much time dealing with the damn ferals."

"That wasn't their fault," Curly reasoned. "We'll explain to the Chief Controller what happened when we get back."

"What happened?" Eddie asked.

"Ran into a horde. Larger'n any I've ever seen before. We had to hole up a couple days before they cleared out."

"They're gone now," Bear said. "So just give us a full tank of gas and our payment, and we'll be on our way."

"We've had our own problems with the Wraiths," Eddie said, addressing Curly. "Which is why we can't let you go. Not tonight."

"You have no choice," Bear warned.

Eddie stepped up to him. Despite being a full head shorter and a hundred pounds lighter, he wasn't intimidated by the hairy mountain of muscle standing before him. "I will not put the safety of my people at risk, whether here or in Haven. Leaving this late in the day is out of the question."

"We have weapons."

"You misunderstand. Our main refueling tanks are offsite," he lied, "and I'm not about to ask anyone here to take the risk of going out to it after sundown. Take the invitation to spend the night. You can return to Haven in the morning, after sunrise. *With* payment." He paused. "And we won't even charge you for the room, meals, and fuel."

The men stared at each other for a moment. Maybe Bear sensed the strength hidden within Eddie, or maybe he was all bluster, but he backed down. "Your choice," he grumbled. "Ain't my blood they want."

Eddie shook his head. He turned to Stephen. "One of the empty rooms in Building 47. They can spend the night there. We'll finalize the details in the morning."

The men exchanged glances again, then nodded.

"We'll pay for the hospitality," Curly said. "Whatever is reasonable."

"Reasonable," Eddie sniffed derisively. "Right."

He watched them go, troubled by the look Bear gave him as they left, and decided to make sure to post a couple armed guards outside their room.

CHAPTER
53

THE FIRST TIME THE POWER FAILED WAS SHORTLY
after two in the morning. Only a few people noticed, those
who were outside patrolling the perimeter, plus a few others
unable to sleep. The lights blinked off for less than ten
seconds before the backup generators kicked in.

Eddie woke, sensing something was wrong, but all was
quiet. He slipped out of bed and padded silently over to the
window in his bare feet. Hannah's faint snores hammered his
eardrums. In the still of the night, he almost believed he
could hear the slow and steady drumbeat of her heart.

He pulled the heavy curtain aside and looked out. He
didn't know about the generators, as his barrack was about
as far away from them as possible, and his window faced the
wrong direction. His view was of the side of the adjacent
building, where Harrison and Bix shared a room. Light
spilled into the passageway from a lamp on the road out in
front. A wedge of the clapboard siding on the opposite
building remained deep in shadow.

But a light was on inside the Blakeley's room, some of it
escaping around the edges of the curtain covering the
window.

Eddie let his own curtain fall back into place, and
darkness returned. He went silently back to his bed, but
didn't sit. Despite the inadequate light, he could see perfectly
well, and he easily found his clothes and put them on. Yet as

quiet as he was, he knew Hannah was awake now. The tone of her breathing had changed, and heart rate had increased.

"I'm just going next door for a few minutes to speak with Mister Blakeley," he whispered. "I want to talk to him about what else we might be able to give Haven to free our boys."

"I wish Bix were here. I wish they all were."

"They're fine, honey. Don't worry. Once we work everything out, they'll send him and the others back."

"Do you trust those men?"

"Not at all, but they hold all the cards." He hesitated at the door, realizing how defeatist that sounded, and he wanted to tell her that the distrust went both ways, so it was a matter of coming to some mutual understanding they could all live with; it was just the way of the world now. "They don't seem to want trouble," he said instead. "They have no reason to hold our people, once we give them what they think they're owed."

"Okay, Daddy. But take your gun."

"Got it. Don't worry."

The low hum of the backup generators reached his ears the moment he stepped outside the building, but his thoughts were elsewhere, and it didn't register that the main powerplant had gone down. He was thinking about the boys still being held in Haven, as well as the rescue crew he'd sent out for the team days before. He had come to accept that they were both lost, but now he had new hope the second team might still be alive. Maybe they had encountered Wraiths, as the Haven men had described, and had been forced to sit tight. Or maybe they'd been captured by a different patrol and were now sitting in Haven waiting for Harrison to return to settle the debt.

The hallway in the second building was just as dark and empty and quiet as his own, but unlike his barrack, this one was filled with ghostly whispers emanating from the locked rooms up ahead. Days before leaving, Harrison had requested Adrian and Jennifer be put in the room across the hall from his own, in part so he could keep an eye on them, but also to keep them away from the rest of the camp. Out of sight, out of mind, as the saying went. The room had its own bathroom, and the door could be locked from either side.

Eddie had put the Haven men in the room beside it.

He hesitated just inside the front door, puzzled. He listened and sniffed the air, but he knew already that neither Harrison nor Harper was in the darkened hallway keeping watch. Over Eddie's objections, Harrison had insisted on not involving anyone else in the camp, concerned that someone might either try to help the men sneak Adrian out, or else bring harm on their Haven "guests" for keeping the boys hostage. He seemed to understand instinctively that Eddie wasn't willing to give Adrian up.

He slipped quickly over to Harrison's door and rapped gently. It rattled loosely in the frame and the knock was loud in his ears. There was no answer. He leaned forward and placed his ear against the wood to listen. Someone was inside, snoring. If Harrison was asleep, then why wasn't Harper on guard duty?

Eddie's skin crawled with the sensation of being watched. He glanced toward the far end of the hallway, but the shadows remained as silent as death.

He turned to face the opposite door. The voices had quieted after his knock, but he knew someone was still awake inside the room. He heard a bedspring creak, then the faintest of scuffs of something brushing across the floor, followed by the rustle of fabric and a soft cough.

A faint band of light seeped out from underneath the door, flickering, illuminating the toes of his shoes. A candle, not lamplight, shifted as someone crossed the room. He reached over and gave it a quick rap.

The footsteps sounded again, louder and with greater urgency. Not toward the door, but initially in a different direction. Then silence.

Eddie knocked again, louder this time. "Adrian?"

The footsteps approached, then stopped on the other side of the door. He reached down and placed his hand on the knob. The door should be locked, and the key was on a hook inside Harrison's room.

"Just checking," he said. "It's Eddie."

The knob was wrenched from his grip and the door flew open. The beam of a flashlight hit him square in the eyes, momentarily blinding him. There was an even brighter flash, accompanied by a flower of pain just behind his eye socket. The next moment, he found himself on his back on the floor of the hallway, the lights on and someone kneeling beside him, shaking him and screaming his name.

"Hannah?" he said, groggily. He raised a hand, confused that he could see only out of one eye, and felt pressure on the blind side of his face. "Bren? What—?" He stopped when the pressure suddenly released and the blindness cleared.

Kaleagh Abramson was kneeling beside him. She tossed away the cloth she'd been holding against his face and leaned in closer. "You were shot," she explained. "Hannah heard it, came and got us. Looks like the bleeding's stopped. You were lucky. It just grazed you."

He reached up to touch the wound, concerned that it was deeper than she'd indicated. The blood was still slick, not yet tacky. He couldn't have been out more than a few minutes, just long enough for Hannah to find him and get help.

"Which one was it?" he asked, frowning in confusion. He tried to sit up, but dizziness swept over him. "The one who shot me? Was it Adrian? How'd he get a gun?"

"I don't know."

"You didn't see anyone?"

He tried to stand, but only got to his knees before falling back, weakened by another wave of lightheadedness and nausea. The door to Adrian's room was open, and he sensed it was empty. He spun around, checking the next door down. It was shut, and it also felt devoid of life. "It was the Haven men!" he yelped. "They must've known we'd try to negotiate and took Adrian! We need to alert the gate!"

"No, you need to lie down," Kaleagh scolded. "You were just shot in the head!"

"You said it grazed me!"

"And you could have a concussion!"

"I'm fine," he declared. There was still time to stop them, but he'd have to hurry. "I know where they're headed."

"They?"

"The motor pool! They need a vehicle."

"Eddie Mancuso! Don't you dare—"

The sound of an engine revving loudly some distance away cut her off. This time, she didn't stop Eddie as he leapt to his feet. He staggered a few steps, bracing himself against the wall, then started to run toward the doors. "I need to get to the gate!"

"Wait a minute!" Kaleagh shouted.

"I'm okay! Wake Harrison up!" he yelled. "Find Harper!" Then he burst out of the building and ran down the steps. He sprinted toward the sound of the engine and saw the truck race past the administration building a couple hundred yards away. One of the sentries had stepped out of the guard shack and was shouting and gesturing for them to stop, but the vehicle only accelerated straight toward him.

"Move!" Eddie screamed. "Get out of—"

The thump of metal on flesh jolted him nearly as hard as a bullet to the chest. He lurched to a stop, saw the guard flew into the air, limbs splayed out. He flipped like a doll and hit the thick lamppost, snapping his spine.

Get up, Eddie whispered. *Dear god get up!*

But he knew he wouldn't. He'd heard the spine snap. The man lay crumpled in a heap on the ground and didn't move.

The truck crashed into the gate, twisting metal and shearing a half dozen posts out of the ground. A second guard appeared and tried to fire upon the retreating vehicle, but he had one hand on the buckle of his loose pants, which had slid halfway down his buttocks. He cradled his rifle in the other arm and tried to fire. The bullets sprayed in a wide arc, producing sparks when they hit the tailgate, but failed to slow it down. With a loud crunch, the gate panel slipped off the front of the truck and slid beneath the heavy tires, emerging out the back a crumpled and mangled mess. It dragged behind for a hundred feet before detaching.

Eddie stopped to verify that the first man was dead. The second guard had abandoned all dignity and made one last attempt to stop the truck. He shuffled forward, pants at his ankles, and fired again, emptying his magazine. He went as far as the reach of the flood lamps, but wouldn't go any farther.

The truck's taillights dwindled into tiny red dots. The engine's roar fell to a growl, then a hum. Then that, too, was lost to distance.

It was at this point that Eddie realized the main generator was offline and they were on backup. He opened his mouth to call out to the guard, who'd bent to retrieve his trousers. A flash of movement caught his eye. The guard didn't even see it coming. His screams tore the night as the Wraith carried him off, but they ended as abruptly as they started, and in the silence that followed came the hisses and growls of the third and final attack on Westerton Army Base.

CHAPTER
54

THE SECOND TIME THE POWER WENT OFF IT STAYED off, throwing the entire compound into pitch blackness. There was no backup for the backup generators.

Eddie spun around without even thinking and sprinted back toward the barracks. Faint starlight was all he needed to see just fine, but everyone else was blind. They stumbled out of their quarters, alarmed by the sounds of the truck crashing through the gate and the gunfire, confused by the absence of light. They were as vulnerable as newborn kittens, and they didn't even know it.

He shouted at them to grab their guns and secure the front gate. "There's been a breach! The gate is down! We're under attack!"

He met Hannah and the Abramson women on the road in front of the barracks, encased in their own little puddle of illumination from Bren's tiny flashlight. "Where's Harrison?" he asked.

"We knocked, but he didn't come out."

He herded them back inside the building and started pounding on the Blakeley's door, shouting Harrison's name. The snoring continued without change. "Stand back," he warned. "I'm breaking it down!"

"You can't do that!" Kaleagh said, but he pushed her away and kicked at the door. It flew open and smashed against the wall. A body lay crumpled on the floor at the foot of the beds, the source of the snores.

"It's Harper," Eddie said, quickly stepping over and shaking him. "He's unconscious."

"Why is he here? And where's Mister Blakeley?" Bren cried. "He's not here!"

Eddie stood up. "Barricade yourselves in here. Block the windows! Do not open the door for anything!"

"But what's happening?" Bren asked. "What about the backup generators?"

"Everything's down. So is the main gate," he answered. He didn't tell her about the dead guard, or the one that had been snatched away. "It's the Haven men. They took Adrian and smashed through. They must have forced Harrison to help them escape."

"And Jennifer. She's gone, too."

"I knew we couldn't trust them," Hannah said.

"Just stay here, honey. I need to get out there and help protect the base."

"I can go, too," Kaleagh said, stepping out into the hallway with him.

"No," he snapped. "I need you to stay with the girls. Please. Try and revive Harper. Maybe he can tell you what happened."

"It's bad out there, isn't it?"

"They're coming. They're probably already inside. Get Harrison's guns and stick together. If anything tries to get in without first identifying itself, shoot it. Don't hesitate."

He hurried out into the night.

Flashlight beams and shouts of concern pierced the darkness from all directions. He glanced over and saw that a crowd of people had gathered by the front gate. Someone was shouting to get a doctor for the dead guard. A group of people had gone out to get the mangled gate panel, circles of light wobbling in the darkness. Eddie wanted to warn them, but it didn't matter at this point. They were all in danger, no matter where they stood.

A vehicle rushed past, heading toward the other end of the compound. He could hear other engines cranking up, running, but still no generator. Without power, they were helpless. The fence alone was little obstacle to the Wraiths. They could come in at any point along the perimeter.

He took one more look toward the front and decided there were enough people to repair the breach, then turned and made for the generator shack, where his skills as a mechanic would be put to better use.

Despite the confusion, most people seemed more angry than scared. Word had already spread that the men from Haven were responsible. Someone had taken the initiative to assign extra guards to patrol the fence line; others showed up on their own at the south gate. Eddie reached the generator shack and waded through the mass of concerned onlookers. Some were children, and he shouted at them to go back to their rooms, that it was too dangerous for them to be outside. A few took off running. Most ignored him.

Two vehicles had been parked in front of the shack, their headlights aimed toward the inert generators. The air reeked of fuel and oil. "What happened?" he asked. "Are we out of diesel?"

"Tank's full," someone replied. "They won't start."

"Neither of them?"

"No."

"Let me see."

He stepped closer, pulled the cap off the tank and sniffed inside.

"Sugar?"

He shook his head, then aimed his flashlight deeper into the darkness behind the hulking machines. "Feed lines have been cut. Who was guarding the shack?"

No one answered.

"Did anyone see who did this?"

Again, silence.

"Are you listening to me?" he screamed. "We need to get power to the fence now! Repair those hoses!"

"We've got the perimeter covered."

"You're not hearing me!"

"We've beaten them back twice already."

"The front gate's gone, and a Wraith took one of the guards!"

"It did?"

"Who was it," one of the youngsters asked, the first indication of concern tainting his voice. "Was it my dad? He was on duty tonight."

Eddie turned and frowned at the boy. What the hell was wrong with everybody?

"We got this covered, Mister Mancuso," someone else yelled.

"The generators are dead! We have no lights! The fence is—"

A gunshot rang out, coming from somewhere off on the north side of the base, near his barrack.

Another sharp report shattered the quiet, but this time from the southeast corner. Everyone's head swiveled. There was a shout from somewhere near the gate, and the chain link rattled as something hit it. Then another. Someone shot into the darkness.

Gunfire began in earnest after that, sounding like popcorn, and it came from every direction.

"Too late! Leave the generators!" Eddie roared. "Grab any weapon you can find! Get to the cars! We've got to get out of here!"

He spun around searching the perimeter for places where the attack seemed lightest. He could see figures climbing the wire, reaching the top, coming over, and he knew they were everywhere. It wasn't just a dozen or two this time. There were hundreds.

He shoved the pistol into his waistband, then grabbed the two nearest children and lifted them up. "Evacuate!" he screamed. "The base is being overrun! Get out now! Everyone run!"

He sprinted back toward the center of the compound, heading for the barracks. He could already hear the screams behind him as the Wraiths took their victims. He could smell blood on the wind. And beneath the screams of terror and pain, he could hear the thick, wet sound of flesh being torn from the bones.

The children in his hands wailed in fright, screaming for their parents. Eddie didn't know where they were or why they'd allowed their kids to wander about unaccompanied. This was what he had worried about, that once people got the treatment, they'd grow reckless. The cure didn't prevent death; in fact, it raised the likelihood. Proof that they had all feared infection more than dying.

He thought about asking the children where their quarters were, but decided that taking the time to reunite them with their families would be foolhardy.

A small military utility truck sped toward them, spraying gravel as it made for the front gate. He saw a man behind the wheel, the frightened face of a child in the passenger seat, and in the split second as they approached, Eddie considered tossing the two children into the small open bed. But the opportunity passed too quickly. The truck roared off, then fishtailed as it tried to make the turn at the end of the road. Both tires on the left-hand side snatched up onto the curb and caught. Eddie watched in horror as the truck lifted up, still moving fast. For a second, he thought the driver would regain control, but the truck didn't fall back onto its wheels. It continued to roll, then crashed into the flag post and stopped, spinning slowly on its roof.

A moment later, a pair of Wraiths were on it, then inside, tearing at the human beings trapped in their seatbelts.

Eddie turned and ran, sprinting between buildings and avoiding the other camp residents. Everyone was in a panic now, screaming, drawing attention to themselves. All was chaos. The barrier was gone. And everyone was just trying to get away.

He rounded a turn and skidded to a stop. The Wraiths were all over the barracks. He was too late.

CHAPTER

55

The TRIAL — IF IT COULD EVEN BE CALLED THAT —
had gone pretty much exactly how the boys had imagined it
would.

"Fucking sham is what this is," Bix complained. "How
much you want to bet they never even cared about getting
Adrian? They probably took Dad and Harper out to the
desert and shot them in the head. Or let them out just past
the outer wall."

"Jesus, Bix," Jonah said. "How could you even think
those things?"

"It's been a week since they left," Finn pointed out.
"You still believe they're coming back?"

"Oh, like you knew this was going to happen."

"I told you then we'd never see them again. I told you
we needed to figure out how to get ourselves out of this, but
you didn't want to listen. We had countless chances to fight
our way out of here, and now we can't."

They had been locked inside a holding cell in the
basement of the courthouse where their case had been heard
earlier that day. The judge was the same woman they'd seen
before. No one stood to defend them, and their self-defense
was summarily dismissed as irrelevant. Shaw had shown up,
but he'd testified as a witness for the other side. He carefully
outlined what the agreement had been, and what had
transpired in the weeks since. "It's an open-and-shut case of
contractual default," he explained.

In his closing statement, Shaw did add one comment to the boys' defense, much to their surprise. He admitted that the men he'd sent with Harrison and Harper were still missing, so it was possible they'd encountered problems on the road that prevented them from fulfilling their end of the bargain.

"Isn't it equally as plausible that your men were victims at the hands of their people?"

"It's possible," Shaw said, "but I have my doubts."

The judge considered this for a moment, then rendered her verdict. "While we must assume your people intended to make good on the promise to deliver full and satisfactory compensation, intent itself has no currency here. It does not erase the debt from the books. And whereas we have forgiven some debts in the past, the law — like our current predicament — leaves us without wiggle room. Justice must be blind and equitably rendered as expediently as possible. So I now find the defendants fully liable for all debts, both previously agreed upon and newly incurred." She banged the gavel once. "As for recompense, how soon can your accountants finish their calculations, Mister Chao? I have an opening this afternoon for serum extractions."

"I must beg the court's indulgence, Madam Chief Controller. We have the initial assessment, but for any addendums, the man assigned to do those calculations is currently outside the wall dealing with a security situation."

She nodded. "Yes, well, security of our beloved community must always take precedence. Very well. We'll hold off sentencing for twenty-four hours."

"Thank you, ma'am."

She banged the gavel a second time, and the boys were taken by force into the holding cell until their next appearance.

Finn went to the door and grabbed one of the bars and gave it an experimental tug. It was solid. Even with his enhanced strength, he might not be able to break it. He repeated the test with each bar, before walking over to the window. One glance told him it was too small for them to use as an egress point. Not even Bix could fit through it.

"What are we going to do?" Jonah asked.

"Well, I'll tell you what I'm going to do," Bix said. "I'm going to tell them I don't have nanites. They won't want my blood if they think it won't help anyone."

"Yeah, I'm not sure that'll make any difference to them," Jonah replied. "Blood is blood. Plus, I have a feeling if you try to tell them about the nanites, their heads will explode. Besides, what else do you think they'll take if they decide your blood isn't worth anything?"

Bix looked stricken.

"Maybe instead of just a kidney, it'll be a kidney, both eyes, all your bone marrow, a lung, maybe your feet—"

"That's not helping, Jonah," Finn growled.

"Do you think he's right?" Bix asked. He went over to Finn and pulled him around. "Do you think they'll dissect me like that? How am I supposed to live? I can't be walking around without any feet."

Finn shook his head. "They could take all your organs, and I still don't think it'd be enough for them. It never is."

Bix reeled back, his face bright red with fury. "Are you saying I'm not worth as much as you, Mister Big Shot?" He pointed at Jonah. "What about him then? Huh?"

"Stop shouting."

"Stop?" he sputtered. "You want me to stop shouting? They're going to take all our blood out of our bodies, and then—"

"It's called exsanguination, and no, they're not. That would kill us, even me. So stop flipping out."

"Stop flipping out? What the hell is wrong with you, Finn? Flipping out is exactly what this situation calls for!"

A guard banged the bars with his nightstick and shouted at them to be quiet. "Don't make me come back in here to tell you again."

"Finn," Bix said, quietly pleading. "We are dead. Do you hear me? We're dead. There's no way out of this."

"You think that means anything to him?" Jonah asked. "He's already died once. You're going to have to try a lot harder to get through to him."

"What are you saying?" Finn growled.

"That you couldn't care less."

"I care."

"Sure you do. If you cared, you'd be scared. If you cared, you'd be worried about what happened to your brother. And what's going to happen to Bren. But all I see you doing is daydreaming about how many of these people you can take out on your suicide mission."

"And what are *you* doing?"

"I can't do a damn thing. But you can. You can show them what you've got, convince them that what we've got in our heads is a lot more valuable than what we've got in our blood."

"They can't have my brain!" Bix wailed. "I need it!"

"Not your brain, dummy," Jonah said, rolling his eyes. "I'm talking about the cure."

"You really don't want to get out of here, do you?" Finn calmly said.

Jonah got off his bunk and walked over. He was still taller, and broader in the shoulders, and yet he somehow felt smaller. He edged in close, until they stood nose to nose. "You've got all this strength, all these abilities, all these smarts. You talk about how you're faster and stronger and better, but you aren't. You've always been less, and now you're even less than ever. You're a failure. Even worse, you're a coward."

"Shut up."

"A loser."

"I said shut up."

"You should've stayed dead, died a hero. Instead, you've turned into someone no one likes, an anti-hero."

Finn slammed his fist into Jonah's face. The punch had been wild, propelled by fury, so it didn't land squarely. Nevertheless, Jonah's head snapped back. He spun around and slammed into the wall. Blood spurted from his nose and a new gash opened up on his cheek.

"Coward," Jonah stubbornly growled, staggering as he tried not to fall. "Sucker punching coward. That's what you are, Finn. You know it. You've always known it. Dying and coming back didn't change that."

Finn screamed and charged. He hit Jonah square in the chest, and the two slammed back into the wall. Jonah's head hit hard, and he slumped to one side. He blinked, somehow still conscious. Bix tried to get between them, yelling for them to stop, but Jonah waved him weakly away. Finn swept an arm in a wide, lazy arc and sent Bix flying across the room. He hit the metal bars of their cell with a loud *clang!* and fell to the floor, gasping and coughing, his breath knocked out of him.

The guard ran back in, bellowing for them to break it up, but nobody heard him. He unlocked the door to the cell and stepped inside. Jonah leaned forward and grabbed Finn by the neck. The lid of one eye was already swollen shut. "Go!" he whispered, as his legs gave out. His grip on Finn's shirt was the only thing keeping him upright. "Now's your chance, don't waste it. Save yourself."

The words cut through Finn's rage like a Wraith's teeth slicing through soft flesh, and he realized too late what Jonah had been doing. The taunting was to get him so riled up that the guard would have to open the door. Jonah had allowed him to attack. Knowing how strong Finn was, he could have easily been killed.

"Go!" Jonah hissed again, and closed his eyes. His head lolled to the side and his grip weakened.

Finn crouched for a moment, frozen with indecision. He was aware of the guard screaming. He felt hands grabbing his shoulders, pulling at him, pulling him away from Jonah, who'd finally lost consciousness. He fell back onto his hands and scrambled away, giving the guards access. Something cold and sharp circled his wrists, binding them together, and he didn't resist. He looked over at Bix and saw how his best friend's body was bent in the wrong places. He saw blood. He tried to see if Bix was breathing, but the men lifted him up and placed him onto a stretcher and wheeled him out of the cell before he could be sure.

Now they were kneeling over Jonah, trying to revive him. Finn watched, still not struggling against the guards as they yanked him to his feet and wrestled him out of the cell, too. His ankles were bound, so the men lifted him up, and he couldn't see anymore. And still he didn't fight or try to escape. He could have easily broken the plastic bands around his wrists and feet; he could have beaten the guards off and run away. But he didn't. Jonah had sacrificed himself to give him one last chance, and he had failed. Jonah had been right. He was a coward, a loser. And now Bix was seriously hurt, maybe even dead, and for what?

Nothing.

After all he'd been through, despite all he'd endured, not a single thing about him had changed. All the things he had always despised about himself, the things he'd always felt were weak or defective, the nanites couldn't fix.

CHAPTER

56

JONAH WAS DEEPLY DISAPPOINTED IN FINN, NOT FOR what he'd done to him, but for what he hadn't done for himself and Bix. But he was equally as disappointed in himself. All he'd managed to do was delay the sentencing by a few days, until both he and Bix were back on their feet again, albeit painfully. And their debt to Haven just kept accruing.

They were back in Holding, except now they were kept separated, each in their own cell, which was sure to exacerbate their debt. Finn had arrived first, followed by Jonah later the same evening. "Fractured cheekbone and eye socket," he informed Finn through the bars, his voice thin and reedy. "Concussion. Bruised lung."

Bix returned early in the morning two days later. His injuries, although bad, hadn't been as severe as Jonah's; his complaints had simply been louder. In addition to a broken rib and a neck strain, he'd bitten his tongue and couldn't chew properly. When he spoke, which was nonstop, they'd had a hard time understanding him. Jonah said it was actually an improvement. The others weren't in any mood for jokes.

Finn figured Jonah would heal completely in a few days — thanks to his nanites — but Bix's recovery would take weeks. He doubted Shaw, or the judge, would have the patience to wait that long to take what they wanted from them. The slowness of his recovery might even make them suspicious that there was nothing special about Bix's blood, and so it could change the entire calculus of their debt repayment in ways he didn't wish to contemplate.

Jonah moped in his cell, punishing himself for badly misjudging Finn's response — not to his taunting, but to the opportunity he'd tried to create — and for the truth it had exposed. He hadn't actually believed what he'd said, but now he had doubts. How was it possible for one person to change so much in such a short amount of time? The Finn he'd known back in the bunker, the Finn who'd defiantly stood up to him in defense of his best friend despite knowing Jonah was far stronger, truly was gone.

As the day wound on, not another word was exchanged between them. In each cell, the solitary square of sunlight coming through the small barred window, slid down the opposite wall, crossed the floor, and disappeared from view. At night, each cell was illuminated by a solitary caged light bulb set in the center of the ceiling, but they weren't timed to come on for another couple hours, so for the last half of the afternoon, their surroundings were just as gloomy as the boys themselves. At last, the door leading from the stairs opened and two sets of shoes scuffed down them.

"Is that dinner," Bix moaned from his cell. He sounded absolutely miserable. "It's Taco Tuesday, isn't it? I hope there's fresh guacamole this time and none of that fake shit."

"Someone here to see you," the guard announced loudly, tapping his nightstick on Finn's cell door.

Finn lifted his arm from his face and sat up on his cot. "Who?"

"Your brother."

* * *

"I don't understand," Harper said. "How could they not be here? They left days ago."

Finn paced the length of his cell, running his fingers through his hair and going over again in his mind everything Harper told him about what had transpired since they'd last seen each other. The fall of Westerton had come as a shock, although not the reason for it. Maybe now Jonah would see why he'd so easily sacrifice Haven's safety if it meant securing his own; their own men had done exactly that to Westerton.

He was relieved that Harper had gotten out, along with Eddie, Hannah, Bren and her mother, and apparently two young boys that Eddie had saved from the massacre. They were waiting outside Haven, he hoped plotting a way for the boys to go free.

"I volunteered to come in alone," Harper explained. "We thought it would be safer for the others to stay outside, but I don't know how long that will last."

"Why?"

"Wraiths everywhere, on the move. I wasn't sure I'd be able to get in. I needed to be escorted the last half mile or so."

"How did Shaw react when you told him what happened?"

"He didn't believe me," Harper said. "He didn't think his men would do something like that. And since they haven't come back, he's even more skeptical. He's sending out a couple guys to check for himself."

Finn rubbed his neck. "Well, it'll buy us a little more time." He shook his head and quickly explained what was going to happen. "A day to Westerton, another to come back again. Add another to search the base, assuming they can get near it. That gives us a minimum of three more days to figure things out."

"What do we tell Bix about his father?" Harper whispered.

"Are you sure they took him, too?"

"Where else could he be?"

"Maybe he got out, just like you."

"No, I was with him guarding the men when it went down, Finn. No one has seen him since. We went back the next day, after the Wraiths cleared out. There weren't any survivors. Nothing but bodies. Besides, if he did get free, don't you think he'd come straight here for Bix?"

Finn let out another deep breath. He knew he was supposed to feel worse about this than he did, just as he should feel better about who had survived, but he couldn't seem to get there. "He might be on foot."

"Everyone's gone," Harper said. "The Largents and Rollinses, Doctor Jadhari, everyone from Bunker Seven. The only reason we escaped is because of Eddie. He got pretty torn up trying to get to a truck, but he'll heal. If it weren't for him, we'd be dead."

"Or infected."

Harper grunted.

"The Largents?" Finn asked. "All of them? Little Mia? Sammy?"

"Yes."

"Are you sure they're dead?"

Harper went over to Finn, sitting on the side of his bunk. He'd taken a piece of paper from his pocket and was staring at it, and he saw that it was a crayon drawing. "They took the cure while we were gone, Finn, so at least we know they're not . . . infected. Almost everyone did."

"What?" he asked, startled. "Everyone took the cure?"

"Nearly all. Jonah was first, asked for his before we left. Eddie knew. So did Bix's father, of course. He didn't want anyone else to know."

The drawing slipped from Finn's hands. He looked up in shock. "Jonah took the cure *before* we left?"

"Yeah, he—"

"Son of a bitch! If I'd known he—"

"It's okay," Harper whispered. "He's fine, Finn. The cure works."

"It's not fine!" He rose from the bunk, shaking with fury, and stomped over to the door. "I could have killed you, Jonah, you son-of-a-bitch!" he screamed through the bars. "How stupid could you possibly be? You should've told us!"

"Told us what?" Bix groaned from his own cell farther down.

"It was my decision," Jonah quietly replied. "We needed more proof before—"

"You didn't know what would happen, not for sure! No one knew for sure yet!"

"Knew what would happen?" Bix asked. "About what? What was Jonah's decision? Someone want to tell me what— *Ah, damn it! Oh shit, that hurts!*"

"Walk it off, Bix," Jonah muttered.

"You know how much it hurts to walk? To lie down? Just breathing hurts like hell!"

"Yeah, well, you know how much it hurts to blow my nose?"

"That's too bad. I was going to ask you to blow me."

"He's nanite-free," Finn announced. "Jonah took the cure. Before we left Westerton."

Silence filled the holding area for several seconds. Bix finally broke it with a string of curses. "You're lucky you're in your own cell, Resnick," he said, his voice trembling with as much anger as pain, "or I'd come right over there and kick your— *Oh, son of a bitch! Goddamn it, that hurts.*"

"Can we put that aside for now?" Jonah asked. "What's happening next for us?"

Harper stepped over to the bars. "Shaw's checking out our story."

"And how's that supposed to help?" Bix demanded. "They want Adrian, and if he's not coming, we're screwed.

405

He's probably the one who caused the mess in the first place."

"It wasn't him."

"Bullshit! *Oh, fuck, that hurt!* No, it was Adrian. He's probably sitting in some hideaway right now, him and his sister, and he's laughing."

"If he's anywhere," Finn said, "it's inside some Wraith's belly."

Harper gave his brother an alarmed look.

"Either way," Bix said, "it ends the same for us."

"If they were attacked, they'll find the truck they stole from Westerton and—"

"Did you see it on the way here?" Finn asked Harper. "If not, then what happened to it?"

Harper didn't reply.

"Yup, they're gone," Bix groaned. "And we're going to die in this damn hole."

CHAPTER

SHAW ESCORTED THEM PERSONALLY FROM THEIR holding cells three days later. By then, Bix was walking nearly upright, although slowly and breathing with difficulty. Jonah was black and blue from his hairline to his jaw, but the worst of the swelling had finally started to recede. He could now see out of both eyes.

"Where are you taking us?" Finn demanded.

"Back upstairs to meet with the Chief Controller."

They went up the back steps and entered the courtroom from a different door than the previous times and were surprised to find it packed with even more people than they'd seen before. Word of their case had apparently spread throughout the Haven community, but so too had rumors of Finn's unusual strength, if the whispers and finger pointing in his direction were any clue.

Finn scanned the gallery impassively, taking in the curious and distrustful stares, but he did a double take when he saw Eddie in the corner near the back. Bren and her mother were to his right, and on his other side was Hannah, her arms wrapped around the shoulders of two small frightened boys.

"What are they doing here?" he demanded, spinning around to confront Shaw. But there was no time for an answer, as the bailiff ordered everyone to rise. Shaw gestured for the boys to keep moving.

They took their usual places behind the right-hand table facing the bench, while Shaw and Harper sat at the other. The courtroom fell silent and the Chief Controller entered. All but the boys were asked to sit.

"The circumstances of this case are highly unconventional," the judge said, reading from her notes. She didn't even look at the boys once. "The details of the case have been heard, the verdict rendered, and the sentence determined. Yet the defendants have yet to be remanded for collection." She glanced up at Shaw. "Would you like to explain?"

"There are extenuating circumstances, Madame Chief Controller. New details have emerged. I would like now to present an *amicus curiae* brief, if the court will so indulge."

"This is highly unusual."

"I understand, Madame Controller, but—"

"What exactly is in dispute here, Mister Chao, the facts of the complaint or the accounting?"

"Both. As you are aware, two men were sent to the isolated community of Westerton to collect on the outstanding debt. We have since obtained strong evidence that their failure to return was not caused by negligence or malfeasance on the part of the defendants or their representatives, but instead appears to have been the result of a combination of factors, both innocent and otherwise."

"Explain."

"First, unbeknownst to us at the prior arraignment, the collection team encountered significant external threats on the road to Westerton, which delayed their arrival there by several days and triggered the filing of the supplemental complaint with the court. Second, there appear to have been criminal actions taken, which have prevented the speedy resolution of this case."

"By whom?"

Shaw glanced toward the boys, his lips pressed into a thin white line. "By my own men, ma'am."

The gallery uttered a collective gasp, and the judge snapped her gavel against the block to silence them.

"Go on," she said, once the court returned to order.

"It appears that Westerton accepted our terms and were prepared to comply. They, in turn, extended a sincere invitation to our men to stay as their guests until morning, as it was too late in the day to safely return. Our men accepted, but apparently had no intention of complying. Instead, they waited until dark, forced one of their residents and a defendant in this case, a Mister Harrison Blakeley, to assist them in stealing a vehicle, and absconded with the payment and another hostage. In the process of committing these unlawful acts, they assaulted at least four other individuals, one of whom is here today, which directly resulted in the deaths of two people, and rendered the community's barricade against the ferals to fail. The community, in such a vulnerable state, was attacked and destroyed. The handful of survivors are here today to offer corroborating testimony."

"How many casualties are we talking about?"

"Seven survivors and close to eighty deceased or turned, including twenty-seven women and eighteen youth."

Another gasp rippled through the courtroom. The judge allowed the commotion to grow for a moment as she considered these new details. But then she banged her gavel and called for order once more.

"And what of the men you sent and now believe committed these heinous crimes?" she asked. "Where are they? And what is this evidence you have gathered establishing their guilt?"

"Our investigation located the stolen vehicle abandoned just east of Salt Lake City; it had run out of gas. The body of one individual was found inside, Haven resident William Carelli, still strapped into the driver's seat."

"Curly?"

He nodded. "The body had been partially consumed, suggestive of a feral attack, and other evidence — the significant amount of blood present at the scene, numerous human tracks and bloody handprints — further suggests no one escaped."

Bix, who had been staring intently at Shaw as he gave this testimony gasped, and the judge signaled for him to be quiet. "That's my father!" he panted. "My father—"

"Order! Bailiff control the witness! Mister Chao, please continue."

"The rest were either turned or killed and their bodies carried off, although it could not be determined whether it was by ferals or carrion feeders. A search of the surroundings yielded no additional clues. Given this new evidence, we ask the court to consider these extenuating circumstances, grant the defendants clemency, and commute the charges."

"Thank you, Mister Chao." She turned and addressed the boys directly for the first time. "Any reason why I should not accept this request?"

The fact that they were being asked for their opinion left them momentarily speechless. Harper was the quickest to recover. "No, ma'am."

She turned to him, frowning. "Are you a party to the original arrangement?"

"No, ma'am."

"Then sit down. You cannot speak for or on behalf of the defendants."

She pursed her lips, challenging him to defy her, but he didn't.

"Mister Chao, as a party to the case, you cannot file an *amicus curiae* brief. Therefore, the material presented today cannot be admitted into evidence."

"But—"

"Quiet, Mister Chao! This is my courtroom, and I expect all who come before me to follow the proper protocol."

"Yes, ma'am."

She sighed. "Disregarding for the moment the original agreement, we must still account for the extraneous debts incurred since then."

"We would request just one pint from each, Madam."

"That seems insufficient."

"From *all* parties, ma'am," he quickly added, "including the gentlemen to my left and the other six survivors. Ten pints in total."

A low rumble of disapproval passed through the audience.

"What the fuck, Shaw?" Bix shouted. He tried to step across the aisle to the other table, but only made it halfway before stalling in pain. "You just said we're not guilty!" he gasped.

"Order!"

The bailiff approached the boys' table once more and glared at Bix. Shaw gestured frantically for the boys to keep quiet.

"No more outbursts," the judge snapped.

"My father's dead because of your people!" Bix grunted.

"Order! *Order!* Control yourself, young man, or I will hold you in contempt!" She lifted the sheet of paper before her and glared defiantly at it.

After several minutes, Shaw cleared his throat.

The judge peered over her glasses at him, the muscles in her face thrumming with tension. "What is it, Mister Chao?"

"Madame Chief Controller, in support of my motion, I would like to call a witness."

"I already told you, the motion is dismissed. We are not retrying the case."

"No, ma'am, but I thought that, in view of the circumstances, we could—"

"You thought wrong. There is procedure. There is protocol. And there are laws. What would Haven be without them? Chaos. Anarchy. The people elected me to uphold them, no matter the circumstances." She paused a moment, then added: "Accounts cannot be allowed to remain unbalanced. We cannot simply erase the debt from the books, especially one of such magnitude as this."

She let the paper slip from her fingers and turned her gaze to the boys. "I am truly sorry for the loss of your friends and families. The death of even one person is heartbreaking. The death of an entire community is an unspeakable tragedy and a terrible loss to the living. I personally cannot imagine how we could ever make it up to you, but I give you my solemn oath that our accountants will consider the full measure of your losses and provide fair and equitable recompense in time. Mister Chao and his designates will be held fully accountable."

"What?" Shaw exclaimed.

"All debts must be considered and repaid individually, sir, by those who incur them. You know this. You handpicked the search team, so their actions fall to your account." She turned to the boys, adding, "Your own debts to this community are not forgiven. The previous verdict is upheld. There will be no clemency. You will each surrender *four* pints of blood immediately, then, in two weeks time, one kidney and one—"

"No!" someone behind them shouted, and the gallery erupted in uproar. "This is wrong!"

The boys turned to see Eddie push his way through the crowd, which was rising to its feet.

"Order!" the judge demanded. "I said order!"

"These boys owe you nothing!" Eddie yelled. "You've kept them prisoner here. And now, because of your twisted system of justice—"

"Officers! Restrain this man immediately!"

They were on him in a flash, but Eddie easily shrugged away the burly hands gripping his arms and continued to wade through the mass of people like he was walking through a field of grass. "Our entire community was wiped out! There is no number, no value you can place on people's lives! Nothing will ever repay our losses. Nothing!"

"I will have order in this court!"

The gallery surged forward, propelling Eddie with them, pushing and shouting, trying to get a better view, indignant, outraged, defiant. Nobody had ever seen anything like this before, not since Haven was formed more than three years before and its system of rules was ratified. Two armed men reached for Eddie, and he pushed them away, too. A third dove for his legs, tripping him. Several people fell in the scrum. The pile writhed like a single amorphous entity, and then a guard's body was ejected from the center of it, flipping end over end over people's heads. Once more, Eddie rose to his feet.

Finn leapt the moment he saw a gun in someone's hand. The explosion was deafening, and he felt the heat as the bullet passed close to his face. More people screamed. They charged the thick oaken doors, but since they were meant to open inward and the crowd was pushing against them, they wouldn't budge.

The judge stood up and tried to slip out through her personal entrance into her chambers, but that door was also blocked. One of the lawyer's tables tipped over and crashed to the marble floor. People fought like crazed beasts, tearing at each other with their bare hands, looking every bit like Wraiths. No one heard the pounding and shouting coming from the other side of the main gallery doors.

Shaw grabbed Jonah's arm and gestured frantically to follow him away from the melee. Jonah in turn grabbed Bix. They made their way to the far back corner of the courtroom, to the hidden panel where they had entered moments before.

"Finn!" Bix shouted. But Finn was facing the other direction, straining his neck, trying to see over the crowd. "Finn!"

"Go!" Eddie shouted at them. "I've got the others! We'll find you!"

Finn spun around and pushed his way over to Shaw. They'd almost reached the door when it burst open and dozens of armed men in riot gear surged inside. A concussion grenade went off, and the courtroom filled with smoke. People fell to their knees, choking on the noxious gas. Shaw and the boys were immediately surrounded and forced onto the ground.

With the crowd falling back into submission, the din began to fade. Somewhere outside the building, a siren sounded.

"Stay down!" someone growled, and shoved his knee into Bix's back, directly onto the injured rib. He screamed in agony, and when Finn tried to assist, another guard slammed the butt of his rifle into his temple. He dropped to his knees, stunned.

Everything was a blur after that. People kept shouting. Hands kept grabbing. Finn was lifted up. He felt weak, unable to move. He watched the floor tiles pass beneath him as he was hauled out of the courtroom and down the hall toward the stairwell. Black boots ran past, heading in the opposite direction. Then he was abruptly dropped and shoved against the wall.

"Finn?"

He blinked and sat up with help from Bix and Jonah.

"Jesus, they tased the shit out of you," Bix said. He pulled off his shirt and pressed it against the side of Finn's head to soak up the blood, muttering how he'd ruined more good shirts this way. Behind them, another phalanx of people ran past, screaming, ignoring the Westerton group in the chaos.

"What happened?" Finn asked. He felt groggy, but he was recovering quickly. "What's going on?"

"It's the ferals," Shaw said, crouching beside Bix. He slipped a knife from a sheath on his belt and cut Finn's restraints. "I should've seen this coming. We had ample warning."

"What warning?" Bix asked, confused. "What should you have seen coming?"

"The Wraiths, thousands of them. They're on the outer wall. They're trying to get into Haven!"

CHAPTER

"You're on your own," Shaw cried. "The wall's in trouble. I need to help defend it."

"Wait!" Finn said. "What did you mean they're on the wall?"

"No time to explain!" He rose to leave, then reconsidered. "Look, you boys probably just want to wipe your hands of this place. Maybe you're thinking this is your best chance to get away, and maybe you will, but we could really use all the help we can get."

"They need shooters over by Coronado Street!" someone shouted down the hall. "Gate's down! Outer wall's coming down! They're starting to climb the inner wall!"

"We can't protect the entire perimeter!" Finn said. "We need to leave. Now!"

"The buffer area between walls is partitioned," Shaw hurriedly explained. "The dividers aren't as high or as strong, but they'll slow them down and limit the spread. But we have to move quickly!"

"We don't owe you anything," Finn growled.

"If they're on Coronado, then there's no way out of Haven," Shaw replied. "You can't run. Now, you can stay and do nothing, or you can stay and fight. Either way, you're staying."

"What about the sewers?"

"Not an option. They've all been sealed shut."

"Get to the armories!" someone yelled. The hallway was starting to clear, so there was no question the man was addressing them. The siren outside continued to wail, and the distant sound of gunfire grew more persistent. "Emergency orders are in effect over all of Haven, people! Move it!"

"If we stay and fight," Bix said turning back to Shaw, "then that wipes the slate clean. Right?"

"Bix, look around us," Jonah said. "There's no more slate. Nobody cares about that anymore."

"Maybe not right now, but what about afterward?"

Shaw nodded. He grabbed Finn under the arm and, with Harper's help, got him to his feet. "After today's ruling, we can be sure about one thing: the debt's not coming off the books until it's paid."

"Does that include yours?"

"By the time we get this under control again — *if* we do — and order is restored, we'll all be long gone. I'll personally help you get out."

"*We?*" Finn said.

Shaw gave them a dark look. "You heard the Chief Controller. Do you know what the cost of eighty lives is? I can't have that all on my head."

"So, it's okay when it's not your pound of flesh," Finn demanded through clenched teeth.

"Or pint of blood," Bix added.

"Can we discuss this another time?" Harper cried. "How far are the armories?"

Shaw pointed northward. "There's one located by each gate. Just follow the crowds." And with that he was gone, slipping between the last few people sprinting down the hallway.

"You're not actually thinking about fighting with them," Bix asked Harper.

"We're not," Finn replied for him. "We need to find the rest of our people and get out of here."

"We don't have a choice, Finn," Jonah argued.

"There's four thousand people inside Haven. Four more won't make any difference."

"Make that ten more," Harper said, and nodded toward the other end of the hallway, where Eddie and the rest of their crew were making their way toward them.

"There's no way out," Jonah told the others, once they joined up. "The Wraiths are all around the entire perimeter. Outer wall's been breached in at least one place. Shaw says we should fight."

"I say we leave," Finn countered.

"They need more help at the front gate," Kaleagh said. "That's why they diverted us to come in the back way this morning."

"Then that's where we get out."

"You just heard Shaw tell us Coronado's fallen. That's the other gate!"

"I'm not fighting for these people," Finn insisted. "If we have to crash through the wall someplace, then we'll do it."

Bren gasped. "No! What happened to Westerton will happen here if we do that!"

"They did it to us first!"

"Then everyone here will die!"

Finn sniffed. "Not all of them."

The others gawped at him in disbelief.

"I can't believe you just said that," Harper whispered.

"What do you want me to—"

The building shook from an explosion somewhere nearby, knocking them off balance. They ran to the cracked window at the end of the hallway and looked out. A few hundred feet beyond the stark line of the outer wall grew a column of smoke, thick and brown, roiling with dust.

Flaming debris rose on the updraft before raining back down.

"What the hell?" Bix shouted over the warble of the siren, now much louder.

Another fireball streaked across the sky, coming from somewhere behind them. It left a white trail and hit even farther out in the city. The concussion rattled the window a half second later, threatening to shower them with glass, and a new column of smoke began to rise.

"Those idiots are going to push them right toward us!" Eddie said.

Tracer fire lit up the sky, crackling the air.

"They're going to run out of ammo shooting like that," Jonah added.

Another explosion, this one farther away and out of view, accompanied the roar of a vehicle racing by on the street below.

Eddie stepped away from the window. "We need to stay and fight. We'll head for the armory by the main gate."

"And what am I supposed to do with two teenaged girls and these boys?" Kaleagh said. "They can't fight!"

"We can shoot, Mom."

"Oh, can you now, Bren? Can the boys? They're half your age!"

"First things first," Eddie said. "Without weapons, we're all helpless."

Another explosion, much louder and closer, finally sent the shattered glass crashing to the floor. They looked out the opening and saw a building a few blocks away erupt into flames. "That was inside the wall!" Hannah gasped, as glowing embers fluttered down all around.

"Time to go," Jonah warned. "If the Wraiths don't get us, these idiots will."

"I agree," Eddie said, breathlessly. "We don't have time for discussions. We need to save ourselves, and that means getting guns."

"I just had a thought," Bix said.

"No time!"

"Just hear me out. We can't shoot them all. We can't blow them all up. We can't beat them all back into submission. But what if we didn't have to?"

"Spit it out already!"

"We knock them out, like with those boxes Adrian had."

"We do have one in the truck," Harper noted.

"Yeah, nice thought," Jonah said. "Too bad we don't have a few thousand of them. One's not going to do us any good."

"It's enough to save us, though," Finn said.

"Adrian had dozens of them at his ranch," Bix said. "And he said there were hundreds more where he got them. Maybe they have some stashed here."

"If they had them, don't you think they'd be using them right now?"

"There might be another way," Harper said. "What if we can use Haven's cell towers to transmit the signal?"

"They haven't used those towers in years," Finn said.

"That's not true," Harper countered. "Curly told me Haven uses the local cellular network for short range communications inside the wall. It's powered by solar panels and backup diesel generators. If we can somehow tap into them and broadcast the signal from the box, it'll knock out the Wraiths everywhere within range!"

"And anyone with activated nanites," Finn said, "like me and Eddie."

"It doesn't matter if we knock out half the community, as long as we knock out *all* of the Wraiths! We just need to get to the QuanTel modulator in the truck."

"And hook it into the network. By the time we figure out how to do that—"

"Mister Largent showed me how Bunker Ten used the mobile radio to do it."

"Bunker Ten didn't even make it five hundred feet!"

"It's a good idea," Eddie said, "but Finn's right. Setting it up, testing it, we don't have that kind of time. We don't even know if it'll work. We stay and fight. Agreed?"

Everyone nodded but Finn.

"These people want to collect our organs," he growled. "They're predators. In my book, that makes them no better than Wraiths."

CHAPTER

59

HARPER SLOWED SLIGHTLY TO GIVE BIX TIME TO CATCH up to him. "Need any help?" he shouted over the barrage of sirens and explosions.

Bix clutched his side, gasping for air. His face was ashen and dripping with sweat, despite the winter chill. But he shook his head and waved Harper on, too proud to accept the assistance and more than just a little annoyed that it wasn't his best friend offering it.

"You're holding up better than I would be," Harper said, as he jogged along beside him.

"Not really in the mood for a pep talk right now," he replied through gritted teeth.

"Fair enough."

Still, Harper felt compelled for a reason he didn't understand to make some kind of connection with Bix. He didn't know if it was guilt over his brother's behavior, or because of the sense of abandonment they shared. "I'm sorry about your father," he said. "He was an honorable man."

Bix grunted. "If you only knew."

"All I know is that without him, we wouldn't have gotten this far figuring out how to eradicate the Flense. Someday, everyone will understand how much of a hero he was."

"Heroes always die in the end," Bix grumbled, as he angrily wiped Finn's blood off his hands. "Every single fucking time. That's how the world works now. The only guys who survive it are the bad ones." He glared at the two boys far ahead of them, his jaw clenched in rage.

"Well, I don't plan on dying here today."

Twenty yards ahead of the rest of the group jogged Finn, Jonah matching him stride for stride, despite his injuries. The two could be seen arguing as they ran. No one else could hear what it was about, but they could all guess. Jonah was understandably angry at Finn for refusing to fight. But then again, was it really that unreasonable for Finn to want to save himself? Haven hadn't done a thing to deserve their help. In fact, it was Haven who owed *them*. Still, it was a stupid thing to argue about now.

Kaleagh and Bren Abramson were thirty feet behind them, and Eddie trailed them by another twenty, the two young boys jiggling in his arms as he ran. Hannah tried to stay with him, but each time she glanced back to check on Bix, she'd lose ground, and her father would shout at her to keep up. She would, for a bit, but then she'd fall behind again. That was one reason why Harper stayed with Bix, to keep an eye on the entire lot, make sure they stayed together. The other was to give himself a little more time to think about Bix's idea. If there were only some way to make it work.

Except he just couldn't seem to focus long enough to figure it out. Another bomb would detonate, and he'd start to wonder if the world would ever find peace. They'd passed a shop, and his thoughts would fly off in a completely different direction. He'd think about the items filling the window, knickknacks and toys and curiosities. Where did they come from? Who had owned them before? Why bother with them now? Dealing kitsch was such an odd thing to consider, something familiar yet so out of place in this ruthless world, where a moment of distraction could kill you. He never would've thought people would engage in civilized commerce like this ever again. It was so . . . so banal, so normal.

Especially in a place whose penal system used blood and organs for compensation.

Which then made him wonder about the proprietors of those shops. What did they take for payment? A vial of concentrated blood? A little bit of bone marrow?

The shop windows were dark now, their owners undoubtedly on the wall fighting for their lives and livelihoods.

His ears rang from the din bombarding them from all around— the sirens, the nonstop gunfire, the thunder of bombs detonating, shouts of anger and desperation and terror. Vehicles roared past, people inside them, others riding on top, some shouting into portable radios, large blocky handsets that had long since become obsolete in a world where anything older than eighteen months and larger than a deck of cards was considered laughably old-fashioned. Except now, old was back in vogue.

At last they reached the main gate, where they found Garth directing people into positions of need along the wall. His mobile radio buzzed and chirped from all the cross-traffic.

"We're here to help," Eddie said.

Garth gave them a dubious look. "Why?"

"Because you need it."

"I'm not sure that's—"

A frantic squawk from his phone interrupted him. The message was garbled, but the panic in the speaker's voice was unmistakable. "Say again!" Garth shouted.

"—ing in! We've taken — streets away from the — many!"

"What are they saying?" Eddie demanded.

Garth pressed his ear tighter against the device. "Repeat last!" he ordered, and stepped away from them.

But the person was gone, their fate unknown.

"The truck we came in on this morning," Eddie shouted, jockeying to stay in front of Garth. "Where is it?"

"Are you planning to help or leave?"

"We're helping! Just tell us where the truck is!"

After the briefest of pauses, Garth said, "Impound yard." He leaned his head to the side to listen to another transmission, cursed, then gave a reply to the person on the other end.

"Where's that?" Eddie asked again.

"What?"

"The impound yard! Where is it?"

Garth frowned. "One block east. Follow the wall! Don't even think about driving it out of the lot. The place is surrounded by chain link and barbed wire!"

"Good. Now, where's the armory?"

Garth pointed in the opposite direction. "Follow those people."

"We'll get guns," Eddie told Kaleagh, "you take the kids. Get them back to the truck. You'll be safer there. Bren, Hannah, I need you to watch the boys."

"We can fight, Dad!" Hannah begged.

"But the boys can't, and they need protection. Please, honey, just go! It'll be safest there for all of you."

"It's not fair!"

"Come on," Bren said, and grabbed Hannah's arm. The young boys were terrified, and huddled against her side.

The rest hurried over to the armory and collected weapons and ammunition. But when Eddie headed toward the wall, Finn held back, shaking his head.

"Coward," Jonah scowled. "All this talk about—"

Eddie pulled the boys apart. What he'd seen in Finn's eyes wasn't cowardice. He wasn't sure what it was, but he knew it wasn't that.

"We can't hold them off," Finn said. "It's only a matter of time before they get inside."

"We'll stop them."

"No, we won't. How long before they reach the impound lot? What happens when they do?"

Jonah flinched, but didn't answer.

"Go," Kaleagh told Finn. "Take care of my girl."

Again, Eddie turned back for the wall, but this time Harper hesitated. "I'm going with Finn. I have to try something. It's our only chance."

"Oh, for crying out loud!" Jonah yelled. "Our only chance is fighting!"

"Two less shooters won't make a bit of difference," Eddie said. He turned to Bix. "Or is it going to be three?"

Bix chambered a round and nodded grimly. "Screw them. I'm going to kill me some Wraiths."

"Okay then. Harper, whatever you try, I pray it works. Good luck."

"You, too."

They found the girls standing outside the locked impound yard, no way to get inside. Finn forced the gate panel away enough for everyone to squeeze through, then bent it back into place.

"I need the Bunker Ten backpack," Harper told Finn. "It's in the back of the truck." He gave his pistol to Bren, then helped Hannah and the boys climb into the cab.

Finn reappeared a moment later and shoved it into his brother's hands. "Next time, get it yourself."

"What are you going to do, Harper?" Bren asked.

"Still figuring that out," he replied. "I need to find an access point for the network."

"I'll come with you. Just tell me what I can do."

"It's too dangerous, Bren. Just stay here with Finn. Lock yourselves inside the cab. And stay alive."

Finn held the gate open for Harper to slip through. He watched him run off alone back in the direction they had come, then he turned to the yard, fingering the ignition key for the truck Harper had given him. Like his brother, he wasn't sure what he was going to do.

* * *

Harper found Garth again and told him of his plan. The man gawped like he was insane and ordered him to get on the wall and help defend the city. "We've got multiple breaches all around the perimeter!" he barked. "They're inside Haven!"

"Then this is our only chance!" Harper shouted back. "I need a hard access point to your communication network!"

"Why?"

"Just get me there!"

Shaw took only a moment to decide. He led Harper to a shack just inside the inner gate. "There's a control panel there on the wall. You'll have to snap the lock to get inside. But if you so much as knock out our comms, I'll personally—"

"He won't," Bren said, stepping inside the shack. She had Seth's laptop in her arms.

"I told you to stay with the others!" Harper said.

"And she told me you couldn't do this on your own," Finn said, following Bren. He swept the surface of the small desk clear and set the modified microwave oven down on top."

"I don't need those."

"Finn has an idea, Harper. Just give him a chance to explain."

Harper's brow furrowed.

"Look, I'll never get a Genius Internship," Finn said, "and I'm certainly not doing this because I've changed my mind about anything, but I do want to live. I want us *all* to live, even the people of Haven."

"I know, but—"

"Just shut up and listen for once," Bren said. "Believe."

Harper hesitated, then he stepped aside. "Okay. But for the record, I've always believed in you, Finn. Now, tell me what you need."

"An electrical outlet for the microwave."

"Behind the chair," Garth said, pointing. "You want to tell me what you mean to do?"

"There's no power," Finn said, checking. "Without electricity, this isn't going to work!"

"But the sirens are still going," Bren exclaimed.

"They're on a separate circuit," Garth said. "All of the vital systems are. But that won't help you. The cables are buried, and there's no way to tap into them, not unless you want to go back to the city center!"

"I don't care where it comes from, I just need power! What about portable generators? We can't run the—"

"Inverters!" Harper shouted. He grabbed Garth's arm. "Get me a car! Something large, like an SUV or a full-sized pickup. Luxury brand would be better!"

"What are you thinking?" Finn asked.

"Lots of late-model year cars came with built-in current inverters, direct to alternating." He pushed Garth toward the door. "Find us something with a standard electrical outlet built into it! Go!"

The man stumbled toward the door, but Finn stopped him one more time. "Give me your phone!"

"You can't have it!"

"It's connected to the network, right?"

"Yeah, but—"

Finn snatched it out of Garth's hand. "Go! Hurry!"

"Okay, Finn," Harper said, as he watched the man run off down the road. "What's the plan?"

"You want to transmit a signal through the network, right?" he muttered, as he asked Bren to boot up the laptop. He pointed to the coiled extension cord hanging by the window. "Keep an eye out for the car. As soon as it's here, plug in the microwave. And pray the cell towers don't fail."

"Finn, please."

"There's no time to explain!" He went and checked out the door. The scene was less chaotic than it had been just a moment earlier. Nearly everyone from the town was now on the parapet of the inner wall, firing down the other side at the invading Wraiths. He tried to spot Bix, but the smoke was too thick.

"The laptop battery's low!" Bren shouted from inside. "I don't know how long it'll stay on!"

"We just need a few minutes!" Finn shouted back, and hurried out to the edge of the road. The street to his left was nearly empty. A woman with a rifle sprinted across it, heading toward a set of stairs that would take her to the top of the wall. About a tenth of a mile off to the right, just past a set of warehouses, a van suddenly appeared. Its tires squealed as it made the turn out of the parking lot onto the road. Finn's breath caught in his throat when the van nearly tipped over. The engine revved, and the vehicle fishtailed several times before the tires regained traction, raising a cloud of blue-white smoke.

"He's coming!" he shouted to the others inside, and was just about to step back in when he spotted several people dash out from a side street and run directly into the van's path. It swerved sharply, careened onto the sidewalk, and ran straight into a lamp post, shearing it off at the base. A stack of cardboard boxes went flying. The vehicle emerged a split second later, veering like crazy as Garth tried to regain control. There was a loud *bang!* followed by the patter of a blown tire. Pieces of rubber flew into the air. The people he'd just missed changed directions and began to give chase.

"Wraiths!" Finn shouted. "They're coming!"

Harper ran out of the shack with the end of the extension cord. "I got the microwave hooked up to the laptop.

It's booted up, but you've got to hurry. The battery's flashing red!"

"Is the program loaded up?"

"What program? I don't know what—"

"The cure!"

"I don't see how this'll work. The signal can't escape the—"

"Never mind! As soon as Garth gets here, plug this end in!" Finn shouted, and ran back into the shack.

Harper spun around, and his eyes widened as Garth pinballed down the road toward him. He'd missed Finn's warning about the Wraiths, but he saw them now. The blown tire dragged on the van, causing it to list heavily to one side. Each time Garth overcorrected, the bare rim scraped the curb, sending out a shower of sparks and slowing him down even more.

Now a hundred yards away. Then eighty.

Sixty.

Another screech of metal against concrete as the rim caught up on the curb once more, then dropped into a drain opening. The van lurched to the left and began to flip. A door popped open, ejecting Garth straight up into the air. He spun like a rag doll several times before crashing to the pavement with a gut wrenching slap. The van continued to tumble toward the shack. Now twenty five yards. Then twenty.

It came to rest on its side more than a dozen yards from the door of the shack.

"Go!" Finn roared.

"But—"

"The outlet's probably in the wall in back somewhere!"

Harper sprinted toward the van, eying the smoke pouring out from under the hood. Somewhere, an alarm chimed that a door was open. Would the cord reach?

He didn't dare look to see how far away the Wraiths were. He knew they'd stop at Garth's body first, but only just long enough to realize he was dead. It wouldn't take them long to resume their attack. He yanked on the back door handle, but it wouldn't budge. He struggled a moment longer before Finn appeared and knocked him aside. He curled his fingers beneath the edge of the twisted panel and pried. The door came away grudgingly, yielding a terrible sound that was certain to draw the Wraiths' attention.

He snatched the cord from Harper and told him to get back inside the shack. "There's too many files! You know which program's the cure, not me!"

He didn't wait to see if Harper understood. He jumped inside the van and crawled around, searching for the outlet. The interior was quickly filling up with smoke. He was vaguely aware that the engine might blow at any moment, but that was the least of his worries. He'd been certain about his plan from the moment he conceived it in the motor pool — Bix's plan, actually, if he was being honest about it — but the self-doubt had returned with a vengeance in Harper's presence. Now he wondered if he'd decided to try it just to spite his own brother or sabotage him into failing. Was he really that petty, resenting him for trying to be the hero?

At last he found the outlet and jammed the plug into it. "It's in!" he screamed. "Hit it, Bren!"

Only now did he take a moment to glance out through the front of the van. Through the shattered windshield, he could see the cluster of Wraiths crouched over Garth's body, saw that he was still moving, and he felt a stab of guilt for the poor guy. Then he vaulted out through the back door and sprinted toward the shack.

The microwave oven sat on the desk. The LCD panel blinked a steady 0:00. Inside, sitting inside the oven, was Garth's cell phone radio, still connected, still receiving and transmitting. Harper seemed to have intuited what Finn was planning. He reached over and shoved a pen into the door's safety mechanism to defeat it, so the signal could reach the cell tower without being blocked.

"Hurry!" Bren yelped from the doorway, her voice choked with terror. "They're coming!"

Finn reached toward the laptop, but Harper stopped him. "That's not the right program!" he said.

"Well find it!" Finn shouted, and stepped over and yanked the shack door shut, momentarily forgetting the cord. He glanced down, afraid he'd severed it, but the numbers on the oven's LCD screen continued to blink.

"Hit it!"

"This isn't the right one!" Harper replied, frantically scrolling through the files. "It's MDR-14, but someone moved—!"

"Are you sure? It should be right there on top, the last program used!"

"It's not!"

A loud boom came from the door, and the shack trembled. Bren screamed and fell into a ball in the farthest corner.

"Run it!" Finn bellowed. "Whatever's on top! Just do it!"

"We don't know what'll—"

Finn stepped over and stabbed at the return key, his eyes on the LCD screen. The display faltered, and the numbers went dark.

"The cord! We're not getting any power!"

Two more bodies hit the side of the shack, one near the door, the other by the adjacent window. A face appeared in the bottom pane, a leering white grin and bloody teeth. Hands pawed at the thin glass, the flesh scarred and raw.

There was a beep, and sparks flew from inside the microwave. The phone began to emit smoke.

Another body hit the door, and the thin aluminum panel crumpled inward.

"They're coming in!"

There was a loud electrical pop from the microwave, and the phone burst into flames.

The shack door shook again, then popped open, slamming against the wall.

The thing on the step was a monster straight out of a nightmare. Gore clung from its teeth and dripped from its mangled jaw. Its nose was flattened and bloody from the assault on the shack, and there were several deep gashes on its face. But the most horrific part of its appearance was its eyes, each one a blackened soulless bottomless pit, a tiny pinprick of piss-yellow glowing at the center.

The killer hissed once and charged.

CHAPTER

THERE WAS A BLAST, AND THE KILLER DISAPPEARED behind a cloud of red vapor. Harper lurched back, stunned by the concussion of the gunshot. He tried to get up and his feet tangled in the extension cord. The microwave slid off the desk and crashed to the floor.

"Stop!" Finn gasped, clutching his head. He tried to stand and collapsed.

"Finn?" Harper yelled. "Bren, you shot Finn!"

"F-finn?" Bren stammered. "Oh, god, did I—"

Finn raised a shaky hand and shushed her. He crawled to the doorway, his body trembling from the effort, blood dripping from his hair. The Wraith had been blown ten feet back by the blast and now lay in a heap on the gravel. The top of its head was gone. Bits of brain matter and bone were everywhere.

"Finn?"

"I'm okay, just . . . . No! Don't touch me! I'm covered!"

"Then what is it?"

"Just stop. Listen."

Above them, the rattle of gunfire had begun to grow sporadic.

"They're running out of ammo," Harper said. He tugged at his brother's clothing, ignoring Finn's warning, searching for where he'd been shot.

Finn shook his head. He pushed himself shakily to his feet, stepped outside, stumbled to his knees, and fell. This time, he stayed down, too weak to stand. He knew the blood on his face and in his hair wasn't his own. So why did he feel so weak?

"Finn? Bren?" Harper said, drawing their attention.

The Wraiths that had attacked the shack were still standing, but they seemed to have lost interest in them. They shambled aimlessly about, slowing, until they came to a stop and stood motionless. Their eyes focused on nothing at all.

"Give me the rifle," Harper whispered to Bren, extending his hand behind him. There was a crash, and when he turned, he saw Finn lying across the threshold, his body seizing.

"Finn!"

He took a step toward his brother, but a new sound drew his attention, raising the hair on the back of his neck. One by one, the Wraiths within sight fell, their bodies collapsing to the ground. They, too, began to convulse.

"I guess it worked," Finn muttered through clenched teeth. His shaking had vanished as quickly as it hit, but now he was gulping for air, like he couldn't catch his breath. "Whatever it was."

"Finn? Honey?" Bren said. She went to him and cradled his head on her lap, rocking him, ignoring the blood. She looked over at Harper, tears in her eyes, pleading. "What's happening?"

Finn shook his head. "I don't know. I think I'm . . . dying."

"What program did you use?"

Harper said nothing.

The reports of gunfire from the wall had nearly stopped. People were shouting, although not in fear. They sounded surprised.

Finn pushed Bren's hands weakly away, ignoring her, and tried to sit up again. Thick plumes of black smoke spewed from the van. The door alarm still chimed. Flames licked the cab. Then, with a roar, the fire funneled into the back like a chimney, and the alarm went silent.

"They're gone," Harper said. "I don't know what you did, Finn, but—"

"We," Finn coughed. The air coming from his chest sounded wet. He was drowning in his own fluids. "We did it. We cured them."

He closed his eyes and slipped back into Bren's arms.

"But did we?" Harper whispered. "And at what cost?"

CHAPTER

IT WAS NEARLY IMPOSSIBLE TO HEAR THE VERDICT through all the chatter, but for those who missed it, the tight smile on Shaw Chao's face and the way he patted Eddie's shoulder was enough to know that the Chief Controller had defied every protocol and applied every loophole they could find to grant his request for clemency. It took some creative accounting, but the debt sheet was wiped clean. Not a single drop of blood would be taken from any of them, and not a single organ would be harvested.

The gallery ignored the judge's halfhearted attempts to restore order, although she didn't seem to mind very much this time. Haven's residents were talking excitedly amongst themselves, trying to understand the implications of what they'd just heard from the Westerton group. No one wanted to believe the truth about the nanites, especially since none of the blood samples taken from at least a dozen people showed any sign of them. But they couldn't deny that something had changed, and they had no reason to refute what the Westerton group claimed, not after Harper explained how he, Finn, and Bren had thwarted the attack. But what was even more exciting was the possibility of a future without Wraiths, although Eddie warned it would be a long road to get there, one almost certainly to be fraught with untold obstacles along the way. He was sure, however, that by working together they would be able to eradicate the disease that afflicted the rest of the world. They would be able to restore humanity in time, and this time do it right.

Eddie couldn't stop grinning. He didn't care that his strength was waning. And his hyperacute hearing. And his superhuman eyesight and sense of smell. After almost a week, those attributes were already becoming a distant memory. All the traits he'd variously cursed and cherished, wished he'd never gotten and feared he'd lose, were slipping quietly away. He couldn't remember feeling so alive.

The people of Haven had always suspected something had been done to their bodies, they just didn't know what or how. Just as they knew instinctively that certain abilities, certain resistances to disease and recovery from injury, was innate in some of them and not in others, and that it was all somehow linked to the fateful day the world had begun to devour itself, like the ouroboros, the proverbial snake that devoured its own tail. They had suspected things, of course, and known that there was something about the blood and organs of the healthiest people among them. But instead of trying to understand why, they'd chosen not to question their good fortune and learned to leverage the advantage, bartering their health, and inadvertently creating an entirely new system of equity for those who lacked the benefit.

Eddie went on to warn them that the effects of the cure were highly focalized to Haven. The Flense still afflicted the rest of the world, including the rest of Pocatello surrounding them. But in that moment of epiphany, no one seemed to care about that. They had confronted the evil assaulting their home with every expectation that their fate was sealed. And now they'd been granted a reprieve, one they never expected. More importantly, they'd been given a reason to hope. They would not let the opportunity go to waste.

Starting tomorrow.

For today, however, they were just happy to be alive.

"So, what do we do now?" Bix asked, as the crowd began to dissipate from the courtroom.

"Seems pretty obvious to me," Eddie said. "We have to figure out a way to repeat what happened here, repeat and expand."

"The microwave's fried. So is the laptop and the programs on it."

"Thankfully, Harrison had the forethought to make a backup copy," Eddie said. "Harper's got the drive. The rest of the experiment shouldn't be too hard to replicate. So I'm going to stay here and work on it with Jonah and Haven's engineers. Jonah wants to try and build a new transmitter, something portable that won't fry the circuitry, like it did with Bunker Ten's radio or our microwave. After we figure that out, we'll take it out onto the road. We'll start curing the world one small piece at a time, one Wraith at a time, no matter how long it takes."

As for the Wraiths they had already cured, that was a problem Haven was still struggling to wrap its collective head around. They suddenly had thousands more souls to care for, the vast majority already showing signs of severe psychological trauma from their experiences. Their difficult journeys were just beginning, too. It would take years for them to move past all they'd done while under the control of the Flense. If ever.

"Guess there really never was a Bunker Twelve," Bix said, as he tossed the leader journals and Seth's collected notes back inside the pack.

"I've all been through all four of those books now," Eddie said, "front to back, and there wasn't even a suggestion of one in any of them."

"So where did the idea of a twelfth bunker come from?" Hannah asked.

"I doubt we'll ever know. I guess it doesn't really matter now anyway."

Bix exhaled in disgust. "If we'd only known that from the beginning . . . . I mean, we had the cure with us the whole time. We didn't even need to leave the bunker."

"If we hadn't, Finn never would have found his brother."

Bix glanced over at the twins. They stood at the window and stared out over Haven's rooftops. From the back, they were nearly indistinguishable. In fact, except for Finn's shorter hair, they were identical.

Harper turned his gaze to his brother. There was something on his face that Bix recognized, and he felt his chest tighten. It was the same kind of look a parent has when they gaze upon a cherished child who doesn't realize he's being watched.

"Your father never stopped believing," Hannah said to Bix, as if she knew what he was thinking. To his surprise, she wrapped his arm in hers and pulled him close. "He talked about it all the time at Westerton, about how Bunker Twelve was the key to everything that happened, not just the cure, but the cause. I like to think he's still out there, searching for it. Maybe it was his will that planted the seed of the idea in your head. It was your idea, after all, Bix. Everyone knows it. You deserve as much credit as anyone."

"He did it for Kari."

"And for Adrian, and his sister. He did it for you. He did it for everyone, Bix. So did you."

Bix frowned. He thought about pulling away from Hannah, then realized he liked the way her body felt against his, so warm and soft, and he decided it wasn't worth arguing about. He wouldn't let his grief ruin the moment.

Unlike Bix, Finn was oblivious to the adoration being paid to him. He seemed to be far away, far beyond Haven's walls. Harper would've been surprised to know what was on his mind, but Bix knew, instinctively, and that was the difference between him and Harper. Bix just knew. They had a bond, a connection that not even Finn's twin possessed. It might have become strained over the past couple of months, but it had never broken.

He knew, for example, that Finn was terrified for himself, for his future. His strength was betraying him, just as it was Eddie. Maybe not as quickly, but it was undeniable. He could still do what no less than five strong men could do, but tomorrow it would be four, and then three. And if Eddie welcomed the change, Finn feared it. The last thing he wanted was to turn back into the person he misremembered once being, the person he'd always hated— weak, self-doubting, self-loathing.

But Bix also knew something Finn didn't, that he'd eventually come to understand how much better that person really was than the one he'd become. And how much stronger he was than he knew. It would come back to him, it would just take time.

Finn turned abruptly from the window, startling Harper. There was a new steeliness in his eyes. "I can't stay here," he said. "I have to keep looking."

He hesitated, then turned and rejoined the others. "I have to go."

Bix nodded. "And I'm going with you," he said, before wincing and glancing down at Hannah.

Finn waited for Harper to chime in.

"Do you really have to ask?"

"I wasn't sure," Finn said. "I thought you were done with wild goose chases."

"Not this one."

"I'm in, too," Bren said.

Kaleagh frowned. "I thought we decided there was no Bunker Twelve."

"Not Twelve," Bix said. "His mom and sister."

"How did you know that?" Harper asked, surprised.

Finn cracked a smile, the first since that day. "I think he knew it from the gecko."

SURVIVAL   ISOLATION

BUNKER 12

"THIS CAN'T BE THE PLACE."

The lone Quonset hut, standing like an ugly wart in the center of the barren, windswept lakebed, was the opposite of what Adrian had expected. And now he fretted that they'd traveled all this way, endured so much hardship, for nothing. They had no food left and very little water. He and Jenny would die out here in the desert in the middle of nowhere, all on the flimsiest of clues that here was somehow connected to the feral, perhaps even the source. They would lie down and die, and the damn incessant wind would continue to blow, and in a few days there'd be nothing of them left visible, and their presence on this terrible world would finally be erased. Scavengers would eat while they could, and the sands would bury the rest.

He felt Jennifer lean heavily against him. She'd spoken very little since leaving the army base, now more than two weeks before, and her latest contribution to the conversation was little more than an inscrutable grunt. Adrian lifted the jug of water toward her without thinking. When she didn't take it, he turned and pushed it into her hands, then guided it to her lips, drawing aside the bandana from her nose and mouth so she could drink.

The journey had taken a heavy toll on them both, particularly the last sixty miles of it, after they ran out of gas and abandoned the army truck with the dead man inside of it. Adrian's hands still held the memory of how it had felt snapping his neck, the crunch of the bones grinding together, the soft spine shearing. The light going out in his eyes. He'd done it without thinking, acting only because of the threat to Jenny.

Curly had turned so quickly that there'd been no time to think.

At least the disease hadn't passed to him. He had his sister to thank for that, the cure. And the others.

The man named Bear had died, too, but not by his hand. The Wraiths had taken him while he was outside of the truck with Harrison, searching for the cause of the stall. The large man fought the killers like his namesake, giving them enough time and distraction to plan their escape.

They had come the entire distance afterward completely on foot, and the ordeal was the hardest thing he'd ever experienced in his life. He knew that it was much harder for her, though, burdened as she was in her soul by the sins she had committed. He'd told her repeatedly he didn't judge her, didn't condemn her, no one did. But it was up to her whether she would accept it or not.

He turned back to the fence and leaned in closer to sniff the air. "Can't tell if it's electrified."

Harrison Blakeley stood off to the siblings' left and studied the barrier in both directions, as if he might glean some visual clue confirming that it was safe to touch, which of course there wasn't. The other three fences they had cut their way through hadn't been electrified either, despite posted signs claiming they were. So why should this one be?

He pulled off his glove and swiped the back of his hand against the metal. Nothing happened.

He was relieved, of course, but also secretly disappointed. The building's exceptionally unremarkable appearance and its lack of security were a letdown from what he'd expected to find. Couldn't there be . . . something, something more definitive? Something that said, yes, you've come to the right place?

But he didn't really need it. Proof was for Adrian. Harrison knew he was right. This was more than a forgotten storage shed in the middle of nowhere. For starters, there was that heavy steel door and keypad, which seemed out of place, excessive. Whatever was inside was a lot more important than landscaping equipment, or maintenance supplies, or even weapons. The modest exterior hid a terrible secret.

Well, the clincher was the product manifest they'd found in the truck back there just north of Provo, the one that proved this was the actual building he was looking for. He dug into his pocket and extracted the folded sheet of paper that had lain in the glove compartment of the cargo truck all these years, the very same truck where Adrian had scavenged the knockout devices he'd had at his ranch nearly three years earlier. He flapped it open for Adrian to see. "Building 238-D, just like it says there in the corner."

It seemed the devices had been on their way to Bunker Ten from here when the Flense hit. So this had to be at least a storage facility. But it was also the backup production site Seth Abramson had once mentioned to Kaleagh?

He let the paper go and watched it flutter off into the desert, where it was soon swallowed up in a veil of dust raised by the stiff breeze. He didn't need it anymore. It had served its purpose.

Adrian reached out and gave the fence a shake, startling Harrison. The motion propagated in both directions, rattling the warning signs attached to the wire every ten meters or so along its length:

GROOM LAKE RESEARCH INSTALLATION
AUTHORIZED PERSONNEL ONLY
DEADLY FORCE AUTHORIZED
AUTHORITY: DOD 18 USC §1382

The noise carried, and he'd instinctively reached behind him for his pistol, but the sound quickly died, summoning nothing out of hiding. Given the utter desolation of the building's location, he'd be surprised if it had. In fact, the last Wraiths they'd seen had been the ones that attacked their truck the night the engine ran dry. Bear had died before finding out where he'd cut the fuel line.

"This sure doesn't look like anyplace special," Adrian mumbled. "It's very small."

"Looks can be deceiving," Harrison replied.

"Well, the only other place is underground. Are you saying it's underground?"

Harrison reached into his backpack for the wire cutters, then set about making an opening for them to crawl through. He unconsciously hummed as he worked, a song dredged up from his childhood. He'd been thinking a lot about the past during their grueling march, about his family. About regrets. It surprised him how much he'd willfully suppressed from that part of his life, before the Flense, so focused had he been on making himself invisible, him, the boy, on just surviving. He thought about how he should have done more then, when he'd had more chances to stop it, how everything might've ended up differently had he just stopped hiding.

Jennifer quietly picked up his tune, croaking the lyrics of the song in a voice made rough by lack of use. Harrison turned his head and silently regarded her for a moment, at first in irritation, then wonder at the English version, and he was buoyed by a new memory, his sister singing it to him, long after their mother no longer could. She stood swaying in the breeze as she sang, her eyes glazed and focused on nothing, her bandana rippling in the wind: *"Morning bells are ringing. Ding ding dong."*

When the tuneless drone faded into a whisper, he turned back to the task at hand.

"Why come here now?" Adrian asked. "Aren't you worried about your boy, up there in Haven?"

Harrison continued to cut, and he didn't think the man was going to answer at first, but then he paused and leaned back on his haunches. "I used to think Bix needed a father figure, but I was wrong. He needed a friend. All those years on the road, that was the one thing he lacked growing up in the back of a van. He had his mother, and I see now that she was really all he needed for a parent. Or, rather, that he never actually needed one at all."

"A friend?"

"Finn. Seeing how much his accident affected Bix, I finally realized it was me who was redundant, expendable. But Finn's back, or at least on his way back. As long as those two stick together, they'll be fine. Bix will be fine. I know that now. He doesn't need me."

He paused again, before adding, half jokingly, "Besides, I've got you two lost causes to watch over now."

"Why *did* you bring us with you? Tell me, honestly. We've only slowed you down. What do we matter to you now that you found this place?"

Harrison considered the question as he resumed snipping. Bending over at such an awkward angle made it hard to breathe. Also, like them, he was weak from the journey, hungry, thirsty, and tired.

"Do you remember our conversation," he said at last, "those first couple of days back in Bunker Ten, when you told me about the horde you followed out of Salt Lake City? How you found the truck and the knockout devices and realized what they could do? It was then that I knew you had a role to play in all this. That's why I wouldn't let them kill you."

"Yeah, I remember," Adrian eventually said. "But it doesn't answer my question. What role?"

"I told you then that there are people who go through life little more than bit players and extras."

"Drawing no one's attention," Adrian added, remembering, "just filling out the scene, hiding in the background. But then something happens, and the scene shifts, and you realize that some people aren't minor characters after all."

Harrison nodded.

"But I don't see how I am more than a minor character in all this. Or my sister."

Harrison chuckled dryly. "Not you, me," he said, immodestly. "It took me a long time to accept that. I didn't want to. But even minor actors depend on a supporting cast to realize their true potential. Perhaps even more than the star."

He made the last few cuts in the fence, rolled the jagged edges apart, careful not to cut himself, and tossed the tool through, followed by the backpack. He stepped into the compound first and gestured for the siblings to follow.

Adrian hesitated. He kept expecting something dramatic to happen— an eruption of gunfire, perhaps, or an explosion from a buried mine. But there was nothing. Harrison crossed the open ground to the building without incident and stopped before the entrance.

Joining him before the solid steel doors, Adrian wondered if the man had planned for this contingency, too. This barrier seemed beyond their means to get past, far too solid to pull down or snip through. Until now, Harrison had seemingly foreseen every other challenge they'd encountered since his return from Haven, including the abduction and the attack on the road. He'd prepared accordingly, secretly stashing supplies and weapons inside the truck that Bear had forced them to steal. There were moments when he wondered if Harrison had actually *wanted* the escape to happen, might even have planted the seed of the idea in Bear's mind. He'd certainly resisted very little. Curly had put up a stronger resistance.

"How do you expect to get inside then?" he asked. "Blowtorch? Bomb?"

"Bare knuckles."

Adrian frowned. "Knocking?" He pointed to the sand and debris piled up against the building. The hardened drifts were undisturbed all around the foundation. "There's no one here. No one's been here for years."

"I'm not so sure about that," Harrison said, and redirected Adrian's attention upward, toward a small camera mounted tight against the eave, out of the weather. A tiny green light glowed patiently beside the dark, unblinking eye of a security camera.

"Well, I'll be damned."

"Bring her forward," Harrison instructed, his gaze still locked on that stoic mechanical eyeball. "They need to see her."

"They who?" Adrian asked, but he obeyed nonetheless, gently guiding Jennifer into position directly in front of the camera.

The iris continued to gaze impassively upon them. The light continued to glow. The wind and sand blew across the desert, and nothing changed. For more than a thousand days at least, nothing had changed.

"I know you're in there," Harrison exclaimed. He reached back and pulled Jennifer's face covering down. "This woman was infected. And now she's cured. Do you understand? We've rid her of the Flense. And we're going to cure everyone else, too. Isn't that what you want?"

"There's no one here."

Harrison stared at the camera, willing it to blink.

"If anyone's even alive in there—"

The hiss of an airlock unsealing and a loud click came from somewhere behind the door. An alarm rang, and a flashing red light came on directly overhead.

Adrian stepped back, instinctively shielding his sister. Harrison reached out and drew them close again.

The door released with a clang and a final puff of escaping air. Sand trapped in the seams blew outward, then cascaded to their feet. The light on the camera went dark, and the alarm fell silent. Harrison stepped forward and brushed the loose dirt away with his boots, then reached forward and pried the door open.

All that emerged from the darkness within was the dank smell of a place that had sat undisturbed for a very long time. He wondered if this was what Tut's tomb had smelled like when it was first opened.

Minus that faint metallic overtone.

"No," Jennifer moaned, and began pulling away. She shook her head, her eyes suddenly wide with fright. "No."

They went in anyway, lights flickering on in sequence as they descended a metal staircase in the middle of the shack, down into the ground beneath the desert, through another long corridor, toward the sound of machinery coming from behind a massive steel door at the tunnel's end. It, too, opened when they reached it, and the smell of metal became nearly overpowering.

"Oh dear god," Adrian gasped. Harrison didn't hear him. He didn't try to stop him from chasing Jennifer as she ran whimpering back the way they had come. His mind was broken by what he saw. It made no sense at all, this scene. It was nothing like he'd expected.

The hall was as large as a hangar for an airship, and indeed what occupied the very center of it looked like some kind of spherical flying vessel. From the top throbbed a massive ribbed hose several feet in diameter. It snaked toward the ceiling, where it split into a hundred smaller hoses, each of which split again into hundreds more that were no larger than the width of his pinky finger. But it was what was attached to the other end of those conduits that defied all comprehension.

After getting over his shock, Harrison's first coherent thought was that he'd been wrong, that this wasn't a manufacturing site at all for the nanites, but some sort of testing facility. But then he saw it, how it really was where the microscopic devices were made. He supposed he'd always known the truth about that particular conundrum, even if he didn't consciously understand why. Now he did. Because, there was simply no known manmade technology, no assembly line had been invented or process conceived, not even at the pinnacle of human advancement, that was efficient enough to produce the trillions of nanites to be administered into every single person alive on the planet before the Flense. This was far beyond such capabilities. For the terminus of each of those ten thousand hoses did not arrive at some sort of high-precision microscopic printing mechanism, each one painstakingly constructing each snurb subunit from its molecular constituents, but rather an entire biological factory with all its impossible complexity. Hanging in open space from the rafters hundreds of feet above the floor, feeding the solitary collection vessel before him, were ten thousand naked human beings.

If you enjoyed the BUNKER 12 series, then make sure to
read the companion series THE FLENSE

This four-book epic pre-apocalyptic technothriller follows the
exploits of French biomedical investigative reporter, Angelique de
l'Enfantine, as she scrambles to uncover the cause of a series of
mysterious and deadly global tragedies known as the Flense. But
the closer she gets to uncovering the terrifying truth, the greater
the risk grows, both to herself and to all of Humanity.

THE FLENSE series consists of four full-length novels, available
in ebook and print. Check it out at:

https://amzn.to/32lxAHg

Or scan this QR code with your smartphone:

SAUL TANPEPPER is the creator of the acclaimed cyberpunk dystopian series, GAMELAND. A former army medic and PhD scientist, he now writes full time in several speculative fiction genres, including horror, apocalyptic, science fiction and paranormal. A frequent world traveler, his works are heavily influenced by these experiences and his background as a biotechnology entrepreneur. He currently resides in California's Silicon Valley with his wife of more than twenty years and his two children. He is the author of the story collections *Insomnia: Paranormal Tales, Science Fiction, & Horror* and *Shorting the Undead: a Menagerie of Macabre Mini-Fiction*.

For more information about this and his other titles, or to receive updates about promotions and upcoming books, please visit Saul's website and subscribe to his private newsletter, *Tanpepper Tidings*, at:

www.tanpepperwrites.com

Made in the USA
Las Vegas, NV
09 December 2023

82407368R00270